The Lifestyle

The Lifestyle

TAYLOR HAHN

ANCHOR BOOKS
A Division of Penguin Random House LLC
New York

AN ANCHOR BOOKS ORIGINAL, JUNE 2022

Copyright © 2022 by Taylor Hahn

Library of Congress Cataloging-in-Publication Data
Names: Hahn, Taylor, author.
Title: The lifestyle / Taylor Hahn.
Description: First Anchor Books edition. | New York : Anchor Books hardcovers, a division of Penguin Random House LLC, 2022.
Identifiers: LCCN 2021036084 (print) | LCCN 2021036085 (ebook) | ISBN 9780593316351 (hardcover) | ISBN 9780593315118 (trade paperback) | ISBN 9780593316368 (ebook)
Subjects: LCGFT: Romance fiction.
Classification: LCC PS3608.A47 L54 2022 (print) | LCC PS3608.A47 (ebook) | DDC 813/.6—dc23
LC record available at https://lccn.loc.gov/2021036084
LC ebook record available at https://lccn.loc.gov/2021036085

Anchor Books Hardcover ISBN: 978-0-593-31635-1
eBook ISBN: 978-0-593-31636-8

Book design by Steven Walker

anchorbooks.com

Printed in the United States of America
10   9   8   7   6   5   4   3   2   1

To Crystal Hana Kim, for your friendship,
encouragement, and radiant light

The real evils, indeed, of Emma's situation were the power of having rather too much her own way, and a disposition to think a little too well of herself; these were the disadvantages which threatened alloy to her many enjoyments.

—Jane Austen, *Emma*

The Lifestyle

Chapter 1

Georgina Wagman's life was so good she felt bad about it. Not so bad she'd change anything but bad enough she'd made it her mission to help others reach their potential in love, career, and epicurean delights. So it was with the best of intentions that she ordered four boxes of the richest, crispiest cannoli in New York City for the junior associates working late on Friday night and hand-delivered them office to office. How could she have known they'd give everyone food poisoning—the Italian bakery was A-rated by the health department!—or that the thirtieth-floor restrooms were closed for cleaning? Building management should have waited until after hours for that. Everyone knows lawyers work through dinner.

Sweaty and groaning, the associates had scattered thirty minutes later—some to the privacy of their apartments, others to the stairwell in search of a restroom on a different floor—except one first-year associate named Meredith De Luca. When Georgina had stopped by Meredith's office with the box of cannoli on display, she'd politely declined.

"I don't have much of a sweet tooth," she'd said.

"Only bad cannoli are too sweet," Georgina had insisted.

"Anyway, I'm a vegan," Meredith had said, and that put an end to that.

All of Georgina's fellow partners at the law firm of Ryan, Dunn & Chandler LLP were assigned a junior associate to mentor, and Georgina had landed Meredith. While most of her colleagues fulfilled their obligation by begrudgingly taking their mentees to lunch on the firm credit card once a year after their performance reviews, Georgina considered herself a Sherpa leading Meredith on a treacherous expedition up Mount Everest. She'd framed Georgina Wagman's Top 25 Tips for Being a Star Associate Without Missing Sleep and presented it to Meredith on her first day in a gift bag and tried not to be offended when she never hung it up. Meredith accepted her advice with grace, if not enthusiasm, but Georgina was determined their relationship would become more than a formality. If only Meredith would ask a question or two, seek her help and counsel, then she could prove her trustworthiness. But Meredith wore her red hair and tight black skirt suit like an electric fence, forcing everyone to keep out. She never attended firm happy hours or holiday parties, and she'd declined every one of Georgina's thirty-seven lunch invitations. Was that Georgina's fault for choosing the wrong restaurants? Now that she understood Meredith's palate, she'd pick somewhere with salty vegetables on the menu.

If Meredith was hoping Georgina would eventually get the hint and stop trying to be her fairy godmother, she was wrong. So wrong. Georgina Wagman would not go down without a fight, especially when her intentions were good, which was always.

If only they'd been a little less good in this particular instance, Meredith De Luca wouldn't have been the only associate to stay late in the office.

Chapter 2

Georgina looked up from her computer at a knock on her office door. Nathan smiled in his favorite gray suit and light pink tie. "I heard you tried to kill the junior associates," he said.

Nathan was her partner in more than law. They'd met as first years—when Georgina was Meredith's age—and married five years later. Last year, they'd both made partner. Nathan worked in the Corporate department, specifically Structured Finance. While she didn't know per se what "structured finance" was, she had no problem faking it when she helped Nathan wine and dine clients. She'd memorized one *Wall Street Journal* article on solar energy securitization and found a way to work it into the conversation whenever someone mentioned the price of oil falling, which they always did. That was good enough. As long as she laughed at their jokes, those men didn't care much what she had to say anyway.

She was a litigator. People assumed lawyers had a well-rounded practice of law, but they were wrong. Just as Nathan only spent his days "structuring finances," her only focus was *advocating*—a fancy word for arguing. She advocated on conference calls, advocated over email, advocated in briefs, and occasionally advocated to a judge, although that happened a lot more on TV than in real life, it turned out. She'd become a lawyer because of Ally McBeal. It was an embarrassing but true fact, like that hummus gave her very bad gas.

She covered her face. "Don't say that! They're going to sue me. Oh God, are they going to sue me?"

"They won't sue you," Nathan said. "They're afraid of you. Especially now that you tried to kill them."

"Stop saying that!"

"Relax." Nathan hitched up his pant legs and sat on the corner of her desk. "People get food poisoning. It happens."

"Not to me." She returned to her computer. "I'm googling remedies and bringing them to their apartments tomorrow morning. And I've got Dr. Frasier ready to make house calls if they need her."

"The junior associates are capable of buying their own Pepto Bismol," Nathan said. "And they do not want a partner showing up unannounced at their apartments, trust me."

Her fingers paused in their frantic search for the best nausea-quelling tea. He was probably right about that. They didn't like it when she stopped by their offices, always hastily stacking their messy papers and putting their shoes back on while she pretended not to notice. "I have to do something. I feel awful."

"Why don't you get them a special treat? Hmm." Nathan made a show of tapping his chin as he brainstormed options. "I don't know, maybe . . . a cannoli?"

She picked up a red pen and threw it at him.

"I know what to do," she said. "I'll give them a sick day."

"Tomorrow's Saturday."

"Lawyers work on Saturdays."

Nathan laughed and shook his head. "*You* work on Saturdays. Hey—" He checked his watch. "Aren't you late for something?"

"Shit!" She stood up so fast her chair fell backward. "I have drinks with a client. Want to be my wingman?"

"I can't."

As she stuffed her laptop and legal pad into her briefcase, Nathan righted her chair. He helped her into her red pea coat and kissed her hair.

She turned to smile up at him. His face was pale, square, and defined, like a sandstone sculpture carved with ninety-degree angles. Every woman at the firm agreed he was handsome, which they told Georgina often. She liked to hear it—it made her proud.

"But this client has no boundaries," she said. "Maybe if you're there, she won't tell me everything about her sex life."

"Wish I could help. I'm taking three guys from Morgan Stanley to the Knicks. You can fill me in on her sex life when we get home."

"It's better if I drink enough wine that I can't remember the details."

When Nathan grinned, two parentheses appeared in his smooth cheeks. "Do you tell her about our sex life?"

"I would love to, but it's usually tough to get a word in edgewise." Also, there wasn't much to tell, but she didn't want to hurt Nathan's feelings. Their sex life was perfectly fine, thank you very much; it just didn't inspire stories. She didn't tell her friends about Swiffering the kitchen, did she? Not that sex with Nathan was like Swiffering the kitchen. If given the choice between those two things, she would definitely choose sex with Nathan. Or probably. Both were rewarding in their own way. She only meant sex with Nathan was a regularly occurring activity that was productive and enjoyable but not surprising enough to talk about. But frankly, she didn't know a single married couple whose sex life was surprising, including her client, whose stories were not so much about having sex as they were about not having sex and the vibrators she used instead.

Georgina gave her surroundings the once-over to make sure she hadn't forgotten anything. When she became partner, the firm gave her a sizable budget to decorate her fancy new office. She bought mauve-colored velvet chairs, an acrylic desk, a gold-framed print of Jackson Pollock's *Lavender Mist*, and a vintage Turkish rug in faded blue. Even though she'd made it her own, she felt like an imposter in there, astonished it belonged to her. That was how she felt about Nathan, too. He was too perfect. Her life was a beautiful glass ornament hanging by a thread, and somewhere scissors waited.

"You'd better go," he said.

"Right." She pecked his clean-shaven cheek and smelled the overpowering scent of Tide. Nathan used too much detergent, but at least he did his own laundry, unlike some husbands she knew—her best friend Norah's, in particular.

Unfortunately, Norah's marriage was the product of Georgina's matchmaking prowess. On their first day of law school at Fordham, Georgina sat beside Norah in the front row of property, having noticed her quiet beauty at orientation, which she seemed determined to hide under too-long bangs, oversize sweaters, and clunky Doc Martens. For the rest of the semester, Georgina observed her taking notes by hand while other students stared at the Internet. She left her textbook closed during class and finished the midterm an hour early.

Yet never once did she raise her hand.

Norah was exactly the type of project Georgina loved to collect, so she decided to become her best friend. She swore to inspire in Norah the one thing she needed—confidence. No, bigger than that—gusto. With a little help, Norah would rule the world.

But Norah was wasting her time dating a quiet guy named Felix, who wore a backpack and grandpa cardigans, and radiated intensity like heat waves from summer asphalt. He lived in the northeast corner of the library, hunched over a textbook with a stack of note cards and a moat of crumpled granola bar wrappers, refusing to join the class at Professor Hops to rehash every exam until they were too drunk to remember the questions. While Felix was cute, with black hair he spiked slightly to the side with gel—not an atrocious hairstyle for 2005—and defined triceps peeking from beneath his short sleeves in hot weather, he was unworthy of Norah. She deserved someone compelling, someone who could make her laugh. Someone like Ari— a life-of-the-party college baseball player who looked like he'd accidentally wandered into torts on his way to an open casting call at the modeling agency. So when Ari asked to join Norah's study group, Georgina invented the teensiest lie that Ari wanted to join because he liked her. Truthfully, she suspected Ari was failing. She'd never seen him crack a book. But who cared? There was a saying: people who get As in law school become judges, people who get Bs in law school become attorneys, and people who get Cs in law school become rich.

What Georgina hadn't predicted was that Ari would impregnate Norah by the end of their first year, that Norah would drop out because they couldn't afford two tuitions and a baby, and that twelve years of marriage later, Ari would still behave like a twenty-two-year-old whose greatest achievement was a grand slam in the 2002 College World Series, despite the fact that he now had three thriving, healthy children. Norah's circumstances were drawn by Georgina's hand, and she wished she could erase them, or at least rewrite them.

Ironically, Felix became Georgina's second-closest friend after Norah left school. Once she'd gotten to know him—and convinced him to trade his backpack for a messenger bag—she swallowed her mistake like a dry, bitter pill. Felix's outward intensity was the byproduct of the immense pressure he put on himself to succeed, with an older brother already the top hepatologist in Los Angeles and Korean immigrant parents he couldn't bear to disappoint. Felix was not unworthy. The world was unworthy of Felix.

His tenacity had paid off, securing him a job offer from the best corporate law firm in the world. He'd spent four years practicing in the Seoul office, where he spoke the language yet felt culturally American, and four more in the New York office, earning a quarter-million dollars a year and living in a luxury high-rise on Twenty-Third Street. But after eight straight 2,800-hour years, he'd confessed to having increasing panic attacks, terrified he'd die the next time his heart seized, his lungs emptied, and his brain drowned in static. One Tuesday, in a moment of clarity, he'd left for a sandwich and never went back. After putting his belongings in storage, he'd moved to Costa Rica for six months. Felix called it a breakdown, his mother called it a vacation, Georgina called it funemployment.

There, he'd met his girlfriend, Alina, who'd been attending a surf camp alone. They'd decided to move in together before they'd flown home. When Georgina had gently suggested they slow down, Felix insisted he needed to be with someone who lived life on her own terms and did whatever made her happy whenever the mood struck. He admired her free spirit and bravery. But when Felix started wearing Alina's personality like he'd worn his navy suits, Georgina worried he'd replaced old pressures with new ones. First, he'd forced himself into the role of ambitious, cutthroat corporate lawyer to please his family, and now he forced himself into the role of contrarian hipster to please Alina. That was his modus operandi. He'd once loved a playwright named Salmon, for whom he'd become a sober vegan cat person. Then there was Lindsay, a second-grade teacher from Louisville, who'd convinced him to take improv classes at the Upright Citizens Brigade Theatre, and Georgina had to suffer through way too many amateur performances of "Scenes from a Hat" and "Weird Newscasters" with five-dollar PBRs from the booth in the back.

Improv was not the life that suited Felix, just as doing her husband's laundry was not the life that suited Norah. Perhaps the life that suited them best was the one Georgina had destroyed.

In the elevator to the lobby of Georgina's office building, she requested an Uber, and it pulled to the curb on Seventh Avenue between Forty-Second and Forty-Third Streets just as she walked outside. Ubers were usually minutes away in Manhattan. It was too easy. She preferred things to be a challenge, found gratification in fixing problems—her own and everyone else's. In her marriage, she was the one who googled "why is my TV blue" and fiddled with the remote for an hour while Nathan told her to *just call someone*. Where was the fun in that?

The back seat smelled like cologne and old french fries, so she rolled down the window and held her face in the fall breeze, smiling at the neon lights of Times Square at night. If anyone asked her about working in Times Square, she'd scoff. Too crowded, too smelly, too noisy, no good food. But those lights still gave her a private little thrill. *I'm here*, she'd think. *This is my life.*

She was born in her parents' bed in a three-bedroom apartment on the Upper West Side of Manhattan to a nurturing father who adored her and a mother who was flighty but fun. As pot-smoking, war-protesting, peace-preaching 1970s hippies, they'd sent her to a cooperative neighborhood school where the parents took turns as the teachers, the cooks, and the principals. Sort of like a grocery store, except the vegetables were human children. Her mother served a yearlong shift as the school treasurer until she spent half the annual budget on a garden before any parents realized they'd never nominated someone to water the plants, which all died. None of the kids received grades until Georgina realized this would prevent her from competing for the city's best high schools and demanded them. She didn't have many friends after that.

After four years of memorizing textbooks at Eleanor Roosevelt

High School, four more years of memorizing heavier textbooks at UVA, and three more years of memorizing case briefs at Fordham, she'd graduated with a JD and a job offer at a real law firm that would pay her enough to cover her loans, live in a "one-bedroom" in the East Village—in other words, a three-hundred-square-foot cube with a plastic accordion partition separating the kitchen from the bed— and go out for dinner and drinks with Norah whenever she could escape her toddler. Georgina had felt like she'd stepped onto the set of a movie, and she was the leading lady.

She was the star student in the school of romance, too. At nine years old, Georgina was the least surprised person in the apartment when her parents divorced. It didn't take an advanced degree, or even an eighth-grade diploma, to see that they lived fundamentally incompatible lives. Her dad got home from his job as an insurance claims handler at Travelers at five fifteen on the dot and put his feet up with exactly one beer, a bag of tortilla chips, and his maps. He was an amateur cartographer who'd spent four thousand hours drawing North America by the time she finished fifth grade. But her mother preferred to start projects she didn't finish. Georgina couldn't remember all the times she'd come home to her mother repainting the kitchen until she'd get bored and go drink wine spritzers with Priscilla, the hair colorist and animal rights enthusiast who lived next door. Georgina would listen to them laughing through the walls while she finished painting the kitchen until well past her self-imposed bedtime. She loved her parents, she just . . . didn't want to be them.

Theirs was a passionate, explosive romance. Like a firework, it burned bright but extinguished fast. Engaged in three weeks, married in three more, and a baby within the year. Whereas other kids yelled, "Yuck!" whenever their parents kissed, Georgina was used to it. Her parents were always kissing, touching, giggling, and escaping to the bedroom. They agreed on one thing—their desire for each other—and nothing else. Not money, not work, not where to live, not how to raise their child, not on who should be president. They didn't even agree on whether to pull the plug should either be in a horrible accident. When she'd started dating Nathan, that was one of her first questions.

"If you were hit by a bus and you were ninety-nine percent brain-dead, would you want your wife to pull the plug?" she'd asked him over a bowl of rigatoni at Union Square Cafe.

"Definitely," he'd said. "I wouldn't want my family spending their life savings just to keep me a vegetable."

She'd smiled and exhaled. That was her answer, too, and her father's. But her mother believed in miracles.

She'd studied her parents like Jane Goodall had her chimpanzees, spying on them with a Styrofoam cup pressed against the door as they argued, taking notes in her black-and-white composition book on which she'd written *SCIENCE EXPERIMENTS—TOP SECRET!!!* in purple gel pen. She would learn from their mistakes so as not to repeat them, because even though she didn't cry when they broke the news, or when her mom moved to North Carolina, or when she and her dad celebrated that first Thanksgiving alone, it hurt. Her parents had decided to get married, decided to have a baby, then decided to give up. It wasn't fair. It had felt like her interests didn't matter enough, like she didn't matter enough. And although she'd grown up and understood not everything in life was fair, the truth was she still felt that injustice at thirty-four. The memory of every message delivered from one parent to the next gave her a nervous pang in her gut. Every milestone in her life cleaved in half because her parents couldn't stand to share a single celebratory meal. Watching so many adults she respected fall in and out of love and marriage should have made her more empathetic to her parents, but it only made her more resolute. Divorce was perfectly fine for everyone else, but she knew better.

So she did the opposite of her parents in every possible way. She turned her back on chemistry so intoxicating it made her drunk, ran from relationships that were too hot and cold. She dated for years, not weeks. On first dates, she grilled men like they were murder suspects while they sweated through their collared shirts under her unrelenting interrogation. What were their goals? How did they like to spend Saturdays? Were they morning people or night owls? Spenders or savers? Kids? How many? How often did they go to the dentist? How often did they expect sex? Were they haphazard dishwasher loaders? Would they want her to quit her career after becoming a mom? And so on. The ones who were only looking to hook up never made it to dessert. Through that strategy, she'd landed Nathan, who was perfect. Good intentions plus careful planning equaled guaranteed success.

With fifteen minutes until she'd meet her client in the West Village, she called Norah to rehash the cannoli fiasco. Norah had a habit of answering the phone by launching into the middle of a conversation, expecting Georgina to catch up. "*Scuba diving!*" Norah answered.

"Ari's going scuba diving?" she guessed. "Where?"

"Does it matter?" Norah asked. "He doesn't even know how to scuba!"

"You have the power to say no to this. You're his wife."

"Okay, Esther Perel," Norah said, and Georgina could hear her eye-roll. Norah and Ari's marriage had always been like driving on a winding road in bad weather. Their oldest daughter, Rachel, had grown from "spirited child" (Norah said that was code for *recalcitrant*) into a rebellious preteen with a glare that could stop a trained killer. Their middle son, Simon, had mild dyslexia and required therapies that strained their finances, and Hannah, their youngest, was deathly allergic to almost everything, which they'd learned the hard way when Ari fed her stone fruit before the pediatrician's chart said he was allowed to. Norah raised the kids full-time, so their lifestyle was carefully budgeted to remain within Ari's salary. In one of the most expensive cities in the world, that wasn't easy. They'd recently moved to Jersey City to save money, but now they fought about commuting, too. Lately, life's challenges seemed to poison every one of their interactions, and Georgina wasn't sure they'd survive it—or whether they should.

Their problem was they had no reason to be together other than the kids. At least in the beginning, they'd had fun. Ari took Norah to rooftop parties in Bushwick and the five-dollar nosebleeds at Mets games, invited her tubing with floating coolers in Hudson Valley, and introduced her to the best tacos she'd ever had in Rockaway Beach. Maybe when two people had as much sex as they'd had, a pregnancy was inevitable. Norah, who hadn't lost her virginity until her senior year of college to someone called "Zephan" after a Model UN summit in Zurich, had become insatiable. Ari "knew what he was doing," Norah said, and while she didn't want to think about where he'd picked up his particular skills or how many times he'd practiced them, she was happy to reap the benefits of his hard work.

But they had no energy or privacy for sex anymore. At their therapist's recommendation, Norah and Ari had scheduled one hour for sex on Sunday and Thursday nights, but the first night, Hannah ran screaming into their room and puked all over the bed, and the second night, Rachel had started cooking a box of macaroni and cheese, but got distracted watching TikTok videos and ended up setting off the building's sprinkler system. Norah had to talk to the firefighters in ill-fitting lingerie she'd ordered on Amazon, and gave up after that.

"So why don't you say no?" Georgina asked.

"Because I'm picking my battles," Norah said.

"This seems like a good one to fight over."

"You don't have kids," Norah said. "You don't get it."

The day Norah found out she was pregnant, Georgina held her

while she sobbed for hours. It was terrifying, and she wasn't even the pregnant one. Would Ari leave, or would he help? How would Norah get money to support the baby? What would her parents say? They'd expected her to marry someone Indian and Hindu, but Ari was white and Jewish. "This is their worst nightmare," Norah had said with tears streaming down her cheeks. "They'll disown me." They hadn't, in the end. It was impossible not to be thankful for a baby as cute as Rachel, who'd been born with thick brown curls and a grumpy-old-man frown.

So Georgina didn't get it, she supposed, but it pained her to think of everything her best friend had lost that day.

"Anyway," Norah said, "when we got married, I promised him I'd never stifle his adventurous spirit. Don't you remember his annual treks to Myrtle Beach to support the local beer economy?"

Georgina forced a laugh, but she was sick with guilt. This was all her fault. Was it too late to right her wrong? No. It was never too late. Any problem could be fixed. These were exactly the circumstances when divorce made sense: they were two fundamentally incompatible people who'd had six months of nonstop hot sex, and it should have ended there, but Ari's super-sperm had other plans. Passion was never the basis for a long-term relationship—Georgina had learned that the hard way, and now so had Norah. Felix may not have been wild in bed, or outside of it, but he was selfless and loyal. If he and Norah were married with kids, he'd do anything to help her finish school, and he'd never go scuba diving unless it was an organized excursion on a Disney cruise with the whole family. Georgina decided then and there to try to get them back together. Sure, Alina and Ari would have to go, but nobody liked them anyway. Alina would prey on her next lost soul, and Ari would be happy spending the rest of his life picking up aspiring Broadway dancers on Tinder.

"Are we still meeting tomorrow?" Georgina asked.

"Yes," Norah said. "Mama needs a bottle of wine."

"What am I going to drink?"

"*Ha ha.*"

She promised to text in the morning and spent the rest of her Uber ride brainstorming how she could convince Felix to tag along without him discovering what she was up to.

Georgina's client, Suzanne, waited at a bar on West Tenth called Casa Amici. A few minutes earlier, she'd sent Georgina a text message: *I ordered you a cocktail but I drank it. Where are you???*

Inside, the air was hot and thick. Georgina hung her scarf and coat on the communal hooks and pushed through crowded patrons until she spotted Suzanne in a bright purple pantsuit with an empty barstool beside her. "It's taken!" Suzanne barked at a hopeful twenty-something in over-the-knee boots.

When she got close enough, Georgina touched her shoulder. "I am so, so sorry."

Suzanne looked up from her phone. "I could fire you for this," she said, but thankfully she was smiling.

"You will not believe what happened." Georgina sat and pointed to Suzanne's drink. "Can I have a sip of that?"

Suzanne nudged it closer. "Have it. I've got another one coming."

"We've got this insane case going on. Everyone's working around the clock. And I wanted to cheer up the associates after they had to cancel their Friday night plans, so I ordered them cannoli from Angelo's in Little Italy—" She swigged what turned out to be a strong margarita. "Thanks, I needed that. Anyway, they all got food poisoning. How long have you been waiting?"

"Only fifteen minutes. How sick are we talking?"

Georgina grimaced. "Someone threw up in the copy room."

"Yeesh. I hope you've got a good carpet cleaner."

"I'm more worried about a good lawyer."

"I think you've got a few of those around," Suzanne said. "Isn't that why you charge the big bucks?"

Georgina arranged her face into an innocent mask, as though she had no idea she billed Suzanne hundreds of dollars per hour to defend her chain of jewelry stores accused again and again of ripping off Yurman, Gucci, and other top-tier designers.

The bar was packed and loud. When Georgina said, "Tell me what's new," Suzanne didn't hesitate to shout, "Philip and I started swinging!" and a few people nearby turned around with curious amusement.

"I swear to God," she went on, possibly unaware of her eavesdroppers but more likely enjoying them, "it's the best thing that ever happened to us. We should have done this from day one."

"You're not serious." Georgina pictured swingers more like a fringe group of radicals and Freudian fetishists in leather straps and purple lipstick, but Suzanne wore J.Jill! Women in sensible heels couldn't be swingers, could they?

"Dead serious," Suzanne said. "If I saw one more of Philip's shavings in the bathroom sink, I was going to push him out the window. We hadn't had sex in two years. *Years*, Georgina. YEARS. Now we're like horny teenagers at prom. Our relationship is better than when we first started dating."

Georgina sipped her margarita. "To be clear, by swinging, you mean—"

"We get together with a small group of friends, have a few drinks, pair up, and screw each other into marital bliss."

"Why not try therapy?"

"We did. We tried everything. We went skydiving—nothing like a near-death experience to bond you for life, right? You know what's a real bonding experience?" Suzanne attempted to wink, but both of her eyes closed, one only managing to squint slightly more than the other. "Fucking the neighbors."

Georgina had to laugh. She was fond of Suzanne and reveled in her outrageous gossip a lot more than she'd let on. Hanging out with her was like smoking cigarettes behind the gym with a cool senior, if the senior wore pearl earrings and a satin headband. "Isn't that awkward when you see him taking out the trash?"

Suzanne made sultry eyes. "It turns trash duty into foreplay."

"Have you tried scheduling sex?" Georgina asked. "My best friend said couples should put an hour for sex at least twice a week into their calendars. Just don't put it on the office-wide one."

"Scheduling sex kills the chase," Suzanne said. "Swinging invites the chase to your house for cocktails."

Georgina laughed again, but it rang out a little frenetic. She cleared her throat. "Don't you worry sleeping with other people will make things worse?"

"We're not *sleeping* together," Suzanne said. "You make it sound like an affair. Swinging is a mutually beneficial arrangement. And no—swinging has accomplished in one month what a lifetime of counseling never could have."

"It just sounds so . . . counterproductive," Georgina said. "Sex with other people is the number one thing to avoid in my book."

Suzanne shrugged. "I don't know what else to tell you. You need to trust me on this one. Philip is downright romantic these days. This morning, we had sex in the shower before work. When's the last time you did that?"

A small frown possessed Georgina's face as she thought about Swiffering the kitchen, which she'd done more recently than she'd had sex with Nathan. Was it Sunday? No, Friday. Or maybe Thursday. Whatever day it was, it happened after two *Seinfeld* reruns, and Georgina never took her sweatshirt off. "I wish I could remember."

"Honestly, you need to try this," Suzanne said. "It's life-changing."

Georgina laughed. "You're my client! If I were bad in bed, that would definitely be bad for business."

"I'm not the only swinger in New York City." Suzanne lifted her eyebrows until they disappeared under her bangs. "Let's just say there's a certain very short, very rich man whose schlong is about as long as he is."

"Well, *now* I'm intrigued," Georgina said. "But Nathan and I are doing fine. I haven't considered pushing him out a window once, I swear."

Suzanne fixed her with a cheeky look. "You're missing the point. We're not swinging to let other people into our marriage. We're swinging to keep them out. It's prophylactic. It's like . . . a divorce condom. Swingers divorce at significantly lower rates than monogamous couples. I'm not making that up. You think I didn't do my research? Google it."

A soap-opera-star-looking bartender dropped off a plate of crostini and a bowl of olives. The way Suzanne was eyeing him, Georgina thought Suzanne might invite him to her next party.

"Not that I'm *hoping* your marriage goes south," she went on, "but if it does, you know who to call. Are you game for one more?" Without waiting for her answer, Suzanne ordered another round. Georgina was going to say yes anyway.

An hour later, she kissed Suzanne's cheek goodbye and waved down a conveniently passing yellow cab. Before she could go home, trade her suit in for sweatpants, and get in bed with her favorite movie, *The Lincoln Lawyer*, she had to swing by the office to pick up a binder that she'd realized during the second margarita she'd forgotten and written BINDER on her hand with the bartender's pen. Law firms didn't recognize a meaningful distinction between Wednesday and

Saturday or Tuesday and Sunday. She didn't mind, but even if she did, there was nothing she could do about it, so she tried not to dwell on it too much. For lawyers, weekend work was as routine as running the dishwasher.

In the back seat, she couldn't help but dream of Nathan as her head lolled against the window. Ari's scuba trip and Suzanne's swinging had cast her fortune in a particularly dazzling light that night. Nathan would never leave her at home with three children. And he never left his shavings in the sink! Her eyes welled up just thinking about him, and it definitely wasn't the margarita talking. *Perfection* was the word that came to mind, as if she'd imagined him into existence, and the world had schemed to bring them together. Their last names both started with a *W*, so their first year they sat together at every alphabetically arranged event. People started asking if they were dating before they were, planting a seed that grew into an inevitable tree from which she'd never climbed down. They were Michael Douglas and Annette Bening in *The American President*, fighting for justice by day and ballroom dancing in black tie by night.

Admittedly, structuring finances and defending patent-infringing jewelry stores wasn't exactly fighting for justice. Often it wasn't clear what she was fighting for except the win itself. That was why she took her mentoring role so seriously. She wasn't saving the world one jewelry store at a time, but at least she helped young women succeed.

The cab driver pulled over beside a hot dog stand on Forty-Second and Seventh before Georgina, lost in fantasy, realized they were back in Times Square. She paid the fare while a family of tourists wearing hats from the M&M's store waited on the curb to replace her. She was in such a happy mood she said, "Enjoy your trip!" as she passed, and they stared as if a subway rat had started belting out Kelly Clarkson.

She rode the elevator to the reception area, a spacious, window-wrapped room with white marble floors. In the middle, a vase of

fresh hydrangeas and a thin Apple monitor decorated the desk usually manned by the head assistant, Danielle. Since it was late, the
room was empty, and pictures of Danielle's two-year-old son floated
across the screen as her computer hibernated. For once, the office
was peaceful. No ringing phones, no cursing partners, no constant
stream of the Outlook email chimes that haunted Georgina's dreams
at night.

Two hallways stretched on either side—one to the left toward
the Corporate wing, where Nathan's office sat, and one to the right,
toward Litigation. She hurried down the right corridor. If she could
grab her binder and catch a subway right away, she'd be home in bed
with *The Lincoln Lawyer* in twenty minutes tops.

As she walked, motion-sensored lights clicked on every six feet
and, when she pushed open the door, inside her office. Binder in
hand, she hurried back toward the elevator bank but paused at the
end of Nathan's hall when she noticed his light was on. Something
must have come up in one of his matters. If a client unexpectedly
demanded a conference call or had some crisis—surely relating to
the falling price of oil—Amar'e Stoudemire himself could not have
peeled Nathan from his desk. It was annoying when she had made
them dinner reservations, but she admired his work ethic.

She'd say hello. The lights clicked on as she walked, illuminating
empty office after empty office. Her stomach clenched with guilt as
she thought of the associates she'd poisoned, but there was nothing
she could do about it now. She'd find a way to make it up to them.
Soup from Katz's? Tea from Lady Mendl's? Some tequila to kill
those stomach bugs? But their absence did give her an idea. Suzanne
thought she and Nathan needed to spice it up? Nothing like an office
romp to prove her wrong.

Also, margaritas.

She paused before a reflective window to apply a little lipstick and let down her hair. Her face had a slight cartoonish quality to it, her eyes and mouth disproportionately large for an otherwise small person. People told her she looked like a Disney princess—Belle because she had a pale complexion, long brown hair, and light green eyes. Hers was a friendly, approachable appearance, which must be why tourists constantly stopped her to ask for directions. But right now, she was trying to go for sexy, and her navy skirt suit, beige flats, and white shirt weren't doing much for her in the seduction department. She'd have to do better. She mussed her hair, undid the top buttons, and tugged her breasts higher in her bra cups to give herself some meager cleavage. Feeling particularly wild, she slid off her underwear and stuck it in her bra for Nathan to find. Good thing she'd been forcing him to eat all those beets recently, or he might have had a heart attack. She'd never done anything remotely close to this daring before.

Outside of Nathan's door, she said, "Knock, knock!" and pushed it open.

What she registered next were fragments: desk, woman, naked bodies, red hair swinging back and forth. That was an important detail, the red hair, though Georgina couldn't immediately put her finger on why. Her brain had gone on break, probably to have a cigarette. Between the woman's thighs, there was a man's head, and Georgina registered its dark hair, neat and clipped short.

She gasped as she realized what was happening. Two associates had broken into Nathan's office to have sex!

"Excuse me," she said from the doorway.

The trespassers froze. The woman was perched on the right side of the desk with her bare legs wrapped around the man's shoulders. The man was on his knees, gripping her hips. Georgina looked at their faces. The short hair currently clenched in the woman's fist was Nathan's, of course. She was less surprised than resigned, as some part of her brain had registered who it was as soon as she'd walked in.

And the red hair belonged to Meredith, her reluctant mentee, whom she'd hoped wanted to emulate her, only not so literally. Refusing that cannoli was a wise decision in more ways than one, it turned out. No man's face could go between those legs if she'd eaten that thing.

Georgina ran her eyes down the length of Nathan's naked body and watched as he deflated and fell limp. What a peculiar heartbreak, to watch her husband lose an erection at the sight of her. It made her lungs feel tight and empty, as if she needed to take a breath but there was no air in the room. There were several seconds of dead silence, like everyone understood whatever happened next would be agonizing, but if they stayed perfectly still, the pain wouldn't notice they were there.

"Georgina," Nathan said, his features pulling together in a pucker of excruciating pain. Her brain sizzled like someone had dumped water on her circuit board, causing her impulses and emotions to go haywire and fire randomly. It shouldn't have been funny, but wasn't it? Wasn't it so ridiculously hilarious to hear her name spoken out of her husband's mouth when it was that close to someone else's vagina? She couldn't control the urge—she laughed. It was a high, shocked, disbelieving laugh, like the kind reserved for watching dads fall off rooftops into swimming pools on *America's Funniest Home Videos*.

She looked from Nathan's face to Meredith's. Why did it have to be so pretty? Her lips resembled pale pink rose petals, and her skin glimmered like moonlight where it curved over her cheekbones. Her brown eyes were sweetly fearful, as if she were afraid Georgina might hurt her. As suddenly as Georgina's laughter had come, it left. She sank to the floor, her body too weak to stand. This was the worst moment of her life. A voice in her head repeated that fact—*This is the worst moment of your life, this is the worst moment of your life*—as if she'd woken up in the hospital, drugged and disoriented, and a nurse was saying, *You were in a bad car accident*. But instead it was, *You caught your husband cheating*.

No! she said back. *This isn't real, this isn't happening, this is impossible.* If she said it enough, she could will it into the truth. Alternate realities were real. She'd read an article about it in *National Geographic* once. Every action had infinite outcomes, all of which played out in parallel universes. Somewhere, Nathan had gone to the Knicks game, so couldn't she just hop on a flight to the next dimension?

But it was useless to deny it. Her perfect husband had cheated. There was Meredith on the desk, hugging her knees and crying like a naked baby. Should Georgina wrap her in a blanket or slap her across the face? And there was Nathan, zipping his pants and buckling his belt, muttering to himself. In the grand finale of her emotional fireworks show, fury rose up in place of her anguish like blistering red sparks as the next thought struck her: *Somewhere in the multiverse, I'm in bed watching Matthew McConaughey right now, you bitch!*

That sent her into a rage.

Chapter 3

Beside her was a bookshelf full of Nathan's deal toys—Lucite and marble trophies from clients to commemorate an investment or acquisition. Breathing hard, flaming blood pumping, she grabbed one and chucked it against the wall. She'd never thrown anything before, but damn, it was effective. The glass detonated into sharp fragments that flew against the opposite window, and Meredith screamed while Nathan yelled, "Jesus!" and they ducked to protect their faces. Another deal toy on the shelf caught her eye, a blue glass globe. She heaved it onto the floor. Beside it, another, and another, and another, endless deal toys, and she snatched them all and hurled them as fast as she could like a game of endless Skee-Ball.

"Stop!" Nathan was shouting. "Jesus, stop!"

But her arm was possessed. She couldn't stop grabbing and throwing, grabbing and throwing until every deal toy was gone and the floor glittered, a mosaic of glass, blue and green and gold and black. Floor-to-ceiling windows reflected the three of them—Meredith's naked terror, Nathan's helpless panic, her own heaving rib cage as she panted. But beyond the mirror, lower Manhattan sparkled before the endless darkness of the ocean. Her breathing slowed. It was comforting, like watching the horizon on a bumpy car ride. Nothing was more beautiful than New York at night.

Nathan spoke in her ear. "Georgina, please," he begged. "This is nothing. I don't know what I'm doing. This was never supposed to happen." He lifted her hands, pressed them to his lips. She was too exhausted to yank them away, but his close proximity revealed red splotches scattering his bare chest. That always happened after he came.

"Can you both get dressed?" she asked. "I can't look at you."

"Yes, sorry, yes." Nathan dived for his shirt on the floor at the same time Meredith scrambled off the desk for her abandoned dress. Their bodies collided, knocking Meredith into a seven-foot stone giraffe statue Nathan bought to decorate his office. A bizarre choice, but Nathan said it reminded him of going to the Topeka Zoo with his parents when he was a kid growing up in Kansas. Meredith yelped and grabbed the giraffe's neck for support, but it crashed to the floor with her arms trapped underneath it.

She screamed. Her body writhed and her bare feet scraped at the floor for traction, but her arms were immobile. "Oh my God, get it off! Get it *off*!"

It took both Nathan and Georgina to hoist the statue upright again. As Meredith cradled her left arm and sobbed, Nathan prodded the giraffe's neck as if to test its sturdiness. Georgina knew what he was thinking—first Meredith would sue the firm for sexual harassment, then for personal injury. She'd allege there was an unsafe condition on the premises, and she wouldn't be wrong. Right now, Georgina could kill them both.

Meredith sniffed. "I need to go to the hospital. My arm is broken."

Georgina wanted to say something nasty, like, *Bone for a bone, eh?*, but she was too tired. "You won't be able to put on your dress. Here—

wear this." She took off her red pea coat and held it open while Meredith teetered to her feet and gingerly slid her arms into it. Georgina did the buttons as tears silently flowed down Meredith's cheeks.

"I didn't think you'd be here," Meredith whispered.

"Trust me," Georgina said. "The feeling is mutual."

With their nakedness gone, it was easier to focus. From Nathan's coat closet, she retrieved his size twelve running shoes and knelt at Meredith's knees to slide them on her feet. "You can't wear your heels," she said, "or you might fall and break your other arm."

With her mascara-smeared face, tangled hair, too-big coat, and clown-size shoes, Meredith looked like a complete and utter train wreck. One part of Georgina took pleasure in this and hoped a crowd of tourists would be waiting outside with cameras. But another part was heartbroken. This was a collapse of everything she had wanted for Meredith, and for herself, and for their relationship. Hot, stinging tears blurred her vision as she reached forward and tied the belt of her formerly favorite coat around Meredith's waist.

Nathan gathered shards of glass into a coffee mug. There were thousands, and Georgina wondered whether he'd stay all night to clean them up instead of risking anyone discovering what had happened.

"We're leaving," she said.

Nathan straightened. "Let me. This is my mess."

"I'm your mess now?" Meredith asked. "Good to know."

"That's not what I meant," Nathan said with an edge of impatience. "It's just—she shouldn't have to deal with this."

"I can handle putting her in a cab," Georgina said. "It's better than walking out of here alone."

"No," Nathan said. "I don't feel right about this."

"*This* you don't feel right about?" she laughed. "Excuse me, but you have questionable morals." She pressed her hand into Meredith's lower back. "Let's go."

In the elevator, they were joined by a building security guard. The three of them stared resolutely ahead in the longest elevator ride of Georgina's life. Her mind looped frantically with the same two thoughts: *Nathan cheated, I'm a fool, Nathan cheated, I'm a fool.* She tried to take deep breaths, but the noise of her own mind overwhelmed her attempt at calm, like when she tried to work while someone in a nearby office played loud music.

Nathan cheated.

I'm a fool.

On the curb of Seventh Avenue, she put Meredith into the first taxi that passed, which she'd have hurled her body in front of, unwilling as she was to wait for a second, and ordered the driver to New York–Presbyterian Hospital. Her level of assistance was downright saintly under the circumstances, wasn't it? Had she been hit by a city bus that very moment, she would have been shocked to find herself anywhere but on a red carpet at heaven's Pearly Gates. That had to cancel out the cannoli debacle.

"Georgina!"

She recognized Nathan's voice calling after her and turned.

He jogged toward her. "Can we please talk?"

She laughed and gestured around. Tourists paraded by, men wearing sandwich boards handed out flyers, and hot dog carts scented the air with salty steam. Everywhere, cars honked, street performers drummed on plastic buckets, and teenagers shrieked. "Here? In the middle of Times Square?" She crossed her arms. "Sure, say what you need to say."

Nathan's grave expression reflected neon-green light from the jumbotron above the corner of Forty-Second and Broadway. His pale pink tie hung loose, and his hair stuck up in the back where Meredith had gripped it. It was impossible to look at him and not see his tongue moving between her legs. That was *Georgina's* tongue. It was only supposed to do those things to *her* body. And it didn't even do it very often!

"I didn't mean here," Nathan said. "Can we go home? Or . . . somewhere?"

"Under no circumstances am I going anywhere with you," she said. "I can't look at your face without wanting to throw up. And I didn't eat a cannoli!"

"But I need to explain," he begged.

She closed her eyes and drew a deep breath. "There is nothing you could say to make this better. So please go. Now."

"You should have the apartment," he said. "I'll go to a hotel."

"No. I am not crawling into your bed tonight, regardless of whether you're in it."

Nathan nodded at the sidewalk. "I understand."

Her blood boiled. She hated it when he played the martyr. But as he walked to the subway entrance across Seventh Avenue, where the S would shuttle him to Grand Central and the 4/5 would carry him to Eighty-Sixth Street, a sudden need to cling to him possessed her, as if when he disappeared, so would their life together. "Wait!"

He stopped. The light on Seventh Avenue had just turned green, and taxis, tour buses, and black executive cars formed an impenetrable danger zone between them. Across the vehicles, they stared at each other, and the tragedy of this night hit her with the force of oncoming traffic. She wanted to fix this like she fixed every other problem, to conceive the perfect plan to make everything better again, voilà! But for the first time, she couldn't imagine how to do it.

When someone stepped on her toe, she yelled, "Watch where you're going!" before realizing it was a child in a Planet Hollywood hat. The parents shot her exhilarated looks, their Angry New Yorker fantasies coming true. *This is not a movie!* she wanted to snap. *I'm just a real-life woman scorned.*

When the light turned red again, Nathan crossed the street toward her amid the wave of pedestrians. She'd lost the passion of a moment ago, now feeling nothing but cold and numb and tired.

"What is it?" He looked innocent and hopeful, as if she might have changed her mind, decided to come home and forget this night ever happened.

Her throat swelled painfully as she held back tears. "I don't understand. Why would you do this?"

Nathan's nostrils flared in and out, and he bit his lips together so hard the skin around them turned bone-white and bloodless. He was trying not to cry. She'd only seen him cry once before, when his mother was diagnosed with breast cancer. But she'd recovered—she was thriving. Could they come back from this? It depended, she supposed, on whether they'd caught it early enough and how far it had spread.

"I don't know," he said. "That person up there—that was someone else. That's not who I am, or at least, not who I want to be."

She sniffed and lifted her chin. "Okay. I will take that under advisement."

When he'd sulked off, she wiped her face. Times Square hotels surrounded her. From the corner looking skyward, she could see the lanterns on the Knickerbocker rooftop, the two-story red *M* for Marriott, and the Hyatt Regency's spire. *Pick one*, she told herself, *it doesn't matter which*. But she couldn't move. The prospect of letting herself into a sterile box with one tiny window and drinking room service wine alone sounded almost worse than going home to her own apartment, which her pride refused to do.

She'd call someone. Her mother was probably at the only gay bar in the Outer Banks with her neighbors Clark and Marcus. What was she going to do? Send a car?

She could go home to her father's apartment, sleep in her childhood bed, and let his partner make her lemon crepes and Thai tea in the morning. Buppha was the best cook in the world. She smelled like doughnuts freshly powdered with sugar and gave the tightest hugs. Georgina had set them up—her greatest accomplishment in matchmaking thus far. After Buppha had taught a Thai cooking class for a bridal shower Georgina hosted, she'd booked her to cater her dad's fiftieth birthday party, and they'd been together ever since. The union was a win-win-win: her father was blissfully in love, Buppha became the nurturing mother she'd never had, and she got to relish in the satisfaction of a job well done. Nevertheless, while the pancakes sounded nice, the smothering pity from them both would be unbearable.

Norah. She would call Norah. She dug for her phone and started to dial before it occurred to her that if she went to Norah's, she'd have to confess what happened, and she wasn't ready to do that. Even with close friends, she had a complex about revealing that the men she dated were anything but perfect. Whenever she and Nathan would argue, she'd skim over the details with Norah, only approximating the real issue, ostensibly so Norah wouldn't get too angry at Nathan and never forgive him, causing Georgina to be embarrassed for having done so herself. Norah put Georgina's marriage on a pedestal, and despite knowing it was petty, she liked it up there. It was cushioned, and the view was nice. She got to freely express her opinions about Norah's problems without looking like a hypocrite, and Norah needed her advice. How would she be in a position to help her best friend fix her marriage if her own had suffered a grisly death before it was buried in an unmarked grave on the side of a road?

Besides, she'd rather not sleep on a trundle bed in a *Frozen*-themed bedroom. One humiliation was enough for the night.

Felix, as cozy and warm as a pair of sweatpants, was the perfect person to call. He was a judgment-free zone, the kind of friend to nurse your hangover even if you drunkenly snapped at him the night before. At least she could tell him the truth about what happened without worrying what he'd think.

With shaking hands, she found her phone and dialed. Felix answered on the first ring. "I was just thinking about you," he said. "Wasn't this the weekend we were going to go to Hudson for leaf-peeping?"

That would have been her preferred kind of peep show. "I forgot," she said. "Sorry." The words came out nasally and thick.

"Whoa," he said, "you okay?"

Hearing his voice, the pain she'd been ignoring surfaced. It stabbed her chest, and she doubled over, trying not to scream at the top of her lungs. The affair was real now that she had to say it out loud. She couldn't pretend. Around her, strangers bustled and laughed and held hands, a thousand miles away from her agony. "I walked in," she began, but it hurt to speak. *Breathe*, she told herself. *Breathe.* She grabbed a napkin from a nearby hot dog cart with a mumbled apology and blew her nose.

"You're scaring me," Felix said. "Do you want me to come get you? Where are you? It's loud."

She tried again. Her throat was so swollen that her voice was nothing but a quiet rasp. "I found Nathan—"

"I'm coming to get you. Are you at a bar?"

"No. No. It's fine. But can I . . . can I come over?"

"Of course," he said. "I'm at home."

She caught the next cab, and by the time it reached Seventy-Second Street, Nathan had called four times. She'd punched *decline decline decline decline* like it was the parachute release on a plummeting aircraft. Could there not have been a less polite button for circumstances like these? *Die, motherfucker*, maybe? *See you in hell, dickhead?*

He wasn't a dickhead, though. That was the thing that made the events of this night so shocking, among all the other adjectives she could choose to describe them. Life-altering. Devastating.

Pornographic.

Nathan wasn't perfect. She had to admit that now. He was an oppressive neat freak and spent way too much money on his haircuts. If someone at work outperformed him, he would dissect it ad nauseam until her ears would bleed if she heard the offender's name one more time. Despite being good-looking and successful and well liked, he was insecure, so she played along and told him his haircuts were worth every penny because she understood that was how married couples survived a lifetime together—a series of small forgivenesses, small sacrifices that didn't mean much to one person but meant a lot to the other. This was different. How could she forgive this, even if it was just another product of Nathan's insecurity? Maybe she should have seen this coming. Nathan needed to feel wanted, and he wanted to feel special. What had Meredith given him that she had not?

She groaned and let her head fall back onto the headrest. "Why?" she whined aloud.

"It's the fastest way to Riverside," the driver said.

"Huh?"

"The West Side Highway."

"Oh." Her phone rang again. This time, she pressed *answer*. "Are you in love with her?" she asked.

Nathan audibly exhaled. "Thank you for answering."

"I asked you a question."

"No. I swear it wasn't like that."

"Then why? Please give me a satisfactory explanation."

"She wanted me," he said. "I wish I had a better reason. It was just sex."

"That's bullshit," she snapped. "You already have sex. With me. Your wife. This was about sex with *her*. Why?"

People had sex for a million different reasons. Even the people doing it with each other had different agendas. But what did Nathan want that he didn't have already? Comfort? Distraction? Ego stroking? Or was it just dick stroking? He'd never been that driven by sex. He didn't ask for it or expect it all that often. But that seemed ridiculous now. Of course he wanted sex with a hot twenty-five-year-old. He was a human being. In believing Nathan wasn't overly sexual, and that sex wasn't their marriage's focal point, maybe she'd diminished that side of him, so he'd gone looking for it elsewhere.

Was this her fault?

"Can we please have this conversation face-to-face?" Nathan asked.

She lifted her thumbnail to her mouth and realized her fresh manicure was already gone. She'd bitten it all off. "I'm not ready for that. Please don't call me again. It's the least you can do."

She hung up. Her taxi exited the West Side Highway on Ninety-Fifth Street, the off ramp's high stone walls blocking her view from both windows until they crossed through Riverside Park, where the streetlamps gently lit the sliver of trees.

A Turkish café called Beste occupied the bottom floor of Felix's building. They went so often for brunch, afternoon tea, or evening wine she knew the menu by heart. It was closing, but the owner waved her inside anyway. She ordered a dozen pieces of baklava before letting herself into Felix's building with the key he'd given her to water his plants when he and Alina went to Tulum over the summer. That trip alone told Georgina Felix was madly in love with his new girlfriend, as his idea of a vacation wasn't an outdoor beach club but a thousand-year-old city with more museums and crumbling temples than a person could reasonably visit in their lifetime.

Inside, a curving staircase led her to the fifth floor, where she knocked twice on the door to apartment A before pushing it open.

That small emblem of closeness to someone—letting yourself inside their home—meant more to her tonight than ever. She wasn't alone. She had people. In the entryway, her briefcase fell from her limp fingers, and she reached for her coat before remembering with a cold, tight ache in her chest why she wasn't wearing one. Meredith was probably sitting alone in the emergency room of Presbyterian, crying and in pain. The vision made it hard to hate her. Meredith was so young, and even though her self-imposed distance gave off a pretentious vibe, she seemed lonely.

"Hi." Felix stood down the hall. "You okay?"

This time, she just shook her head. In three strides, he'd closed the gap and hugged her. She clutched the back of his sweater and pressed her face into his shoulder until she started to feel embarrassed and pulled away, though he would have held her like that all night if she'd wanted him to.

She sniffed and said, "I brought you some baklava."

He laughed gently and shook his head. "Only you would bring a hostess gift in a crisis. Did you eat dinner?"

"I had a margarita for dinner," she said.

"I ordered Broadway Pizza," he said. "Come on."

She followed him into the kitchen and collapsed on the bench in his breakfast nook. He and Alina had found the pot of gold at the rainbow's end with this apartment, a classic six now divided into two units. It had a soaring bay window overlooking 101st Street in the kitchen, high tin ceilings, detailed molding, and herringbone floors, and it must have been one of five apartments in Manhattan with a wood-burning fireplace. If she could snuggle up on his couch with a blanket and a crackling fire, she'd stay until all her problems floated away like smoke up the chimney.

While Felix warmed her a slice of pizza in the microwave, she rested her cheek on a place mat. Her body was impossibly heavy, a case of canned goods she'd been forced to carry up a mountain. "He cheated on me," she said. It felt good to say it out loud, as though she now owned this fact.

The microwave beeped, and Felix carried her slice to the table on a blue ceramic plate. Broadway Pizza was usually her favorite, but she had no appetite. The orange oil pooling in the pepperonis made her stomach turn, and she nudged the plate away.

"I'm so sorry," Felix said. "I wish I had something better to say."

"Are you not surprised?" she asked.

"Of course I am," he said. "I like Nathan. I thought he was a good guy."

"Good guys cheat, too."

"I guess that's true."

He stared at the table for a while, then glanced up at her. Felix had overly expressive eyebrows like a puppy's. He was capable of looking innocent and guilty, adorable and strong, all at the same time. At his heartfelt, aching expression now, she wanted to take his face in her hands and comfort him, but remembered she was the one who needed the comforting.

"Do you mind if I stay here tonight?" she asked. "I can't go home."

"I hoped you would," he said. "I made up the bed. You can stay as long as you want."

"Where's Alina?"

"She went to a gallery opening downtown."

They were quiet. From outside, the distant sounds of traffic on Broadway drifted through a cracked window. Georgina poked her pizza crust, but it had already turned rock-hard from the microwave. Felix took a baklava piece from the box and contemplated it.

"I feel like I'm not saying the right things," he said.

She rubbed her face. She was desperately tired. "There's no script for this."

"Do you want to talk about it?"

"There's not much to say. I walked into his office and found him with a junior associate. How cliché, right?"

"Don't do that to yourself." Felix set the baklava back in the box and got up to look in the fridge. "Do you want something else? I have ice cream. Beer. Tea? How about some tea? I'm going to make some tea."

He was filling the kettle when Georgina pressed herself standing. "Honestly, I want to go to bed, if that's okay. We can talk tomorrow."

"At least let me bring you a cuppa." He'd adopted that word from Alina, who'd spent most of her adolescence in London. Georgina tried to smile her thanks.

In his guest room slash office slash Alina's yoga studio, she unzipped her boots to reveal mismatched socks. One had small palm trees on it, the other red and blue stripes. She'd picked up the habit in the fourth grade when she considered it a fashion statement, and could never convince herself to stop. She justified it as saving time by skipping the sock-folding step of laundry, but really, she liked having this secret on her feet. It was exhausting to do her hair and put on makeup and don a suit every day to look the part of Put-Together Professional. Her socks were like a rebellious middle finger to all of that. Nathan had never understood it and made comments whenever they went through airport security together. Her college boyfriend said it was his favorite thing about her, though, and that had made her feel seen.

The room was small and stuffed with plants and books. On the writing desk sat a small but mighty clock, whose ticking pecked at her brain. After Felix delivered her tea, a pair of boxers, and one of his worn-out Fordham Law T-shirts, she tossed and turned on the daybed well past midnight. In the apartment upstairs, a couple argued, made up—or so the thirty seconds of creaking metal suggested—then played a game apparently involving dice. In a fit, she threw back the covers, searched online to find Felix's management company, and emailed the landlord, threatening to sue for the breach of the covenant of quiet enjoyment, demanding $1,500 off the rent, and signing it as Felix's attorney. Then she turned the window unit to high, though it was forty degrees outside, and collapsed back into bed.

During the delirious hours that followed, slipping in and out of anxious wakefulness, she devoted all her energy to not thinking about Nathan or Meredith. Instead, she thought of John Grisham novels. The recipe for chicken piccata. Her escape plan if a tsunami hit Manhattan. Tsunamis generally and how terrifying they were. She dreamed of a wave, as tall as the Empire State Building, stampeding the city, churning cars and bodies, obliterating skyscraper after skyscraper until there was nothing left.

Chapter 4

After a few hours of sleep during which she dreamed fitfully about drowning in a tsunami with Tom Cruise's character from *The Firm*, Georgina rose and went to the kitchen in search of coffee. She wore Felix's clothes and the underwear she'd had to pluck out of her bra and put on in the back seat of her cab last night. That had to be rock bottom. Nowhere to go but up, right?

Despite her anxiety-ridden insomnia, she did wake with a slightly more optimistic perspective. Nathan wasn't leaving her—he'd made it clear Meredith was a mistake. There was something empowering about that. If he wanted her forgiveness, he would have to earn it, and she had all the say in how. She could make him perform circus tricks or sing opera if she wanted to. She could do anything she damn well pleased, and he couldn't say a word about it. Whatever happened next was up to her. That was how she liked it.

Felix's kitchen was small by any normal standard, but typical for New York. Two people could fit comfortably inside of it, but three would be a crowd. It had an antique, avocado-colored stove, butcher-block counters, and indoor plants occupying half the shelf space. Georgina was holding a particularly wilted one to the tap for a drink when light footsteps approached and she braced herself. Alina breezed in wearing a loose rose-colored T-shirt and black underwear. The fluid motion of her limbs paused when she spotted Georgina, and she pressed a delicate hand to her chest. On each finger, she wore a silver ring.

"Oh," she said. "You scared me." Alina was from Bulgaria, but spoke with a lyrical English accent. "I didn't know we had company."

Georgina put on the most dazzling smile she could muster before sunrise. "Please, I'm hardly company."

Felix and Alina's cohabitation put Georgina in an impossible position. It forced her to spend time with someone she didn't particularly like, while simultaneously reminding her she wasn't doing enough to befriend Alina considering how serious Felix obviously was about her.

It didn't help that Alina was always tan, tousled, and glistening, as if she'd slept on a surfboard. Her scent reminded Georgina of a new age bookstore—incense and damp earth. Maybe a little weed. She was one of those women who could make a sweatsuit look cool, whereas Georgina resembled a 1980s gym teacher. Beside Alina, she felt instantly insecure even on the best of hair days.

"Can I make you a cup of coffee?" Georgina asked.

"Thank you, but I don't drink coffee." Alina withdrew a pitcher of lemons bathing in blue water from the fridge. "Blue spirulina," she explained, catching Georgina watching. Alina was "very into gut bacteria."

"So what are you doing here?" she asked.

"Sorry, I thought Felix would have told you," Georgina said. "I needed somewhere to stay last night."

"Is everything okay?"

"Um—" She did not want to have this conversation with a woman she barely knew. Rather, hadn't gotten to know. But Alina would find out anyway, she supposed, and she couldn't hide there forever with no explanation. "No, not really."

She watched as Alina lifted one leg onto the counter to stretch her hamstring and found it impossible to look away from her smooth muscles. Could one meditate their ass to perfection? She'd have to try that sometime.

With one cheek pressed to her knee, Alina asked, "Did something happen with Nathan?"

"Yes."

Alina returned her feet to the floor and bent down, wrapping her elbows behind her thighs. Her underwear narrowly covered her crotch, revealing not a stray hair in sight and not a bump of razor burn either. The woman was superhuman. Her skin was like untouched, sparkling amber. "I don't mean to push you," she said, her mouth nearly at her ankles. "But you can talk to me. People like to tell me things because I don't judge."

"How's that possible?" Georgina asked. "Everybody judges. You're judging me right now for drinking this coffee."

Alina straightened. Her face was flushed. "I don't care whether you drink coffee."

"Then why don't you drink it?"

"I drank tea with my grandmother. It has a strong emotional pull for me." Alina grabbed her right elbow in her left hand to stretch her triceps. Her arms were powerful and defined from the perfect Chaturangas Georgina had seen her demonstrate on the living room floor, sometimes right in the middle of a dinner party. "Coffee doesn't satisfy me in the same way."

"Has your grandmother passed away?"

"No. She's in Bulgaria," Alina said. "Would you like some breakfast?"

"Oh, you don't need to—"

"I don't mind." Alina opened the fridge again and pulled out eggs, a bag of spinach, and a square of feta cheese floating in milky water. Georgina's stomach responded with a growl, and she remembered she never had dinner.

"Thank you," she said. "Can I help?"

"No worries. Make yourself comfortable."

As Alina cracked the eggs into a bowl and stirred in feta, Georgina filled her mug with more coffee and cupped its warmth close to her chest. Felix's apartment was either soupy with steam from the radiator or arctic levels of freezing, and this morning, it was the latter. Alina poured the egg mixture into a hot pan, where it sizzled.

Perhaps driven by the tension Georgina felt when it was too quiet, or perhaps because she did need to talk about it, she blurted, "Nathan has been having an affair." Alina was sautéing the spinach, and it was easier to confess to her back than her pensive, inscrutable eyes.

"How do you feel about it?" she asked.

"Angry, obviously."

"I don't think that's obvious," Alina said. "There are lots of ways a person could feel."

Georgina stared through the window over the kitchen sink, where the sky was just beginning to lighten from navy to violet. She hadn't stopped to think about how she felt. In fact, she'd been actively trying not to think about it. It was true she was angry, but why, exactly? And who was she angry at? Nathan or herself? In a course she'd taken in college called the Psychology of Relationships, she'd learned *anger* was a secondary emotion that protected hidden, vulnerable emotions like *fear* or *humiliation*. The litmus test was to pinpoint the raw feeling present in the moment before anger took its place. She closed her eyes and remembered applying lipstick and tousling her hair. She'd been giddy, about to win Wife of the Year. She pushed open the door and—

"I feel like I had the rug pulled out from under me," she said, "and I'm humiliated. And I feel like I've been deprived of a say in my own life. I don't like feeling that way. It terrifies me that this could happen again and it's totally out of my control."

"Those are all valid feelings." Alina switched off the burner and scooped eggs and spinach onto two plates. While it steamed, she sliced a tomato and salted it. "Do you want to forgive him?"

"I don't know," Georgina said. "I'd feel weak forgiving him and moving on. Like I was too afraid to be on my own."

"Are you?" Alina asked, glancing over her shoulder.

Georgina tried to imagine leaving Nathan and starting over. He'd move out or she would. Either way, she'd live alone, cooking for one or eating at the office because she'd have no one to go home to. She'd have to start dating again, creating web profiles on Match.com or whatever apps people in their thirties and forties used these days. She had no idea what they were called, it had been so long. She'd go on months or years of awkward dates, returning to that vulnerable period in her life when she'd worried about whether men were interested in her or would return her texts. She'd have to start shaving her legs every day again, and waxing, too. Maybe she would find someone new, or maybe not. There was a good chance she'd never have children if she started over at nearly thirty-five, unless she moved fast and married the next suitable man. Meanwhile, Nathan might end up with Meredith or some other pretty twentysomething girl who wanted to date a grown-up with a successful career. He'd be married again in a year, with a baby in two. It always worked like that, didn't it? He would have a thriving second family while Georgina spent her sixties on singles' cruises in the Bahamas.

"I guess I am," she said. "Is that awful?"

Alina handed Georgina a plate. "That's natural. When I left my country, I was terrified to start over."

"That's way more intense than what I'm going through."

"Trauma is trauma."

Instead of sitting at the table, they ate leaning against opposite counters. Perhaps sharing a table, just the two of them, would have been too intimate. On the other hand, they were already having the most intimate conversation Georgina could imagine. She hadn't told her best friend the basic facts of what happened last night, and here she was confessing her soul to this near stranger who wore earrings made of feathers. Even though Alina and Felix had been together over a year, she'd never tried to get to know Alina beyond the obvious. She'd had one dinner with the happy couple when they'd first returned from Costa Rica, heard Alina talking about sound baths, and figured that was all the information she needed.

But Alina was easy to talk to. From then on, Georgina resolved, she would treat Alina as a friend.

"This is delicious," she said. "Thank you."

Alina crossed her long, bare legs at the ankles. "I believe food is medicine."

Georgina wasn't sure what that meant but smiled and nodded nonetheless. "You're very wise."

"After what I've been through, it's easier to have perspective."

"Do you want to talk about anything?" Georgina asked. "I'm happy to return the favor, although I should warn you I'm not the therapist you are."

"I've dealt with my trauma, and I'm at peace with it."

Alina finished eating and began to rinse the dishes. Georgina chewed slowly, prolonging the meal, curious to hear what she would say next. She wanted answers, and Alina had all of them.

"After Communism fell in Bulgaria, my father sent my mother and me to live with his brother in London, and my uncle believed that gave him permission to treat us however he liked."

Georgina's fork hovered near her lips, and she set it back down. "I had no idea."

"You never asked," Alina said, washing her hands.

They were both silent as Georgina finished eating and Alina wiped the counter with a towel. Nothing remained to keep her in the kitchen, but Georgina didn't want her to leave. "How'd you learn to be so enlightened about everything?" she asked.

"I spend a lot of time meditating."

"On what?"

"The point of all of this." She gestured vaguely around the room.

"Do you have any wisdom for me?" Georgina asked, and forced a laugh to give the impression she was joking.

"I have noticed Nathan doesn't seem happy," Alina said.

Georgina looked up from the coffee mug she was refilling for a third time. "Unhappy, how?" He had seemed perfectly happy to her. What was there to be unhappy about? Everything had been fine.

"When you're looking at him, he has a pleasant expression," said Alina. "But when you look away, his face goes blank."

Georgina's fingers tightened around her mug. "Are you saying that's an excuse? Just because he's sad he can do whatever he wants?"

"No." Alina scooped her hair on top of her head and began tying it in a knot. Despite Georgina's sharpened tone, Alina remained calm. "I'm not trying to minimize your feelings. I'm just saying he might have some, too."

Outside the window, the city was coming to life—neighboring televisions switching on, children chattering on their way to the park, the *pfsst* of city buses stopping on the corner. Across town, Nathan would be waking up, too. When his alarm went off every morning at six, he threw the covers back dramatically like he was in a Broadway musical, swished Listerine until his teeth turned blue and his eyes watered, then put on sweatpants and left to jog Central Park. The whole routine lasted eight minutes. Eight minutes together and he'd be gone.

Or that was what he did on a normal day. Today, maybe he would lie motionless in their dark bedroom for hours, thinking of Georgina and how he'd ruined everything, drowning in sickening guilt. She hoped he was suffering. Would that change if there was some truth to Alina's observation? But if he was so unhappy, was cheating his only option? Why not retail therapy, for example? That was Georgina's go-to, and it worked just fine. She planned on retail therapy after breakfast. At the very least, she deserved a new coat.

"Even if he's secretly miserable," Georgina said, "that doesn't make this right."

"Right or wrong is not the way to view this situation," Alina said. "Some people make the choice to be nonmonogamous, and it isn't wrong for them."

There we go, Georgina thought. That was the Alina she'd been expecting. Down the hall, Felix's alarm rang, and she silently implored him to get up and tune in to Alina's moral nihilism. Though Alina had earned a spot on speed dial for Georgina's next crisis after their morning therapy session, that didn't change the immutable fact that Alina thought Dumbo was a suburb, whereas Felix dreamed of leaving the city to raise his family in Hudson. They were wrong for each other, just as Norah and Ari were wrong for each other. She suspected Alina could see that as well and her relationship with Felix was some sort of pet project to liberate him from his earthly restraints. And as for Ari, well . . . he'd sealed his fate when he flew to Vegas for *WWE SmackDown* on Rachel's first birthday. Georgina's plan to reunite Norah and Felix, already sketched in her mind, solidified.

"Nathan didn't exactly ask my opinion in advance," she said. "If he had, I'd have said no. Call me a moralistic goody-goody, but this one's pretty black-and-white."

Alina shrugged and glided out of the kitchen, less of a stranger than when she'd arrived but just as mysterious.

Chapter 5

Georgina liked errands, calendars, and checklists. She liked them so much she frequently volunteered to take care of tasks on other people's to-do lists in addition to her own. When she'd first learned about the website TaskRabbit, she'd briefly considered quitting her legal career and Rabbit-ing full-time. What a recipe for personal satisfaction. But that winter, cronuts were all the rage in New York City, and standing in line at 4:00 a.m. in twenty degrees to buy fried croissants wasn't exactly the dream.

If only Nathan had chosen a Monday to cheat, Georgina would have had a Tuesday full of back-to-back conference calls, meetings, emails, deadlines, and to-dos to distract her late into the night. Nathan knew she turned to productivity in times of stress, so it felt like a personal affront that he had chosen a Friday night to get caught cheating. Monday was a perfectly good day to have an affair. Better, even, than Friday, because no one expected sex on a Monday. Fridays were for wine and lovemaking. Mondays were for Thai food and *Law & Order: SVU*. Now she needed to fill a completely empty day, but she was already so on top of her errands that she had no more errands to run.

How early is too early for that drink? she texted Norah.

Never too early for mimosas, Norah responded.

They arranged to meet at ten thirty at Postino's, a wine bar with a small brunch menu on Lexington. In the meantime, Georgina busied herself by studiously reading the deposition transcripts she'd picked up at the office last night. She represented a network of sperm banks being sued by a woman who'd given birth to a child with a rare genetic disorder called Larsen syndrome, which caused skeletal malformations and breathing problems. It was caused by a mutation of the *FLNB* gene. The woman wanted to prove the gene mutation was inherited from the father. Georgina wanted to prove the gene mutation was on the mother's side or spontaneous. It had turned into a class action lawsuit—now the woman argued to sue on behalf of hundreds of other mothers who had used sperm from the same network and given birth to a child with a genetic disorder, alleging a major cover-up scheme in which the sperm bank's doctors destroyed the results of genetic tests and switched blood samples to hide genetic history that didn't pass their standards. It was tragic, to want a child so badly only to face daunting and lifelong health care and a messy legal fight. Her heart tightened when she thought of those mothers and their babies. But she doubted the existence of a nationwide blood-sample-swapping conspiracy. The simplest explanation was usually the right one. The sperm bank didn't hide anything. Tragedies just happened.

But proving that fact had become inseparable from proving herself. This was Georgina's first trial as a new partner, and the pressure to win was suffocating. Every day, senior partners stopped by her office to ask how it was going, then they'd give her double finger guns and say, "Knock 'em dead!" before stopping by the next partner's office, probably to gossip about whether she was ready to take on such a significant case alone. She'd thought so—she'd fought for the case—but now she worried she'd set something in motion that had grown bigger and stronger than she would ever be.

Anyway, losing might have been a foregone conclusion. The sperm bank ran a standard genetic screening on the blood of all donors, which tested for more common disorders like cystic fibrosis and sickle cell anemia. But the *FLNB* gene mutation could only be detected through targeted screening, which the sperm bank did not do. But that was not dispositive of liability—if the mother tested negative, that did not prove the donor had the mutation, because it could also develop spontaneously. The absence of this test just made Georgina's job a thousand times harder, and the genetic counselor with three Stanford degrees she'd hired as her main expert witness had been no help. In his deposition, he'd unequivocally admitted the necessary blood test was both "simple" and "inexpensive," which wasn't even the question. *"Could the mutation be determined through a blood test?" "Yes. And by the way, it's both simple and inexpensive! I'll tell you that for free!"* Plaintiff's counsel had latched onto that sound bite and run with it.

Worst of all, Meredith was one of the junior associates on the team. Georgina had staffed her specifically to spend more time together, knowing there would be late nights in the office with pizza, traveling for depositions, and a two-week trial in Michigan next summer. She couldn't kick her off now—that would be victim blaming and against everything she believed in. She would have to put a smile on her face and deal with it.

Reading the transcript, she could barely stand it. Her expert witness was giving their entire case away. When asked about the likelihood of the mutation developing spontaneously, he'd said, "I'd be guessing, but I'd say unlikely." She wanted to go back in time and wring his neck. In their practice sessions, she'd told him a hundred times that if he could not answer with a reasonable degree of medical certainty, then don't. A guess was not evidence.

She slammed closed her binder and pushed it off the bed.

It was only eight forty-five. She decided to walk to kill some time and clear her head. Fresh air was good for the soul, wasn't it? After a quick shower, during which she used Alina's bath products and wondered if she'd come out miraculously transformed into divine Mother Earth (she didn't), she hurried into the same navy suit and white button-down she'd worn yesterday. In her purse, she scrounged for lipstick and concealer, and twisted her hair into a bun. Nothing like business formal on a Saturday to make a woman feel like she had her life together. At least, that was what she told herself.

The walk took an hour, and her feet ached by the time she arrived. Inside, Norah sat at the far end of a communal table decorated with miniature pumpkins and fake red maple leaves, dressed in a black blazer over a plain white T-shirt and jeans, with a long gold teardrop necklace. Thanks to her natural eye for fashion, she was one of those people who could create an ultra-cute outfit at TJ Maxx for thirty dollars and receive compliments for the rest of the year. Georgina, on the other hand, usually convinced herself she should "take more risks" with her wardrobe and ended up with a wacky colorful blouse in the back of her closet with the tags still on, then stuck to her navy suit. Between Norah's straight-across bangs, heart-shaped face, and rose-balmed lips, she looked like the most popular girl at summer camp when she glanced up and smiled.

Georgina smiled back but lingered at the door until Norah mouthed, *What are you doing?* and waved her over.

Stalling, that was what. Telling Felix and Alina had been one thing, but this was her best friend. There would be no going back after Norah knew the truth. Not that Georgina would ever pretend Nathan's affair had never happened, but it was nice to have the option.

She caught the server's eye as she joined Norah. "I'll have what she's having."

"A personal crisis?" Norah asked dryly.

"I meant the drink. You're having a crisis?"

Norah grimaced. "This morning, I was running errands with Hannah, and I really had to use the bathroom, so I found a Starbucks—" The server appeared with Georgina's mimosa, and Norah held up her glass to request another with an embarrassed little shrug before continuing her story. "And Hannah opened the door while I was peeing and made a run for it. Everyone in need of a caffeine fix saw me naked from the waist down."

Georgina bit her lips, trying not to laugh.

"It's not funny," Norah said.

"It is actually pretty funny," Georgina said. "Sorry."

"And this happened immediately after Hannah's soygurt exploded in my purse, which is the only thing I've bought for myself all year."

"Soygurt?"

"Soy yogurt," Norah said, lifting her bag to reveal the chalky blue stain on the inner lining.

"Soy is bad for you," Georgina said. "Something about the estrogen levels."

"Please don't start. Soygurt is basically the only thing Hannah can eat."

A woman wearing red lipstick brought them a small basket of muffins, and they both ordered the ham-and-cheese omelets.

"So did you tell Ari and his scuba trip to pound sand?" Georgina asked.

Norah glanced up and arched one eyebrow. "Little surfing pun there?"

"Did you like it?"

"Too soon," Norah said. "And no. The thing you will never understand until you have children is that some things are worth putting up with to keep your marriage together."

You'd be surprised, Georgina thought.

"He can go on his little scuba trip," Norah said, "and when he gets back, I'm Wife of the Year and we're spending the holidays at home instead of schlepping all the way out to Long Island where his mother will say I'm getting jowls."

"She does not say that to you!"

"That's how she greets me." Norah lifted her fresh mimosa, made a face, and drank. "Wait until she tastes the food I bring. She thinks cinnamon is too spicy." She lifted one side of her mouth and nodded as if to say, *I'm not joking.* "Speaking of, do you and Nathan want to come over for dinner next weekend?"

At the sound of his name, Georgina's hand slipped on the stem of her mimosa, and it spilled across the table. "Sorry! Shit, sorry." A busboy in untied Converse hurried over with a towel. "Sorry again," she mumbled, futilely trying to soak up the spill with a sopping-wet cocktail napkin.

When he'd left, she remembered the question. "Um, like a dinner party?"

Norah laughed. "I'm flattered you think I'm capable of that. I can't find enough clean forks to feed my kids most nights. No—my grandmother is flying in from India after Thanksgiving, and if I can't prove to her that I can make her recipes, she'll move in with me. So it's nothing fancy, but I'm doing a little dry run."

Georgina spread butter on a muffin for an excuse to look nonchalant. "Are you inviting Felix?"

"I wasn't planning on it." Norah narrowed her eyes, dubious. "Do I need to?"

"Could be nice," Georgina said. "I was chatting with him last night, and he said he missed you."

Her expression was skeptical, but mildly entertained. "He did? Why?"

"Why wouldn't he miss you?"

"Several reasons," Norah said. "We barely speak to each other, being the first."

Georgina's muffin was now so buttered it was inedible. "He'd like to change that, I guess."

"Weird," she said. "What did you guys do last night?"

Georgina took a deep breath. It was time to confess. Tell Norah all about Meredith and say goodbye to her cushy pedestal forever. And she definitely would—in five minutes tops. She put on a bright smile. "Have you been thinking more about going back to school?"

Norah paused with a muffin halfway to her mouth. "When was I thinking about going back to school?"

"I thought you mentioned something . . . that one time. Was it Labor Day weekend?" Georgina shrugged. "Anyway, have you?"

"Are you crazy?" Norah asked. "I don't have time for law school. I don't even have time to apply for law school."

"You'll make the time," Georgina said.

"That's easy for you to say. You're Superwoman and I'm"—she looked around the restaurant, then pointed at the Converse-wearing kid in black, who balanced a swaying, overfull tray of wineglasses—"like that guy. Barely managing to avoid disaster."

"Nathan's having an affair," Georgina blurted. The words had tumbled from her mouth before she could stop them. It wasn't right to let Norah think her life was in control when she'd never felt more out of it. At least the truth was laid bare now. The woman in red lipstick mercifully returned with their omelets, and she started scarfing it down for something to do with her hands.

Norah stared with her mouth open for a full minute. "Are you sure?"

"If I'm wrong, I need a brain scan," Georgina said with her mouth full. "I walked in on them."

Out of nowhere, a thirtysomething man in a backward hat and plaid shirt pulled out the chair beside them. "This conversation looks too serious, ladies! Lighten up. I'm Jared."

He extended his hand to Norah, who glared at it murderously. "My best friend is having a crisis. Can you please, for the love of God, leave us alone?"

Jared sulked off, not bothering to push in his chair, and joined his friends at the far end of the communal table. A few seconds later, his buddies shot bitter glares in their direction.

"See, why can't you stand up to Ari like that?" Georgina asked.

"How come you let me prattle on about my stupid life while you were sitting on this?"

"Your life isn't stupid."

Norah pressed her hands to her face. "Tell me everything. Who? What were they doing? Oh my God. I can't believe this. Fuck men. Do you know what I mean? Fuck. Men."

"Her name is Meredith De Luca," Georgina said. "First-year associate and husband stealer extraordinaire. And he was going down on her. With the lights on, by the way, so unless she's the bravest woman in the world, this wasn't their first time."

Norah pressed both hands to her mouth. When the server passed, she said, "We're going to need more mimosas. But hold the orange juice. And make it wine."

"You read my mind," Georgina said.

"Is he—I mean—leaving you for her?" She grimaced. "Sorry. Couldn't come up with a less horrible way to say that."

"He says he's not in love with her and it was a mistake."

"That's good, right?" she asked gently.

Georgina nodded, pushing egg around her plate. "But Meredith is in love with him."

"She said that?"

"She didn't have to. Her face when I walked in?" Georgina raised one eyebrow to make her point. "No. Nathan's not that good."

Norah, who'd been vise-gripping Georgina's forearm, let go and laughed. "Stop."

"His technique is more like a cat cleaning her kittens," Georgina said. "Long, slow lapping. *Soothing* would be a good way to describe it."

"I'm sorry—" Norah was biting her knuckle with tears in her eyes. "I shouldn't be laughing right now."

"I'm not terribly concerned about protecting Nathan's feelings at the moment."

"Do we think it's better or worse that they weren't having sex the old-fashioned way?" Norah asked.

"If it's not my vagina, it's pretty bad regardless," Georgina said. "Although I'm not sure I'll ever be able to kiss him again."

"How are you so calm about this?" Norah asked. "I'd be lying down in the middle of Broadway right now if I were you."

"Last night, I was not calm. But this morning, I woke up and decided I'm not going to let this ruin me. I never wanted to get divorced. I was happy. Why should he get to derail my life?"

Norah shook her head with an amused smile. "Only you would turn a cheating husband into a women's rights issue."

Georgina raised her fresh glass of white wine. "Frankly, I think I speak for women everywhere when I say fuck him and the fact that men can cheat on their wives who've done nothing but support them, then divorce those women while they go marry younger and hotter and their wives have to start online dating a bunch of catfishing creeps with coin collections."

"Hear, hear!" Norah cheered, and Jared and his friends sneered. "So what's your plan?"

Georgina sipped the wine. The drinks were going to her head, and yes, it was eleven in the morning, but she was not going to let herself feel bad about that after what she'd been through. She felt lighter, relieved to laugh about this absurd turn in her life. "I don't have one yet. But when I do, it'll be good."

"Are we talking revenge plot?" Norah's cheeks were growing flushed, her eyes bright. "We could frame him for a crime. Ten years max jail time."

"Do you want me to end up a mini-docuseries? Next."

"You could put a GPS tracker in his briefcase," she said. "Take away all his independence."

"So I'll be his mother," Georgina deadpanned. "I hear that's great for a marriage. How about a Renaissance-era torture device? Except I'll call it an *enhanced marriage technique*."

"Or you could sleep with someone," Norah said. "Rebalance the scales of justice."

"Getting warmer," Georgina said. "But I'd need Nathan to find out about it. Would I do it and then tell him? Or get his permission first?"

"You'd have to time it so he walked in on you," Norah said, "like a surprise party!"

"I could tell him I've earned the right to one affair," Georgina said, "and I'll let him know when I've found the right candidate."

"A getting-laid layaway plan!" Norah exclaimed, and clapped.

They laughed until Georgina was short of breath and her eyes stung, but at the same moment, they seemed to remember the circumstances underneath their brainstorming and sobered. Norah cleared her throat. Georgina wiped her eyes. There was one muffin left, and Norah nudged it. "Want to split it?"

The half muffin crumbled on Georgina's plate as she poked at it. "It's not about punishing him or getting revenge. I'm worried Nathan's been unhappy. Alina mentioned something."

"We listen to Alina now?" Norah pointed her fork in Georgina's face and scowled. "And you told her about this before me?"

As suddenly as if the roof had caved in, the past twelve hours crashed down upon her. She covered her face with her hands as a raw, choking sound escaped her chest, and began to sob. "I'm sorry," she said between gasps. "I'm sorry."

Norah came to sit on her side of the table and held her shoulders. "Finally," she said. "I was worried there was something wrong with you."

They sat for a long time, Georgina crying and Norah rubbing her back, until her tears dried up and she was left with a puffy face and an exhausted headache. She blew her nose in a cocktail napkin. When she forced herself to speak, her voice came out swollen. "What if I've made Nathan miserable?" she whispered.

"Impossible. You're perfect, and everybody knows it."

"If that were true, he wouldn't have cheated."

"So go to counseling," Norah said. "Figure out what went wrong and move on. It's nothing to be embarrassed about. Ari and I go to counseling."

"I'm not embarrassed about counseling." The cocktail napkin in Georgina's hand was wet and cold as she held it to her nose and blew again. "It's just not enough. Doing trust falls at a retreat upstate isn't going to change anything. This will happen again."

Norah gave Georgina's shoulders a little squeeze. "I can't believe I'm defending him right now, but people do make mistakes and learn from them."

"What would you do if it were Ari?"

"I can't answer that," she said quietly. "It's too painful to think about."

"You two are still together," Georgina said, shredding the edges of her sodden napkin, "after everything you've been through. Tell me your secrets."

"There is no secret, and there is no magic potion. I wish there were. I'd be first in line."

Georgina peeked up into Norah's eyes like a child getting caught trying the dog's treats—she shouldn't, but she couldn't help herself. "My client told me swinging saved her marriage."

Norah snorted. She thought Georgina was joking, but she wasn't. The realization had struck her somewhere after the first glass of wine with the heart-vibrating sensation of a giant gong. It was perfect. She could save her marriage and feel in control of it, too. There would be no more secrets, no more lies, and no more surprises. If sex was what Nathan wanted, she would hand it to him on a silver platter, a home-cooked meal she'd whipped up from her own recipe. *Voilà*.

When Norah saw Georgina was serious, her expression fell. "Oh my God. You're not actually considering that. Are you absolutely insane? You want to have sex with dirty old men?"

Georgina lifted her chin. "I like older men."

"I'm not talking Idris Elba," Norah said. "I'm talking saggy butt. I'm talking grandpa."

"I wasn't planning on swinging at a nursing home," Georgina said, "although I bet that would be wild."

"I'm serious." Norah fixed her with a glare that cleared up the mystery of where Rachel got hers from. "Think about this later, without the wine."

"I don't need to," Georgina said, waving her wrist in the universal sign of check requesting. "This is what I'm doing. Nathan and I need to spice up our sex life, clearly, and this way, I get to do it, too. All is fair."

Norah recognized her imminent defeat and shook her head skyward. "This is a really bad idea," she groaned.

"When are my ideas ever bad?" Georgina asked.

The bill came, and she signed it with a flourish.

Chapter 6

"I knew it!" Suzanne screeched when Georgina confessed her change of heart. They were sitting on a park bench in Columbus Circle, facing the center fountain. After Georgina said goodbye to Norah, she wasted no time before calling Suzanne and begging her to meet, offering to bring a pick-me-up from Café Boulud. "It'll be the best decision you ever made."

Georgina pulled the lid off her latte and blew. "Tell me more about what it's like."

Suzanne dunked a chocolate biscotti into her black coffee. "Saturday night, we went to a party in Brooklyn. Our friends rented out a *wedding venue* for a sex party. Isn't that so delightfully ironic? I met this guy named . . ." She paused and squinted into traffic. "Actually, I can't remember his name. Anyway, they were the most mind-blowing orgasms of my life."

As in, plural? That didn't sound so bad.

"I think I saw an alternate dimension," Suzanne said.

"But what actually happens at these parties?" Georgina asked.

"Other than the obvious? We usually play games. Maybe everybody wears a blindfold, or my favorite—Name That Fantasy."

Georgina laughed. "Can't say I've played that one before."

"Pretty straightforward sex game," Suzanne said. "Everybody writes down their fantasy on a card. One by one, someone reads them out loud, and we try to guess who it belongs to. The person who gets it right performs it. Or there's a slightly different version that's more like twenty questions, but that one takes too long, in my opinion. Anyway, that's how I ended up acting out a leather daddy fantasy onstage. I swear you could have sold tickets—I was that good."

Georgina's face must have betrayed her panic.

"I don't mean to scare you," Suzanne said. "The experience is what you make of it. If you want to go and watch but not participate, that's fine, too. Some people do that."

"You let people *watch*?"

"You say that like it's weird."

"I'm just trying to establish a new normal," Georgina said. "I'm not looking for crazy, *Fifty Shades*-type stuff."

Suzanne crumpled up her biscotti wrapper and threw it toward the trash can, but missed by nearly four feet. "Then you're not doing it for the right reasons."

A pigeon pecked at Suzanne's crumbs for a while.

"I was wrong when I said Nathan and I were doing fine," Georgina said quietly. "Very wrong."

"Did something happen?"

She nodded. "I woke up from that fantasy."

The two women shared a moment of silence buried under the city's sounds. Georgina sensed Suzanne watching her, but couldn't meet her eye or she'd cry again. It was that way with the events of last night—if she let herself look directly at them, the devastation would overwhelm her. Swinging offered a chance to look elsewhere, to focus on the solution. If it saved Suzanne's marriage, why not hers? She held that hope in the palm of her hand like a rare, exquisite stone. All was not lost.

"I'm joking," Suzanne said eventually, and rested her gloved hand on Georgina's. Occasionally she put aside her outrageousness for a minute and became this hopeful, endearing person Georgina liked a lot. "There are lots of reasons why people swing, and they're all good. We don't just hump each other at the parties—we talk. We're friends. And everyone gets something different out of it. Some couples aren't attracted to each other anymore, but they love one another or have kids and want to stay married. Some couples are voyeuristic, and they get off on it. Some couples want to reinstate some competition into their relationship because it makes a stale marriage feel young again. And for some couples, it builds trust—give your partner freedom, but by your own rules. It's not one-size-fits-all."

Georgina sat on her hands to suppress her urge to take notes. "And it works?"

"In more ways than you'd expect. Not only do I feel more confident, more satisfied, more erotic in my relationship with Philip, but we're finally communicating. We couldn't talk about what to have for dinner without cold shoulders and snide comments. Now we actually express ourselves, and even better, we listen. Totally foreign concept, right? But we had to learn how to tell each other what we were comfortable with in the experience, and that's bled into how we operate elsewhere."

"How fast did it work for you?"

"You're very focused on the destination without paying attention to the ride," Suzanne said, and winked with both eyes again. "Pun intended. Think of your most embarrassing fantasy, and you can have it. Easily. Just say the word. Sometimes you don't even have to say the word. At a sex club in Brooklyn, they have rooms for every fantasy you could ever imagine, and you just walk in."

Georgina laughed. "I'm looking for more of a . . . swingers bunny hill."

"Now *that* sounds like a game we need to play at the parties," Suzanne said. "But sure, you can pizza your way down the mountain, and I'll go black diamond. It's not all group sex and whips, okay? What you need to find is a group of couples interested in exchanging partners every so often, and you can get to know each other and see if you're a good fit."

"Yes, exactly," Georgina said. It would be just like when she ran a case—if she controlled the schedule, the content, the staffing, she'd control the outcome. The win.

"Frequent sex makes you live longer, you know," Georgina said. "Studies show that."

Suzanne threw her hands up in a hopeless gesture. "Who's the expert here?"

Sitting still for too long in the autumn air, she'd begun to shiver and her latte had gone cold, but she couldn't leave yet. She closed her eyes and mustered up the courage to ask, "Was it hard the first time?"

"Oh, it was *very* hard," Suzanne said, elbowing her in case she missed the joke.

"Seriously," Georgina pleaded. "Help me."

Suzanne's cheeky grin faded. "It was hard and really, really scary. I just wanted Philip to love me, and he wanted to do this crazy thing called swinging, and I felt so rejected by that. I thought, okay, if I do this once, he'll realize he actually wants me all to himself and being with someone else wasn't as great as he thought it would be. Obviously, that didn't happen. But I was thinking too much about him and not enough about me. Sex feels good, and it turns out lots of men like having it with me. Now I've started making demands and feeling desired, and honestly, I'm a whole new person."

"I can tell," Georgina said. "You've got a glow about you."

"That would be the morning sex I just had." Suzanne nudged Georgina with her shoulder. "Let me know if you need an introduction to the right people. And don't forget to get yours, my friend. Promise me that."

Georgina watched Suzanne cross Fifty-Ninth Street in her peach-colored poncho and plaid scarf. If Suzanne the Talbots catalog model could do it, so could she. The bedroom was just like the courtroom, wasn't it? Just another place to fuck or be fucked.

She picked up Suzanne's littered wrapper and sank it cleanly into the can.

Georgina sent Nathan a text: *I'm going to the apartment. If you're there, leave.*

Their building was a fourteen-story postwar flat façade on the corner of Eighty-Sixth Street and Madison. When she arrived, she found her favorite doorman on duty. "Mickey, I brought you this," she said, handing him an everything bagel with scallion cream cheese and a carton of orange juice.

"You're too kind to me, Ms. Wagman." He scrunched up his deeply lined face. "I'm not supposed to eat on duty."

"I won't tell if you don't." She leaned over his podium. "Do me a favor, and call my cell if Nathan comes in?"

Mickey paused with the bagel already halfway to his mouth. "Everything okay, Ms. Wagman?"

"Oh, fine." She smiled. "I'm planning him a surprise party. Give me a call, got it?"

But when she got to the tenth floor, she discovered her bribery was a waste of a perfectly good bagel. Nathan was sitting on the couch.

"I asked you not to be here," she said.

"I had to see you," he said. "Can we please talk?"

Their apartment was just the same as it had been when she left for work yesterday morning. The tile in the entryway was still black-and-white. The fireplace that didn't work still had candles in it. The built-in bookshelves in the living room remained color coordinated, and the retro clock above the mantel was predictably five minutes slow. But everything seemed strange and off-kilter, as if this weren't her apartment, rather a movie set made to resemble her apartment. *That's because home is a perception*, she told herself, *and I have a new perspective.*

She set down her briefcase in its usual place beside the door. "I'm going to change my clothes."

In the bedroom, she stripped out of yesterday's suit and dumped it in the dry cleaning hamper, but it might as well have been the trash. She couldn't ever wear it again. The necklace, too, had been a gift from Nathan for her birthday years ago, but she'd never be able to look at it without remembering how she'd grabbed it as a reminder that their marriage was real when she'd first walked into his office and seen Meredith naked on the desk.

From her dresser, she pulled a pair of black leggings, a red turtle-neck, and matching socks for Nathan's sake. Her hands shook as she pulled them on. She'd wanted more time for this conversation, to think about what she needed to say, to prepare for what he might say. But at least—at least—she was armed with a way out of this mess.

When she returned to the living room, Nathan stood at the window, looking out.

"Start at the beginning," she said.

He turned around. "Can you sit?"

"I feel better over here."

They stood ten feet apart like bookends, separated by something impenetrable.

"Meredith started flirting with me," he said. When she snorted, he hurried to say, "I'm not putting this on her, trust me, I'm just telling you how it started. About a month ago, she asked me to go to lunch to talk about her career. I said fine. I go to lunch with associates all the time."

"But Meredith is a litigator. That makes no sense."

"I thought the same thing, but she told me she was considering crossing over to the dark side, I think is how she put it."

For some reason, the knowledge that Meredith wanted to leave Georgina's group—leave her—hurt worse than learning about the lunch. She sat on the far end of the couch.

"We went to the sushi restaurant at the W."

"It's called Blue Fin," Georgina blurted. The details were important. They would never have this conversation again, so they needed to nail it the first time.

"Right." Nathan started to pace with his hands in his pockets. He wore his suit pants from last night, and she wondered whether he'd slept at all. "We went there. And I could tell—" He ran one hand through his hair and tugged at the back. "This is going to sound really bad, because I swear to God I don't look at what the associates wear, but I could tell she'd dressed up. She wore this hot pink, tight, sleeveless dress, and I noticed—"

Georgina knew exactly the dress Nathan was talking about and remembered the day Meredith had worn it. She'd looked tall and stunning, the pink color clashing with her red hair in the most electrifying way. One part of Georgina had thought, *I've got to talk to her about her sexy clothes in the office.* Another part of her had thought, *You go, girl.* That had all been for her husband. This cruel truth sucked the gravity from the room, giving her the sensation of floating through her life without anything real to hold on to.

"Noticed what?"

"That she was staring at my mouth." Nathan's chest caved as he let out a single sob. "It sounds so stupid. I'm such a fucking idiot."

He began to move around the room with agitated strides, jerking his limbs and pounding a fist on his thigh. When he spoke, it was argumentative and muttery, as if he were having this conversation with himself, trying to work out the details and convince himself it wasn't so bad. But he was losing that battle, and that made him more hysterical. "Nothing happened at the lunch. It was just the way she looked at me. I don't know. It felt like she thought it was a date. When I paid the bill, she said thank you like she owed me something, like I was being a gentleman. But that was just the firm credit card. And on the way back to the office, she kept bumping into me. But it's Times Square, it's crowded, okay? But I knew she was doing it on purpose."

Heat flooded Georgina's cheeks. "You should have cut it off."

"I worked late that night, and she came to my office. She closed the door when she walked in, and I thought that was weird. She said she had a friend who was starting a platform for crypto exchange, and it was going to be huge, and would I like to set up drinks with this guy because he was looking for a lawyer. Should I have said no? Fuck, I should have said no. But that's my job. That's what I do."

Without warning, Nathan left the room, leaving her alone with his words hanging in the air. He returned a minute later with two glasses of water and set one on the coffee table in front of her. In a few gulps, he emptied his.

"A couple of nights later, we go out with this guy—"
"Where?"

"It was a wine bar on Seventeenth and Irving. She picked it. Not the type of place I'd take a client. The tables were too small, and it was dark. The guy was just a kid, big ideas but no real funding. Honestly, it was a waste of time, but between the two of them, I felt fucking ancient. They wanted to drink for free, and I wanted to impress them, and we ended up getting pretty hammered." Nathan sat on the ottoman and put his head in his hands. "We shared a car uptown. It was freezing outside, and she had bare legs. I shouldn't have noticed that, but I did. I gave her my coat and she used it like a blanket, and I felt . . . I was really drunk. And in my head, it all made sense. It was a good idea. Haven't you ever had that experience? No. Don't answer that. I'm not trying to get your empathy."

Georgina's body was stiff, as if with rigor mortis, but her heart pounded as though it were trying to break free. She knew what was coming next. "So you went up to her apartment."

He nodded. It was possible she was going to throw up, and she wondered vaguely whether she'd make it to the bathroom, but at the same time, it didn't matter. There was little to hide anymore.

"Who asked who?"

Nathan pressed his temples. "She told me her neighbor was creeping her out. Sometimes he would wait outside her door and ask for legal advice. So I said I'd better walk her up. It was the right thing to do—she'd had a lot to drink, and that was my fault—but I also *wanted* that to be the right thing to do. I was justifying it in my head as we went upstairs."

"Were you thinking about me?"

"Honestly, no," he said. "I was a man, and she was a woman I was attracted to, and you didn't exist."

A hard pressure pushed the tender space underneath Georgina's rib cage until she couldn't breathe. Nathan's words—*you didn't exist*—were the most painful she'd heard in her lifetime. They made her body feel like a locked cupboard and she was screaming from inside. More than almost anything, she wanted to matter to people.

"Inside, she went to go change. And I thought, okay, whatever she comes back wearing will tell me what this is. Maybe she needs a friend, maybe she's going through something. I should have left, obviously." He shook his head at the floor. "Her apartment was disgusting. She's a total slob. The whole place was really . . . sad."

Nathan returned to the window and slumped against the frame. Sweat darkened the back of his shirt, his sloping figure silhouetted by the gray sky beyond.

Quietly, Georgina asked, "What did she come back wearing?"

He gazed out the window for a while, then said, "Nothing."

She closed her eyes, and for a long time, they were silent. It was at least clear Nathan didn't love Meredith—he'd been honest about that. This wasn't about her, not specifically. In the span of two days, he'd slipped from perfect husband to cheater, and all it took was a hot pink dress and a few glasses of wine. If it was so easy the first time, it would be easy the second time, and she could never, ever let herself be blindsided like this again. The only way to make sure Nathan didn't break the rules anymore was to change them.

"How many times were you together?" she asked.

"Four," he said, and let out a loud, gnarled yell of frustration. "A *first-year associate*."

"You're the married one," Georgina said. "And you're a partner, and you're ten years older. This is on you."

"I know."

"You had a million chances to walk away."

"Yeah. I know."

She wasn't sure she could handle the answer to this question, but she had to ask. "Why didn't you?"

Nathan sat beside her on the couch, and he smelled like a bar. "Don't you ever wonder whether your choices were the right ones? What if there's someone out there who's a better match for you, or a city where you'd be happier, or a job with less stress?"

"I was happy," Georgina said. "This was the life I wanted."

"I ask myself those questions a lot," Nathan said. "I wish I didn't, but I do. And Meredith was a chance to be a different version of myself, and I took it."

"You want to be someone else—"

"No." He shook his head, gesturing at himself, his suit. "I want to be this person. I'm just not. It got the best of me."

That was validating. People did want the best life for themselves even if it didn't come naturally. They made choices to improve their shot at success, like she planned to do now with their marriage.

"Did I ever tell you about the time I almost got arrested?" he asked.

She looked up from her water glass. "What? No."

"I was in high school. A bunch of us broke into a theme park one night, and we were drinking on the roller coaster tracks. When the cops came, everyone ran. My best friend fell off and broke his leg, and I didn't stop to help him so I could get away. They all spent three nights in jail except for me—I never confessed. I've been thinking about that a lot. I'm not a good person, Georgina. I'm just pretending to be."

Surprising herself, she reached over and squeezed his hand. There was furious anger, and there was love. They could coexist. In a way, they weren't that different. "You're a good person," she whispered.

Nathan knelt on the floor and grabbed her hands and kissed them. "I need you. You're perfect, and I need your goodness to rub off on me. Please give me that chance."

Begging on his knees, he looked so unlike himself. His usually smooth face was shadowed and lined, and his neat hair stuck up in all directions at once. She took no pleasure in seeing him that way. She was happy when he was happy, when they were happy.

"We can't go back to the way we were," she said, "but we can't move forward either. At least, not like this."

"Can you ever forgive me?" His voice was that of a small, scared child.

"I don't know," she said. "But I don't think forgiveness is the answer anyway."

Nathan looked apprehensive as Georgina explained how Suzanne and Philip had saved their relationship, that it was stronger than ever, that they were thriving through a newfound trust and appreciation, a sense of shared adventure. She hit all the right points, sounding more like a therapist than a desperate, brokenhearted woman. All she needed was a PowerPoint presentation and a laser pointer, and she'd have been leading a restorative couples retreat.

"You want an open marriage?" he asked when she'd finished. "That doesn't seem like you."

"It's not an open marriage. You can't sleep with whoever you want. We'd do this together, to bring us closer. I want us to have passion and trust. Don't you?"

Nathan contemplated her face, then his expression relaxed. "You would do that for me?"

That answer, right there, confirmed she was making the right decision. This was what he wanted. But she couldn't let him know how far she was willing to go to make him happy, even after what he'd done, so she said, "It's not just for you. It's for me. It's for us."

Chapter 7

The sun set as Georgina walked through Central Park to collect her things from Felix's. Her breath clouded the cold air before dissipating into the twilight. Through the tree trunks and gaps in gray buildings, she occasionally caught a glimpse of orange over the Hudson, hoarding all the warm light and leaving the rest of the city in violet shadow. The snapshot was beautiful but fleeting, or beautiful because it was fleeting.

Her marriage had taken on a memorialized, frozen quality. It was no longer an ongoing, present reality but a bittersweet memory stored, like framing a photograph of your first house. She would never live there again. She could only hope her destination would be even better.

She picked up her pace to make it to Felix's before dark, walking so fast and hard on the pavement her legs grew tired and her neck damp under her scarf despite her wind-chilled cheeks. She was overwhelmed with urgency now that she had found a way out of this mess. If she didn't act now, right now, it would be too late. She'd lose her nerve. With no outlet, her anger would fester into resentment, and soon she and Nathan would be like Ari and Norah, unsure why they were together but for the piece of paper that tied them. Every word out of Nathan's mouth would become annoying, his post-workout smell would become repulsive instead of familiar, and his habit of narrating his morning routine ("Hot shower time!") would become embarrassingly childish instead of endearing. They'd lie beside each other in bed each night with the comforter forming a valley between them, not touching, not kissing, definitely no sex, ever. Eventually, coldness would become routine until someone couldn't take it anymore and moved out. That was exactly what happened to her parents. It was exactly what had happened to almost every divorced couple she knew, the slow decline from tolerance to indifference to hatred of a person once cherished.

But if what Suzanne said was true, swinging offered her a way to change their fate. Felix would think she was crazy. And maybe she was, but people did crazy things for marriage. People moved across the country, people had children they didn't want, people bought houses they couldn't afford. For fifty years, Georgina's grandmother had gotten out of bed every morning at 5:00 a.m. to put on makeup before her husband woke up and saw her bare face. *That* was crazy. This was rational.

Why shouldn't this work? It didn't require any mental gymnastics to understand the benefits. Sex with one person, one body, for two-thirds of one's life was unnatural! That wasn't how the cave people did it. That wasn't how the animals in the jungle did it. They just *did it*—free fucking for all! Of course, she had watched Animal Planet and noticed the forlorn expression in the meerkats' eyes as they were mounted from behind, but that was beside the point. She was not a meerkat. She'd liked sex a lot back in her heyday. But at some point, she'd graduated from having clothes-tearing, door-smashing, making-out-down-the-hallway, horny sex. She was getting older, her hormones were dying, and she was busy. She didn't even have sex on top of the covers anymore. It was too cold.

But what if she and Nathan could reclaim that part of themselves, a part they'd never shared with each other? How could that not help? They'd have a naughty, thrilling secret to look forward to on Friday nights instead of working past eleven with green curry delivered and *The Late Show* on low volume in the background. Maybe she'd buy lingerie for the first time in ten years. It would be exciting. And to be touched by someone who hadn't hurt her would feel nice, too. There was no downside she could see.

When she arrived at Felix's, he wore a smeared apron that said *Looks like Someone Kneads a Hug!* underneath a smiling, googly-eyed cartoon loaf of bread. He held a wooden spoon in one hand and a burned oven mitt in the other, and the apartment smelled like onions sautéed in butter. Seeing his face instantly made the weight pressing on her shoulders feel lighter.

She pecked his cheek and took off her coat. "I came to get my stuff. Smells amazing in here."

"You're not staying?" he asked. "I made salmon risotto, and I was going to serve you Chianti in front of the fire. I thought we could have a *Law & Order* marathon."

"I won't say no to any of that." Georgina waved to her new friend Alina as she passed the kitchen on her way to the guest room, Felix trailing behind.

"But you're going home already?" he asked. "How's that possible?"

"Nathan and I talked, and we have a solution we agree on." She yanked the sheets off the daybed. "I'll wash these and bring them back tomorrow."

Alina poked her head around the door. "Wine?"

"Please," she said, and accepted the glass. She sipped and set it on the desk to finish packing the spare toothbrush Felix had given her, the makeup she carried around in her purse for emergencies, and her binders from the office. "Thanks for letting me borrow your blow-dryer, by the way."

"No problem," Alina said. "I don't use it."

She glanced up at Alina's perfect, frizz-free waves cascading down her shoulders. Of course that was how it air-dried. If Georgina let her hair air-dry, it resembled the texture of the steel wool she used to stuff mouse holes in her apartment. She wasted twenty minutes every morning blowing out her hair with a round brush—no wonder Alina had time for Chaturangas.

"So what's the solution?" asked Felix. "Must be a good one."

Georgina zipped her shoulder bag in one clean swipe. "We're becoming swingers."

"Swingers," Felix repeated. "As in—"

"A couple that swings."

"And by *swing*, you mean—"

"I assure you it has nothing to do with a jungle gym," she said. "More of a playground for adults."

Felix and Alina exchanged a look. She had a secretive smile on her face, and he wore a bashful one.

"What?" Georgina asked.

"We know a thing or two about that," said Alina.

It was a good thing Georgina wasn't holding her wine, because she would have dropped it on the rug. "Get out!" she said. "You do not. Felix? You're a swinger? But you like 'game nights.' How is this possible?"

He tried and failed to suppress his grin. "We're not *swingers*. Come on, let's go eat. *SVU* is waiting."

Georgina watched, stunned, as Felix took Alina's hand and led her toward the kitchen. They were whispering to each other and laughing. Twelve hours ago, she'd thought of swingers as mythical, sexual counterculturists. Now three people in her inner circle were members of this illicit underground society? Was she about to learn Norah was the tooth fairy and Nathan the Zodiac Killer? None of this made sense. Even accepting his new hipster vibe, Felix was not the swinging type—this screamed Alina. Swinging was just Felix's latest chameleon trick. Was the problem that he loved in spite of himself? Or could Felix assume his partner's desires so easily because he had no idea what his own were?

But watching them kiss in the hallway now, Georgina couldn't deny their magnetic chemistry and found it hard to look away. This was further evidence that her theory was correct. Swinging brought couples closer together. Georgina and Nathan had never romantically kissed in the hallway, but they'd start now, right?

She followed them into the kitchen and sat at the same breakfast nook where she'd rested her cheek on the table and cried just twelve hours ago. That already felt like a different lifetime in another universe. Tonight, she held her head high. "Spill. I need details," she said.

The two of them exchanged another look, and Alina nodded.

He scooped asparagus onto three mismatched plates. "We've been to a couple of clubs. We're not regulars or anything."

"What kind of clubs?" Georgina asked.

He looked up with a brow raised. "What kind do you think?"

She glanced between them. "Dare I ask whose idea this was?"

"Mine," Alina said. She carried a wooden salad bowl to the table and began massaging olive oil into kale with her hands. "When I was in graduate school, I was in an ethically nonmonogamous relationship. We both agreed to have multiple partners at the same time. It was the most empowering experience of my life—to communicate my needs without feeling sorry for having them. I was so tired of that.

As a woman, I constantly felt like my opinions and my expectations didn't matter as much as my male partner's. I'd be upset, and somehow I'd be the one to end up apologizing for the way I 'handled' it. In navigating these relationships, I learned how to say what I wanted without feeling bad about it or worrying that what I wanted was wrong somehow." She tested a piece of kale, then continued massaging. "Ever since, I've been open with my partners up front that the occasional extracurricular activity was part of my lifestyle."

Georgina considered Alina's off-the-shoulder sweater, her silver rings, and her unplucked eyebrows. She'd never thought they'd had anything in common, but Georgina knew too well the feeling Alina described. Wasn't that exactly the dynamic playing out now? Nathan acted on his desires like they mattered more than Georgina's, and now she was the one trying to make peace again. Maybe she needed swinging more than she'd thought. She sipped her wine. "What kind of extracurriculars?"

Alina lifted one shoulder in a delicate shrug. "Felix and I have been to three clubs in the last year. We talk about it before we go, then talk about it again. What we're going to do, what our boundaries are, who we are looking for, what to do if someone wants to leave. It makes our bond stronger. Do you think this needs more salt?" She handed Georgina a softened piece of kale.

It was perfect, of course. Lemony, garlicky, and salty in equal proportions. "Delicious. Do you mean, like . . . an orgy? Because that's not what I want."

Alina laughed like Georgina was a child who'd said the darndest thing. "Not an orgy, although there are those. We dance, we find a couple we're both attracted to, and if they're interested in us, we might book a private room for the four of us. But we've also just flirted and gone home. It's more about the energy and the intimacy you find in trusting each other enough to go there together. Wanting your partner to have their needs met is the ultimate selfless act."

From the counter, Felix started coughing into his fist. "Wrong hole," he wheezed.

Alina smiled cheekily.

Felix filled a glass of water from the tap and drank the entire thing in a few gulps, gripping it with both hands. He cleared his throat and wiped his face with a dish towel. "Dinner's ready," he said. His voice was flat and raspy.

After he carried three plates of risotto and asparagus to the table, Alina scooped a heap of salad onto each one. Felix passed out forks, then sat facing the window. He avoided Georgina's eye. There was a moment of pause in which no one touched their food. Was Alina going to recite a Buddhist prayer? Perhaps an ode to Mother Earth? She waited, but when Alina took the first bite, Felix followed, and the moment passed. She attributed the awkwardness to Felix's discomfort in talking about his sex life, and dug in.

"I feel like a 1950s sitcom husband coming home to dinner on the table," she said. "I could get used to this."

"We enjoy cooking," Alina said. "It relaxes us."

"You're both excellent." Georgina covered her full mouth with her fingers. "If I were at home right now, I'd be eating week-old spaghetti, so thank you."

"Felix is teaching me how to make maeuntang, and I'm teaching him how to make sarmi," Alina said. "Our favorite dishes to eat when it's cold outside."

"Add it to your list of extracurriculars," she teased.

Felix had already cleaned his plate. He biked twenty miles up the Hudson every morning, so he ate like a linebacker. Wanting him to join the conversation, Georgina prodded him with her elbow. "I see you hated it," she said, but he didn't respond or even look up.

"Do you have any more questions for us?" Alina asked.

Georgina's eyes lingered on Felix for a few seconds longer. Something was bothering him. He must have been embarrassed to have his secret exposed, so she did him the courtesy of leaving him alone to stare into the salad.

"I'm not ready for the club scene you're describing," she said. "My friend suggested I find a small group of people with . . . shared interests . . . who get together for . . . hobby nights?"

"You need to get comfortable with the language," Alina said. "But sure, I can hook you up with that."

"You can?" She hadn't known where to begin searching for her new friends. Joining Suzanne's group was out of the question—there had to be something in the lawyer's code of ethics about that. Craigslist? she'd wondered. The dark web? But it turned out her sexual Narnia was separated by only one degree. The swinging gods were surely smiling down upon her.

"We'll even join you," Alina said. "Don't you want to, my love?"

Felix hesitated so briefly Georgina would have missed it had she not known him so well. "Definitely," he said. "I'm in."

"With who?" Georgina asked. "Who are these people?"

"They're industry types," Alina said. "The leader is Quincy. He was an adjunct professor in artistic brand design at Parsons while I was there. He's not what you'd expect. When I first saw him, he reminded me of a Vegas magician." She paused to nibble the end of her asparagus. "He's lovably eccentric. His wife I don't know well, but I think she used to be a chorus dancer on Broadway."

Georgina barely tasted her risotto anymore, already too busy trying to envision herself swinging with this Quincy person. But her fantasy had a blurred, indistinct quality to it because she still had no idea what *happened* at these gatherings. She wouldn't, she supposed, until she experienced it for herself. She wasn't accustomed to that level of unpredictability. In fact, she'd spent her whole life trying to avoid it.

"And there's my good friend Laila, who is an acupuncturist. I met her through her husband, Jeremiah, who was a design consultant at my last company and Quincy's protégé. Everyone met through industry connections, though there's one guy named Marco who does something with the stock market. I'm not sure how he ended up there, but he's pleasant. Seems shy."

"So you've been?" Georgina asked. "To their parties?"

"I used to go regularly with my former partner," Alina said. "Years ago."

Felix got up to clean the dishes.

"Can I help you?" asked Georgina.

"It's fine," he said, and dropped his plate into the sink with a dangerous clatter.

Georgina sipped her wine and dabbed her mouth. With Felix so distant, she'd begun to feel like she was on a date with Alina, and between the wine and the sexually charged conversation, it was a pretty good one. She leaned in. "Are they . . . attractive? Am I allowed to ask that?"

"It's like dating," Alina said. "Some nights you'll have a conversation with someone and feel chemistry, other nights not. You're never obligated to be with someone if you're not vibing with them. But on the whole, yeah, everyone in the group is attractive."

Georgina leaned back in her chair. "You've sold me."

Alina used her knife to curate a bite of asparagus, risotto, and salmon on her fork. She ate European-style, her fork in her left and her knife in her right. It made her look skilled and sophisticated, her plate neat at the end of a meal. Georgina was a messy eater, a trait only her father found endearing. She looked down to see that she'd somehow managed to smash half an asparagus into the table with her elbow. Those qualities—her messy eating, her mismatched socks— were the parts of herself she strove to hide. They were embarrassing. Having spent her life trying to be perfect, she didn't know how to stop. As discreetly as she could manage, she wiped the table. "Let me do the dishes," she insisted.

When the pots and pans were drying, Georgina suggested a rain check on *Law & Order*. "I'm exhausted," she said. "This has been the hundred-year weekend. I just want to take a bath and go to bed."

"I'm about to do the same," Alina said, and kissed Georgina's cheek.

"Enjoy," Georgina said a little stiffly, knowing that whereas her own bath plans included trying not to drop her phone in the tub as she answered emails, Alina's would include luxuriously lounging with candles, incense, and rose petals, masturbating while the saxophone played. She was a walking, talking wellness blog. It was infuriating. "Thank you for your help tonight. And this morning."

"My pleasure," Alina said. "Soon to be yours."

"Let me walk you out," Felix said, and he trailed her to the door with a wooden muteness.

In the small entryway, Georgina took her time buttoning her coat, occasionally shooting him glances. "Are you okay?" she asked. "I swear I didn't come over here to cause trouble. I just needed my binders."

"I'm worried about you," he said.

"No need," she said. "I know what I'm doing."

"I don't think you do." Felix tipped his head back against the wall, staring at the ceiling. His Adam's apple was defined in his smooth neck. She admired his features as if through a window, a beautiful gift that didn't belong to her. His strong shoulders. His dark, thoughtful eyes. Any woman would be lucky to have him, but after today, she could understand why he'd chosen Alina. Alluring and confident, she knew exactly what she wanted. But this evening's revelation had only strengthened Georgina's suspicion that the two were misaligned. Felix didn't seem as enthralled with swinging as Alina did.

She whispered so Alina couldn't hear. "Do you not like it? Tell me the truth."

"Of course I do," Felix said. "And it's important to her. She was up-front about that. But it's hard—for me anyway. Jealousy doesn't go away because you've decided to do this. Just do me a favor and take some time before you rush in."

"Time for what?"

"To grieve?" he suggested. "To think about it? Twelve hours after your husband cheated isn't the time to be making life-changing decisions."

If he thought he was talking her out of it, he was wrong. The more she felt compelled to explain herself, the more resolute she became. "Or it's the best time," she said. "I can't stick with the status quo. There is no status quo."

"You're leaping into this because you want it to fix everything, but this is for couples who already have a secure foundation. It tests you, that's all I'm saying."

She lifted onto her toes to hug him. "Message received. As far as good intentions go, we're both right. So let me try this my way."

Felix laughed. "Don't worry. I wouldn't fool myself into thinking you'd listen to me."

She pecked his cheek. "Because you're not half as conceited as I am."

"I do know what I'm talking about, unfortunately," he said more quietly. "I've been cheated on a couple of times."

She whacked him with her glove. "And here I thought you told me everything. Who?"

He kicked the baseboard gently. "It doesn't matter."

"Do you mean Norah?"

Felix's mouth twisted into a self-effacing grin. "No. She didn't cheat. She just dumped me savagely."

"She did not."

"She left me a voice mail while she knew I was taking my con-law final. Does that not seem savage to you?"

Georgina toyed with the pom-pom on her knit hat. "Maybe she was a chicken because she knew she was making the wrong decision."

"I don't have a ripped back and a butt chin like Ari," Felix said. "Pretty sure she made the right decision."

With a coy lilt in her voice, she said, "I wouldn't be so sure."

Felix made a face. "What's that supposed to mean? She's got three kids with the guy."

"She told me you were the best kisser she ever had." That was true, Norah did say that.

He laughed. "Well, I'm terrible now. All teeth."

"I'm sure they love teeth at the sex club," Georgina teased. Felix instantly lost his humor and said goodbye. His sudden shift left her unsettled as she rode home in an Uber, but not enough to change her mind. Suzanne and her husband hadn't had a secure foundation— they'd been tightrope walking on a G-string before swinging. Felix was cerebral, inclined to overanalyze. But Georgina was a doer, an action-taker. She wasn't going to agonize about this decision when there wasn't anything to think about. It was this or nothing.

On Monday morning, Georgina dressed carefully in a new navy suit with a long jacket that ended below her hips and a pleated skirt instead of her usual tapered knee. It reminded her a little of something she'd seen Elaine wear on *Seinfeld*, but the '90s trends were making a comeback, she supposed. While she'd once appreciated Meredith's beauty with a kind of motherly pride, it had overnight become a threat. She sat at the mirror applying makeup for much longer than usual. Around her eyes she used a copper eyeliner usually reserved for holiday parties and filled in her lips with a powdery red. If Nathan noticed her heavy hand, he didn't comment.

Meredith's role in the whole affair was in a significant way Georgina's fault. She'd hired her, for one thing, and brought her into their lives. She'd convinced Meredith she was special with constant flattery and encouragement. Hers was an ego Georgina had nurtured. Cringing, she remembered telling Meredith, "If you work hard, you can be me someday." She didn't mean literally! If only she'd done more to teach Meredith the difference between the kind of attention she wanted and the kind that wasn't worth it.

Meredith needed her more than ever.

On the other hand, she would have expected Meredith to at least understand that seducing your boss's husband was a major no-no. That was pretty standard stuff.

Georgina bought coffee from Starbucks at eight thirty before catching the 4 train to Grand Central and sorting emails on her phone. It was strange how normal the morning seemed considering how much had changed since she'd done this commute last. By the time she arrived at the lobby of Eleven Times Square, she'd nearly forgotten to be anxious about what she'd arranged, and considered that a testament to her plan's early success.

Upstairs, bangs and grunts and shuffles came from the office next door to hers as two men from Office Services moved furniture. They were her heroes, Jax and Louis. They fixed everything, moved everything, fed everyone, set up and took down every client event or attorney happy hour, and made her printer run smoothly when all she could get it to do was whine and jam. Louis was in his fifties and only as tall as Georgina's shoulder. Jax was in his twenties and inhumanely hot. It was cruel, the way that he looked. While in bed with Nathan, she'd fantasized more than once about feeling the scrape of his stubble on her thigh and the press of his full lips on her neck. Today, he wore a faded denim button-down rolled up to his elbows, and she hung in the doorway to watch his forearms flexing for a few seconds before announcing herself.

"Everything all right in here?" she asked.

Seeing her, Jax smiled to reveal straight, white teeth. "I told you not to get all dressed up for me again," he said. "People are starting to ask questions."

"This isn't for you," she teased. "It's for Louis."

Louis made an exaggerated show of pretending to faint. "I got dressed up for you, too, Ms. Wagman. I wore my tuxedo." He leaped out from behind a stack of boxes on the desk. "My Canadian tuxedo!"

She laughed while Jax gave her a subtle eye-roll. "Here," she said. "I brought you Starbucks to say thanks. Sorry to spring this on you last minute."

"We're just doing our job, Ms. Wagman." Louis tipped an invisible hat and took the coffee. "But I appreciate it, ma'am."

"Please. You're making me feel a hundred years old," she said.

Jax leaned close enough that she could smell a spicy scent on him. "I must say you look very good for your age."

She fought a smile. "Are you almost done? She'll be here soon."

"Just about finished, ma'am," Louis said. He pointed at the newly installed computer in what was formerly an empty office. "Did what you asked. You'll be able to see the computer screen from the hall-way."

Georgina raised one eyebrow, hoping she appeared casual and sly instead of nervous and overbearing. "Just between us, right?"

Jax's perfect mouth quirked into a one-sided grin. "What's just between us?"

She double-flicked her eyebrows. "Exactly."

Right at nine, Meredith wandered into view looking lost, and Jax and Louis jumped out of the way to make room. She wore a loose black dress with one sleeve scrunched up above a white plaster cast from her knuckles to her elbow. On the side, Georgina saw a heart drawn in red Sharpie and a message that said: *Unstoppable!!!* She wondered who'd written it and whether they knew the truth behind the accident.

"Welcome to your new digs!" Jax said.

Meredith glanced at the wall to the right of the door, where a nameplate now read *Meredith De Luca.* "What's going on? Danielle said—"

"I told you I was going to upgrade your office!" Georgina raised her arms like Vanna White. "Ta-da!"

"What happened to your arm?" Jax asked.

"I broke it skiing," Meredith murmured, peering into a cardboard box that now held her files.

Jax leaned into Georgina's ear. "She's not too happy to be sitting next to the boss."

"Would you be?" Georgina whispered back.

"I'd sit next to you all day," Louis piped up.

"Meredith, come into my office while they finish up here?" Georgina walked next door without waiting for her answer.

A few seconds later, Meredith trailed in and closed the door behind herself. "I was going to resign," she said.

"You were?"

"*Am.*" She stared at the floor, her red curls falling into her face. "I *am* going to resign."

"I don't accept." Under the cover of her desk, Georgina gripped the edge of her chair to keep her hands from shaking, wearing a smile so frozen it probably looked clownish. "I'm still your mentor. As hard as it is to be in the same room as you, I care about your career, maybe more now than ever. What you did, it doesn't just affect me. It affects you. Every time something like this happens, it's the woman whose career is derailed. Nathan is the one who is married, Nathan is your boss, Nathan is older—although I hesitate to say wiser after the last two days. But do you see him quitting?"

Meredith didn't react. The age difference between them seemed suddenly significant, as if Meredith were her teenage daughter and Georgina was lecturing her about hanging out with the fast crowd.

"I promise you the thought of quitting has not occurred to Nathan for a second," Georgina said.

"It would just be easier," Meredith said.

"For who?"

"All of us."

Meredith's un-casted hand rested on the door handle, and she kept glancing over her shoulder.

"I don't want to be having this conversation either," Georgina said. "But please have a seat. This is important."

For a few seconds, Meredith closed her eyes and held her face to the ceiling like she was praying for the fire alarm to save her.

"Please," Georgina said.

Meredith walked to the closest velvet armchair as laboriously as if she were moving through mud.

"The way you're avoiding eye contact," Georgina said, "it's like I've done something to offend you. Isn't it the other way around?"

Meredith looked up, and Georgina wished she hadn't. It hurt to see her face. Her skin, as luminescent as the star of a face wash commercial. Her small mouth, shining with red gloss. She appeared impossibly young for a woman who'd accomplished what she'd accomplished—who'd done what she'd done.

"I'm sorry," she whispered, and began to cry. What started as elegant tears leaving a silky trail down her cheeks soon turned into face-contorting sobs and gasping hiccups.

Georgina pulled a travel pack of tissues from her desk drawer and tossed it to Meredith, who tried to catch it with her uninjured arm but missed. She fished it off the floor and blew her nose unglamorously. Of all the situations Georgina had found herself in since Friday night, this was the oddest. It was satisfying to see the woman who'd seduced her husband reduced to ugly, hacking sob-coughs under her own commanding stare, but it was also having the unintended consequence of making her feel sorry for Meredith, which was not at all what she'd wanted from this conversation. Meredith had fucked up—royally—and she didn't get to pity her way out of it. This was a mistake she had to learn from, and it was becoming more and more apparent with every chest-shaking sob that Meredith wasn't capable of that on her own. Mentoring her was an opportunity, not just for this girl but for every woman who'd been sidelined from her career over sex while the person she had sex *with* marched merrily along, consequence-free. Women's rights were at stake, and Georgina was the coitus crusader.

The swinging suffragette!

She stood up. "We're not going to be a big, happy family. But I'm not running away to hide, and neither should you. So long as you don't tell anyone, and you keep your head down and work hard, people will know you for the reason you want and not the reason you're trying to avoid. Okay?"

Meredith blew her nose again, but it did little to make her voice sound less congested. "And you're not going to tell anyone either, right?"

"Not unless you piss me off." Georgina tried to smile to show that was a joke, but the result felt more like the face she made when she stubbed her toe.

She let Meredith clean herself up for a second before shooing her out. Louis and Jax had finished their setup next door, and all was quiet, or as quiet as it could be with the background bustle of Times Square thirty floors below. She turned her computer on, opened Outlook, and stared at the screen. She'd accumulated seventy-five new emails since she'd last checked in the elevator on her way upstairs. Some announced themselves as highly important with red exclamation points, others simply said, "Call me." The first one she clicked on was from opposing counsel in the sperm bank case—a man who'd asked her the first time she'd talked to him whether she was an attorney or returning a call for her boss. His email was a mess of run-on sentences and intermittent phrases in bold and underline. It would be a small triumph for her to fire back a quippy response, to conquer what she could control after control in her own life had been savagely stripped away. That relief was right at her fingertips. And yet her hands were numb, and her chest drew breaths in shallow gasps. An earthquake of emotion was oncoming, and she'd just given her only tissues to Meredith.

Right when she was on the brink, her phone buzzed and lit up with a message.

It was from Alina.

We're in.

And just like that, she could breathe again.

Chapter 8

Norah called later that evening as Georgina was cleaning the kitchen, and Nathan sat at the table, marking up a brief and drinking a beer. She mumbled some excuse about a new workout trend called skateboard Pilates, then got down to business. "Felix called. Apparently, *he's* a swinger? Or did I dream this?"

"When did you talk to Felix?" Georgina asked.

"He called me this morning."

"To tell you this?"

"To say hi, I think," Norah said. "So it's true?"

"To say hi, huh?" Georgina teased. "I'll bet he did."

"You're dodging. Answer my question."

"One second." Georgina pointed at her phone and mouthed, *Norah*, to Nathan before retreating to the bedroom, a tidy space with light gray walls and white bedding on a dark wood four-poster. "Are you alone?"

With three children, Norah wasn't even alone when she used the toilet or showered. She remembered Norah ranting once after Rachel, at age five, wrenched the shower curtain aside and pointed at

Norah's crotch, yelling, "What is that furry stuff!" like it was trying to kill her. "I'm hiding in Rachel's closet," Norah said in a way that suggested she did that every day.

"Apparently, Alina's been doing it for a while," Georgina said.

"No surprise there," Norah said. "But *Felix*?"

She walked into the bathroom and began to clean her face with a makeup remover wipe. After a long day at work, her heavy makeup looked morning-after-ish. "I was as shocked as you are. But this is good. It proves my point."

"Wow," Norah said. "So you're really doing this?"

"It's official. Nathan and I hashed it out on Saturday," she said, "and we both agree this is a healthy solution for us." Her tone came out more defensive than she intended, already prepared for Norah to try to talk her out of it by texting her photos of saggy old man butts.

But to her complete shock, Norah said, "I want in," and Georgina dropped her plastic container of face wipes, which landed facedown on the floor like a wet diaper. When she could speak again, she said in a dazed voice, "I don't think I've ever been this happy in my life."

"I couldn't stop thinking about it," Norah said. "Ari and I—we're in a really bad place. I haven't told you the full extent of it because I'm too embarrassed."

"You know you can tell me anything."

But Norah said nothing. Georgina sat on the edge of her bathtub and gripped her phone, waiting. Could they tell each other anything? Hadn't she hesitated in confessing the truth about Nathan? She couldn't expect Norah to be honest about the problems in her marriage when Georgina acted like her own was so blissfully perfect all the time.

"Did you walk in on Ari going down on a hot twenty-five-year-old?" she asked.

Norah laughed. "No."

"Did he cheat with any person of any age in any position?"

"No," Norah said. "I don't think so."

"Then you're way ahead of me."

"There's more than one way to be a shitty husband," Norah said. "Ari resents me. He didn't want to get married at twenty-three, and he can't get past it. Yesterday, he got passed over for partner—"

"I didn't know Ari was up for partner." Though, it didn't surprise Georgina that he wasn't promoted. Ari worked at a medical malpractice firm owned by his uncle. It was the only job he could get after being unemployed for six months postgraduation. He seemed to be the worst lawyer at the firm, and only five lawyers worked there.

"Well, he was," Norah said. "But Carl got it."

"Who's Carl?"

"Carl Eschelman."

"Am I supposed to know who Carl Eschelman is?"

"I'm telling you right now—Carl. Carl Eschelman," said Norah. "What more do you need to know?"

"So you're giving Ari a pity swing?" Georgina asked. "Is that what you're trying to tell me?"

"No, God, no! I'm saying that to Ari, this is my fault. He's obsessed with the fact that Carl wears nice suits, like if he didn't have to *clothe his freaking children* he would have made partner. It would help if he didn't spend all day trolling the Eagles on Twitter!"

"Did you tell him that?"

"Of course not. But I think this could help us. We're desperate. I need Ari to stop seeing me like the bad guy and start seeing me like a woman again. There's so much tension in our house, it's impossible to see through it. Maybe we just need to start having fun again. Is that crazy?"

Georgina set her phone on the counter and turned it on speaker.

"Not at all," she said, squirting face cream into her palm. "But you can't start swinging just to convince Ari you're a cool wife. You need to do this for *you*."

"Aren't those the same thing?"

"No. Ari treats you like a left foot because you're acting like a left foot."

"What does that mean?"

"He walks all over you without appreciating you," Georgina said, walking into her closet to trade in her plaid pencil skirt and white button-down. "That makes you akin to his left foot. But you need to become his penis."

"If I knew what you were talking about, I suspect I'd be offended," Norah deadpanned.

Georgina grabbed the Fordham T-shirt she got for free at orientation, now thin from thirteen years of wear, and flannel pants from a drawer. "He cherishes it, he's afraid of losing it, and he respects the power it wields over him," she said.

There was a pause. "Be the penis," Norah repeated.

"Be the penis," Georgina said again. "It's impossible to start seeing your left foot as your penis without major surgery or a traumatic brain injury. It won't just happen on its own. You need to force Ari to see you as a different person by actually becoming one."

Norah snorted. "You want me to become a different person? Okay. That's . . . rude."

"I mean you should start swinging to start feeling sexy and confident, and when you start seeing yourself as a total badass, Ari will notice. That will change your marriage."

Cozy and free of her restrictive waistband, Georgina flipped out the lights and walked back into her bedroom. She was relieved to be at home with her creature comforts, and now she could finally, finally get in bed, turn on *The Lincoln Lawyer*, and let Matthew McConaughey lull her into sleep with his deep, gritty, calming voice. All was right again.

"Ari is lucky to have you," she said, "but for some reason, you see it as the other way around."

"Maybe you're right," Norah said, but she sounded slightly less convinced, even though she was the one who originally suggested it.

"I'm definitely right."

Through the line came a clatter of wood and the scrape of hangers across a metal pole.

"MOM, GET OUT!" Rachel yelled. "GET OUT OF MY ROOM, YOU CREEP! I'M CALLING THE POLICE, STALKER!"

Norah snapped, "Who puts this roof over your head?" then growled into the phone, "I am the left foot."

"Be the penis!" Georgina said, and quickly hung up as Norah started to unleash on her twelve-year-old.

In bed, she grabbed the remote from her nightstand. Other than a bottle of unopened hand lotion and a silver lamp, the nightstand was bare. No framed photograph of her and Nathan on their wedding day. She wondered whether that was a bad sign and resolved to add one tomorrow.

"I saw that on a T-shirt in Venice Beach once," said Nathan. She looked up to see him leaning against the doorframe. He wore a white undershirt with navy slacks and bare feet. He had nice feet for a man, long and soft, with high arches and relatively little toe hair. "What was that about?"

She leaned back into her stack of pillows and smiled. "Norah wants to join us. With Ari, obviously."

"Won't that be awkward?"

"We're all adults here," she said.

Nathan sat on her side of the bed and rested his hand on her leg through the covers. "Can I ask you a question?"

"There are some things you need my permission for, Nathan. But asking a question isn't one of them."

He stared at the black rectangle of the television. "Why is this so important to you?"

"Because I don't like to be wrong," she teased, poking his leg with her foot.

"I mean it," he said. "What is it you want out of this?"

She pushed herself upright and drew her knees to her chest. "I don't understand what you mean."

When Nathan looked back, he wore a watchful, nervous expression. "I mean, what do you want?"

She played with a tassel on their quilt. "I want you to be happy, and Norah, and Ari—sort of. I want everything to be good again."

"That's what I thought you'd say. You worry more about other people's happiness than your own."

"Other people's happiness makes me happy."

"For now." Nathan appeared to consider a few different ways to say the next thing he was going to say. "You don't ever wonder . . . whether you've made a mistake? Choosing me? And now you're . . . doubling down?"

"No," she said carefully, "but now I'm worried you are. You think we made a mistake being together?"

"No, no—" He moved closer and rested his hands on her knees. "That's not what I was implying. I just wanted to make sure that, after all this, it's me you're going to want."

The tension that had crept into her back released, and she exhaled. "Have you just now realized this means I'll have sex with someone else? I figured you'd want to watch or something."

Nathan made a quick movement with his cheeks. Like a smile, but not. "Yeah," he said. "You're right."

He went to the bathroom to get ready for bed. His bedtime routine involved "brushing his teeth" in front of CNN for twenty minutes, the toothbrush remaining stationary in his cheek while he muttered things like, "The Russians must find this hilarious." Then he'd scrub his face ferociously, like it was covered with tar, and collapse onto the mattress with the exhausted groan of a man who'd labored in the mines for forty years. Finally, he'd pull out his Kindle, queued exclusively with nonfiction books about the economy, which he'd narrate with his own commentary, sighs, laughs, and grunts of *for fuck's sake*.

Georgina watched him move around, thinking about his question. Had she ever wondered if she'd made a mistake choosing Nathan? Only one memory surfaced. They were at the wedding of a colleague five or so years ago. The reception was on a terrace downtown with a view of the sun setting behind the Statue of Liberty. Every couple was dancing except for them. Nathan spent the whole night schmoozing clients and sucking up to partners instead. He was doing his job, she'd told herself. She liked ambitious men. Romance wasn't her thing. She was too practical to waste time with that nonsense.

Still, while eating her rubbery chicken breast alone in her assigned seat, she had wondered. But just for a second.

Chapter 9

Saturday was Georgina's thirty-fifth birthday, and Nathan had made a reservation for six at Menerbes, a swanky French Mediterranean restaurant in the Meatpacking District. When they arrived a few minutes early, Norah sat alone at a round table in the corner. She wore a black, off-the-shoulder top with an earthy lipstick and her hair in a sleek low ponytail, sipping a glass of white wine as she read a book. One of the classics, surely—Nora Roberts, Danielle Steel, Nicholas Sparks. Norah drank those novels like the elixir of life. It couldn't have helped her relationship with Ari to have a constant stream of beautiful romances as her marriage yardstick. Ari would never sail across a treacherous squall to save Norah from a cave and make love to her on a sandy shore. Norah needed a novel about a husband who spent all day on Reddit learning how to build a DIY squat rack and a wife who changed their dynamic through swinging.

She was so engrossed she didn't notice their approach. "Hi," Georgina said, and Norah jumped, snapped her book closed, and shoved it in her purse, but not before Georgina glimpsed a shirtless hunk on the cover. "Where's Ari?" she asked.

"The babysitter was late, but he's on his way." Norah half rose to hug Georgina, her waist trapped by the table. "Happy birthday!"

"Thank you." Georgina pulled out the chair beside her. "I'm feeling not a day over thirty-four."

Norah smiled, then her eyes fell on Nathan, and she turned stony-faced. "Hello, Nathan."

He did something strange with his hands and sat beside Georgina without saying anything.

The restaurant was a gorgeous open space with giant palms, black booths, and ceiling-high mirrors reflecting the candlelight. Based on the gold-wrapped gifts and cakes on neighboring tables, Georgina's wasn't the only birthday. It gave the room a celebratory atmosphere with full-bodied conversation and touches of laughter. She relaxed into her chair. "This is perfect."

Nathan lifted her hand and kissed it. "I owe you perfection. Happy birthday."

A man with gelled hair in a white shirt and black vest took their drink orders just as Felix, Alina, and Ari arrived. Felix was dressed in a wine-colored sweater with brown chinos and glasses, looking like a model in an eyewear catalog. Alina wore a shapeless beige cotton dress that would have looked like a potato sack on anyone else, but she carried it like couture. And Ari, as usual, looked heart-stopping in a rumpled white oxford and dark jeans with his wavy hair swept back. Physically, Ari only had one less-than-perfect quality: his ears. They were freakishly small, like they belonged on a Cabbage Patch doll. Georgina suspected he grew his hair out to cover them up but couldn't blame his vanity too much because she'd have done the same thing.

"You three clean up nicely," she said.

"Sorry we're late," Felix said, bending to kiss her cheek. "This is for you. From us."

In his outstretched hand, he held a cylindrical package wrapped in brown paper and tied with red string. After everyone had settled around the table, Georgina used a knife to slice it open and screamed with delight. It was a glass prayer candle, but instead of a saint on the jar, it was Whitney Houston, who was, as far as she was concerned, also a saint. If it wasn't Whitney, it wasn't worth it. "Oh my God!" she said. "Where did you find this masterpiece?"

Felix beamed. "I made it."

"He spent a lot of time on it," Alina said, and Georgina couldn't tell whether she'd found Felix's crafting nice or annoying.

"I will treasure this forever," she said, and pressed her lips to the glass, warm from Felix's hand.

"I'm glad," Felix said, then smiled at Norah. "Hi there. Long time no see."

Norah looked shy as she smiled back. "Way too long. It's great to see you."

Georgina observed them grinning at each other with barely masked glee until Ari said, "Happy birthday, Georgina. My present is my presence—a.k.a., priceless."

She rolled her eyes hugely, making sure he saw. That had been their relationship forever—giving each other endless shit. She'd think it was fun if she didn't have Norah's honor to protect. "Next time, get me a lottery ticket," she said. "It's much more valuable."

Ari chuckled and flipped open his menu. "So," he said, "oysters for the table?"

"Quit it," Norah snapped, and Georgina saw Ari flinch from an unseen jab.

"What?" he asked. "We aren't going to talk about the elephant in the room?"

"I'll have oysters," Nathan chimed in, oblivious to the mounting tension. "How many do we think? Two each?"

Ari leaned back and slung his arm around Norah's shoulder. "How many does it take to get everyone in the mood?"

"I take it this means you're in," Georgina said.

Felix looked up from his menu. "Wait. You're doing it, too?"

Norah straightened and set her shoulders back. "Yes. We are."

Something in Ari's nonchalant posture and cocky grin fell for a split second, but Georgina caught it. It was a break from his usual toughness. For a moment, he'd looked . . . scared? He must have been nervous. That was normal. She was nervous, too. They all seemed to be. A shiftiness possessed the table.

Ari recovered. "When your wife says she wants to swing, you don't say no, you say when."

"I don't know," Felix said. "I don't know. I just don't know."

When their server walked by, Felix ordered a strong drink. "Manhattan, please," he said. "But light vermouth. Actually, just whiskey. On the rocks. Please. Thanks."

"Make that two," Ari said.

"Three," Nathan said. "And a dozen oysters."

Norah, Georgina, and Alina decided to split a bottle of sparkling rosé. After he'd gone, everybody glanced around the table. It felt as if they were sizing each other up, looking at one another in a way they never had before. Physically, sexually. Not as friends but as people who had the requisite parts to fuck.

"Maybe we need some ground rules," Georgina suggested, "if we're going to do this together."

"Absolutely," Alina said. "Every expectation, every boundary needs to be out in the open. Personally, I have never had any problem engaging in the experience with friends. It's better, in some ways, because you trust one another already."

"I want you guys to come to my kids' birthday parties without remembering what I look like naked," Norah said. "You guys are off limits for me."

"Me, too," Georgina said.

Norah elbowed Ari. "Hello?"

"What?" he asked. "I'm not allowed to think about it?"

"There's nothing to think about," Norah said. "You're not having sex with my best friend."

He gestured across the table. "What about Alina?"

Norah narrowed her eyes at him. "Off. Limits."

Ari lifted his menu and began to read it petulantly. "Gee. This is fun. Glad I agreed to do this."

"You should consider yourself lucky," Norah said, and snapped open her menu to hide her face.

"Everybody at this table is off limits," Georgina said. "Understood? Now, what's everybody getting to eat?"

"I'm debating the rib eye," Nathan mused. He seemed to have no idea there were anything but pleasantries being exchanged at the table. "Anyone want to share the burrata?"

"I'll share it with you, buddy," Felix said. That Felix had dropped a "buddy" showed how desperate he was to change the subject. "I'm going with the burger. Can't go wrong."

"You always get the burger," Alina said. "Try something new."

Felix frowned. "You're right. I'm boring."

Georgina had a sneaky feeling that was exactly how Felix ended up becoming the occasional swinger. "Oh, but the burger is so good here," she said. "You have to get it."

His frown deepened. "Okay. I will."

"Why don't we all let Felix get whatever he wants?" Norah asked loudly.

"So long as it's not anybody at this table," Ari said, and glared at Georgina with the glint of a challenge in his eyes. She narrowed hers back. What was he getting at? Was he that eager to sleep with someone at this table? Was it *her*? If that were true, why was he looking at her like he wanted to pick a fight?

"I changed my mind," Nathan announced. "Market fish."

Their server returned with a silver ice bucket of sparkling rosé and three cocktails, all balanced expertly on a black tray. When he'd finished doling them out, he whipped out a pad from his front pocket. "Are we ready to order?"

"The french onion soup, please," Felix said, and Georgina watched Norah's mouth twist into a thoughtful frown.

"I'll have the burger," Norah said. "Felix, you can have half."

"The steak," Ari said. "Still mooing. Thank you, good sir."

Alina ordered the mussels, Nathan the fish, and Georgina the gnocchi. After he'd gone, she clapped her hands. "I'm exercising my birthday right to change the subject. Let's play a game. I want to hear the best birthday present everyone has ever received. Me first." She picked up Whitney Houston and smiled. "This candle."

"Hold on," Felix said. "I don't think we're finished here. I'm no pro, but I have been to one of these clubs before, so that makes me the closest thing you've got to an expert—"

"Alina's probably the expert," Georgina corrected.

"Alina will agree with me on this one. There's more we should discuss—" Felix paused to take a swig of his whiskey. "There's not much privacy at these things, if you catch my drift. So as much as I don't want to ask, I need to. Are you comfortable with"—he whispered the last part—"watching each other?"

Georgina tried to lighten the mood. This was her birthday, after all. "Felix, you old dog, you. I didn't realize you were into that kind of thing."

"I'm not," he said without wasting a breath. "But some people are."

"Felix is right," Alina said. "But it's not how he makes it sound. The purpose of a communal space is to feel the sexual energy and the eroticism of the environment."

Even Nathan was listening now. He and Georgina looked at each other. This wasn't the swingers bunny hill she'd initially imagined, but she was more determined than ever now that her friends were on board, too. Swinging could fix not only her problems but everyone's. Her posture perked as it occurred to her that Norah and Felix would be at the parties together, experiencing the "sexual energy and eroticism of the environment." What better place to rekindle an old flame? She sipped her sparkling rosé and cleared her throat.

"We're getting ahead of ourselves," she said. "Alina is introducing us to a more exclusive group, right?"

"Of course," Alina said. "We're invited to a party next Saturday at my friend Quincy's apartment. You will have complete autonomy and privacy, if you want it."

Their server delivered the oysters. He pointed at the tray and listed the names, but Georgina wasn't listening. She buzzed with too much excitement at the possibility of Norah and Felix together. Although, she remembered ruefully, they had just agreed to be off limits from each other. Then again, weren't rules like these made to be broken?

"We're not signing anything in blood," Georgina said, "and we're not selling our souls to the devil. This is something we're all trying. Let's keep an open mind and have fun. If it's too much, we can quit. Okay?"

Norah squeezed Ari's hand. "Agreed."

Ari's eyes searched hers. Quietly, as though he wanted only her to hear, he asked, "You really want to?"

She nodded. "I do."

"Me, too," Nathan said.

Everyone looked to Felix, who gave a thumbs-up as he swigged his whiskey.

"It's normal to be nervous," Alina said, "but ask yourself, what is it you're afraid of? Is it touching a stranger? Or are you afraid of your own desires?" She ran her index finger along the curve of Felix's ear as she spoke, and although she wanted to, Georgina tried not to look away. The truth was she wasn't comfortable with her own desires, but embarrassed by them. She wanted more than she got from Nathan. Sometimes when they were having sex, she would imagine ridiculous things, like Matthew McConaughey as a bartender who spotted her across the room and fucked her in the wine closet. Lately, she'd been pretending he was her boss, going down on her at ten o'clock on Friday night in the office. All her fantasies shared Matthew McConaughey in common. She should buy a vibrator, she'd think occasionally, and visit a website selling sex toys but never buy anything. Then for weeks, she'd see vibrator banner ads on every website and feel humiliated and stupid. If she was going to swing, she'd have to confront that shunned side of herself. Could she do it? Could she lay bare her desires in front of friends and strangers alike? In front of herself?

The idea terrified her. But it also gave her a pleasurable thrill, like when she typed in the first few letters of *Babeland* into her browser, before she chickened out.

A little smile of secret delight forced its way onto her lips as she raised her glass. "Here's to our last party with clothes on."

Chapter 10

When Alina first described the couple hosting the party on Saturday night as "industry types" she'd met in grad school at Parsons, Georgina envisioned Instagram influencers squatting in a graffitied Williamsburg factory with exposed pipes and factory windows reinforced with chicken wire.

She was wrong—very, very wrong.

At eight o'clock on the dot, Georgina and Nathan's Uber dropped them off in front of a non-graffitied, redbrick building with two-story arched windows in the most expensive part of Tribeca. Georgina knew for a fact from a feature in *Marie Claire* that her middle school idol Brooke Shields lived in this exact building.

"When you said Alina hooked us up with these people, I was expecting something a little more VW van," Nathan said.

"Do you think we're too early?"

"We're right on time."

"Exactly. Let's walk around the block."

"We don't need to play hard to get," Nathan said. "They know what we've come for."

She glanced longingly down the block, but the temperature got the best of her. She hadn't wanted to show up at a sex party wearing a puffy coat and a knit hat her mom had made, so she'd dressed in black leggings with black stilettos and a black blazer over a black turtleneck. It was a little bit dominatrix, a little bit spy, and a lot freezing. "Fine," she said. "It's the penthouse."

Nathan pressed the touch screen beside the door, and they were quickly buzzed in. The entryway was empty and elegant, with polished concrete floors and orange filament bulbs dangling on ropes from the high ceiling.

"Should we have brought something?" Georgina asked. "A gift?"

"These folks aren't wanting for much," Nathan said.

"But I feel rude. I can't believe I didn't think about it."

"What would you have brought to a sex party?"

She followed him into the sleek elevator. "I don't know—chocolates? Condoms? Chocolate condoms? What are the rules?"

Nathan grinned and pressed the button for PH. "We're about to find out."

When the elevator doors opened directly into the loft, her mouth fell open. The space was at least two thousand square feet, with a wood-beam ceiling and iron columns and gleaming slate floors. All four walls had arched windows as tall as a city bus. Outside, the Hudson reflected the lights of Jersey City and the Chrysler Building glittered. She'd lived her entire life in New York, and still, the view stunned her.

"This place is insane," she said.

"Thank you kindly, strangers!" said a voice.

She turned to see a jolly-looking fellow approaching. He was blond and pudgy, in his late forties or early fifties. "I'd like to say I built it with my own two hands," he said, "but the builder was actually the owner of a dozen shoe factories back in 1885. John-Paul Franklin Capistrano was his name."

"He certainly had an eye for design," Georgina said.

"Oh, that?" The man smiled and rubbed his palms together. "That was my wife and about a dozen architects."

The square room was divided into four parts—living room, dining room, kitchen, and study—using artfully arranged furniture and light fixtures to create the illusion of walls. The décor was industrial-chic, with stone vases, tall iron bookcases, and worn leather furniture. She was admiring what she thought might be a real charcoal Degas sketch when the man stuck out his hand.

"Quincy," he said. "These are my stomping grounds."

Nathan, who could smell a fresh client from three miles away, leaped forward. "Nathan Wagman. I'm in structured finance if you ever want to talk shop. This is my wife, Georgina."

"Very nice to meet you both, and welcome. Can I offer you a drink?" Quincy asked, gesturing toward a display of paper-thin tumblers prefilled with a finger of whiskey. "I hear this is your first party."

Georgina took two glasses and passed one to Nathan. "Any advice for us rookies?"

"I've been doing this a long time," Quincy said. "Best advice is to get a mentor. It helps you navigate the rules, and if you ever get into trouble—"

"Trouble?" Nathan interrupted.

Quincy clapped him on the back. "Not the kind you're worried about, mate. What we're doing isn't illegal! I mean if it ever gets complicated for you."

Georgina and Nathan met eyes. She looked quickly away and sipped her drink. They would be fine. How could things get more complicated than they already were?

"What do you mean by a mentor?" she asked.

"We all have mentors here," he said. "Someone who started in the

lifestyle before you and has some wisdom to share. You'll find someone, don't worry. Usually, the right match finds you, much like at the
parties."

Quincy winked. She smiled politely back, but Quincy wouldn't
be her match that night. Blond-haired men reminded her of oversize
children. Put a baseball cap on their head and a pair of cleats on their
feet, and you might as well pick them up from soccer and feed them
ants on a log before homework time. The image wasn't exactly getting
her in the mood.

"I'll also tell you this," Quincy went on. "Share your experiences
openly with each other. You don't want a veil of secrecy between you.
The lifestyle is meant to be shared."

"You tell your wife what you did with . . . other women?" Nathan
asked. Georgina had an unpleasant flashback to Nathan detailing his
tryst with Meredith and decided she would decline to follow that particular nugget of wisdom.

"It's inspiring, mate, you'll see. We end up tearing each other's
clothes off during that conversation. It's like watching porn with your
wife as the star."

"Do you have enough bedrooms in this place?" Nathan asked,
looking around the loft like the fire chief, squinting and sizing up the
walls. "I was told this wasn't a . . . group thing."

Quincy laughed. "I'm getting the sense one of us is more excited to
be here than the other. Don't worry. It's always like that the first time.
Ease into it. Maybe you two don't do a full swap tonight."

"A what?" Nathan asked.

Georgina had learned everything she needed to know from Reddit. "*Full swap* means the couple is open to having intercourse with
other people, either in the same room or different room. *Soft swap*
means no sex, but kissing, touching, oral. Or you can watch. Some
couples enjoy having another couple just watch them."

"The mentee becomes the mentor!" Quincy cheered. "You can make this experience whatever you want it to be. But yes, we've got bedrooms upstairs, although one is technically a gym. My wife has dibs, though. She likes the mirrors."

Nathan lifted his whiskey to drink, but noticed it was already empty. "I'll just—" He hurried off toward the bar before bothering to finish the sentence.

"He's a little nervous, I guess," Georgina said.

"We're nice, I promise. Can I introduce you to the others?"

Quincy waved over a trio, two men and a woman. As they shook hands and exchanged hellos, Georgina soaked in their appearance. She'd had preconceived notions about what a swinger should look like—pierced nipples, severe bangs, always nude—but Suzanne's velvet headbands and pantyhose had proven her wrong. So she wasn't surprised when these three turned out to be ordinary. No whips and chains in sight. The woman had long braids twisted into a high knot on her head and wore no makeup. She could have been Rachel's fifth-grade teacher. For all Georgina knew, she *was* Rachel's fifth-grade teacher, in which case, Norah was headed for an interesting evening.

"Laila," she said. Alina's friend, the acupuncturist. "This is my husband, Jeremiah." She pointed toward the first man on her left, who wore a blue T-shirt and jeans. Jeremiah's neighbor wore a lumpy sweater that looked hand-knitted, and said his name was Marco. The quiet stockbroker. He had fluffy hair and extremely white teeth.

"Thanks so much for letting us join the party," Georgina said.

"Are you kidding?" Laila asked. "Fresh meat!"

"We'll all be fighting over you tonight," Marco said. "Trust me."

"How are you feeling?" Jeremiah asked.

"Excited?" Georgina said. "Curious? A little too sober?"

They all laughed, and Jeremiah hurried off to fetch her a refill. A wave of relief loosened her shoulders. Not so bad to be the guest of honor. Her new acquaintances—soon to be much closer than that— were warm, encouraging, and laid-back. They could all be friends, like Suzanne said, talking intimately about their relationships at the parties, and maybe going to a kickboxing class together the next morning. Attending this party had been the right decision. There was not a doubt in her mind.

Across the room, the front door opened and her friends walked in. "Excuse me," she said, and rushed over to them.

Alina wore a leopard catsuit with her hair pulled into a tight ponytail at her crown. As she slinked past Quincy, she kissed him on the cheek. "Hi there."

Quincy beamed. "Welcome back, my friend. We've missed you."

"I stopped coming to the parties because I was experimenting with celibacy for a while," Alina explained to Georgina. She turned back to Quincy. "Meet my partner, Felix."

Though Felix shook Quincy's hand, there was a stiffness to his greeting. Georgina tried to catch Felix's eye, but he avoided her.

Behind him, Ari bent his head to step through the door, even though its steel frame was four feet taller than he was. "Nice place," he said, shaking Quincy's hand. "What did you say you do?"

"I'm the global head of advertising for a media company," Quincy said.

"Huh." Ari frowned as he gazed at the high ceilings. "What's it called?"

"AT&T."

Georgina choked on her cocktail.

"Like, the phone company?" Ari asked.

"Well, we do much more than that," Quincy said graciously.

Ari knocked on the wall like he was searching for studs. "I'd have thought being a lawyer beat working at the phone company. Serves me right, I guess."

Quincy, appearing unsure whether to show Ari one of his pay stubs or ask him to leave, turned to Georgina, who rolled her eyes for his benefit. He returned the gesture with a humorous shrug. "Drinks, everyone?" he asked.

Chapter 11

Georgina and Norah escaped to a quiet place by the window to talk. Outside, a fancy yacht packed with partygoers and flashing disco lights glided along the Hudson. Their first year of law school, the student bar association hosted Barrister's Ball on one of those party yachts. Everyone called it *law school prom* because that's what it was, except everyone was above the legal drinking age. Having sworn off dating for law school, Georgina had asked Norah to be her date, but she'd been thrilled when Ari had asked Norah to dance. She'd collapsed into an empty folding chair near the dance floor to rest her sore feet and watch Ari and Norah attempt to swing. A funny coincidence, in retrospect. She'd noticed Felix sitting by himself with a slice of cheesecake, also watching Norah. That was the first night they'd exchanged anything more than stilted conversation about what time they'd left the library. Felix confessed that he'd sensed her pulling away, and Georgina did not confess that Norah was being pushed away or that she was personally doing the pushing. How sorry she felt now, how angry at herself. If only she'd have ordered Felix a shot of tequila and told him to buck up and get out on the dance floor, things might have been different. But they were here now, in a place where anything could happen. Energy hummed through the room like the vibration of bass notes.

"Are you having fun yet?" Georgina asked Norah.

"Great time," Norah said. "Fantastic time, actually."

"You are? You're not nervous?"

"I'm drunk, if that's what you're wondering." Sipping her whiskey through a straw, Norah pointed at Nathan. "Look! He's on the verge of a panic attack." She imitated his face, wide eyes darting left and right. "He needs one of these," she said. "Quincy's got some top-shelf shit."

Georgina leaned against the window, surveying the crowd. "Who here would you pick to be with?"

With zero hesitation, Norah pointed. "Who's that tall drink of water?"

It was difficult to see across two thousand square feet in the soft lighting. Georgina squinted. "Don't know him."

"He's gorgeous," Norah said. "I pick him. His hair/T-shirt combo screams, 'I'm amazing in bed.'"

"Go for it," Georgina said. She looked away, but found her eyes drawn back a moment later. Something was familiar about that hair/T-shirt combo. She did another double take—and her hand flew to her mouth. "Oh my God." She leaped behind a concrete beam to her immediate left. "Get over here!" She grabbed Norah's wrist and tugged.

"What's wrong with you?"

"I know him," Georgina whispered, "from college. Oh my God, this cannot be happening. Of *course* he would become a swinger."

Norah peered around the beam. She seemed unable to control the volume of her voice and practically shouted, "Of course who would become a swinger?"

"Whitaker Nolan," Georgina said. She poked her head around the beam above Norah's like they were a comedy duo. It was definitely Whitaker. Brown, messy hair that looked fresh off a motorcycle. Yesterday's stubble like a layer of sand on his jaw. Thumbprint chin, smooth forehead, easy smile. "Whitaker Nolan," she said again.

She'd met him her third year at UVA during a benefit for Legal Aid she'd organized as the Future Lawyers Association president. Whitaker Nolan, with fewer salt-and-pepper strands at his temples or crinkles around his eyes, had walked right up to her and asked how he could help.

"All the roles are assigned," she'd snapped. "I'm afraid if you want to look good for grad school, you're going to have to try harder."

"I was trying to look good for you, actually," he'd said. "Is it working?"

"So far, my first impression is *expects to be seated even when late*," she'd said coolly, then attempted to lift a banker's box of wine bottles for the reception and nearly fell over backward. He'd reached out and caught her bare arms. As soon as his skin made contact with hers, they'd met eyes and she'd known she was in trouble. Succumbing to that feeling was precisely what she'd sworn to avoid.

"So you were, what, study buddies?" Norah asked.

"It sort of started that way," Georgina said, "but we never got much studying done."

A few days after the event, she'd learned he was in her comparative politics class. She'd been so singularly focused on her notes and her textbook that she'd barely have been able to pick the professor out of a lineup, let alone a classmate. But he'd walked up to her seat after dismissal and asked if she'd help him study for finals.

She'd pretended to organize her pens. "Why?"

"You know everything," he'd said, "and I'm failing."

"What's in it for me?"

He'd smiled and shrugged. "We'll have fun."

Turning away so she could avoid the temptation of his face, she'd slipped her arms into her navy J.Crew blazer and told him she'd think about it.

"You look like you've seen a ghost," Norah said. "Are you okay?"

"More like someone from a past life," Georgina said, "who is apparently alive and well."

Norah looked him up and down. "*Very* alive and *very* well. So you, what, dated? I can't see you with someone like him. I picture all your boyfriends as some variation of Nathan in different shades of blue suits."

"We didn't date," Georgina said. "We were just horny kids."

Remembering the filthy, dirty things he'd say to her and the dirty things she'd say back, she had to laugh. Observations about his "cock" and its varying degrees of hardness fell off her tongue like she was ordering coffee from Starbucks. She and Nathan had never dared speak that way with each other, their sexual language limited to "Does that feel good?" and other attentive but pointless assurances.

"We had sex so many times one day, I got a raging UTI, and he had to take me to the emergency room." An unexpected lump formed in her throat as she remembered how many times she'd insisted he leave her there, but he'd stayed all night, holding her hand as she cried in the waiting room, clenching her legs together to try to stop the pain.

She swallowed the memory with a cool drink of her cocktail.

"Screw Nathan," Norah said. "You should have married him."

"Like you said, he was not my type," Georgina said.

"Are you crazy? He's everyone's type! Look at him!"

"I wanted someone less—" But she couldn't think of the right word.

Norah looked amused. "What, less hot?"

"Nathan is handsome!" Georgina said, and shot her a glare.

"There's handsome," Norah said, "then there's hot. Let me guess what was wrong with him. Ooh, I bet he liked to sleep in."

Georgina lifted her chin. This conversation wasn't fun anymore. "He was a loose cannon." And he did like to sleep in—past eleven sometimes.

"You sound like my mother."

"He skipped a semester to go *hiking in Nepal*," Georgina said.

"What a criminal," Norah deadpanned.

"He moved to Peru after graduation without a job! He didn't know where he was going to live. He wanted to *volunteer*."

Norah pretended to wipe sweat off her brow. "Sheesh, he sounds like a good person. Glad you got away."

"Can't be that good," Georgina said. "He's here, isn't he?"

Norah lifted one eyebrow. "And we're what, holographs?"

"What's that supposed to mean?"

"You've always taken the safe path," Norah said, patting Georgina's shoulder, "but you're a swinger now. It might be time to admit you're just as bad as the rest of us. It's freeing, I promise."

For the next hour, Georgina avoided Whitaker as skillfully as a cat did a flame. Whenever he looked in need of a refill, she excused herself from the bar for a restroom break. When he attempted to catch her eye, she faked a sneeze. When Quincy invited his guests to the living room for a toast—"To freedom, to sex, to the freedom to have sex with your friends!"—Georgina positioned herself behind a human-size sculpture of a crane, its neck just thick enough to hide her face. But when he insisted on introducing the newcomers, she was stuck.

"A fellow creative," Quincy said about Alina, "and a bunch of lawyers, which might come in handy should the need for hush money ever arise. If you haven't had the pleasure yet, please meet Norah, Ari, Nathan, Felix, and—where is she?" Quincy peered around until his eyes landed on Georgina. "Ah, there she is. Hiding in the corner—a vision in black—Georgina! Come on, Georgina. None of us bite!"

"Speak for yourself," said a voice she recognized as Whitaker's dry, flirtatious one. Before she could stop them, her eyes flicked in his direction, and their gazes locked. Somehow he'd become more attractive than when she'd last looked at him five minutes ago. He'd always had a blithe, warm quality to his face, but now there was a ruggedness layered on top of it, like he really had hiked in Nepal and built bridges in Peru, he wasn't just a boy who dreamed about those things. Without breaking eye contact, one corner of his mouth lifted in a private smile meant only for her. He slowly raised one hand and held it there, not quite a wave, but a hi. He'd gotten a tattoo on the inside of his forearm. It was a minimalist design of intersecting straight lines. It bothered her. Not because he had it—it was sexy—but because she didn't know what it meant. He had a secret. Back then, they'd shared everything—their bodies, their fantasies, their fears. But this was evidence that he'd shared experiences with other people, other women probably, and as much as she tried not to care, she cared.

Still, she managed to keep her face passive as she looked back to the crane.

"For our new friends," Quincy said, "I'll say a few words about how this works. You and your partner need to decide in advance what your expectations and limits are and communicate those clearly to whoever you choose to spend your time with. Do you kiss on the mouth? Do you play in different rooms or the same room? Are you comfortable with intercourse? What kind of contraception do you use? Are both partners playing or is someone here to watch? Et cetera. We've all got different answers to those questions, and all answers are welcome here. We are sex-positive people. Martin, for example, prefers to watch his wife play with other couples, so if you're with them, you'll be four to a room, three playing together, if you're comfortable with that, of course. My wife and I only soft swap, but we've got an affinity for toys and other machinery." He smiled across the room at a woman with waist-length black hair and a long neck who gave off a distinct witchy vibe. "If you and your partner don't have the same rules," he warned, "make sure you're at least comfortable with each other's rules. Nothing will ruin a party faster than miscommunication and disrespect. All of us are in committed relationships—we've got to go home together at the end of the night. Don't forget that."

Georgina's body tightened as she glanced at Nathan. It might have been the first time in her life she hadn't done her homework. But considering the position she'd found him in, nothing was off the table, was it? That wouldn't be fair.

Her friends looked similarly squeamish as they whispered to each other—only Alina appeared cool and unfazed as she braided Quincy's wife's hair in an armchair by the fire. Somewhere around nine o'clock, the party atmosphere had shifted from friendly to seductive. Someone had dimmed the lights. The music had changed from James Brown to a smooth, rhythmic pulse. Eyes in the room were like lassos drawing her in, and it made her heart race.

"What do you say?" Quincy asked, lifting a blue glass bowl from the coffee table. "Should we go old-school tonight?"

"When are you not old-school?" an older man sitting cross-legged on the couch asked. "We heard you only do it with the lights off."

Quincy chuckled. "What can I say, I desperately need a tan. But what I'm suggesting is a key party. It might take some pressure off our new friends. No one will be the kid who isn't picked for kickball, and yes, Martin, before you ask, that kid was always me."

Martin must have been the older man on the couch, because everyone looked at him and laughed. Norah had been right about one thing—Martin was less Idris-Elba-older and more saggy-butt-older. He was the only person there Georgina could definitely, without a doubt, never be with. His frail, grandfatherly frame recalled images of her pop in swimming trunks doing water aerobics with the old ladies in his nursing home and eating soft potatoes that didn't require teeth. But the others were attractive, as Alina had promised. Even Quincy's boyish, excitable grin had grown on her. She could do this. No matter whose keys she picked, she'd be pleased. Unless they were Martin's, in which case, she'd fake a stomachache and leave.

A loud *thunk* came from across the room. Someone had dropped a heavy object. That someone turned out to be Norah, who looked mortified at the unwanted attention. Perhaps she was less enthused about the key idea. It did make the next step feel more real. Coming inside had been one thing, going upstairs another.

Georgina caught Norah's eye and tried to beam her a silent message of strength: *Be the penis!* Norah stared back with wild eyes, and she wondered whether this was all too much. But then, Norah considered Ari's face for a few seconds before fishing in her purse and extracting her keys.

They would do this together. They had to. Georgina reached into her purse and touched the miniature wooden gavel on a key chain her father had given her as a law school graduation token. She and Norah stepped forward and tossed their keys into the blue bowl with a clatter. For a minute, Georgina enjoyed the glory of triumph—then spotted Norah's Hobby Lobby key chain card. Norah needed sexier keys by next Saturday.

"Now everyone knows what to hunt for," Quincy said, and everyone laughed again, but Georgina sensed he wasn't joking.

The seasoned partygoers deposited their keys without much fanfare, and Ari and Nathan did so with macho strides, though their hands tremored as they reached toward the bowl. There was only one person who hadn't budged from his hiding place in the corner—Felix. Perhaps Quincy noticed, too, because he said, "Grab your refills, your toys, whatever you need, and we'll start."

Georgina slipped away from the crowd to join Felix as the low rumble of conversation returned. "Are you okay?" she whispered.

He closed his eyes and tipped his head back against the wall. "I don't know."

"What's wrong?"

Felix drew a deep breath and sighed. "Remember when I said I was cool with this?"

I remember you pretending to be cool with this, she thought. She put her hand on his shoulder. "I remember you said it was hard. Harder than Alina made it sound."

"I'm trying. It never gets easier for me."

"You don't like seeing Alina with other people?" she asked. As the question occurred to her, she realized that of all the thoughts and worries and fears looping through her brain in the days leading up to this party, how it would feel to see Nathan with someone else wasn't one of them. What did that mean?

"It's *being* with other people," he said. "I don't want to. I just want her."

Georgina gave his shoulder a little squeeze. He was so loving it made her heart break. "So leave," she said.

"I can't do that either." He nodded toward the other side of the room, where Alina now leaned so close to Quincy's wife it seemed they were about to kiss. "This is who she is. She was up-front about that. And I like that she sees life differently. She's taught me a lot. Who am I to try to change her?"

"In the matter of sex, Felix, you're allowed to have rules for your partner."

"Not about this," he said. "I'll lose her. She wants to be with someone exciting."

"You are exciting!"

Felix made a grunting sound of humorless self-deprecation. "Right. I'm about as exciting as a reusable water bottle."

"The ozone is excited about reusable water bottles," Georgina said. "You need to find your ozone."

"I thought I did." Felix pretended to bang his forehead repeatedly against the wall. "What am I going to do?"

"This isn't just about whether to leave a sex party or not," Georgina said. "You need to decide whether what she wants is more important than what you want. How much are you willing to give up for her?"

"All of it?"

"Why?"

"I love her?" Felix said. "Do I need a better reason?"

"Oh, Felix," Georgina groaned. "You love too much. That's your problem. Remember when you adopted that three-legged cat with Salmon?"

Felix's mouth pressed into a grim line. "I hate cats."

"Exactly. Only this time, it's swinging. If you want to be here because you want a new experience, try to have fun. But if you're only doing this out of sacrifice, you need to leave."

For a while, he stared into the fire. "No," he said. "This is what I want. I do like it, I just had a moment of . . . something."

Georgina rested one hand on his chest. His heart pounded through his sweater. "Are you sure?"

He nodded. "You know I take a while to open up."

She didn't know that, actually. He wore his heart on his sleeve. The problem was that everyone could see it but him.

Her newfound appreciation for Alina vanished, replaced with a fiercely protective instinct. Felix clearly didn't want to be there, and he'd been pretending this whole time. How could Alina not see that? Or did she see it but didn't care?

Georgina cared. Felix deserved someone who cared.

Then an idea struck her.

"Wait," she blurted. "What if you drew Norah's keys? They're the ones with the Hobby Lobby card. Alina said there's more trust when you're with a friend, right? You won't feel so much pressure. You two can . . . see where things go." *And then fall in love and live happily ever after!* she declined to add.

Felix looked skeptical. "Wouldn't that be weird? Ari's not my friend, but he's also not *not* my friend. And what about the off-limits rule?"

"I promise you he is too busy thinking about his own keys to notice," she said. "It's perfect."

Quincy tapped a spoon against his glass from the center of the room. "Everybody ready?"

Georgina raised her eyebrows at Felix. "Ready?" she whispered.

After a pause, he said, "Yeah. Okay."

"Felix will go first!" she announced, and everybody's heads turned. She looked straight at Alina as she said, "He's very enthusiastic about being here."

"Take it away, mate," Quincy said.

Felix gave Georgina one last beseeching glance and walked to the bowl. With his hand hovering over it, he hesitated for so brief a moment that she must have been the only one to notice. Then he reached in and pulled out a blue Hobby Lobby tag.

There was a smatter of applause. Norah's head swiveled left and right, as if waiting for someone to object, but everyone smiled encouragingly. Everyone except Ari. He looked stunned with a mushroom crostini halfway to his open mouth.

"The bedrooms are upstairs," Quincy said. "Choose whichever one calls your name. Who's next?"

Anxious to cause a distraction so Felix and Norah could escape before Ari intervened, Georgina said, "Me. I'll go."

"Mine's the one with the BMW, FYI," Quincy said, and everyone laughed, though the joke was getting old.

She walked forward. The glass bowl held twenty-two pairs of

keys, and one was Whitaker's. The possibility of choosing his was too bright and burning to think about, like trying to stare directly at the sun. She'd have to pick the keys least likely to be his.

She could rule out Nathan's, her own, and the feathered ones that obviously belonged to Alina. One had a Mickey Mouse figure and another a silver Eiffel Tower. Neither of those seemed Whitaker-ish. Someone cleared their throat—Georgina was taking too long.

She spotted a ringless black key fob for a Porsche. It definitely belonged to a man, and that man was definitely not Whitaker. Porsches were showy, and he was the opposite of showy. In college, he'd used a bath towel for a curtain.

She reached down and grasped it. When she straightened, her eyes were drawn to Whitaker's like magnets. He suppressed a smile and shook his head. He knew exactly what she'd done.

"Over here," said a voice, and it turned out to be Marco's, the quiet guy who did something with stocks, according to Alina. Perfect. Wouldn't be the best sex of her life, but that wasn't what she'd come for, was it?

She exhaled and nearly laughed with relief. "Lucky me," she said.

Marco offered his elbow, and she took it.

Chapter 12

Georgina and Marco entered an upstairs bedroom. It was train themed, with a large print of empty tracks across a desert hanging above the bed and lamps made of iron railroad ties. Quincy must have designed this one himself. It looked like an eight-year-old boy's drawing of an adult's bedroom.

Marco reclined on the bed and folded his hands behind his head. He appeared comfortable, like he'd been there dozens of times before. "So tell me about you."

From the corner by the dresser, Georgina could not look at him as she said, "I'm a lawyer, and I live on the Upper East Side."

"No, no," Marco said, "tell me something interesting."

She frowned at him. "Being a lawyer was the most interesting thing about me until I became a swinger."

"Tell me about that, then." Marco scooted over to make room for her and patted the empty space. "We need to get to know each other."

Slowly, she perched on the corner of the mattress, pressing her hands between her knees. She hadn't realized how nerve-racking this was going to be. That seemed ridiculously naïve and stupid now. She felt like she was losing her virginity all over again, except this time it wasn't to her first boyfriend, Daniel Albright, while his parents were at work and his little brother was downstairs. This man was a complete stranger. "Isn't that what the sex part is for?" she asked, and heard the slight tremor in her own voice.

"Partially. But we don't need to rush into the physical aspect. Tell me, why'd you join the lifestyle?"

"To save my marriage," she said. "Isn't that the reason we're all here?"

"Not in my opinion." He rolled onto his side and propped his head on his hand, facing her. "Everyone wants something different out of this. Me? I'm looking for companionship. I'm voracious for human connection."

"So we're just going to snuggle tonight, are we?"

He smiled, revealing white teeth straight out of a Crest ad. "Whatever you want."

"I'm not looking for anything fancy," she said. "I think it's best if I just get my first time over with."

"We can do better than that." In one swift motion, Marco was off the bed and disappearing into the closet. He rooted around, shuffling and pushing aside hangers. When he reappeared, he held a silver box in one hand and a pair of gold handcuffs in the other. "Every room at Quincy's has a treasure chest. How about we trade fantasies? I tell you what I want to do, then it's your turn. Of course, you're welcome to go first."

"You can go," Georgina said in a rush. "It's fine."

"Okay." Marco twirled the handcuffs on his index finger. "I want you to wait in the hallway until I call you in."

She nodded. Her body was stiff as she pressed herself standing and left the room. In the hallway, she gave herself a pep talk. This had been her idea. Nathan hadn't chickened out with Meredith.

He'd gone through with it—four times. Maybe it would help if she lowered her expectations. She shouldn't expect her first time to be life-changing—losing her virginity hadn't been. The sex had been terrible—more like a fist poking her stomach from the inside, making her feel like she needed to pee. Not until Whitaker did she discover sex wasn't supposed to be like fumbling around naked in a light cardio class at the YMCA, but a skin-melting, sweaty, aching, out-of-body experience.

Thinking about Whitaker, it struck her again that he was somewhere in this penthouse apartment. Not a ghost, or a memory, or an apparition. The real him. She never thought she'd see him again in her life, then ran into him at her first sex party? It was less of a coincidence and more of a cruel joke. But she wasn't surprised he'd become a swinger or that he cavorted with artists and "industry types." She had a feeling someone said to him, "Hey, swinging is fun, you should try it," and he said, "Sure, why not?" and never looked back.

Nor was she surprised that he'd only gotten hotter with age. Unfortunately, he'd always had that aging-like-a-fine-wine, Clooney-esque promise to him. The real surprise, the true slap in the face, was that he lived in New York City and seemed to have his life together.

She leaned her head against the wall, closed her eyes, and whined to whoever was listening, "Why? Why tonight? Why is he here?"

Then, as if a message from God, music answered from inside the bedroom. Loud, synthy, late '80s funk. Was that . . . Wait. Was that "Nasty" by Janet Jackson?

She looked over her shoulder at the closed bedroom door. Electric keyboard bopped behind it. A feeling so high and surprising made her laugh as Janet started to sing, *Hey, who's that thinkin' nasty thoughts? (Nasty boys!)*, and the volume cranked up to full blast. Immediately, her nerves dissipated. Anything with a Janet Jackson soundtrack had to be fun, right?

"Hello?" she called. "Can I come in yet?"

"Yes!" Marco yelled.

She pushed open the door to Janet singing, *Who's jamming to my nasty groove?*

Me! she thought. *I am!*

Inside, Marco stood on the bed wearing a trench coat over his bare, hairy legs.

"I'm not here!" he instructed. "You're just walking down the street. Pay me no attention."

Okay. This is unexpected, but I can't say my interest hasn't piqued.

She closed the door and meandered across the room like an aloof pedestrian.

"You're a sweet, innocent girl," Marco said, "trying to make it in the city, on your way to work as an assistant for Mr. Scary Wall Street Guy."

She tried to make her face appear sweet and innocent, playing with her hair and humming as she walked around in circles. Beneath the act, she was giddy with Janet and the unexpected but not unwelcome strangeness of this entire affair. She had to see where this was going.

"You're walking to the subway," Marco said. "You're running late and you're super sweaty under your pink fluffy sweater."

Okay, this is taking a slightly gross turn. Do I smell, too?

"You're running down the subway steps, you're about to miss the train, and you see me standing at the turnstile!"

As Janet chanted, she looked up at Marco, looming tall on the bed in his trench coat—which he had just jerked open to flash his humongous erection. It was staring straight at her like the head of a pointy greyhound. She couldn't help it—she leaped back and slapped her hand over her mouth. It was so big! So pointy! And . . . had he *shaved?*

"Good," he grunted. "You're scared. But wait! You're not scared, because you're a trained cage fighter. Come get me, you tough bitch!"

Marco jumped off the bed and landed on all fours in the middle of the room. "Please don't kill me!" he begged. "I've got kids at home!"

A huge, ecstatic smile overcame her face. Was a grown man role-playing a perverted subway flasher on the floor of a train-themed bedroom to Janet Jackson's greatest hit of all time?

Suzanne was right. This was fucking liberating. She could do basically anything and it would not be weirder than what was already happening.

"Stay down!" she yelled, and dived across the room to snatch the handcuffs from the dresser. "If you move, I'll break your neck!"

"No, please!" Marco rolled on the floor while his erect penis waved around like a trumpet in a marching band.

"I'll do anything!" he begged. "Anything!"

"Shut up, you pervert!" Georgina threw her body onto Marco's back to push him flat on his stomach.

"Ow, my dick!" he yelled.

"I hope it gets ripped off!" She grabbed his wrists and cuffed him. "These innocent city girls don't need another disgusting perv like you!"

Marco lifted his face from the floor and whispered, "Now press your heel into my ass!"

"Won't that hurt?" she whispered back.

"Just do it!"

Slowly, she pressed her stiletto into his ass cheek. "You don't mean your ass*hole*, do you?"

"No, this is good," he whispered. "Harder!"

"This is what it will feel like when you get stabbed with a fucking toothbrush in jail!" Georgina stepped onto his other cheek in her stilettos, holding on to the bedpost to keep from falling.

"Gargh!" Marco screamed. "I deserve it, make me bleed!"

She stepped off, and Marco turned to flash her a grin before he rose to his feet, trench coat open, and started to dance around the room. Watching him, she couldn't help but laugh with light-headed elation. Without stopping to think, or worry, or feel embarrassed, her body started to move. The funky melody, the sassy chanting, the electricity, all of it lifted the burden of shame and hurt she'd been carrying around like a backpack full of bricks, and it floated away. To where? She didn't care. All that mattered was Janet, nasty boys, and dancing.

They played the song through one more time, and when it ended, Georgina's cheeks hurt from smiling and her breath came in winded gasps. "You're a freak, Marco," she said.

He looked up at her from where he lay sprawled on the floor, naked and panting. "The correct phrase is *Nasty Boy*."

They grinned at each other, and she understood what he meant about human connection. They were bonded for life.

"Now," he said, pulling on his pants, "what can I do for you?"

"Anything I want, huh?"

"Anything," Marco said, then frowned as he buckled his belt. "Actually, I don't do blood stuff. Or pee."

Georgina's smile fell right off her face as a vision of Quincy in a Satanic blood ritual crossed her mind. "Not what I'm in the mood for, but thanks for the terrifying visual. Are there people I need to steer clear of?"

"Cynthia," he said. "Do not follow her into a bathroom."

"Yikes." She looked at the four-poster bed, thinking. Scheming, more like. Marco's invitation had opened up a world of possibilities. What did she want most? Was it just an orgasm? The thrill of a new man's hands? Or was it more sinister, like revenge? Marco seemed sincere—whatever she wanted, she could have. But revenge wouldn't satiate the true need that had opened up inside of her since she walked into Nathan's office that night. Hurting Nathan wasn't it. She wanted to feel . . . bad. As bad as Nathan had been. She wanted them to be equals again.

She peeked up at Marco from beneath her lashes. "Would you mind calling me Meredith?"

He didn't hesitate. "My pleasure, Meredith. And who am I?"

This was her chance! "Matthew McConaughey."

Without missing a beat, Marco rubbed his palms together and grinned with one side of his mouth, drawling, "All right, all right, all right," in a Texas accent. The man was a pro. "What else would the lady like?"

She grabbed his hand and marched him out of the bedroom. "Come with me downstairs, Matthew McConaughey."

In Quincy's living room, three leather couches faced inward to form an incomplete square. Georgina stripped to the red bra and underwear she had dug out from the back of her top drawer earlier that night, hoping they still fit and hadn't been eaten by moths, and tried to arrange herself in an alluring position on the couch.

Marco sat beside her. "Are you an exhibitionist?" he whispered, temporarily breaking character.

"Just a woman who wants to know what it feels like," she said. "Can you pretend you're my secret lover and we're sneaking around while my husband is at work?"

Marco relaxed seamlessly back into Matthew McConaughey's swagger. He slung his arm over the back of the couch, nodding around the loft. "This is quite the place you got here. I like your vibe, great vibe, chic, edgy vibe. I dig it. It's sexy. It makes me feel sexy. What about you? Well, you're always sexy."

Georgina laughed. Marco was so good at role-playing he could even nail Matthew McConaughey, riffing in the same dry, sneaky voice. She couldn't believe how free his willingness to play along made her feel. She could be anyone, say anything. Words came out of her mouth, and she didn't worry about what Marco would think. "I'm so lonely in this big, empty, cold apartment." She pretended to pout. "Good thing I have my hot yoga instructor to keep me company while my controlling husband is gone."

Marco/Matthew tilted his head to the side and smiled Matthew McConaughey's slow, charming smirk with precision. "I teach hot yoga? All right, all right, all right. I can dig it. Good for the body, good for the soul."

"I don't mean you're my 'hot yoga' instructor, I mean you're my *hot* yoga instructor."

"Even better, baby doll," Marco/Matthew said in a voice like warm molasses. "Is that offensive if I call you *baby doll*? I think that's offensive. You're a woman. A human being. Flesh and blood. And beautiful flesh at that."

"What do we do now?" Georgina whispered.

"You tell me," he said. "How about a kiss?"

She looked down at his mouth. It was a fine mouth, and it would have been a fine kiss, but she wasn't interested. Kissing was romantic, and she didn't want romance.

It was the game that had caught her attention.

"No need," she said. "And don't forget to call me Meredith."

"What time's your husband coming home, Meredith?"

"Ten minutes."

"A quickie then, huh? I'll see what I can do."

Her heart started to pound. This was it. No turning back. She would have sex with a man she'd met at a party less than two hours ago, and she was married. It was wrong.

It was undeniably hot.

Marco slid between her legs until his body was parallel to hers. "What happens if we get caught?"

"My husband will kill you," she said. "So you'd better hurry up."

She reached down and pulled her underwear to the side with one hand, his hips closer with the other. In seconds, he'd freed himself and put a condom on—this was not his first rodeo.

"Are you ready?" he asked.

Her breath caught at what would come next. She closed her eyes and thought of Nathan. The man who'd brought her to this place, this penthouse, this crossroad. The man whom she'd trusted to love her, who'd made her feel like an unwanted, humiliated idiot instead. That pain kept pummeling her at unexpected moments, trying to beat her to the ground, but she kept kicking it away. This time, she didn't fight it. She let it swell within her and ebb away. He couldn't take this moment from her. It didn't belong to him. This was hers— her game, her terms, her power. When she started to cry, she didn't bother to hide it.

Marco pulled away. "What's wrong? Too fast?" He wasn't Matthew McConaughey anymore.

"It's not that." She laughed a little and sniffed. "I'm crying because I'm relieved. Thank you. Thank you for this night. It was unexpectedly freeing."

He relaxed. "You're welcome. We don't have to make love. This was fun."

"No." She reached up with both arms and hooked them around his neck, pulling him back down on top of her. "I'm ready. I want to."

Marco's energy shifted. He transformed from the guy who liked Janet Jackson dance parties to the guy who had sex with a lot of women and knew how to please them. He reached a steady hand underneath her waist and swiftly hitched her hips up to his, holding them with a strength she didn't know he had. His mouth slid across her collarbone and over her breasts, kissed her skin between hot breaths. For the first time in years, she felt the pulse of anticipation, the thrill of newness, the audacity of desire. She opened for him, gasping when he thrust into her, and he stopped, pulled back, waited. In answer to his question, she drew him deeper. She did not want to stop, could not stop. Her body became a campfire that had jumped out of its pit, and lit a bush, and then a tree, and burned the whole fucking forest to the ground.

"You've got to be kidding."

Marco froze. Georgina froze. They turned their faces toward the voice, and there stood Nathan, fully dressed in his jeans and tweed overcoat, keys in hand. His expression sickened. "What the fuck is this?"

She smiled and waved. "Honey, you're home!"

Chapter 13

Georgina opened her eyes to a dark bedroom. The clock on her nightstand said six-fifty. Beside her, Nathan slept on his back. He was a silent sleeper, like he was dead. That was how she knew he was faking when she'd gotten home last night. She could hear him breathing.

He'd stormed out without another word after he'd caught them. Had she ruined swinging already with what she'd done?

If so, it had been worth it.

Had last night been a fluke? She couldn't believe the things she'd said and done—role-playing, crying, letting her body feel good without reservation. Hopefully she hadn't ruined their arrangement, because she wanted to go back.

She wanted more.

More of what? She didn't know. But if she kept going to the parties, she'd find out. She was too naïve to desire anything specific yet, she could only desire *desire* itself. And that seemed like a good start.

She was dying to find out how the night had gone for Norah, and with three kids, Norah was guaranteed to be awake. By now, she'd have cooked three different breakfasts, washed two loads of laundry, and attempted a twenty-minute YouTube workout, which usually ended with Hannah crawling all over her, thinking they were playing.

Georgina left Nathan asleep and walked to the kitchen to call her. Through the sliding door to a small terrace overlooking the alley between Eighty-Sixth and Eighty-Fifth Streets, the sky was beginning to lighten from navy to misty gray. She hunted around the fridge for smoothie ingredients as the phone rang.

"I only have five minutes," Norah answered.

"You okay?" Georgina asked.

Through the line, pans clattered. "I'm only on breakfast number one. Super late today because Hannah was up all morning puking."

Among a zillion minor allergies, Hannah was dangerously allergic to eggs, gluten, dairy, and nuts. A porridge of mashed banana and rice milk was about the only food she could tolerate. Simon, her five-year-old, was in a bacon phase, in which he refused to eat anything but bacon. But her oldest, Rachel, had recently decided to become a vegetarian because of "Big Pharma." Her twelve-year-old reasoning made a few leaps here and there, but everyone was proud of her budding passion for social justice. Norah had to use a different set of pans for Hannah's porridge than those she used for Rachel's eggs, which couldn't dare touch Simon's "evil, drug-peddling meat." Her kitchen looked like the office of a crime scene detective, with color-coded Post-it notes stuck on every dish like clues that only led to more dead ends.

"Ouch." Norah swore under her breath. "Oil splash."

"I was calling to see how you liked last night."

"It was good," Norah said, then she muffled the speaker and yelled, "*Simon! Breakfast is ready!*"

"That's it? You're not going to give me the juicy details?"

The metallic clank of silverware being dropped onto ceramic plates. "*Come get it! NOW!*" Norah yelled. "Sorry, what?"

"I asked if you were going to give me any juicy details," Georgina said, pulling a cutting board from the cupboard to slice some strawberries.

"You want juicy details about Felix in bed?" Norah asked. "SIMON! DO YOU WANT YOUR FOOD HOT OR NOT?"

Georgina raised her voice. "Maybe this isn't a good time. Call me later!"

"This is a fine time," Norah said. "And Felix is great. I just didn't think you'd want to hear about his penis."

Simon must have entered, because in the background, he announced, "I have a penis!"

"We're teaching him to use the real words for his body parts," Norah said. "Hold on." She murmured away from the phone, "Sit down—not on the floor, the table."

Simon answered, "There better be six pieces of bacon or I will starve *all day*."

"It's a BLT," Norah said. "It has three pieces of bacon inside of it."

"I'll take the B but not the L or the T," Simon replied.

Norah returned to the speaker and said, "He's impossible, but he's hilarious. It's so hard not to laugh."

Georgina sensed her time was limited and cut to the chase. "Were you mad he picked you?"

"No, that was a good idea. We had fun. Felix is so sweet."

"You act like you haven't known him for twelve years," Georgina said, peeling her banana.

"You know what I mean. We're not really friends, not like you two," Norah said. "It's like when you've been around someone a bunch of times and you don't know their name but you have to pretend you do because it's too late to ask. That's how I feel around him."

Georgina broke the banana in half and dropped it into her blender as she asked, "So did you . . ."

Muffled voices argued in the background, and Norah snapped, "*Simon! No hot sauce!* Remember last time?" Then she was back. "Have you-know-what? *Y-e-s.*"

Georgina heard Simon yell, "That spells *yes!*" She dumped a heap of Greek yogurt over the fruit. "And? How are you feeling?" she asked.

"Let me go in the other room." The kitchen noise faded, and a door closed. When it was quiet, Norah said, "I'm ecstatic, to be honest."

"That good, huh?" Georgina asked. Then came the sound of Norah peeing. She'd closed herself into the bathroom.

"I guess," Norah said, "I mean . . . sex is pretty standard at this point."

"Until last night," Georgina said, "I might have agreed with you. But then I put a grown man in handcuffs and watched him dance around naked to Janet Jackson."

The toilet flushed. "I'm going to need more context."

"I drew Marco's keys, and when we got upstairs, he suggested we trade fantasies. Guess what his was? Pretending to flash me before an '80s dance party," she said, slicing strawberries into juicy chunks that bled onto her fingers.

"You're lying," Norah said.

"I am one hundred percent serious. And honestly, it was life-changing."

"Oh my God. I don't even know what to say. What was yours?"

She glanced down the hall. It was dark—no sign of Nathan. "I made him pretend he was Matthew McConaughey. A little more straightforward, I guess. How's Ari handling it?"

When Norah spoke, it was with half-enunciated, garbled words. Apparently, she'd started brushing her teeth. "Eh. He—ahee—*Weh Win*. Wuk?"

"Um—what?"

Norah spit. "He's acting like we did nothing but watch an episode of *The West Wing* last night," she said. "Are you sure this is going to work?"

"Not if you pretend it's not happening. Quincy told me the couples are open with each other about what they do at parties. Tell Ari about your night. And make it hurt a little."

Norah made a noncommittal grunt. "We'll see. I can't believe you used to date that gorgeous guy, by the way."

Georgina held her phone with her shoulder while she scooped coffee beans into the grinder. "I told you we didn't date."

"Then why'd you look like you were having a heart attack?"

She thought she'd hidden it better than that. "Because he almost ruined my life by trying to convince me to call off law school and move to Peru with him. It was just an unfortunate coincidence."

"Or a message from the universe," Norah said.

"And the message says . . . ?"

"You tell me," Norah said. "Shit. Simon is screaming. He definitely used the hot sauce."

She hung up.

The apartment was quiet and dim in the early-morning light. Peaceful. Pre-Meredith, Georgina made a point to never turn on the coffee grinder or blender before Nathan woke up. Small signs of respect went far in a marriage. But Nathan had shown her a big sign of disrespect—indeed, the biggest.

The injustice got the best of her.

She cut through the tranquility by turning on both ear-rattling buzz saws together and leaving them on for thirty extra seconds.

Nathan hadn't slept in since the morning after the firm holiday party when they were first-year associates ten years ago, where he'd had six tequila shots at the karaoke afterparty. But by ten o'clock, he hadn't emerged from the bedroom, and Georgina was beginning to panic. Whenever she was distracted by her own problems, she found relief in doing something nice for somebody else, so she decided to visit her father.

In her running shoes, leggings, and a hoodie, she walked through Central Park to Seventy-First and West End, where her father and Buppha lived in the same apartment of her childhood. It was the parlor floor of a brownstone that hadn't been updated since the '70s. The walls were wood paneled and the couches a burnt-orange plaid. For years, Georgina had begged him to pull up the thick blue carpet to see whether there were wood floors underneath, but he insisted it would be too drafty, and she supposed the apartment would lose its charm. But for the giant elk head in the living room, it was actually pretty groovy.

On the way, she stopped in Zabar's and bought chocolate babka and cinnamon rugelach for Buppha, even though Buppha's was better. Everything Buppha cooked was better. When she arrived at their building, she smelled garlic and pancakes wafting through the open windows. Suddenly, her father yanked open the door, holding a watering can.

"Dad!"

He set down the can and raised his arms in a double-handed, overhead wave like he was on the other side of a football field. "You got my message?"

"Yes!" she lied. "Had to come right over!"

"Perfect timing," he said. "Buppha made brunch."

"I was hoping you'd say that." She hugged him. Her father was around her height, with a W-shaped hairline and red cheeks. "Hi, Dad."

"Sweetheart, I'm so glad to see you." He grasped her shoulders and kissed her cheek before hobbling into the foyer.

"What happened to your leg?"

He paused. "I thought you got my message?"

"Right, I mean," she quickly recovered, "what *exactly* happened?"

Her father waved one hand and grunted. "Buppha made me go to yoga."

Inside, the kitchen was warm and the fragrances comforting. Buppha stirred a saucepan that steamed and popped, wearing her usual brightly colored pants and knitted poncho. When she saw Georgina, she tossed aside her wooden spoon and ran for a hug. The way Buppha moved through the world could only be described as *acrobatic*. She leaped, jumped, twirled, bounced. Now she catapulted herself into Georgina's chest and squeezed. "I said to your father, 'Don't bother her! She's too busy for us boring people!' But I'm glad he called you because now here you are ready to eat khao tom and banana roti with an old lady and a one-legged man."

Her father swept pieces of mail and days' worth of the *Times* off the kitchen table for Georgina to sit. "Tell me more about this accident," she said.

"Your father tried eight-*ankle* pose instead of eight-angle," Buppha said, having returned to her cooking. "Now he's got one ankle."

"So you can't go to Thailand?" Every winter, they headed off to warm, muggy paradise until April, where they stayed in Buppha's seaside village with the rest of her family.

"We'll leave in a few weeks," her father said. He hoisted his foot onto a stool and slapped it with a frozen bag of peas.

Buppha served them bowls of khao tom, a steaming rice soup with ground pork and an egg cooking in the broth. "Be careful," she warned. "It's hot. How've you been?"

"Oh, you know," Georgina said, thinking of everything she could not say. "Busy with work." She spooned broth into her mouth so she didn't need to go on.

"And Nathan?"

She just smiled and nodded.

"You two need to get out more," Buppha said. "Every time I talk to you, it's work, work, work. Have some adventures, go on vacation!"

"Maybe," Georgina said. "This soup is to die for."

"I could live on this," her father agreed.

Buppha tasted it and frowned. "Too much ginger. Not enough fish sauce."

"It's perfect," Georgina said. The table was silent for a minute as they ate. Then her father perked up and suggested, "Hey, if you two need a vacation, come to Thailand for a while. We've got plenty of space in our house."

"Yes, yes, yes!" A little piece of ground pork flung off Buppha's ceramic ladle as she waved it around. "We can eat, explore, drink beers, and relax."

Georgina poked at the egg yolk, releasing it into the broth. "Oh, I don't think so."

"Why not? Ten years and you've never come," Buppha said. "It's about time."

She couldn't imagine going on that sort of vacation with Nathan. Theirs were usually meticulously planned trips to European cities with historical monuments and cathedrals to check off the list, their feet so sore by the end of the day they'd skip dinner and go straight to bed. Even their honeymoon involved a five-hour walking tour of Edinburgh's underground tunnel system, which was supposedly haunted and scared her so much they slept with the lights on. "I've got a huge case at work," Georgina said, "so I doubt I'll be going on vacation for a couple of years. Sorry."

Buppha clucked her tongue. "The problem is you and Nathan are both workaholics. There's no one to balance you out. It's unhealthy."

"You're not wrong," Georgina said. "But I can't. What have you been up to?"

For the rest of brunch, Buppha chatted about her village, airline customer service, her fall garden, and the Green Party while her father laughed along and Georgina slurped every last bit of her soup. It was a peaceful distraction, and she wished she could stay all day and listen to their idle chatter in the warm, savory-smelling kitchen, but by noon, it was time to face Nathan.

"I should go," she said. "I've got tons of work."

"But it's Sunday!" Buppha protested. "Stay for roti. We can drink champagne and listen to Céline Dion." Buppha was obsessed with Céline Dion, who'd coincidentally been Georgina's first concert when she was ten. Georgina wanted to take Buppha to Vegas to see her perform, but work always got in the way.

"Rain check?" she asked, rising to clear her plate.

Buppha grunted.

At the front door, Georgina kissed their cheeks and told them to call her before they left for Thailand. She turned to go, but paused with one foot on the top step. "Hey, can I ask you two a question?"

"Uh-oh," her father said. "It's usually a bad sign when lawyers want to ask me questions."

Buppha swatted his arm. "You don't need our permission."

After a pause, Georgina asked, "Why'd you two never get married?"

They looked at each other and, in the same moment, broke into conspiratorial smiles. The entryway around them was filled with photographs of their adventures. Their coats hung together on the

same rack, and Buppha's knickknacks were strewn among her father's old furniture. Maybe their lives were so intertwined that a piece
of paper meant nothing.

"We're together because we want to be together," her father said,
"and no other reason."

"Every day, we ask ourselves, are we happy?" Buppha said. "Today
the answer is yes. If the answer is ever no"—she gave a theatrical
shrug—"I'll kick him out."

Her father put his arm around Buppha's shoulders. "And I'll
starve to death."

"How'd you survive before me?" Buppha asked.

"On the fuel of my own stubbornness."

"Not much has changed, then," she said.

When they started rubbing noses, Georgina knew it was her cue.
"Bye, lovebirds."

She took the long way home, strolling the meandering paths
through Central Park without using her phone as a guide. Every
once in a while, she'd look up in search of the Met's flat stone roof to
make sure she was heading in the right direction. She passed families
and tourists and joggers. She passed Belvedere Castle and watched
a couple sharing popcorn, and she passed Turtle Pond, where she
bought some to feed to the ducks. The whole time, she thought
about her parents and what her father had said about being with
Buppha because he wanted to and no other reason. Could she say
the same? Was she with Nathan because she was happy, or was there
some other reason? But she couldn't think of what that other reason
would be, except she had a feeling that if there was another reason,
it had to do with her need to be right. Especially when it came to
relationships. She'd rejected Whitaker despite being desperately
in love with him because he didn't fit her husband-prototype. He
was a wanderer with no career plan, and he liked sleeping on top of

the blankets, which was bizarre. She was practical with a savings account and liked sleeping under the blankets like a normal person! So she'd chosen Nathan because not only did she love him—although not "desperately," she supposed—but because he never asked her to put law school on hold to move to the jungle in Peru with him. Nathan would never go anywhere that required a vaccine or a propeller plane.

That made her think of Thailand and Buppha's invitation. She closed her eyes and tried to picture her and Nathan tangled in the bed of a secluded villa, their bare skin tan and warm against white sheets. In their private pool, they could go skinny-dipping and watch the sunset with wine before showering together. But the fantasy was out of focus, the colors wrong, Nathan's face blurry. The images inspired nothing. No excitement or longing. If anything, they made her uncomfortable.

Then Nathan morphed into Whitaker, and she saw it all. Every sexy moment. He'd kiss her awake and pull her body into his. He'd make a joke about morning breath, and she'd laugh, not caring whether she had it. He'd give her two, probably three, orgasms that were so loud the guests next door would call the police. She'd explain to the police that everything was fine, and no, they had not heard there was a college girl missing in the area, and no, they hadn't heard anybody screaming. It would turn out the neighbors were very religious, and that would make Georgina feel a little embarrassed but also naughty, so they'd have sex again in the shower, and she would try to keep it down. Over breakfast, they'd have champagne, and when Whitaker would rub sunscreen on Georgina's skin, it would feel like foreplay. In the evening, she would put on a white eyelet dress and red lipstick because she would want him to think she looked sexy, and he would say so. They'd hold hands over the dinner table while the sun went down and share a cigarette because they could be bad on vacation. She saw it all, even the way he looked at her.

When Georgina got home, Nathan sat at the breakfast bar in the kitchen, wearing plaid flannel pants and bedhead, reading the paper and drinking coffee.

She pulled out the stool beside him. "You slept late."

He didn't look up. "I didn't sleep well."

"Because of last night?"

"Obviously."

Gently, she rested her hand on his. She was prepared to apologize for what she'd done. It was unproductive and vengeful and not reflective of why she wanted to swing. Anyway, that was the speech she'd practiced, and she opened her mouth to give it, but Nathan spoke first.

"I didn't know how bad it would feel." He lifted his face, and to her shock, it was clear he'd been crying. "I knew what I did to you was wrong, but until last night, seeing you with him, I didn't realize what it would actually feel like to be you, walking into my office."

"Like having your internal organs dragged out of your mouth and diced up while they're attached?" Georgina offered.

He let out a small, weak laugh. "Yeah. Like that."

Nathan got up to refill his coffee and poured her one, too. He put an ice cube in it to cool it down, then sat and took her hands, looked her straight in the eye. "I'm so sorry. I can't begin to describe how much I hate myself. What that must have been like for you—and now you want to do this to save us. Even after what I've done. I don't know what I did to deserve you, but I swear I am devoting my life to making this up to you." He nudged the mug of coffee toward her. "Starting now."

She laughed. His boyish pajamas and hair poking in funny directions made her heart ache for when love was simple between them.

"I will do anything to make you happy," Nathan said, and he looked like he meant it. "If swinging is it, okay. But if you're just saying that because you think I need it, we don't have to ever go again. In fact, I don't want to go ever again if that's the only reason."

Georgina considered his face. Two weeks ago, she'd have done almost anything to keep her life uncomplicated. A handstand on the edge of the Grand Canyon would not have been out of the question. He was offering that life to her now. *Let me earn your forgiveness*, he was saying. *Let me love you*. So why did it feel like uncomplicated was so unappealing? Because it was too late, she told herself, they couldn't go back to the way things were. That was all. But another voice told her that wasn't the explanation. Last night had introduced her to a part of herself she'd been ignoring, and now she couldn't pretend they didn't know each other.

"Actually, I had a good time last night," she said. "I'd like to keep going. I promise I won't stage any more walk-ins."

He searched her face. "Are you sure?"

"I am."

"You're braver than I am," he said, and looked down at the counter. "I chickened out."

"Do you want to stop?" she asked, while a voice in her head chanted, *Please say no, please say no*.

"No," he said. "I think this could be good for us. I don't want to feel like I'm stifling you. And I . . . I guess I needed an outlet. And this way, there are no secrets between us."

Georgina squeezed his hand. They would never have achieved that level of honesty, that fast, without last night. Months of counseling couldn't have gotten them there. It was a relief, to feel no barriers left between them. They were not perfect, but they were imperfect together. In a way, this was rock bottom—not that Friday night. They were deep in a hole, with nothing left but each other, clawing their way out.

Nathan suggested he make dinner reservations somewhere new and went back to reading the paper. For the rest of the afternoon, Georgina prepared for a deposition at her dining room table, but her mind kept wandering back to that villa in Thailand with the private pool she would never get to see.

Chapter 14

As Meredith's official firm mentor, it was Georgina's responsibility to conduct her annual review. That process involved collecting feedback about Meredith from other partners and senior counsel, having a one-on-one meeting to communicate that feedback constructively, and taking her out to lunch at a fancy restaurant the firm would pay for.

Meredith's review had been long scheduled for the following Wednesday at eleven thirty. Georgina couldn't get out of it now. That would be suspicious. Nor did she want to for reasons not entirely selfless, but not completely selfish either. The feedback she'd gotten about Meredith was good but not great. Partners said she could be competitive, not sharing credit where credit was due. *Not a team player*, one said. *Works hard but not efficiently*, another said. *Seems like she's trying to prove something.* The most searing, especially considering what Georgina knew, was a senior partner's one-sentence review simply stating: *Meredith is not entitled to special treatment.*

Georgina would relish in a smidge of delight delivering that news.

It wasn't all bad, though. Everyone agreed Meredith performed her assignments well and on time, which was all that mattered. Despite a lot of bluster about being a good citizen and team player, the firm was a business, and it had a bottom line. So long as Meredith billed hours and made money, she satisfied expectations. But mediocrity was not the future Georgina had wanted for Meredith. Rather, she'd dreamed of Meredith becoming a star associate and someday partner thanks to her mentorship and influence. So she was gripped in the claws of a dilemma—wanting Meredith to suffer, wanting her to grow, and wanting to be a woman who helped women.

Georgina printed out Meredith's review. Then she hid behind her computer to check her makeup in a handheld mirror and refresh her lipstick. Yes, she'd be a role model for Meredith, but the woman had slept with her husband.

A reluctant knock on the door. *Knock . . . knock . . . fine, one more knock.*

Georgina cleared her throat and plastered on a smile she hoped wasn't maniacal. "Come in!"

Meredith pushed open the door. "Is this still a good time?"

"Indeed. Please have a seat." She wondered if they were going to speak to each other like students in Miss Manners classes the whole time. *How do you do?* she nearly asked.

Meredith sat on the edge of Georgina's guest chair and folded her hands. Her left arm remained casted. It was like a giant neon sign with a loudspeaker attached to it, shouting, *You walked in on me and your husband!*

Georgina laughed for no reason. She wasn't sure what to do but start talking. "So you've had a productive first year. The general consensus is that you do quality work and everyone appreciates your follow-through. You meet deadlines without rushing or making mistakes."

"That's nice," Meredith said, and smiled. Georgina was startled by her ability to remain nonchalant. Inside her chest, her own heart thumped against her ribs almost painfully, but Meredith sat there like she was waiting for her manicure to dry, not moving, not even fidgeting.

"And one partner was particularly impressed by the motions in limine you wrote in the *Bank of Switzerland* case," she went on. "He said your understanding of evidence law was beyond most first years he'd worked with."

"I appreciate that," Meredith said.

Georgina frowned. She wasn't sure what she'd expected. Meredith was historically guarded and unfriendly, but shouldn't she be a bit more . . . appreciative? She didn't need groveling, but come on. A little humility would be nice. A little humanity at least.

"The only aspect of your review that's more on the constructive side is that several partners felt you should try to be more of a team player," she said carefully, and watched for Meredith's reaction, but there was none.

"Okay," she said. "What does that mean?"

"It means offer to jump in and help your classmates, go to firm events, be supportive when others have done a great job and deserve the credit," Georgina explained. "A good firm citizen. I guess some people felt you were trying too hard to stand out. But sharp elbows won't help you win the race. Working as a team will."

Meredith's back straightened a touch. "Thank you. I hear you."

That's it? Georgina wanted to ask. But she gave Meredith a stilted smile. They stared at each other for a few seconds.

"Right," Georgina said, and stacked her notes. "These are for you to keep. Shall we go to lunch?"

"We don't need to—" Meredith started to say.

"We're going to lunch!" Georgina cut her off in a rush. "Sorry . . .

sorry. I mean, we have to go to lunch. So let's just go. I'm hungry anyway."

Meredith stood up and straightened her pencil skirt. "I'll go get my coat."

After she'd gone, Georgina nearly burst into tears. It was much harder than she'd expected to look into Meredith's eyes and tell her she was doing a good job, and to be rewarded with coldness. Maybe she should cancel lunch. Meredith would probably be relieved. But she lifted her coat from the hanger on the back of her door and buttoned it up. If she hid from this lunch, she wouldn't be letting Meredith down—she'd be letting herself down. Meredith wasn't the one with something to prove. She was. She needed to show Meredith that she was fine, that she was strong, that this hadn't ruined her or her marriage.

Before stepping into the hall, Georgina took three deep breaths and sipped some water to calm her throat. *Don't think about it*, she told herself. *Don't think about it or you'll cry.*

She opened the door.

Georgina took Meredith to a restaurant a few blocks away that served Italian food to the business crowd. During lunch, it was difficult to get a reservation, but the place was probably empty for dinner. The interior was formally decorated but without much character, with white walls, wood floors, and black tablecloths, a bit like a hotel lobby.

They were quiet on the walk over except for Georgina's occasional small talk about the firm holiday party, which she'd helped plan for the last six years. It was early November, and the committee usually started arrangements by Halloween. This year, the afterparty would be bowling instead of karaoke since the number of "Piano Man" renditions she'd tolerated in her career was a cruel and unusual punishment. Meredith received this information with a polite smile and nod.

A young man in a bow tie seated them at a table for two, surrounded by other people in suits. Meredith squeezed some lemon into her water and started perusing the menu. Longingly, Georgina glanced at the wine list. That would make this painful lunch a little more tolerable. Before the affair, she'd hoped she and Meredith could become friends who'd sneak out for a wine lunch on Fridays occasionally, and Meredith would think she was the coolest partner in the universe and tell everyone how cool she was. Now a wine lunch would be medicinal. But she couldn't reveal her weakness and tore her eyes away.

"The linguine with clams—" Georgina started to recommend, then remembered Meredith was a vegan. "I mean, the spaghetti is excellent. Oh, that's not vegan either, is it. Soup?" Her eyes were desperately scanning the menu. "Right. Broth. Um—"

A waiter couldn't come soon enough. When a woman also wearing a bow tie introduced herself and offered to answer questions, both Georgina and Meredith ordered their lunches without appetizers or beverages. It seemed the illusion was over. Even the office was more fun than this.

Then Georgina had an idea to get the conversation moving back in the right direction. "Hey," she said. "We've got a bunch of depositions coming up in the sperm bank case. There's no reason why I should take all of those myself, and the experience will be great for you. Why don't you take some?"

Meredith thumbed the rim of her water glass. "Whose deposition would I take?"

"How about one of the named plaintiffs?"

"That's an important one. I can't."

"The named plaintiff depositions are usually straightforward. Just facts. You don't have to worry about combing through their research or hunting for bias like with experts. I promise."

She thought about it for a while, then nodded. "Okay. Thank you."

"I'll have you take Kathleen Duncan's," Georgina said. "She wasn't the original plaintiff, she was added late, which means she was probably recruited by the firm and doesn't know much about her claim. You can suss that out."

Her plan worked. When the woman in the bow tie returned with their plates—Georgina's clam linguine and what appeared to be a heap of plain lettuce for Meredith—they ate while Meredith asked questions about deposition strategy and what was going on in the case. It was the first time Meredith had ever expressed interest in what Georgina had to offer as a mentor. This was the relationship she'd craved. The best relationships in her life were the honest ones, in which both sides bared their true selves, even if their true selves were awful and the process was excruciatingly painful, because on the other side, an alliance emerged.

They finished eating, and Georgina paid the bill. As they were putting on their coats, Meredith said she had to stop at CVS and couldn't walk back to the office together. It might have been an excuse, but that was okay. They'd accomplished enough.

But as Meredith turned to leave, Georgina threw out her hand and touched Meredith's arm. "Wait," she said. Meredith stopped and looked at her, but Georgina wasn't sure what to say. It was just that she had so few answers about what had happened. Nathan hadn't told her any details beyond the first night. Where did they go to be alone? How did they communicate? Did they go on dates or just have sex? And did she want to know the answers to those questions? Or would it hurt her progress, forcing her backward while she was trying to move forward?

Meredith stared at her with an alarmed expression, seeming to sense a shift. "Is everything okay?"

"I have a question," Georgina said quietly. "And I think you owe me the answer. Is it over?"

Meredith looked down, but not before Georgina saw her eyes well up. Tears fell to the floor like raindrops. "Yes."

"How do I know that's true?"

Meredith wiped her face with both hands, childlike. "He told me it was a horrible mistake and we shouldn't speak anymore. He said you two were working on your relationship. I can show you the email."

"An email?" Georgina grimaced. "Nathan is afraid of conflict."

She sniffed. "It's okay. I deserve it."

"No, you don't."

When Meredith lifted her eyes, the two women held each other's gaze. They would never be friends, but they would be something.

Chapter 15

When Georgina returned to the office after lunch with Meredith and plopped into her chair, emotionally exhausted from the last hour, she had an unexpected email that made her body buzz like she was licking a battery.

> Dear Georgina,
> Quincy tells me you need a mentor. I am great at mentoring.
> Whitaker

She stared at it for a full minute. The message stared back. Before hitting Reply, she peeked into the hallway to make sure no one was looking. It was empty, but she closed the door just in case. Emailing Whitaker felt illegal, though it was fine. Perfectly fine. A kindness, even. One should stay connected to old friends.

> Whitaker,
> While I don't "need" anything from you, Quincy indeed recommended I find a mentor, and I would appreciate your services.
> Georgina

She clicked Send and tried to focus on the brief she'd been editing before Meredith's review, but his response was nearly instantaneous. The back-and-forth that followed left her breathless and sweating. That was how all of their exchanges ended, back then.

Dear Georgina,
It would be my pleasure to service you.
WN

Mr. Nolan,
You are emailing me at work. Watch your language.
Georgina

Dear Georgina,
I thought you were the boss?
WN

Whitaker,
I need to set a good example.
The Boss

Dear Mentee,
As do I. 277 Essex at 8. I'll show you how it's done.
Your Mentor

Mr. Mentor,
Should I bring Nathan?
Georgina

Dear Rookie,
You can, or you can come alone. Up to you. We won't be attending a party. Think of it more like a seminar.
Professor W
P.S. Nathan should get his own mentor.

Dear Professor,
See you at 8.
Teacher's Pet

Before her next meeting, Georgina had to go to the bathroom to put a wet paper towel on her neck.

The afternoon had passed in a distracted blur. She'd tried to work through her backlog of emails, but her fingers kept wandering over to Google and typing in Whitaker's name before she could stop them. She'd learned that he didn't have any social media accounts but found his wedding announcement and his wife's Instagram. It shouldn't have surprised her that he was married—swinging was a game for couples—but it had seared through her like a flaming iron poker nonetheless. In her mind, Whitaker wasn't the marrying kind of guy. That was the most painful discovery—not that he loved somebody else but that she'd been wrong about his character. If she'd known he wanted to get married someday, would that have changed their future?

His wife was an urban planner, according to her Instagram bio, which was the right mix of adorable and witty. She was beautiful and her name was Mei and she liked to wear lots of gold jewelry. An hour had passed while Georgina clicked through Mei's photos, and when she'd realized it, she was so humiliated she'd turned her computer off and started studying a legal treatise she'd never once opened.

At seven, she went to the bathroom to freshen up. She sprayed dry shampoo in her hair and tipped her head upside down to shake in some volume. She powdered her face, reapplied blush and lipstick, and tweezed a few eyebrow hairs. But appraising herself in the mirror, she felt like an overzealous try-hard and used toilet paper to rub most of it off before throwing her hair in a ponytail. If Mei was going to be there, she couldn't look like she was trying to impress Whitaker, which she wasn't trying to do anyway.

Her Uber driver—Jasper he'd said his name was—braked in front of 277 Essex a few minutes after eight. "Have a good one," he said, but Georgina didn't move. Outside waited a closed storefront, its metal curtain padlocked into the cement. Beside it was a steel door on which blue electrical tape secured an advertisement for a dentist. Or was it an electrician? Somehow it was both.

"Something wrong?" he asked.

Whitaker's in there, she told herself. *Go.*

"All good," she said, and climbed out. The night had turned freezing. She held her coat closed at the neck as Jasper sped away. Alone, she turned to face 277 Essex and noticed a crack of light between the door and its frame—the dead bolt was engaged, preventing it from closing. Now that she was on the street, faint bass notes vibrated the air. It must have been one of those trendy speakeasies. Behind this crummy, unmarked storefront would be a luxury lounge serving top-shelf liquor.

She lifted her chin and strode forward, but when she pushed open the door, she stood under the unforgiving light of a fluorescent bulb in a cramped mudroom littered with discarded mail and dried leaves. No beautiful aspiring actress waiting to take her coat or bouncer asking for a secret password. But a second door waited ahead, also propped on its dead bolt. As she walked closer, the music got louder, and she realized it was a remix of "Higher Love," her favorite Whitney Houston song.

She touched her fingertips to her lips and felt them curve into a smile. A gut feeling told her Whitaker had bribed the DJ to play that song at the moment of her arrival. It had always put her in the party mood.

The door opened, and there he was. His brown hair swept to the side, slightly ruffled, like he'd just run his fingers through it and it stuck. His gray button-down was rolled to the elbows, and he wore army-green chinos over brown boots and glasses with black frames. She'd always thought he looked sexiest in glasses. The brown leather watch on his wrist she recognized from college. He was the type of person who could wear the same watch for a lifetime, especially if it meant something to him.

"I worried you'd see the sign and think I was trying to wire your jaw," he said.

"I've always wanted a smile that glowed," she said.

Whitaker grinned. "I assure you it already does."

His eyes resembled clouds hanging over an East Coast ocean in the morning. When he leaned down to kiss her cheek, she tensed. *Do not enjoy this*, she told herself. *Do not enjoy this!* His lips were warm and the scent of his skin familiar.

Damn it! She enjoyed it.

"Can I take your coat?" he asked.

Georgina reached for the top button of her beige trench, then stopped. They were alone in a low-lit hallway. Better keep it on to be safe. "No, thank you."

"It's warm in there."

She peered around his shoulder. "What is 'in there'?"

"Indoor soccer," he said. "Didn't you get my email?"

"Are the players naked?" she asked.

He laughed. "Try not to gawk," he said. "The rookies always gawk."

Georgina raised a brow. "You take a lot of women to indoor soccer, huh?"

"This is a first," he said. "But you can always spot a rookie."

"With your experienced eye," she said.

Whitaker leaned against the wall and dug his hands into his pockets, never taking his eyes off her. His expression was relaxed and open, like he was staring at a beach. He took in her face, nodding ever so slightly. "I can't tell you how good it is to see you again," he said. "Ever since I moved here, I'd hoped. Only I thought I might run into you during rush hour at Grand Central, not necessarily at a sex party."

This confession made Georgina's insides feel like hot soup, but she tried to cover it up by keeping her tone light. "Of all the places I could imagine, a sex party is exactly where I thought I'd run into you."

Someone opened the door at the end of the hall, and they both jumped. It was an older man in a suit, staring at his phone. As he passed and wished them a good evening, Georgina saw red lipstick on his jaw and collar.

"He doesn't look like he's been watching indoor soccer," she teased.

"European rules," Whitaker said. "Ready? Your foam finger awaits."

She followed him toward the final door, managing to check out his butt only once. He shouldered it open and let her pass, watching her face with an amused little smile. Inside, a topless hostess greeted them, and Georgina couldn't help it. She gawked. Despite its modest entrance, the space was cathedral-size. Rows of doors, some open, some closed, led to private rooms off the main floor, and velvet couches surrounded the center like spectator seating. People in varying states of undress lounged with cocktails, some engaged while others watched. From the ceiling, a man and a woman dressed in black feathered bodysuits with wings performed acrobatics in giant silver lyras.

"I warned you," Whitaker said, and gently closed her jaw with his fingertip. Even that simple touch sent goose bumps down her neck. Meeting him may have been a mistake. A dangerous mistake.

She cleared her throat and looked away from his face. "Where are we?"

"It's a sex club."

She laughed. "Yeah, I gathered that. I mean, what's it called?"

"La Peluche," he said. "But I don't think you can find it on Google."

The hostess's breasts pooled on the podium, her nipples dangerously close to a row of votive candles. "Reservation?"

"We're meeting some friends upstairs," Whitaker said, and gave a name Georgina didn't recognize. Whoever it belonged to seemed important because the hostess raised her eyebrows.

"Follow me," she said, and led them up a flight of magenta-carpeted stairs lined with more candles.

"This is a fire hazard," Georgina whispered.

"Wait until you see the burning loins," Whitaker whispered back.

A low and jazzy saxophone played upstairs, where the patrons were generally clothed, though the sexual energy was palpable. "Over there," the hostess said, and pointed toward a circular booth in the far corner.

Georgina had begun to walk toward it when she felt Whitaker grab her shoulders and steer her left just in time to avoid a man's bare leg jutting out from under a table. "Watch for flying body parts around here," he said.

At the booth, faces from Saturday night smiled at her. Martin sat closest, then his wife, and beside her sat Mei, whom Georgina recognized from the Internet, except she was even more graceful and alluring in person. She had a pensive face with high cheekbones and a straight nose. Her black hair hung above delicate shoulders, and her crepe top and gold jewelry exuded classic, effortless taste.

When Mei noticed Georgina watching her, she raised her drink with a knowing nod. Georgina looked down at her knee-length black suit and felt like the class treasurer at a summer internship fair.

"The apprentice!" Martin cheered.

"Martin's something of a celebrity around here," Whitaker said.

"I should say so," Martin said. "I've spent enough money at this club. Speaking of, let's get going. I've got a room reserved for nine."

Georgina sucked in a small, involuntary gasp.

"Not for you, dear," Martin said.

"Give her a minute," Whitaker said. "She's a little shaken from the crows."

Everyone at the table shook their heads and rolled their eyes.

"They're ridiculous," Martin said.

"They're terrifying!" his wife said.

"Attention-seeking," Mei said.

"I tried it once," Whitaker said. "Nearly broke my neck."

Georgina laughed. He'd always found a way to make her feel at ease. "I'd pay good money to see that."

Whitaker made introductions, and Martin's wife turned out to be Cynthia, the bloodthirsty bathroom lurker. She was older than the other women, with pointy red fingernails and coiffed silver hair. Only an Audrey Hepburn–style cigarette holder was missing from her polished, retro style.

By the time he'd finished, a waiter had stealthily delivered Georgina a drink. She looked down and saw . . . an appletini.

"Whitaker!" She was mortified.

Whitaker feigned innocence. "What? You don't like it? I asked them to make it extra green." Then he bit his lips together, trying not to laugh.

"I'm not twenty-one anymore!"

"Really? Because you look exactly the same."

She glared at him, but as he lost his own battle to keep from laughing, she found herself losing, too. "Very funny, jerk," she said. "The joke's on you because I'm going to have two and throw up in your back seat."

Whitaker gazed wistfully into the distance. "Ah, good times."

"You deserved it for taking me riverboat gambling."

"I still have that car," he said. "On a hot day, it smells like apple and puke, and I think of you."

She punched his shoulder, then caught Mei's shrewd eye. Her arm fell limp and dropped. She felt like a dog interrupted while eating from the trash.

"Are we going to do this or what?" Martin asked.

"Sorry," Georgina said. "Yes. Do, um, what, exactly?"

"Whitaker tells us he is to be your spiritual guide through the oasis in which we all live," Martin said. "I once did the same for him."

Whitaker leaned forward and stage-whispered, "Martin likes to remind me I owe him."

"What has he told you about the lifestyle?" Martin asked.

"Hey, aren't I the mentor here?" Whitaker asked.

"Of course." Martin bowed his head. "Please. Go forth." He settled back into his seat and folded his arms, observing them like a mildly amusing school play.

Whitaker began to clean his glasses, wearing an overly serious expression on his face. "This is my professorial look. How am I doing?"

She laughed. "Nobody is convinced."

He put his glasses back on, and some part of her wished he hadn't. The more responsible part. The less responsible part was quite pleased. "So," he said, "why do you want to join the lifestyle?"

Georgina looked around to see if anyone else was confused, but they appeared either at ease, intrigued, or bored. "What's 'the life-style'?" she asked. "Do you mean swinging?"

Everyone laughed. What was so funny?

"We don't call it that, sweetheart," Cynthia said.

"That's very seventies," Mei said.

"We call it the lifestyle," Whitaker said, "but yes, it's swinging."

"Right," Georgina said. "I'm here because a friend recommended it." She picked up her appletini to drink, and when she set it back down, it splashed over the edge because her hands had begun to shake. That question was unexpected. Why did her reason matter?

Whitaker looked curious. "Why?"

She returned a casual shrug and played with the stem of her martini glass. "Because she did it, and it saved her marriage." She sensed Whitaker watching her, but she was too nervous to look up. When she did, he wore an earnest expression.

"That's how most of us ended up here, one way or another," he said.

"Does that mean it works?" she asked, hearing the vulnerability in her own voice and wishing it hadn't betrayed her.

"Depends on who you ask," he said.

"I'm asking you," she said, quietly enough that only he could hear.

Whitaker moved his glass of beer in circles on the table, leaving a wet trail of condensation. She wanted to know what he was waiting to say, but Martin had apparently been eavesdropping. "Better than you could ever imagine," he interrupted. "This is everything you want and more."

"How do you know what I want?" she asked, but smiled to show she was teasing.

"You're here to find answers," Martin said, "and you will. But more importantly, you'll be happy, and I can see you are not happy."

"You're very presumptuous, Martin, to assume I want to be happy."

"Everyone wants to be happy, dear," he said. "It's not an assumption, it's an understanding."

"Don't mind him," Whitaker said. "Outside of the lifestyle, Martin's the most expensive psychotherapist in New York City."

"Then I'll know who to call if this goes south," Georgina said. "Not that I'm not enjoying the conversation, but why did you bring me here again?" She looked between Martin and Whitaker.

"Right," Whitaker said. "If you'd like to join our group on a more permanent basis—"

"Oh, please join us, beautiful Georgina," Martin interrupted.

"We have a few unwritten rules we tend to abide by," Whitaker finished.

"Tend to abide by?" Georgina asked. "Or abide by?"

Whitaker glanced drolly at Martin and commented, "Lawyers."

Georgina made an apologetic face and motioned for Whitaker to continue. "Habit. Go on." She sipped her appletini again, which wasn't half-bad.

"The first thing is we only see each other at these sorts of events," Whitaker said. "A party, a club. If you and I had dinner to catch up, for example, it could complicate the dynamic."

She looked up to see if he was joking, but he seemed sincere. Why did he have to use that as an example? It hadn't occurred to her that they could have dinner, but now that he'd mentioned it, it seemed like a possibility, and she pictured them sharing Thai food over candlelight and laughing. They were old friends, so what was the big deal?

"Aren't we all adults here?" she asked. "Can't we tell the difference between a sex party and a birthday party?"

"Sometimes those are one and the same," Martin quipped.

"We're adults," Whitaker said, "but we are also human."

Whitaker gave her a look she couldn't interpret. Heat unexpectedly flushed her neck, and her face burned. She was painfully embarrassed, but why? Did she want to have dinner with him that badly? Two seconds ago, she'd never considered the idea, and now it bothered her that she could never do it. This was a perfect example of how she'd known back in college that their relationship was doomed. It was too painful to want what she could not have. She'd thought he was happy to see her and that he was flirting intentionally, but of course that was ridiculous. He was just an incorrigible flirt. He was married and so was she, and dinner wouldn't have been appropriate anyway. She wouldn't have gone, so none of this mattered. She picked up her drink.

"Got it." She made her voice sound light. "You're officially uninvited from my New Year's Eve party."

"Oh, we have a New Year's Eve party, dear." Martin wore a mischievous smile. "And you are formally invited."

Carefully, she set down her glass. "Okay. What's next?"

Whitaker glanced quickly at Mei. "We change partners."

Georgina raised one eyebrow. "Isn't that the basic concept?"

"I mean we change partners frequently," he said. "Try not to have a preference for any one person. It's more of a sage piece of advice than anything. Martin here has been doing this a long time."

"I'm older than I look," Martin whispered. "Sex keeps my color healthy."

Georgina and Whitaker met eyes. There weren't many couples in the group. If she stayed, they would be together soon. He seemed to be thinking this, too, because he shifted in his seat and looked away.

"Whitaker's making this more complicated than it needs to be," Martin said. "What he's trying to say is don't fall in love. It will fuck everything up."

"I promise I'm doing this to save my marriage," Georgina said, "not to destroy it."

Martin clapped once. "It's settled, then, and I've got a date with destiny." He stood and offered his elbow to Cynthia. "Milady?"

"I should get going as well," Georgina said. "It's a school night."

Whitaker jumped out of his seat. "Let me walk you out."

"You don't need to."

"Please."

She nodded. Their postures were strangely stiff as they walked downstairs compared to the way they'd walked up. As the couches on the bottom floor came into view, Georgina's eyes were drawn to familiar blond hair. Although, without the J.Jill, it was hard to be sure . . .

Then, "GEORGINA!" the woman yelled.

It was indeed Suzanne, naked, dripping candle wax onto the chest of her male companion.

"DO NOT MOVE! I'M COMING OVER!"

Georgina grabbed Whitaker's arm and squeezed. "I just saw someone I know."

"Get used to it," Whitaker said. "I ran into my super. Now he refuses to empty my radiator."

Suzanne jogged toward them, breasts bouncing as she took the stairs two at a time. "She's a swinger for a week and already she's partying at the best club in the city? Why am I not surprised!"

Georgina forced a smile. *Better get used to seeing naked people,* she told herself. *You're in the lifestyle now. It's basically a perpetual women's locker room!*

"Suzanne, this is Whitaker," she said. "Whitaker, Suzanne. Suzanne is the friend I mentioned, who introduced me to the lifestyle. This is all thanks to her."

Suzanne's eyes practically bugged out when she looked at Whitaker. "It is so nice to meet you. Really, really nice. Do you come here often?"

Whitaker smiled politely. "Occasionally. My friend Martin has the sex club equivalent of box seats."

"Oh, I know Martin," Suzanne said in a voice that suggested there was more to this story. "You're playing with the big boys, Georgina, and I mean that literally. Is Nathan here?"

"No, he—"

"No explanation needed," she said. "Good girl. Get yours, my friend!" Suzanne winked with both eyes again and dashed off.

"You sure you don't want her to be your mentor?" Whitaker asked when she was gone.

"She's black diamond," Georgina said. "I'm bunny hill."

"Right," Whitaker said. "Wouldn't want to break something."

"Like what?"

He didn't answer that.

Back on Essex, Whitaker waited with her for a yellow cab to drive by. She could have called an Uber, but didn't. She wanted to stand with him for a while. The street was empty but for the occasional group of young people smoking cigarettes and yelling over each other.

Georgina must have been frowning without realizing it, because Whitaker said, "Something wrong?"

"No," she said. "Not wrong. Just thinking."

"About what?"

"About whether you're angry at me."

"For making me stand out here in the cold?" he asked.

"For not going with you to Peru," she said.

He grinned. "If I say yes, will I get something out of it?"

"I've heard forgiveness can be very rewarding," Georgina said. "Though personally, I prefer getting even."

Whitaker gently kicked the toe of his boot against a green lamppost. "Nah. There's nothing to be angry about. Not then and definitely not now."

"Really? I still curse John Paul Pasteroni for stealing my mechanical pencil in the fifth grade."

Whitaker rubbed his chin in exaggerated thought. "It all makes sense now."

"What does?"

"Why you're so deeply troubled," he teased.

She lifted her chin and folded her arms. "Most people tell me I'm perfect."

He looked at her sideways, his expression playful. "Well, I'm not going to lie to you, am I?"

A block away, a yellow cab turned from Houston onto Essex, and they both jumped to the curb, plunging their hands in the air. Her shoulder connected with his chest, and his free hand wrapped around her back to keep her from falling. For a beat, she sank into the relief of his body heat before scrambling back to the sidewalk with a panicky, "Sorry!"

"A decade later and I still send you running," Whitaker said. "Figures."

The cab forgotten, it rolled behind him and disappeared around the corner.

"Shit!" She chased it for a few steps before giving up.

"I knew you weren't going to come," he said quietly.

She turned. "Then why'd you ask?"

"It was worth a shot."

"But I was going to law school," she said.

"I know."

"I'd already gotten in. I'd borrowed the money. I'd bought a pocket Constitution!"

"Yeah," he said. "I know."

"It wasn't fair, what you did, to be completely honest. You could have canceled your plans and come with me to New York if you wanted to be together." It came out huffier and more petulant than she'd intended. The past was the past. Why did this matter?

He resumed kicking his toe against the lamppost. "The thing was, I already knew I'd give up everything for you."

"So it was a test."

"It was a kid in love."

She turned away so he wouldn't see her blinking back tears. A hard sensation built in her chest, making it difficult to breathe. It reminded her of the night she'd caught Nathan, only then the feeling in her chest had been emptiness. Now it was too full, like the anger she felt that Whitaker had forced her to choose and the fear that she'd picked wrong was enough to tear her open. "I should call an Uber," she said in a traitorous, swollen voice, and looked at her screen through blurred vision. "Two minutes."

"We might freeze before then," Whitaker said.

But at that moment, freezing to death seemed like a reasonable way out of this unwanted conversation. She cleared her throat and tried to sound chipper. "So what did you do in Peru anyway?"

Whitaker leaned one shoulder against the post, like a scene in a Broadway play. "Drank pisco sours to heal my broken heart. Went out too much. Hiked. Did some freelancing and English tutoring. Oh, and I had a blog, but please don't try to find it. I was quite the socialist philosopher."

She pretended to type into her phone. "What was it called? Just curious. Definitely not sending it to everyone I know."

When a black Toyota Camry braked at the curb, neither moved.

She glanced at the car and back. She couldn't leave without asking. "So Mei knows about us?"

He dug his hands into his pockets. "She does."

That was the answer she'd wanted. It proved her existence somehow, that she'd mattered to him enough. "And she's okay with me joining the group?"

"She doesn't have much say in the matter," he said. "We're divorced."

Her body tensed with an exhilarating panic. "But you came to the party together. And you're here together."

"We're still friends," he said. "We decided to stay partners in this."

The Uber driver honked. She was being rude, but she couldn't leave. There was one more question that plagued her. She didn't like how confused she'd felt since she'd seen Whitaker again. Their relationship, if it rose to that level, was defined only by the group. Nothing remained between them but distant history. He'd been significant to her once, and now what was he? Just a person she used to know?

She couldn't look him in the eye as she asked, "Do you think we could ever be friends?"

"We are friends," he said. "We've always been friends. We just lost touch for a while."

Though he'd ostensibly given her what she wanted, the answer left her hollow. Two weeks ago, she'd only thought about Whitaker Nolan when she put on mismatched socks. So that was every day, she supposed. He'd loved her socks. But she never thought she'd see him again, and now that she had, she realized it was better when they remained strangers. With him, it was all or nothing. "Friends" just wasn't enough.

"Friends it is, then," she lied. "But no dinners."

He nodded once, firmly, like closing a deal. "Definitely no dinners."

Chapter 16

Felix and Georgina met for lunch on Fridays. Until it got too cold, they'd buy salads from 'Wichcraft and eat at the little green metal tables in Bryant Park. Now November, they might have one or two outdoor Fridays left, then they'd switch to an indoor market on Eighth Avenue that had food vendors in any cuisine one could imagine.

At noon, Georgina left her office into an invigorating fall day, the weather perfectly suiting her mood. Her first swinging experience had gone better than expected, and she'd conquered a visit to a sex club. She had to congratulate herself. She'd taken a rotten situation and turned it into an opportunity, not only for herself but for her friends, too. As she walked along Forty-Second Street toward Sixth Avenue, she lifted her face toward the sun and closed her eyes for a second to relish the city's sounds, which comforted and excited her.

Then she ran into something hard and reeking of cigarette smoke, which turned out to be a large man's back.

He looked up from his phone. "Jesus fucking Christ, lady, watch where you're going."

"Says the man blocking traffic," she snapped, and carried on.

Felix waited near the subway entrance on the southeast corner, watching a chess match between two old men in tweed. After they bought their salads, they found a table by the corner of the lawn, surrounded by hopeful pigeons.

Georgina unwrapped her plastic fork and began to eat with her winter gloves on. "So," she said, "tell me."

Felix shoveled a conveniently enormous bite into his mouth and shrugged.

"What'd you two do?" she asked.

He looked up at her with an eyebrow raised as if to say, *What do you think we did?*

"Was it a good idea?" she asked. "Picking Norah?"

She detected the smallest hint of a smile as he continued scarfing down his salad.

"Yes!" she said. "You loved it. I can tell. I'm a genius."

He rolled his eyes and laughed. "I wouldn't go that far. But we had a good connection. I've been thinking more about the foundation for exchanging partners. It's primal from an evolutionary perspective, but at the same time, it requires advanced emotional intelligence, like Alina has. Strong empathy for your partner and, I'd argue, more selflessness than the average couple possesses."

"You have to be the most cerebral swinger on earth," Georgina said.

Felix forked the last bite of salad into his mouth and tossed the plastic container into a nearby trash can. "I wouldn't call myself a swinger."

"But you're going to keep going."

"Yeah," he said, "for now."

She peered up at him coyly. "Norah had fun at the party."

He raised his eyebrows, amused but not unhappy. "She told you that?"

"We have no secrets."

"Is that right?" Felix had a curious look on his face.

"What?" she asked. "Do you know something I don't?"

"I don't know," he said. "Do I?"

"She told me you had sex. What am I missing? Did you think it was bad?"

"No, it was fine." He was grinning hugely.

She narrowed her eyes at him. "That's what Norah said."

"I guess it was fine, then."

"If there's one thing I've learned since becoming a swinger," she said, "it's that *fine* is not a word that should ever be used to describe sex."

"Nice?" he suggested.

She laughed. "That's worse."

Felix slid a giant chocolate chip cookie from a paper sleeve and offered Georgina half.

"I'm still eating my salad because I'm not an animal," she said. "Maybe later."

"Suit yourself," he said.

"You can admit it if it was boring," she said. "I won't tell her."

Felix pointed to the remaining half, having already finished his piece in one bite. "It's now or never."

"Have it." She snapped the lid back onto her salad container as her phone began to vibrate with a call from Norah. "Look," she teased, "it's your lover. Hello?"

"It's working!" Norah blurted.

"Hurrah!" Georgina cheered. "But don't sound so surprised."

She carried her empty container to the trash can as Norah continued. "I told Ari all about my night—*very* detailed," Norah said. "At first, he acted like he didn't care. But since then, he's been totally different. He calls me—not texts, calls—to 'ask how I'm doing.'

Weird, right? We had sex *twice* this week, and he did . . . this thing I like—*both times*. And when he came home from work yesterday?" She paused as a siren blared through the line. "He *gave me a gift*."

"What kind of gift?"

"It's this hippie rope necklace with a crystal on the end," she said. "I hate it, actually, but I'm wearing it right now because I will be damned if I don't encourage this behavior."

When Georgina returned to the table, Felix was chewing his cookie absently and watching her with interest. "I should go," she said to Norah. "I'm having lunch with Felix."

"Oh." Norah paused. "Did he say anything about Saturday?"

"He's been a perfect gentleman about it," Georgina said carefully, and raised one eyebrow at Felix, who'd leaned forward to eavesdrop.

"A pigeon pooped on Hannah," Norah said, and hung up.

"What was that about?" Felix asked. His attempt at nonchalance was hilariously transparent. The man was practically whistling.

"Nothing," Georgina said as a small smile crept to her lips. "Nothing at all."

Something was going on here, something highly secretive and suspicious, and there was only one explanation.

Felix and Norah were in love.

When Georgina got back to her office, she had an ECF notice waiting—the auto-generated message sent to all parties when a judge issued a decision. She typed in her password to download the document and skimmed it for the word *granted* or *denied*.

"Shit!" She smacked her palms on the desk. "Shit!"

She'd lost an important discovery motion in the sperm bank case, and now she'd have to make do without the additional medical records she desperately needed.

"Everything all right?" Nathan leaned against her doorframe, handsome in a navy suit and forest-green tie, just like he'd done before sending her off for drinks with Suzanne that fateful Friday night. She picked up her water glass and drained it. Her high from the Felix-Norah discovery had disappeared, and she wanted to be alone and feel sorry for herself in peace.

"I lost a motion," she said. "The client will not be happy."

Nathan closed the door behind him. "I might have news to cheer you up. Want to hear it?"

"Of course." Georgina eyed him. "What are you smiling about?"

"I can't help myself. It's too good." He sat on the edge of her desk. "It's about Norah and Felix."

"Spit it out, then."

"Apparently, it got pretty unorthodox when they were together at the party on Saturday night."

She examined Nathan's face for a hint that he was lying, but found none. "Unorthodox," she repeated. "What do you mean?"

"Let's just say they did something we've never done."

"What, like—" She pointed to the back of her skirt.

Nathan laughed and shook his head. "No. Not quite." He glanced at her speakerphone like the NSA might be listening, and dropped his voice. "But they watched porn together."

For several seconds, Georgina stared at Nathan in astonishment, stunned and ecstatic in equal parts. It wasn't just that she was right. It was the *degree* of her rightness. They'd been to one party! One! And already Felix and Norah were not only in love but their intimacy and downright raunchiness had reached unprecedented levels. She was their naughty fairy godmother.

"How do you know?" she asked.

"Ari told me. He's pretty pissed, to be honest."

Georgina's claws reared on Norah's behalf. "As if he has any right!"

Nathan raised his palms. "Just relaying the facts."

She harrumphed to convey just how she felt about that. "You tell Ari he should be happy swinging is so liberating. He only stands to benefit."

"I'd prefer to stay out of it."

On her desk, she had a fidget spinner for long hours of slogging through briefs. Nathan picked it up and played with it.

"Hey, I want to talk to you," he said.

She returned to her computer screen to clean out her inbox before the weekend ahead. "You want to watch porn together?" she joked absently. But when Nathan didn't laugh, she looked up. Immediately, her mind went to Whitaker. Had Nathan found out about their past? Had he heard she flirted with him just a tad at the club on Wednesday, and somehow figured out she hadn't stopped thinking about him since? How? Who told? She was instantly defensive, wishing she could shine a flashlight in his face and yell, "*Where were you on the night of November 3!*"

Get it together, she chided herself. *You both agreed to this. Sex clubs, flirting, it's all part of the package. Everything is under control.*

She forced a smile. "What is it?"

What came out of Nathan's mouth next was more surprising than if he had somehow read her mind about Whitaker. "We should have a baby," he said.

She could not move as she stared at him, one hand on her mouse and the other holding up her chin.

"You want a baby, right?" he asked. "I mean, with me?"

Compared to all the other shocks she'd received lately, this one was strangely numbing. She had no idea what to say. The thought of a baby hadn't crossed her mind in recent memory and definitely not since Meredith. "Of course I want a baby," she said, "but do you think now is the right time?"

"We're struggling. It might help to remember what we want and what's important in life. Put things into perspective. Don't you agree?" On his face, he wore a boyish expression of hopefulness she found endearing. It softened her slightly.

"But they always say a baby doesn't fix your problems," she said gently. "Everybody says that."

"We're not everybody," Nathan said. "We're better than everybody."

I used to think that, too, she wanted to say. She put her hand on his. "I want us to be smart about this."

"I've been looking for more, and I think that's connected to . . . what happened. I want to focus on moving forward as a family. I'm ready. So—" He flicked the fidget spinner one last time. "Let me know."

After he'd gone, she picked up the toy. Definitely a choking hazard. Obviously, everything in her life would change when they had a baby, but there was one thing in particular she wanted to hold on to.

Chapter 17

Georgina and her friends were invited to a party at Martin's the following Saturday night. Had there been an official vote, it seemed the referendum for their permanent admittance had passed. Georgina was thrilled, Alina was not surprised, Norah was more determined than ever, and Nathan had spent an especially long time choosing his shirt. This amused Georgina, as all of Nathan's shirts were Brooks Brothers button-downs in different colors. Two had patterns, which he called his "party shirts."

It turned out Martin lived in a narrow West Village town house that reminded Georgina of an eccentric, wigged old lady who refused to leave her rent-controlled apartment though she could no longer walk half a block to the bodega on her own. It had character, but it needed help.

As Martin gave her a tour of the first floor, she learned that he lived with Cynthia, a number of adopted cats and dogs with health issues ranging from one eye to three legs, and, depending on their flow of income, three adult daughters.

"Will they, um, be here tonight?" Georgina asked.

"We got them tickets to *Kinky Boots*," Martin said. "Little joke there."

She smiled. "Yes. I get it. Good one!"

Every detail in the house looked original, from the oak banister to the claw-foot tubs to the wood-burning stove in the kitchen. She hadn't even spotted a refrigerator. The crepe curtains hanging over the sitting room window were so threadbare she could see the taxis rolling down Perry Street.

When the tour ended, she spotted Whitaker chatting with Quincy near a stand-up piano straight out of Vaudeville and pulled him aside. "Are the bedrooms as dirty as the living room?" she whispered.

"Depends on your definition of dirty," he whispered back.

She held up a velvet pillow, caked with dust and cat hair. "I mean, do the bedrooms look like this?"

"Martin's house is a stop on every antique tour in the city."

"I don't care if it's from the 1800s, I want to know if it's been cleaned since the 1800s."

Whitaker grabbed her hand and pulled. "Let's get you a drink."

In the parlor room, a carved wooden bar offered bottle after bottle of aged, top-shelf liquor. Georgina picked up a medieval-looking Russian vodka with fuzz growing inside of it. "Martin could open a *very* authentic speakeasy," she said.

Whitaker poured her a glass of red wine from a decanter. "Martin claims he won that in a chess match against a KGB operative. Interesting guy, you should talk to him sometime."

She accepted the glass. "The KGB operative? No, thanks."

Whitaker half suppressed his smile and leaned one elbow on the bar. He wore a gray pullover with dark jeans and the same brown leather lace-up boots. On his jaw, a few gray hairs hid within his stubble. Lines crinkled around his eyes, the ghosts of his chronic amusement. *He's a thirty-five-year-old man*, Georgina thought, and almost laughed out loud. This fact had just occurred to her for the first time. She'd been thinking about him as the same twenty-two-year-old kid who'd used a stack of textbooks as a coffee table, but of course he wasn't. She wasn't either. They barely knew this version of each other. "Do you have kids?" she blurted.

"No," he said. "Do you?"

"No."

They sipped their wine. Georgina made a clicking sound with her mouth. Whitaker said, "Hm," for no apparent reason.

"Anyway," she said, "you were saying?"

"I don't think I was saying anything."

"Right. What's on the syllabus tonight?" she asked. "Safe words? How babies are made?"

"Actually, there is something," he said. "There won't be any keys tonight. You choose your own partner. It's a little weird the first time."

"Oh." Her back straightened. "How do you do it?"

This was a strange question to be asking of her ex-lover. They'd once chosen each other, every day, usually multiple times a day. Now she was asking him for assistance with seducing somebody else.

"Like this." He took her shoulders and gently turned her body so she faced the living room, where the rest of the party drank and talked. "Close your eyes."

She glanced back at him over her shoulder. Their faces were inches apart. "Is this some sort of swingers' game I need to be prepared for?"

"Humor me," he said. He waited for her to obey, then spoke close to her ear. "Pretend you're at a bar, alone or with a friend. It's dark but not so dark you can't see. You're single. You're hot—"

Georgina scoffed.

"Come on, you know you're hot," he said. Her cheeks flamed. "You came here tonight for one reason. You want to take someone home and stay up all night. You with me?"

She squirmed. His hands remained on her shoulders, warm, like his breath on her neck.

"You get a drink and look around for someone attractive. There are a few people who pique your interest. You make eye contact. One lifts his drink, and you walk over. He tells you you have gorgeous eyes and he seems nice, but you're looking for someone less tame tonight."

Georgina was biting her lip so hard it hurt. His closeness felt as real as a physical object between them.

"You go talk to the next guy. He's older than you. He'll know what he's doing. But you want energy. You want somebody—"

"—who will stay up all night," she murmured.

"Exactly. So you talk to the third guy. He's the one you've been looking for. He asks you if you're interested, and you say yes because you deserve what you want. He'll come home with you, and before you close the door, he's got you pressed against the wall."

Georgina opened her eyes and held her body still, but her mind raced. He was the third guy, right? That was an elaborate, sexy—extremely sexy—ruse to get her to pick him?

She turned around. "Who . . . who will you be with tonight?"

"Laila," he said.

Or not.

"It's been a while. It'll be nice to catch up."

Georgina swallowed a gulp of her wine. "You have an interesting way of catching up with old friends. I usually stick to lunch."

He laughed. "I'm very talkative during sex."

"I'm aware," she said, and this nod to their history ratcheted up the tension in the room. She couldn't look at him anymore.

After a few moments of silence in which she pretended to dig a fruit fly out of her wine, Whitaker asked, "By the way, does Nathan know about us?"

"No. He doesn't need to."

"You should tell him," Whitaker said. "Honesty is the best policy. I learned that in kindergarten."

"Adult relationships are a little more complicated than that."

Whitaker leaned toward her with a sneaky smile. His lips against her ear sent goose bumps racing down her neck. "Then how'd you explain the tattoo?"

There it was. It was bound to come up eventually, no matter how resolutely she stared away from it in the shower. She set her shoulders back and picked up her glass. "If you'll excuse me, I need to go find my third guy. And the tattoo is just a tattoo. It's not like it says your name."

While she made the rounds, Georgina kept one eye on Felix and Norah. They were standing in the kitchen with their faces close together, deep in conversation. She'd tried to join them a few times, but they kept excusing themselves for "more ice." As they were both drinking red wine, she found this highly suspicious.

She accosted them beside what appeared to be an authentic butter churn. "Is there something I need to know?"

They glanced quickly at each other before becoming intensely fascinated with the contents of Martin's kitchen. Felix held up a spatula to the light like it might be counterfeit, and Norah squeezed every lemon in the fruit bowl like she was grocery shopping.

"Just hangin'," Norah said.

"Chitchattin'," Felix said.

"You two know there won't be any keys tonight, right?" Georgina asked. "We choose our own partners."

Miraculously, Felix and Norah had an entire conversation without words. Felix cocked his brow, and Norah gave a small shrug. He returned a single nod, and Norah glanced upstairs. They set their drinks on the counter, grabbed hands, and ran out of the kitchen.

"I guess my work is done here!" Georgina said to no one. She toasted herself against Norah's abandoned wineglass.

When she turned around, Ari was watching Norah's ankles disappear onto the second-floor landing. Then he glared at Georgina with eyes like shark teeth. *Take that*, she thought. It turned out she'd had it wrong all her life. Nice boys get porn, and bad boys get missionary with the lights off.

Someone tapped on Georgina's shoulder, and it turned out to be Quincy. Maybe it was the lighting, but his hair looked more brown than blond tonight. He wore a three-piece suit with a pocket watch like an old-timey businessman, and his face was clean shaven.

"Georgina," he said, "would you consider doing me the honor of being my partner tonight?"

It was the most formal invitation for sex she'd ever received. Was she supposed to RSVP by mail?

But she was relieved he asked. It took the pressure off her quest to find the third guy, and though Quincy was a little eccentric, she felt safe with him. "The honor would be all mine," she said, and held out her hand for him to take.

Upstairs, Quincy held open the door to a bedroom with blue carpet, blue velvet wallpaper, and an antique four-poster with blue bedding. It was like being inside a fish tank. Quincy dimmed the lights and sat on a spindly wooden chair in the corner, leaning forward with his elbows on his knees and smiling at her warmly.

"Whatever you're thinking right now," he said, "I guarantee you it's wrong."

"I was thinking you're planning to give me the wildest night of my life," Georgina teased, giving the bed a once-over for bugs before sitting down.

Quincy laughed. "In that case, you are entirely correct."

The mattress turned out to be plush and the bedding lusciously silky. She closed her eyes, suddenly tired. For weeks, months, years, her entire life, she'd been sprinting toward a finish line only she could see. But lately, the road ahead had gotten hazy, and she wondered what she was running toward. Maybe she needed a break. A nap would feel nice, a chance to rest her feet. "Do people ever come to these parties for a foot massage?" she asked.

"I can give you a massage," Quincy said. "I'd love to."

"Are you good?"

"I'm good at the happy endings."

She laughed. "Should have seen that one coming."

Quincy rubbed his palms briskly together. "It's chilly in here. I'll turn the heat up."

He went into the closet and returned with a treasure chest identical to the one Marco found at Quincy's place. "I never go anywhere without my supplies," he said, sitting on the bed beside her. When he opened the lid, she peered inside and saw several tubes of oils and jellies, brightly colored oblong devices, a necktie, fuzzy red handcuffs, what looked like three black hair ties, and a paddle wheel with little tongues on it.

"This reminds me of the time capsule I made in the fifth grade," she said.

"You were a very advanced fifth grader," Quincy said.

"The hair ties were actually hair ties, the fuzzy red handcuffs were bracelets I stole from my cousin, and the tubes were Lip Smackers," she explained.

He withdrew an amber bottle of liquid. "Massage oil?"

She eyed it, chewing her lip. A massage did sound heavenly. "Okay," she said, and reached for the hem of her sweater.

"I'll give you some privacy," he said, and turned around. He was so professional she was beginning to wonder whether he'd expect a tip.

Georgina undressed to her bra and underwear. There was freedom in looking for an experience rather than romance. Suzanne had been right about that. She found herself less self-conscious, more curious. *I'm getting mine, Suzanne!* she thought, and smiled as she climbed onto the mattress. Somewhere, Suzanne was proud.

With her face nestled between two pillows, she heard a squirt of oil and the slick sound of rubbing hands. Quincy started at her feet, pressing his thumbs into her arches and pulling each toe until it cracked. His hands were surprisingly large and capable, his movements deft.

"Have you taken lessons?" Georgina asked. Her voice was muffled by a mouthful of pillow.

"My wife and I dabble in the therapeutic arts," he said. "How are you feeling?"

"Very relaxed, thank you."

His hands worked up the backs of her thighs, skipped her butt, and landed on her lower back, where he fanned his thumbs away from her spine and dug them into her kidneys. The oil was hot and tingly—it must have been spiked. As the minutes passed, she melted deeper into a state of blissful nothingness.

"Can you do this every day?" she groaned, and Quincy chuckled.

He massaged her shoulders, her neck, the base of her skull, then kneaded his way down each arm and finished with her hands, working the tension out of each knuckle carefully. When he asked her if she was awake, she could barely nod.

"Amazing," she managed to say. Her body was supple and warm as she sat up and rolled her neck. "I can't wait to find out what your next party trick is."

"You tell me." Quincy handed her the treasure chest, and she held it in front of her like a baby with no diaper.

He chuckled again. "I'm getting the sense your sex life might be what we in the lifestyle call vanilla."

She peeked inside and spotted two red silk sashes. "You could say my education is fairly elementary." She lifted one from the box and inspected it. "What's this?"

"Do you want me to show you?"

Before her night with Marco, she'd have said hell no without hesitation. She would have been too afraid—not of Quincy but of herself, and how much she might like it, and what that would say about her. What it would say about her marriage. But owning her desires that night had been so exhilarating. She couldn't turn away from them now that she'd had her first hit. The question that remained wasn't whether she had desire, it was what she desired, and who.

"Yes," she said. "I would like that."

"If at any point you're uncomfortable," Quincy said, "tell me and I'll take them off."

"Okay." She lay back on the mattress and waited, watching him. From the box, he withdrew a pink silk mask and handed it to her.

"Put this on," he said.

The mask was soft and cool on her face. She heard rustling as Quincy moved off the bed, and the mattress shifted. She felt his hand on her right wrist, lifting it above her head. His fingers brushed gently against her skin as he wrapped the sash around it. He repeated the ritual on her left wrist. When he was finished, she pulled the sash until it was taut and realized she could only move her arms a few inches. For the first time in her life, she had relinquished control.

For a few seconds, she heard nothing but her own breathing and the sound of her pulse in her ears. Something feathery and light brushed against her cheek. She jumped.

"It's just me."

"I thought it was a mouse."

"I've got a few furry things in the box, but I promise none are alive."

The feathery brush trailed languidly along her jaw, down her neck, across her collarbones, down her breastbone to her belly and the skin between her hip bones. Taking his time, he brushed it between her legs, and they moved slightly apart, her body reacting and wanting more. He swept the feather down each leg through the oil left behind from her massage, and her skin tingled where he'd touched it. Wondering where he would go next and what he might use was thrilling and, frankly, turning her on big-time. She pulled against the restraints, squirming. The mystery itself was intoxicating.

The feather brush left, replaced with the gentle press of something metal and pointy rolling along her kneecap. She gasped. "What is that?"

"It's a pinwheel for sensory awakening," Quincy said. "Picture a pizza cutter, but less dangerous."

Her nerves came alive as he rolled it down her calf. When he swiped it up the bottoms of her feet, her toes curled pleasurably. A small sound escaped her mouth. Quincy's treasure chest demonstration wasn't bad. Not bad at all. It was nice, actually. Quite . . . amazing. She began to feel a warm pulse between her legs. Her muscles grew hot and tense. She ached for the delicate press of fingertips. She couldn't—impossible—from *this*?

Without sight, each sensation was amplified. He moved the pinwheel back up her leg and down the lacy stretch of her underwear, up and down, lighting each nerve on fire. When he moved it away, she nearly yelled at him to put it back. It felt so good. He rolled it up her stomach and over her breasts, following the same path as the feather, but this time pressing harder so the sensation was less teasing, more rewarding. Whenever she squirmed too much, he stopped and waited for her urge to subside, making the pleasure last longer. A new object, this one buzzing, first dragged lightly from hip to hip, then pressed between her legs. A familiar heat built in her toes and rushed along her limbs, this time unstoppable. Her body flamed, then deliciously unburdened.

Chapter 18

The next weekend, Nathan was receiving an award for Corporate Achievement at a fundraiser for an organization called Women We Are, hosted at the Frick Collection. The award was all Georgina's doing. Wasn't there a saying? Behind every man who won a prize was a woman who came up with the idea. Something like that. A few years ago, she'd suggested he join the junior board of a nonprofit and researched the perfect up-and-coming organization. Everybody knew that joining a board was a good way to enter the fundraising circuit in Manhattan and meet high rollers as potential new clients. Also, the firm expected every lawyer to do fifty hours of pro bono every year, and Nathan had done zero for seven years running. It was time he gave back. While it was no secret that Corporate Achievement roughly translated to "Donated Lots of Money," it was something nice to stick on the shelf regardless, and the champagne would be free. With that carrot, Georgina had successfully convinced Felix, Alina, Ari, and Norah to tag along.

Georgina stood in her closet deciding between three different dresses. One was a red strapless silk gown with a slit nearly up to her hip. Too sexy to fight homelessness. One was a formfitting tea-length silk dress with a rose pattern that somehow managed to give her a little cleavage. The third was blue and backless with a straight, high neckline on the front, like the mullet of dresses.

"You'll be gorgeous in any of them," Nathan said from behind.

She turned around and looked him up and down with a theatrical nod of approval. "You look dapper in your tuxedo, and those have got to be the shiniest shoes I've ever seen. I might need sunglasses."

"These have got to be the hottest dresses I've ever seen," he said. "I might need air-conditioning."

For some reason, she and Nathan had lately taken to excessively complimenting each other. It was nice at first, but had become difficult as she'd run out of things to compliment. That morning, she'd moved onto his toenails as a last resort (very clean, no fungus whatsoever). He'd complimented her knees. "They're so straight," he'd said.

She decided on the rose one, and Nathan told her she never failed to make the right decision, though she had a feeling he would have said that about whatever dress she chose.

In the taxi from their apartment to the Frick Collection, Georgina watched the gray town houses and nearly naked winter trees on Fifth Avenue as they drove the sixteen blocks south. It was a short ride. They could have walked, but it was windy and below thirty degrees, though clear and cloudless. One could never see many stars in Manhattan, but tonight, craning her neck to see the sky from the cab, she spotted the brightest few.

"Beautiful night," she said, though it wasn't really.

"Any night with you is beautiful," Nathan said. He reached across the bucket seat and held her hand—cupping it protectively, not interlacing his fingers with hers. She gave him a quick smile in return and searched for the stars again.

When they arrived at the Frick Collection, which looked like a small Luxembourg Palace behind wrought iron gates, a tuxedoed valet helped her from the back seat, and a woman in black waited behind him with a tray of prefilled drinks. Georgina thanked her and took a glass of pink champagne before walking inside to admire the entrance hall's marble floor and carved busts.

"Through there, ma'am," another woman in black said, pointing toward a sign that read *Garden Court*. It may as well have been an elegant haunted house. She entered a long, rectangular room with an arched skylight. A fountain filled with candles cast the black-tie-wearing guests in flickering orange shadows.

Nathan helped her out of her coat. "Be right back," he said, and headed off toward the coat check. Alone, Georgina surveyed the crowd for familiar faces and spotted a few, but no one she was dying to speak to. She looked up to admire the skylights and noticed a small bird frantically beating its wings as it searched for a way out. *Poor little thing*, she thought.

When Nathan returned, they were immediately swarmed by a group of older partners from Keats & Rukoff—Cheats & Ripoff, as everyone more accurately called it. Georgina chatted with them about a recent decision from the court of appeals and new lunch spots in Times Square, but after the fourth man's eyes slid to her breasts, she was grateful when someone grabbed her arm and it turned out to be Suzanne. She'd forgotten Suzanne was a major Women We Are donor.

"Excuse me," she said with a polite smile, and followed Suzanne behind a Roman column.

Mercifully, Suzanne was clothed this time, wearing a matronly beaded black gown and a thick ruby pendant. Still, it was impossible to look at her without picturing her bare breasts bouncing. "Tell me everything," she said.

"There's not much to tell," Georgina said.

"Spare me the coy act!" Suzanne said. "Who was that gorgeous man I saw you with?"

Georgina's face got hot. "Just an old friend I ran into. An awkward coincidence."

Suzanne nodded like she and Georgina were coconspirators. "Got it," she whispered. She drew her fingertips across her lips as if to seal them.

"Seriously, we knew each other in college," Georgina insisted. "It's nothing more than that."

"Just like my neighbor Dick is nothing more than that," Suzanne agreed.

Georgina rolled her eyes and gave up.

"So have you listened to my advice?" Suzanne asked. "Please tell me you're not showing up in a suit and taking notes. You're participating, right?"

Before answering, Georgina glanced around, but the guests close by were minding their own business. "I've had two eye-opening experiences. You were right. About everything. Happy?"

"Ecstatic." Suzanne clinked her glass against Georgina's. "And how's your marriage?"

"What do you mean?"

"I mean, has it spiced up your sex life?" Suzanne asked. "Are you applying your new skills?"

Over Suzanne's shoulder, Nathan was gesticulating to the group of older men. On cue, the men all tipped their heads back in laughter and clapped him on the back. Georgina frowned, watching him continue his animated tale. She and Nathan had barely kissed since Meredith. A peck here and there, but not a kiss. "No," she confessed. "Should I be?"

Suzanne shook her head at the heavens. "Lord help me," she said.

" '*Should I be?*' Have you learned nothing?" She held both of Georgina's shoulders tightly. "Listen. Here's what you've got to do. Take what you saw or did at a party and try it out on him. If there weren't so many people around, I'd tell you about the time Philip and I made abstract body art with edible paint, which basically means I used his dick to paint a picture of a sunset." She paused. "Well, that was pretty much the whole story. I used his dick to paint a picture of a sunset."

"Is it hanging on your wall?"

"Over the bed," Suzanne said. "We tell everyone it's a Gerhard Richter."

Red hair caught Georgina's attention. Meredith had walked in. An email had gone out to the entire firm saying there were extra tickets, and some junior associates RSVP'd yes for the free booze and food. But this was the first firm event Meredith had ever come to—and it was Nathan's. At least Meredith was making an effort to heed Georgina's sage advice about becoming a better firm citizen, but did it have to be this event? Tonight? Now? Looking like that? She wore a mermaid-style emerald dress with her hair swept to the side in voluminous curls like Jessica Rabbit. At the entrance, she shrugged off her fur stole and handed it to the coat check before swiping a glass of champagne off a passing tray and sipping it while she surveyed the scene, appearing at ease and confident standing alone. Within seconds, two men approached her. On the bright side, Nathan wasn't one of them.

"I'm a terrible artist," Georgina murmured to Suzanne, "but I'll try something. I promise. Would you excuse me?"

She swallowed the last of her drink and set it down before marching back to Nathan. "Gentlemen," she said to Cheats & Ripoff. In front of everyone, she wrapped her arms around Nathan's waist and kissed him. It was a hard kiss, their faces pressing into each other without tenderness. "There," she said, and nodded once, having proved her point.

"Bubbly going to your head?" a man asked. It turned out to be Randolph Burton, Nathan's mentor. He was a six-foot-four college football star turned handsome corporate lawyer with veneers and gray streaks in his coiffed hair. Randolph raised his arms and pulled Georgina into a suffocating bear hug.

"You are a force, Georgina," he boomed.

"And you are very strong, Randolph," she said, extracting herself.

"Come," Randolph said, "I want you to meet someone."

He walked over to a small group of people and clapped the closest man on the back. There was so much back clapping at these things. The man was tall with brown hair and a slim-cut tuxedo, and in the same heart-stopping instant he began to turn around, Georgina realized who it was.

It was official. The man could wear a tuxedo.

"Whitaker Nolan, meet Nathan and Georgina Wagman," Randolph said. "Whitaker here is my guest of honor tonight. He's starting an online magazine. It'll be huge, I swear on my firstborn son—and he's the son I like. This could be a good connection for two partners rising in the ranks, eh?"

Georgina held out her hand and hoped nobody noticed the slight tremor. "We've actually—" *Met before*, she was about to say, but Whitaker beat her to it.

"Nice to meet you both," he said. "Randolph raves about you."

For some reason, Nathan looked about as happy extending a hand to Whitaker as he would sticking it in a garbage disposal.

"How do you two know each other?" Georgina asked.

"It's a long story that involves beer," Randolph boomed. "Way back when I still had black hair, I represented a politician who will remain unnamed, who was accused of I-won't-say-what. Whitaker here worked on the campaign."

"Only until I learned about the I-won't-say-what," Whitaker clarified.

"Before everything went to shit, Whitaker used to graciously get us drunk on his excellent beer." Randolph clapped him on the back again, and Whitaker winced. Georgina had the impression their friendship might have been one-sided.

"You make beer?" Nathan asked in the same tone someone else might have said, "You're a flat-earther?"

"It's just a hobby," Whitaker said, and shrugged.

"He's being modest," Randolph said. "Best ale I ever had."

"My brother's got a farm in Vermont, and we started brewing in his barn a while back," Whitaker said. "He does the hard work, but I *did* come up with the name."

Nathan coughed. "Sounds lucrative."

Whitaker dug his hands in his pockets and smiled at Georgina. "Nah. But we do have fun."

"What's the name?" she asked.

"Hopless Romantic."

"Cute," Nathan said dryly as Georgina sank into a vision of Whitaker riding shirtless on horseback, the Hopless Romantic indeed.

"Tell me about the magazine," she said, a little too breathlessly.

"It's just an idea," Whitaker said. "It'll be like Vox for people Randolph's age."

"Ha!" Randolph boomed. "Old as fuck, is what he means. Anyhoo, I'll leave you to it." Then he was gone, leaving the three of them to stare at each other.

"We should talk for a minute," Nathan said, "to keep up appearances."

"It's fine if we chat," Whitaker said. "Randolph introduced us."

Georgina tugged on Nathan's sleeve and whispered, "Are you okay?"

He returned a terse nod. "Perfectly fine."

"You seem—"

"I'm fine," he snapped.

Georgina forced a smile and turned to Whitaker. Her voice came out several notches too loud. "So what topics will your magazine focus on?"

"Politics, economics, and culture. Their influence on one another."

"Magazines are dying," Nathan said. "There's no money there."

"It's not about the money," Whitaker said. "I just think there's a demographic that doesn't have access to content that might expand their worldview. Anyway, it's just an idea."

"Fascinating," Georgina said. She fixed him with the contemplative gaze of Barbara Walters. "Tell me, will it have a blog feature?"

Whitaker suppressed his smile, but he couldn't hide it from his eyes. "The concept of a blog is very early 2000s."

"But they never go out of style," she said, and the effort of trying not to laugh nearly brought tears to her eyes. "You could call it *A Principled Utopia*. That has a nice ring to it."

Nathan glanced at her like he might need to check her forehead for a deliriously high fever. "The man can decide the name of his own blog."

"Oh yes," she agreed. "He certainly can."

Meanwhile, Whitaker shook his head, wearing an amused expression. *A Principled Utopia* was the name of his infamous Peruvian blog, which of course she'd tracked down. And while Whitaker was no doubt the destitute philosopher he'd warned about, the blog unlocked a piece of him she hadn't understood or at least hadn't appreciated. She'd thought she was the only one with ambitions and plans, but he'd had them all along. They just weren't as superficial as hers.

The lights dimmed to signal the start of the program. "Excuse us," Nathan said, and pulled Georgina away by the hand. She looked back only once.

———

After Nathan gave his speech, he and Georgina found their assigned table, where Felix, Norah, Ari, and Alina were waiting.

"Nathan," Ari said, "you looked like a boss up there."

"Thanks, man," Nathan said. "You didn't think my speech was too long?"

"Nah," Ari said, meanwhile Norah met Georgina's eyes and nodded vigorously.

"Norah, you look stunning," Georgina said. "And, Alina, you look like a celebrity."

Norah wore a chic black sheath with her hair in an elegant twist and small gold hoops. Alina wore a violet knee-length dress as snug as a second skin with her hair folded into a bun at her crown and balanced out with a pair of heavy earrings. The only makeup she wore was a swipe of dark wine lipstick.

"What about me, Georgina?" Ari asked.

Ari's chiseled features and olive skin glowing against his white tuxedo shirt could have caused a car accident, but Georgina couldn't give him the satisfaction. "You combed your hair," she said. "I appreciate it. And, Felix, I'm loving the elbow patches."

He grinned. "This jacket was my grandpa's."

"The junior associates tell me the grandpa look is in." Georgina raised her glass of champagne. "Let's have a toast. To my best friends, who always support one another. Thanks for coming to Nathan's night."

"Hear, hear!" Felix said, and the six of them clinked as three caterers dressed like stagehands dropped off their salad plates.

Ari offered Norah the bread basket. "What do you want, babe?"

Norah raised her eyebrows and smiled at Georgina as she answered, "I'll have the focaccia, please."

"More water?" Ari asked as he set the bread on her plate.

"Thanks, honey," Norah said, and Georgina watched in awe as Ari refilled Norah's glass and kissed her bare shoulder. It was like watching a gorilla use sign language for the first time. She laughed out loud, shocked and gratified that the lifestyle had worked such wonders on Ari's behavior already. She must speak to Suzanne about writing a book. They'd put marriage counselors out of business.

Ari wasn't the only one paying Norah extra attention. As everyone chatted through dinner, Felix leaned over often to whisper in Norah's ear. Once, he jotted a note on a cocktail napkin and slid it toward her. Georgina had craned her neck to see if it was a hotel room number, but Norah had quickly stashed it in her purse. She was like the popular girl in the lunch cafeteria with two men vying for her attention, the jock and the valedictorian.

When the main course was delivered, Felix picked up a knife and fork and started to cut his silver dollar of beef tenderloin, commenting on how delicious it looked.

"Those are mine," Ari said in a voice like melted steel.

Felix looked at the fork in his hand. "Oh, sorry, man. Here, take mine." He nudged the unused cutlery toward Ari.

"But you already touched those," Ari said. "That's disgusting, *man.*"

Georgina and Norah exchanged a silent message of alarm.

"What am I supposed to do now?" Ari asked.

Felix set down the knife and fork and calmly said, "I'll get you some new ones. Don't worry about it."

Ari threw his napkin down. "You're trying to take what doesn't belong to you," he said. "That's all I'm saying."

"Did I miss something?" Felix asked, looking around.

Ari slammed one fist on the table, making the ceramic plates rattle. "You know exactly what I'm talking about. It's not cool."

A server stopped by with a fresh bread basket, and Felix asked her for another setup. He tossed it across the table to Ari. "Happy?"

Everyone ate quietly for several minutes. Georgina cut her chicken into the smallest possible bites, stealing glances up at Norah and Felix, who'd stopped whispering to each other and stared at their plates like kids who'd gotten in trouble at the dinner table.

She leaned into Nathan's ear. "Do you know what's going on here?"

One corner of his mouth turned up in a wicked smirk. "Norah told him she and Felix used some sort of futuristic sex toy at the party," he whispered. "I'd never heard of it, but apparently, you have to plug it in."

"Good for them," Georgina whispered, and Nathan gave her a surprised look she didn't have time to interpret before Norah blurted, "I've decided to go back to school!"

Felix held up his hand in a high five that Norah proudly gave.

"Wait," Georgina said. "Did you know about this, Felix?"

He nodded, smiling at Norah.

"Pillow talk," Nathan joked, and Ari's face turned beet red. His hand nearly vibrated as he gripped the fork Felix had gotten him.

"I'm so happy I'll try not to be offended you told Felix first," Georgina said. "You deserve this. This is your time."

"I've been telling her the legal profession is going downhill," Ari interrupted loudly. "No jobs, too many lawyers. And they all hate their lives anyway. Haven't you seen the statistics? Everybody's drunk and high, if they don't kill themselves first."

The mood at the table became instantly heavy, as if someone had draped it with a lead blanket.

Georgina stared at him in astonishment. "How can you say that?" she asked in a hush. "This is what Norah wants. Doesn't that matter to you?"

He shrugged. "It's true. I'm not making that up. I've read it on Above the Law. And other places."

Norah put her hand on his shoulder. "I'm sure he's right. Anyway, I probably won't get in, so let's talk about something else."

"No." Georgina tried to reach Norah's other hand across the table, but it was too far. "You'll get in. I can hook you up with the right people. And when you're done, you can come work at our firm. Consider this my official offer."

"Why don't you give me a job, Georgina?" Ari asked. "I'd make twice as much money as I do now. Best friends support each other, right?"

"We don't hire people who had Cs in law school," Georgina snapped. "If you recall, Norah had straight As until you happened."

"Until *I* happened?" Ari scoffed. "I'm not the one who got pregnant."

A small pop of air escaped Norah's mouth.

"Ari," warned Felix.

"Shut up, *man*. You have no right to talk to me after what you've been doing to my wife."

Felix threw down his cutlery and stood up, his chair legs scraping against the marble floor. He never got angry, *ever*, even when someone cut him off on the subway platform. But his fists were clenched now, and his voice restrained, as if trying hard to keep from yelling. "You have a gorgeous wife and three healthy kids, yet you act like your life is shit. What's wrong with you?"

A small soap opera played out then. Norah watched Felix as he wove through the crowded tables toward the bathroom. Mascara-stained tears streamed down her cheeks. Ari noticed, and lifted her hand off his shoulder. "I can't believe this is happening," he murmured. Then he stood, buttoned his jacket, and strode toward the exit, nearly colliding with a server carrying a tray of dirty plates.

Norah used her cloth napkin to wipe her face. "Excuse me," she said, and ran after him.

"Don't worry," Nathan said. "They're a family."

"I don't think the fact that they have kids is going to save them, do you?" Georgina snapped.

Nathan looked down at the table and nodded. "Right. Stupid me for suggesting it, huh?"

"Wait—" Georgina reached for his arm, but he was already getting up. "That's not what I—" But he didn't stay to hear the rest of the sentence.

"Meant," she finished, and let her forehead fall into her palm.

On her left shoulder, she felt a brush of fabric and turned to see that Whitaker had been sitting behind her at the adjacent table the whole time.

"Pardon me," he said.

Under the cover of their pedestrian interaction, they looked at each other, and the room stilled. Some amount of time passed, but she couldn't say how long. Eventually, as if someone had turned up the volume, the soundtrack of a hundred people having dinner returned, and she forced her eyes away with the difficulty of hauling a tree right out of the ground.

Only she and Alina remained at the table.

"That was awkward," Georgina said.

"They're not on the same page," Alina agreed. "I get the sense Ari doesn't want to be participating in the lifestyle."

"I'd have thought he needed little convincing."

"It's not a safe assumption that all men are only interested in sex," Alina said. "It can be dangerous. Ari may feel that if he confesses his disinterest, it will make him less of a man."

Georgina pushed the last bit of mashed potato around her plate. She wasn't usually in the business of catering to Ari's feelings, but

Alina had a point. Ari had seemed so miserable at the last party, his face like a puppy locked out in the rain. "Ari acts like his feelings are more important than Norah's, and they're not. Just because he's struggling isn't an excuse to be a dick."

"I agree," Alina said, "but if he doesn't want to do this, it will make their relationship worse, not better. What happened tonight is just the beginning."

She couldn't tell Alina that Norah and Ari splitting up would only pave the way for Norah and Felix's romance, so she nodded. "Alina, I might start paying you to be my therapist."

"We're friends," Alina said. "We can talk for free all you want. But I should go check on Felix. You know how sensitive he is."

As she walked away, Georgina slumped onto her elbows, folding under the pressure of what she had created, hoping it wasn't a gargantuan mess. She'd only wanted to fix her broken marriage, and help Norah and Felix get back the happiness they deserved. They were meant to be together. But it was becoming harder to pretend that Ari and Alina wouldn't be affected by her scheming. Once she started talking to Alina, really talking, she discovered Alina's thoughtfulness, and apparently, Ari wasn't just a heartless frat boy but a man who loved his wife and didn't want to lose her.

Then there was the matter of Nathan, who wanted to fix their marriage the more traditional way—with a baby. That was romantic, right? Weren't her ovaries supposed to be aching by now? What was wrong with them?

Georgina was morosely tearing a piece of olive loaf to bits when she felt warmth near her ear. Whitaker whispered, "Meet me in the library."

When she looked up, his back was retreating toward a door off the main hall. There was no one left at the table to lie to about where she was going or who she was going there with. Casually, she stood up, smoothed her skirt, and pushed in her chair, then gave up the act and hurried after him. A car length behind, she followed him through the door and found him waiting by a portrait of George Washington with his perennial hands-in-pockets.

"You rang?" she asked, and tried to smile, but she was so nervous it felt strained.

"It's official mentor business," he said. "I heard what happened at your table, and I don't think your friends are ready for this."

"Tensions are running high," she agreed. "It's complicated."

Whitaker contemplated her face for a while. She squirmed under his gaze.

"I don't mean to pry," he said. "But what's going on with Norah and Felix?"

"They've been getting adventurous, apparently," she said. "Ari's jealous."

"Normally, I'd say good for them. But as your official mentor, I'm saying they've been together twice already, so it's time to change partners."

She sat on the velvet bench facing the portrait. George leered down his nose at her. *You don't approve of the lifestyle, huh, George?*

"This rule of yours doesn't make sense," she said. "They're comfortable with each other. Isn't the lifestyle about finding partners you trust to have new experiences?"

Whitaker sat beside her, not so close that their knees were touching but close enough that she could feel the pull of his body. It was dangerous to be that close to him, alone with him, and she wondered whether this was how Nathan felt around Meredith, like at any moment he might forget who he was and do something stupid, but at the same time justify it. How could desire feel that right but be so wrong?

"My ex-wife, Mei, fell in love with someone in the group," Whitaker said eventually, and Georgina's body stilled. "Oliver. They're not together anymore, but it all started as a preference for each other at the parties."

"Oh." She examined his profile, but it was hard to see his expression from that angle. She didn't expect him to look thrilled about that development, but she wanted to know the degree of his sadness. Specifically, how heartbroken was he on a scale of one to ten? "I'm sorry," she said.

"I started noticing the way they acted at parties. I tried not to, you're supposed to give your partner space, but it was impossible to miss. We all flirt, that's the point, but this was different. They'd disappear together for the entire party. It was like they were waiting for Saturday night just so they could be together."

"I'm sorry," she said again, and started to reach for his hand, then thought better of it. It dawned on her that she and Whitaker were almost guilty of the same, which may have explained Nathan's icy attitude earlier.

"I'd rather not be married to someone who prefers someone else. Call me old-fashioned."

"You're hardly old-fashioned." Her face grew warm as she remembered the un-puritan acts he used to do to her body. "The church elders would have kicked the Whitaker I knew right out the front door."

He laughed, but said nothing.

"I appreciate that you're trying to protect my friends," she said.

"I don't want anybody to get hurt."

She put her hand on the crook of his arm. His muscles tensed under her fingers. Back then, she had been enamored with the feel of his body, and she remembered it now with a satisfying sorrow. "That person is usually you, isn't it?"

Whitaker stood up. "Come with me."

"Where are we going?" she asked. "Not another sex club?"

"Slightly more illegal than that." He took her hand and led her through a second door and up a flight of emergency exit stairs, then another and another. Soon they reached a final door that read *Roof*. He glanced back at her and grinned.

She gaped at him. "We can't."

"Says who?"

"Says that sign right there! And that alarm thingy right there."

"The alarm's not on. I saw an emergency exit propped open for the caterers."

He put his free hand on the lever.

"Wait!" she said, but she had no idea what she was waiting for.

"If the alarm goes off, we'll run. Ready?"

She covered her face with her hands and squeezed her eyes shut. Her heart thumped against her chest as the lever squeaked and pressed. Freezing air whooshed in, and she held her breath, waiting for the alarm that never came.

When she opened her eyes, Whitaker held the door open, cartoonishly pleased with himself.

"This is exactly how I ended up with a tattoo," she groaned, and traipsed outside.

It was the beginning of May her fourth year. They'd woken up to a blanket of snow from a freak spring storm. "I was going to run errands," she'd whined.

Whitaker had smiled, kissed the top of her head, and said, "I bet I can come up with twenty-five things for us to do today that are more fun than errands."

Georgina had looked at him hard. "There is nothing more fun than errands."

After they had baked carrot cake from a box, played tic-tac-snow, walked their friend's dog, gone to the used bookstore, and had sex

in the shower—she'd soon realized twelve of his twenty-five activities were sex in different locations—they'd gone to the botanical gar-
dens and wandered through the humid tropical room until they were
sweating under their coats. A hummingbird feeder hung from the
branch of a gigantic tree with leaves like green sails, and two hummingbirds darted up and down and left and right, angling for the best
entry.

"Did you know hummingbirds' hearts beat twelve hundred times
a minute?" he'd asked. Whitaker was full of strange trivia and always
beat her when *Jeopardy!* was on. He'd never been flunking out of
school, as it turned out. That was a ruse she'd uncovered when she'd
spotted an A+ scribbled on the same midterm paper on which she'd
earned a B.

When he'd said activity number seventeen was to get a tattoo,
she'd thought he was joking, but he had a way of melting her inhibi-
tions. The needle was soon in her hip, tracing a permanent reminder
of the way her heart behaved when she looked at him.

The same skylights she'd admired from the inside formed a pyra-
mid on the roof. Each panel had a handle to open it, and Whitaker
grabbed the nearest one and pulled.

"You can't do that!" she cried out. "It's dangerous."

"There's a bird trapped in there," he said. "I'm letting it out."

She nearly laughed as she remembered the bird inside. Only
Whitaker would sneak up to the roof to free it. This was one of the
reasons she needed him.

To learn how to be free.

He pulled, but the panel was stuck. She watched him struggle for
a few seconds.

"Oh, what the hell," she said, and went to help. Together, they
yanked the window open and rested it on its hinges. Within a
minute, the bird soared through the opening and disappeared in

the black expanse of Central Park at night. Georgina clapped and cheered, freezing but not caring. This was what it felt like to be with him.

So why had she said no? Why not go to Peru? She'd had reasons, but she'd temporarily forgotten what they were.

"Birds have a special place in my heart," he said.

Without thinking about what she was doing, or that she would freeze, or that she was married, or even that she might have forgotten to shave her legs that day, Georgina pulled up the hem of her dress to show Whitaker the black-and-pink hummingbird on her hip, right where she'd left it. The frigid wind burned her bare skin.

"It's gotten a little blurry over the years," she said.

Whitaker looked at it with a pained expression. "It's perfect."

He lifted his hand and gently brushed his thumb across the tattoo. She closed her eyes, feeling the warmth of his skin, imagining they were in bed and he was about to kiss the bird like he had every morning. "Hello," he'd say, "fancy meeting you here."

She opened her eyes and reached for his tie. His hands cradled her face. She felt a wave of helplessness and surrendered to it. He swept his thumb across her cheek and kissed her, first softly, then with a fast-growing hunger that made her sink into his chest with dizziness. His mouth sent electricity through her nerves, stirring intoxicating sensations she hadn't felt since she'd kissed him for the last time the night she said she wouldn't go to Peru.

But then reality bombarded her, and when they broke apart, she took three steps backward fast.

"Georgina!" he yelled, and lunged forward to grab her waist. She looked down. Her foot was an inch from the open skylight.

For a moment, he held her, both of them frozen in shock. Then she smiled weakly and said, "Told you it was dangerous."

He shook his head. "Nothing like a near-death experience to make you see what's important in life."

"And what's that?"

His arms pulled her closer. "Making out. Definitely making out."

"And here I thought it was being a good person."

"No." He brushed his lips against hers. "That's for suckers."

Chapter 19

Georgina and Nathan owned a small weekend house in the Berkshires that offered relief from the city's concrete and noise. It was a classic shingle-style cottage with white trim and a red front door that looked straight out of a Victorian Christmas card in the wintertime. In the summer, the green was so vivid it was as if someone had dialed up the color on photo-editing software, and in the fall, the red and gold leaves seemed to light the world on fire.

After the fundraiser, Georgina needed to get the hell out of Dodge. She couldn't stop thinking about Whitaker or the kiss. If her husband hadn't been waiting downstairs, she'd never have been able to stop. But how could she have been so cruel? She'd been on the other side of cheating. She knew how much it hurt. Nathan's affair was foolish and thoughtless, but hers was malicious. There was no excuse. Nathan wanted a baby and she wanted to, what, run off to Thailand with a sexy ex-boyfriend? A very sexy one? A ridiculously unfairly sexy one? No. An escape to the Berkshires for the weekend would give her the distance she needed from Whitaker to think straight and quality time with Nathan to remind her what she was fighting for.

She called Norah as soon as she woke up on Monday morning. "We're getting our wisdom teeth out."

"Thank God," Norah said. "I was about to sign my kids up for military school. Do they take toddlers?"

"We're getting our wisdom teeth out" was code for "Let's skip town." When Rachel was two and Norah twenty-five, a dentist told Norah she urgently needed to have all four of her wisdom teeth taken out. Rachel was plagued with ear infections and acid reflux, and Ari hadn't yet found a job after graduation. They had no health insurance and lived with Ari's parents on Long Island. The timing could not have been worse.

Norah, it turned out, had been told by a number of dentists over the years that her wisdom teeth were ripe for removal, but she'd always found a new dentist and another excuse to avoid it. It was spring break. It was senior prom. She had to study for finals. She was busy with her LSAT course. It was 1L. She was pregnant.

Norah's ninth dentist had said the teeth could not remain in her head for one more day, lest it explode.

"He actually said your head was going to explode?" Georgina had asked. "You need a second opinion. This guy sounds like a hack."

"He basically did!" Norah said. "They have to break my jaw."

"You shouldn't have waited so long."

"Not helping!"

She'd been terrified, so Georgina had suggested they spend the weekend at a cheap motel in Atlantic City so Norah and her teeth could enjoy one last Jersey Shore goodbye tour on the condition that Georgina personally drive Norah to the dentist on Monday morning. "You'll get plenty of Vicodin," Georgina had said. "It'll be fun."

Ever since, "We're getting our wisdom teeth out" meant something in their lives felt too scary to face head-on, and the only solution was to drink Long Island iced teas out of plastic hurricanes.

"So you're in?" Georgina asked.

"Is it just the two of us?" Norah asked.

"I was thinking everyone," Georgina said. "It could be nice after . . . what happened." She was referring to the fundraiser, which Norah seemed to understand because she didn't press the issue. No one had spoken about the explosion at the table, but in truth, no one had spoken at all.

"I don't know. Ari says he never wants to see Felix's face again." After a brief pause, she said brightly, "On second thought, let's do it. I'll ask Ari's parents to take the kids. They owe me for babysitting their incontinent dog."

On Friday afternoon at three, Norah and Ari's Honda SUV idled behind Felix's 1997 Subaru on 101st Street, the doors and hatches flung open as everyone loaded their bags. When Ari had pulled up the car, Norah hopped out of the passenger seat and announced Hannah was coming. "No comments," she'd said. "Ari's parents are not comfortable with her allergies, and frankly, I don't trust them." So it wouldn't be the luxuriously relaxing weekend Georgina had imagined, but maybe it was for the best that she get used to having a baby around. She'd smiled and said, "The more the merrier."

Now she heaved a cooler of water bottles, cheese, and potato chips into Felix's back seat and slammed the door. "If we don't leave in the next two minutes, it will take us five hours to get there."

"Who's riding with me?" Felix asked.

"We'll ride with you, bud," Nathan said.

Georgina glanced at Felix's packed car. If Alina sat in Felix's front seat and she and Nathan sat in the back with the cooler, there would be no room for Norah, and she was determined that this weekend would be an opportunity for them to spend more time together. After the fight, she wanted Norah to see how supportive Felix was in contrast to Ari's attempt to undermine her professional goals. Georgina grabbed Nathan's hand and pulled. "Let's ride with Ari. I'm in the mood for some . . . Red Hot Chili Peppers!"

Even Ari looked as though Georgina had him confused with someone else. "Um, sure," he said. "But with Hannah's car seat, we only have room for three."

"Norah, why don't you ride with Felix?" Georgina suggested. "Weren't you saying you were thinking about buying a Subaru?"

Norah paused with one leg in the passenger side of her Honda. "No?"

"It's settled!" Georgina shut herself into the Honda and rolled down the window. "Felix!" she called. "Try not to drive like my grandmother. I'd like to get there before we turn forty."

"Are you going to be okay with Hannah?" Norah asked Ari.

"I'll take care of her," Georgina said. "Don't worry."

Norah shrugged and offered Nathan her seat. "I hate the Red Hot Chili Peppers anyway. I bet Alina has cool music."

Felix grinned. "Actually . . . Alina listens to EDM. It's her only flaw."

As Norah walked to the Subaru, she glared at Georgina. "If my ears start bleeding, it's on you."

Hannah fell asleep as the car wove north on the highway, so they rode in silence for the entire three hours to avoid waking her. Every once in a while, though, Ari would murmur under his breath, "Felix? Really?" Georgina watched him in the rearview, his expression furrowed in such concentration he looked as though he were analyzing the complexities of the multiverse. Occasionally, he would catch Georgina spying, and she'd steer her eyes quickly away.

The trees thickened as they continued north on the Hutchinson River Parkway to the CT-15. By five, the sun had set, leaving behind a purple sky above the ridged black horizon of forest. When theirs was the only car in sight, Ari turned on the brights, lighting up the solitude.

At one point, Nathan displayed his phone to show Georgina a white blob with tentacles hovering over the entire northeast. "Big storm coming," he said. "I hope we don't get trapped."

When they arrived, snow fell in a gentle swirl, and the house looked idyllic surrounded by the dusting of flakes on pine trees.

"Why don't you go warm up the house?" Nathan suggested. "I'll get the bags."

Georgina walked as quickly as she dared across the icy path to the front door. Inside, the air was stale, dry, and freezing. She cracked a few windows and lit a fire. Ari walked in holding a zonked-out Hannah, and Nathan followed with duffel bags slung over his shoulder and arms full of groceries.

While cooking a stir-fry in the kitchen, a pair of headlights swung into the driveway. Norah bounded inside a minute later. "We bought out the wine store!" she announced. Her usually bright white teeth were tinged a shade of purple. But spotting Hannah snoozing in her car seat on the floor, her smile fell. "Oh my God. Did she sleep the whole time?"

Ari nodded proudly. "Like a baby."

Norah whimpered. "No, no, *no*. Now she's not going to sleep tonight. We're totally screwed." She shot the wine one last longing look before lifting Hannah and gently waking her up with a sweet song.

Felix had followed carrying two reusable canvas bags. "She's not exaggerating about the wine store. Their inventory was a little low, but still." He removed bottle after bottle and arranged them in a triangle like bowling pins. "Guess we're having fun this weekend."

After everyone settled into their bedrooms, Alina, wearing cutoff shorts while the others were snug in sweats, insisted they start the weekend with a round of shots. Everyone protested, but she wouldn't let it go. Nathan eventually managed to dig up three shot glasses and three espresso mugs, rinsed off the dust, and arranged them in a circle around a bottle of whiskey. Once Alina had poured them—to the brim—they stood shoulder to shoulder and waited for someone to give a toast.

Georgina echoed Quincy from their first party. "To freedom, to friends, to the freedom to have sex with your friends!"

"How about . . . to weekend getaways," Norah said.

"How about . . . I'm so grateful for you guys," Felix said, and Ari rolled his eyes.

"To new experiences," Alina said.

"To dinner," Nathan said. "I'm starving." On cue, the timer of Georgina's stir-fry beeped, and everyone threw back their shots in one choreographed swoop. She was pleased that but for Ari's inability to mask his disdain for Felix, everyone seemed loose and happy. It was the weekend, they were together, and though a storm raged outside, the boiler was doing its job. When Nathan wrapped his arm around Georgina's shoulders, she let her head fall onto his chest and felt briefly content.

By the end of a leisurely dinner around the dining room table, they'd finished three bottles of wine, and everyone was drunk. Norah disappeared upstairs for a while in a futile attempt to put Hannah to bed and returned half an hour later with a wide-eyed toddler.

"I'll play with her," Felix said, and took her into his arms. Soon, he was covering his head with a blanket from the couch before whipping it off and saying, "Boo!" while Hannah rolled on the floor in a giggle fit. Norah observed, her expression both exhausted and adoring. That was what parents should look like. Meanwhile, Ari lounged on an armchair, staring at his phone, and Georgina was infuriated all over again. At him, for being so disengaged, and at herself, for her weakness at the fundraiser when she'd briefly entertained his feelings. He didn't deserve Norah. He didn't deserve Felix as a friend. He didn't even deserve the meal she'd cooked for him, which, now that she thought about it, he did not thank her for!

Snow was accumulating on the windowsills like a scene from a Hallmark movie. "It's beautiful," Norah said. "I want to live here forever."

They assembled around the coffee table on Nathan's suggestion that they play a game.

"Not cards," Norah said. "Cards are boring."

"Spin the bottle?" Georgina teased.

Ari snorted. "What is it with you trying to get us to hook up with each other?"

Georgina shot him a glare. "You caught me, Ari. This whole thing has been an elaborate ruse to get you into bed. Shall we go upstairs, then?"

"How about truth or dare?" Felix asked. When everyone stared at him, he said, "What?"

"Are you a fourteen-year-old girl?" Ari asked.

"I think it sounds fun," Norah announced. "Felix, truth or dare?"

He grinned. Hannah hung on his back like a baby monkey. "Dare. And make it a good one."

She chewed her lip, thinking about it, never taking her eyes off his. "I dare you to switch clothes with me," she said.

Felix passed Hannah to Ari, but not without kissing her puffy cheek goodbye and promising to play again shortly. He and Norah disappeared into the hall bathroom and a few minutes later emerged, laughing, looking like they'd dressed up as each other for Halloween. Felix wore Norah's tie-dyed zip-up hoodie and purple leggings, which now bulged in the crotch, and Norah swam in his Public Radio Nerd

T-shirt, wearing his glasses that must have made her blind. Everyone but Ari started cheering.

"These are comfortable," Felix said. "I think I'll keep them."

Norah had to Frankenstein her way back to the table. "I've got to take these off, sorry. They're making my eyeballs cramp." She handed back his glasses and reclaimed Hannah.

"Who's next?" Felix asked.

With no humor in his voice, Ari said, "Me. I'll go."

"Okay. Truth or dare?"

"Truth."

"Wimp," Norah teased, and Ari flinched.

Felix thought for a few seconds while sipping his wine. "Hm. Okay. Well . . . what is your deepest, darkest secret?" he asked, then shook his head at the ceiling like he could not believe he'd just said that. Georgina patted his foot to let him know she'd heard worse.

Ari fidgeted with a throw pillow as he said, "I've never told anyone this before, but I guess now's as good a time as any."

The air in the room seemed to stop circulating. Nathan looked at Georgina, and his expression was apologetic, as if this were his confessional. Under the coffee table, Norah squeezed Georgina's fingers so hard it hurt.

Ari took a deep breath. "After Norah—I mean *we*—got pregnant, I proposed."

"I think we know that, man," Nathan said.

In the awestruck hush of a guest at the royal wedding, Norah whispered, "I don't think he's finished."

Ari scratched at the coffee table with his fingernail. He wasn't looking at anyone. "My parents didn't want us to get married. Like, really, really did not. They told me to transfer to a different school without . . . without saying goodbye. They even filled out my applications to a bunch of California schools. They figured you'd have an abortion if I did that."

Norah stared at him in astonishment. She opened her mouth, but no words came out.

"I told them to fuck off," Ari said. "I didn't use those exact words, but that was the gist. They cut me off. Said I had to pay them back for college, law school, rent. I'm still paying them five hundred dollars a month. Probably will until the day they die."

"But I thought they loved our kids," Norah said. "They're taking Rachel and Simon ice-skating tomorrow. Who goes ice-skating against their will?"

"My parents know how to hold a grudge. The ironic part is I didn't want to go to law school. My dad made me, and now I fucking hate it, and I'm paying for it when I could be using that money for my kids." He shook his head and looked up at Norah. "If I could give you my degree, I would. In a heartbeat. It should have been you."

Norah and Ari held each other's gaze for a long time, her face wet with tears, his pained. Everyone needed to leave them alone, but as Georgina rose from her spot on the floor, Ari spoke. "Norah," he said, "truth or dare?"

"No, Ari," she whispered, and her voice broke.

"Please," he said. "I'll make it easy for you. Pick dare."

Norah shook her head, desperate not to play.

"Please," Ari said again, and his face had never looked so pleading and anxious before.

"Okay," Norah whispered. Tears slid down her cheeks. "Okay. Dare."

"I dare you to ask me whether I ever wanted to share you with anyone," he said.

Norah coughed out a single sob. "Ari."

"Please," he begged. "I need you to know."

She took a deep breath and asked with her eyes closed, "Did you ever want to share me with anyone?"

"No," Ari said. "I never wanted to do this. I only thought you did, and I was trying to save face because I'm a prick. It's been excruciating. I know I don't deserve you, but I also don't want anyone to have you but me."

Hugging a finally dozing Hannah, Norah sat beside Ari and held his hand. He sank his face into her neck and embraced them, his wife and his child. That was Georgina's cue. She looked up at Nathan and nodded, and one by one, everyone left the room.

Georgina cleaned up after the others went to bed. Watching snowflakes drift past the window over the sink, she washed the wineglasses and scrubbed the pans, replaying the scene from the living room over and over again, thinking about how genuine their love looked and wondering whether she'd underestimated Ari, wondering whether she could accept his words, or whether she had some duty to continue hating him on behalf of her friend.

As she rearranged the pillows on the couch and folded the throw blankets, Ari's laptop stared at her from the coffee table. He'd been using it to check the score of some European soccer match, and it was open, waiting. She stared back at it, chewing her lip. If she checked it, she could discover he had a gambling addiction or an Internet girlfriend. It would prove her right. Or she could find nothing and trust his confession. Wasn't either outcome important?

She glanced upstairs to make sure no one was coming before grabbing the laptop and sitting on the couch. The machine was hot on her thighs. Her pulse raced as she opened the browser. She'd never spied before, and it wasn't thrilling, it was terrifying. But Norah was her best friend, and Georgina needed to protect her if Norah wasn't going to protect herself.

She clicked on the history tab to view Ari's recently visited websites. There were dozens. The bank, *The New York Times*, American Express, Reddit, Barstool Sports, and ESPN over and over and over again. Then she saw what she'd been looking for—or was it what she hadn't wanted to see? That depended on the version of Ari she wanted to be the real version.

It was a series of Google searches run two days ago. Georgina searched her mental calendar and thought she recalled Norah mentioning Ari having the kids alone that night so she could visit her aunt and uncle in South Jersey.

Games to play at home with your kids
Kid favorite meals
Brother sister fight resolve strategies
Communicate with preteen daughter

and

How to be a great dad

She closed the laptop and set it carefully on the coffee table, as though it were a bomb that might detonate. That was not what she'd expected to find—it was not what she'd wanted to find. The truth was she'd hoped Ari was the selfish, emotionally stunted man she'd pegged him for so she could be right, so she could reunite Norah and Felix without a second thought. But Ari was trying to love Norah in the best way he knew how, and the hatred Georgina had so long felt for him turned inward, directly at herself.

The bedroom she and Nathan shared upstairs was cozy, with thick red blankets and patterned wallpaper. In the daytime, the window above an old writing desk overlooked a sloping hill leading down to a small frozen pond. But now all Georgina could see were heavy white flakes piled against the pane. Around eleven o'clock, the snow had intensified. The forecast said the storm would continue through the night and into the next day, trapping them inside.

She rolled over to look at Nathan reading a book in the lamplight. He wore plaid pajama bottoms and glasses, and his lips moved as he read the words noiselessly. Georgina slid out of bed and went to the en suite bathroom, where she changed into a pink silk nightie. When she walked back into the bedroom, Nathan took off his glasses. "Yowza," he said.

"It's been a while," she said.

"I didn't want to rush you. But I'm ready if you are."

She walked to his side of the bed with her hands behind her back so he couldn't see what she was holding. She was thinking of Suzanne and her advice to try something with Nathan she'd learned at the parties. Maybe if she and Nathan tried as hard as Ari and Norah, they would bond, too. Other than joining the lifestyle, they'd barely been trying at all, and lately it seemed like the lifestyle didn't even count. She and Nathan never talked about the parties, never tore each other's clothes off like Quincy said they would, and never had morning sex like Suzanne had promised. The lifestyle had brought her closer to someone, but it wasn't Nathan.

"We need to try harder to rekindle our romance," she said. "Don't you agree?"

"Is that a trick question?" he asked.

"I'm serious. The lifestyle hasn't affected our sex life at all. Don't you think that's weird?"

Nathan watched her with a hesitant interest, like she was a strange animal. "We haven't had a sex life, so . . . no."

"That's the weird part," Georgina said, and revealed what she was holding. It was a silk necktie, blue with stripes, that she'd taken from his closet. "Want to play?"

"I don't think we need stuff like that," Nathan said. "Do you?"

"Maybe," she said. "How will we know if we don't try?"

"Come on." Nathan reached for her free hand and swung it back and forth. "Can't I make love to my wife the regular way?"

Considering what she'd done with Quincy—and how much she'd enjoyed it—that felt like a slight. She pulled her hand away. "This isn't regular?"

"I didn't mean it like that." He closed his eyes and pinched the bridge of his nose, always playing the martyr. "I like what we usually do."

"What we usually do is lie next to each other in silence," Georgina said. "The lifestyle was supposed to turn us into teenagers at prom."

Nathan frowned. "What?"

"Forget it," she said, mostly to herself. She stormed to her side, making as much disturbance as possible as she settled in—punching her pillow, shaking out the comforter, elbowing him to scoot over. When she'd switched out the lamp, she lay there breathing heavily into the darkness. But she wasn't sure who she was angry at. Nathan, for shutting her down? Or herself, for thinking a necktie would save them?

The lifestyle had given her pleasure, desire, thrill, and empowerment. It had given her new friends, new experiences, new reasons to laugh. And it had brought Whitaker back into her life. But it had not given her the marriage she'd sought when she'd signed up in the first place.

"I'm sorry," Nathan said.

"About what?" she asked. She was tired, and wanted sleep to close the door on this whole evening.

"That I can't be who you want me to be."

"We need to love each other for who we are," she said, "and not who we want each other to be."

Sleep wouldn't come after that. For hours, she lay there in the dark, staring at the snowflakes suffocating the window as Nathan's breathing slowed and his body sank into stillness.

The next morning, they woke to at least two feet of snow and more was coming. Alone, Georgina brewed coffee in the kitchen and mixed muffin batter as footsteps creaked the upstairs floorboards. Felix trotted downstairs first in a wool hat and gloves and announced he was taking Alina on a walk to see the frozen pond. She appeared behind him wearing barely enough clothes for a balmy spring evening—a short cotton dress and a burnt-orange cardigan.

"Take my coat," Georgina insisted. "You'll die out there."

Norah debuted next and slumped into a chair. "I'm hungover. Alina, I blame you for this."

"A hangover means you're vitamin deficient," Alina said.

"Gee, thanks," Norah said with her eyes closed while pressing her temples.

"When I get back, I'll make you a plant-rich breakfast," Alina offered, and Georgina tried to hide her sugar-filled mixing bowl by throwing a kitchen towel over it.

"Hair of the dog," Felix suggested. He lifted a bottle of champagne and two paper cups. "That's what we're doing."

"That sounds lifesaving," Norah said. "But I don't want to be your third wheel."

"You're never anybody's third wheel," Felix said. "Life is more fun when you're around."

Norah smiled. "Let me get my coat. I'm not as hot-blooded as Alina."

A few minutes later, Georgina watched them through the window over the kitchen sink as they disappeared between the snowy tree trunks. Alone again.

After peeking up the stairs to make sure no one was coming,

she grabbed her phone from its charging cord on the counter. She planned to call Whitaker, apologize for the kiss, and tell him he could not be her mentor anymore. They could not spend time together, even at the parties. The lifestyle would never work for her and Nathan with Whitaker in the picture. He was too distracting, too fun to be with, too tempting.

But when she opened her contacts, she realized she didn't have Whitaker's phone number. Last time they'd spoken, it had been over email. She couldn't put the kiss in writing—she was a better lawyer than that. So she opened a new message from her work address, which had her cell in the signature block, and disguised it to look as professional as possible.

Whitaker—
Please call me at your earliest convenience to follow up on
our last conversation.
Georgina

As she hit Send, Nathan appeared at the top of the stairs. She hastily stashed her phone in the pocket of her robe. "Just in time for coffee," she said. "Although you've missed the mimosa train."

"No one is ever too late for the mimosa train," Nathan said. "You just hop on."

"Well, they're by the pond if you want to join them." Georgina sliced half a butter stick into a saucepan and watched it melt.

Nathan got a mug from the cupboard. As he filled it with coffee, he said, "Hey, about last night."

"We don't have to talk about it," she said.

"I want to." He set down the pot and looked at her. "You're right. I haven't been trying like I promised I would. I'll do better."

"Me, too," she agreed. "I'll do better."

Her phone vibrated in her pocket.

"I'm going to join them at the pond," she blurted. "Can you put these in the oven?"

Without waiting for his answer, she pushed her wooden spoon into Nathan's hand and grabbed his coat from a hook by the door since she'd given hers to Alina. Her phone was as heavy as a brick in her pocket. "The butter goes in the batter. Three hundred fifty for thirty minutes!"

Outside, the snow crunched under Georgina's boots as she followed the path through the trees. When she was out of Nathan's view, she grabbed her phone from underneath his coat and saw a missed call from a 646 number she didn't recognize. She hadn't expected him to call so quickly. She would have practiced what she wanted to say in the shower. But perhaps it was for the best because if she waited much longer, she'd lose her will.

She tapped the number to call back.

"Hi," Whitaker answered.

Georgina hid under the minimal protection of a leafless maple tree, its boughs like snowcapped mountain ranges. "You didn't have to call me right away." She was whispering even though no one could hear her.

"But this is my earliest convenience," he said.

She picked at a piece of bark. "That might have been a little dramatic."

"Is everything okay?"

"I can't stop thinking about last weekend."

After a pause, he answered softly, "Me either. But maybe for different reasons from yours."

"Because you have nothing to feel guilty about," she said.

"If that's how you feel, why'd you do it?"

"Why'd *you* do it?"

"You know why," he said.

Georgina zipped her coat to the bottom of her chin, starting to shiver but not wanting their conversation to end. She had to tell him what she'd planned to tell him. *Do it*, she told herself. *Say it, now.*

But instead, she blurted, "Do you want to have lunch?"

"I thought you were calling to yell at me."

"We're not supposed to have dinner, so I thought . . . maybe lunch."

He laughed. "This is why everybody hates lawyers. Dinner was more of a symbol."

Georgina kicked the base of the tree with her boot. "So that's a no?"

"I didn't say that."

"That's a yes, then?"

"I didn't say that either."

"But those are your only two options," she said.

He was quiet for so long she checked to see whether she'd lost him. "I'm here," he said. He groaned like he'd made a wrong turn and driven a mile in the opposite direction. "Of course I want to have lunch with you. I always want to have lunch with you. But you need to promise me you're really thinking about this. You're not just going to flirt with me forever while I'm pining away for you like a sad sack."

"I promise," she said, and as the words came out of her mouth, she knew they were true. She was thinking about it, although she didn't know exactly what "it" was. She only knew that since joining the lifestyle, something had shifted. The dynamic of her marriage, yes, but also her perspective. From this point of view, her former aspirations looked far less appealing.

When Georgina got back to the house, Nathan was stressed out over the muffins, and she showed him how to scoop the batter into the foil cups without dripping it all over the tray. As she silently worked, he kept stealing glances at her.

"How was the pond?" he asked.

"Pretty," she lied. "Cold. I didn't stay long."

After he slid the muffins into the oven, he touched her shoulder. "Are we okay?"

Her fingers tightened around her spatula. "You had an affair. We're working on it, but no, I don't think that qualifies us as okay. Do you?"

The back door swung open again, and Norah, Felix, and Alina were back, sooner than expected.

"Breakfast isn't ready yet," Georgina said. "Go have fun."

Norah widened her eyes and gave Georgina a subtle headshake. She was trying to send a message, but Georgina didn't understand what it was. Alina announced she was going to take a shower and floated upstairs. Felix was stoic as he hung up his coat and walked into the living room without another word.

"Oh my God," Norah whispered when they'd gone. "The most awkward thing in the world just happened. I wanted to dive into a snowbank and hide forever."

"Do tell," Georgina said.

Norah checked to make sure Felix was out of earshot, then whispered, "I was telling them a story about a girl at school Simon has a crush on. He asked me if we could buy her a tree for Valentine's Day. Like, a full tree. So I found one of those 'adopt a tree in the rainforest' websites and printed him out the certificate, and he asks me every single day if it's February yet."

"Simon, the King of Romance," Georgina said. "I might ask him to be my Valentine."

"Is he available for lessons?" Nathan asked.

Norah pressed her hand to her heart. "I know. It absolutely kills me every time. Felix thought it was adorable, and he was raving about how he can't wait to have kids. But Alina acted like she didn't think the story was cute."

"Did she *hear* the story?" Georgina asked.

"It gets worse," Norah said, and leaned closer. "Suddenly, Alina says, 'I don't want kids.' Just like that, like she was saying no to dessert. You should have seen Felix's face."

"Had they never talked about that before?" Georgina asked.

"Apparently, she wanted them. She changed her mind." Norah sank onto a barstool and put her head in her hands. "I feel so bad. He's crushed."

"Why don't you give him one of yours?" Nathan suggested.

"Trust me," Norah said, "he was so good with Hannah last night, I thought about it."

"What do you think he'll do?" Georgina asked.

"If you ask me," Norah said, "pretty soon, Felix is going to start saying he never wanted kids in the first place. That is the power Alina has over him."

Chapter 20

Georgina woke up earlier than usual the morning of Meredith's first deposition. She had to make it to the Financial District by seven thirty because she'd promised to arrive early and review Meredith's outline. It was nice not to be the one asking the questions for a change. Instead of obsessively checking and rechecking her exhibits, she leisurely got dressed while listening to a Spotify playlist. On the way to the subway, she stopped for coffee at her favorite café and bought a croissant, too, since she didn't care if she dropped buttery flakes on her suit. No one would be paying her any attention.

But when she entered the lobby of 125 Broad Street and spotted Meredith sitting on the couches, she wondered whether her calm had been foolish overconfidence in Meredith's ability to handle this. The woman was a complete disaster. A scrunchie loosely held her knotted hair in a high ponytail she'd clearly slept in and coffee stained the front of her white camisole. Her feet, in scuffed pink Keds, bounced frantically on the marble floor. Georgina's only relief in surveying her appearance was the absence of her cast.

She approached as one would a wild animal. "Are you okay?" she asked.

"I was up all night," Meredith said, her eyes wide and glassy. "I'm freaking out."

Her panic was contagious. Georgina's eyebrows began to sweat. "Do you have your outline?"

Meredith nodded.

"Do you have your exhibits?"

She nodded again, on the verge of tears.

Georgina exhaled. "Then you will be fine. This doesn't need to be the most stunning *My Cousin Vinny* performance of all time. The goal is to create a clean record. Trust your plan."

Meredith buried her face in her shaking hands. "They'll know I've never done this before. What if they object and I don't know what to say?"

"You don't need to argue with the objections unless they're getting out of hand, and if that happens, say you need a break." Georgina sat beside her on the couch. With anyone else, she'd have rested a comforting hand on her shoulder, but touching Meredith felt too much like pressing a finger in an open wound. "You own these seven hours, okay? If you wanted to sit there and stare at each other, you could. I'm not recommending it, but remember—you're the boss in there."

Meredith stared at her lap for a while, then sniffed and began to gather her notes and legal pads back into her briefcase.

"Where are your shoes?" Georgina asked, peering into Meredith's bag and seeing only a wallet, crumpled tissues, and makeup.

Meredith's face drained of what little color it had to begin with. "Oh my God. I forgot my shoes. And my jacket. Oh my God, oh my God, oh my God. They're sitting on my kitchen table."

"It's okay," Georgina said. Getting through the deposition alive was her main concern. "What size are you?"

"Eight," she whispered. "This is so humiliating."

"You can wear mine," Georgina said, slipping off her beige pumps. "They might be a little big."

They traded shoes, and Georgina gave Meredith her navy suit jacket, which clashed with Meredith's black pants, but it was better than nothing. Together, they rode the elevator to the twenty-seventh floor.

"You'll have an iPad that shows the transcript as the court reporter is typing it," Georgina explained. "Read the answer before you move onto the next question. It's a lifesaver. It's too hard to listen when you're nervous and you're thinking ahead to your next question, so if you read the answer, you'll make sure you got what you want. If it's not clear, or if she says something unexpected, ask a follow-up." She wasn't sure whether Meredith heard her advice because she stared ahead mutely, frozen.

When the elevator doors dinged, they stepped onto marble floors surrounded by endless windows facing the harbor. The Statue of Liberty appeared so close they could touch it.

Meredith apparently did not find the view calming. "This is too fancy," she whispered.

"Not as fancy as you," Georgina said, and Meredith returned a small smile.

They walked to the windows, where bright sunlight exposed a thin but noticeable layer of white hair on Meredith's black pants.

Georgina pointed. "Is that . . . cat hair?"

Meredith looked down and gasped. "Daisy! Fuck. My cat. She likes to sleep on my clothes." She frantically swiped at her pants, but the cat hair remained securely attached.

"Come with me," Georgina said, and marched over to the receptionist. "Hi. We're here for the deposition of Kathleen Duncan."

The receptionist was an elderly woman whose silver hair had a purple sheen to it. "I'll let them know you're here."

"Before you do that—" Georgina leaned over the counter to whisper. "Could we use some of your Scotch tape? We're having a little emergency."

"I don't see why not," the receptionist said, and handed it over.

For the next fifteen minutes, Georgina and Meredith hid in the women's restroom, Scotch taping Meredith's pants until all the cat hair came off. Though they didn't speak much, occasionally they'd catch each other's eye and laugh.

"And that's why it's good to arrive early," Georgina said when they'd finished. "Now walk in there like you own the place. You ready?"

After a deep breath, Meredith nodded.

In the conference room, two grumpy-looking men shook their hands and introduced themselves as Kathleen's lawyers. They were white, around fifty, and carried themselves with an impatient demeanor. Those qualities were true of most lawyers Georgina met. Since she spent much of her time in her own office surrounded by junior associates, over half of whom were women, it was easier to forget that the profession remained dominated by middle-aged, privileged jerks. She caught them checking out Meredith before they exchanged a cocky look, and wanted to pick up the pot of hot coffee on the table and chuck it in their faces.

The witness, Kathleen Duncan, sat in the middle chair of a marble conference table. She had wispy blond hair and a pink summer dress she must have frozen in outside, but if Georgina remembered correctly, the witness was from Texas and probably had no winter clothes. Usually, the lawyers taking the deposition had to travel to wherever the witness was located. But for some reason, Kathleen's lawyers had insisted the deposition take place in New York. That was strange, but Georgina didn't press it because she preferred not to travel halfway across the country with Meredith in the most awkward business trip of all time anyway.

When everyone was settled, the court reporter swore in Kathleen, and Meredith began. Her nerves were palpable. She stumbled on

Kathleen's name, asked for her home address twice, then apologized profusely when she started to ask questions about Kathleen's baby, who'd also been born with Larsen syndrome.

"And when did you realize that your baby was sick?" she asked. "Sorry, I don't mean *sick*. I mean, *not right*. I mean, when did you realize there was something wrong with it? I don't mean *wrong*—"

Kathleen laughed and poured Meredith a glass of water. "It's all right, sweetheart. The first sign was that he could not push himself up during tummy time with both of his arms. One of them would give out."

"Tummy time?" Meredith asked.

Good, Georgina thought. *She's asking follow-ups.* Progress.

The deposition droned on for an hour, fairly boring and straightforward. Slowly, Meredith relaxed, her words coming more easily and smoothly. On a break, they ducked into the next conference room to chat privately. From her purse, Georgina pulled out two Kashi bars and a banana. "If I teach you anything," she said, "let it be to never go to a deposition without snacks."

"Thank God," Meredith said. "I forgot to eat breakfast." She scarfed them down wolfishly compared to the prim and proper way she'd consumed her salad during their mentoring lunch.

Back inside, the deposition took a turn for the worse. Meredith missed so many opportunities for follow-up questions and skipped over such key facts that Georgina worried she'd have to step in, which would be embarrassing for everyone, but perhaps she had pushed Meredith too far and too fast. She wasn't ready.

Suddenly, Meredith's slumped-over posture perked. Georgina wasn't sure why, as the witness's answer had seemed irrelevant. Meredith had asked her why she'd chosen this sperm bank out of all the others, and the witness said, "A good friend of mine used it. I met her at camp thirty-odd years ago at Yale Lake."

"Yale Lake?" Meredith asked.

"The one and only," Kathleen said.

"Did you know the other named plaintiff, Missy Weaver, is from Yale Lake?"

Georgina hadn't been sure why Meredith cared so much about Yale Lake, which Georgina couldn't pluck out on a map, but now she was listening, too.

"I did know that," Kathleen said.

"Is that a coincidence?" Meredith asked. Her outline was forgotten. She was on a roll.

"I should think not," Kathleen said. "Our grandmother is from there."

"Your grandmother," Meredith repeated.

"Janette," Kathleen clarified.

"You and Missy share a grandmother?"

"That's how it works when you are cousins," Kathleen said.

Under the table, Meredith pressed her toe into Georgina's. The grumpy lawyers on Kathleen's side of the table maintained their bored expressions, but Georgina noticed them shift. No wonder they hadn't wanted Georgina to fly to Kathleen's hometown—the place was probably crawling with family who'd spill their secret. There was a saying: you don't win a lawsuit in a deposition. And that was true, but they had won something. Something big. If the two named plaintiffs, Kathleen Duncan and Missy Weaver, were cousins, they shared DNA in common. The fact that they'd both had children with Larsen syndrome using the same sperm was a whole lot less suspicious. And named plaintiffs were supposed to be adequate representatives of all the other plaintiffs in the class, the ones who didn't go to court but would get money from a settlement. But if the named plaintiffs were cousins, they had a unique set of facts that didn't apply to everyone. Georgina would easily win a motion to oppose this case as a class action, so instead of hundreds of plaintiffs, there would be two, and instead of tens of millions in damages, the figure would be small.

"One more question," Meredith said at the end of the day. "Why did you and your cousin decide to use the same sperm for your kids?"

"You probably think it's weird," Kathleen said, "but when we were growing up, we felt like sisters. We wanted our kids to really be sisters."

As they packed their briefcases, Georgina should have been ecstatic, and she sort of was. This was her first important case as a partner, and thanks to Meredith, she wasn't losing anymore. But she couldn't help but wonder about those kids. Being a lawyer was all about the fight, no matter the cause, but that didn't make it feel better.

"We need to celebrate!" Georgina said. They were standing on Broad Street, shivering in the late-afternoon sun. "Anywhere you want. How about Manhatta? The view is incredible."

Meredith chewed her lip for a while, considering the question. "Um—"

"Or anywhere," Georgina said. "Eataly?"

"There is one place," Meredith said. "It's sort of a tradition in my family to go there for celebrations."

"Perfect," Georgina said. "As long as it has the heat on. What's it called?"

Meredith smiled, a genuine, unguarded smile. "Applebee's?"

So this was the authentic Meredith, the woman she'd been hiding. She hadn't declined Georgina's thirty-seven lunch invitations because the restaurants weren't trendy or vegan enough. They were too trendy, too vegan, too much. Now she'd offered Georgina an invitation, and though knowing Meredith, really knowing her, would be painful and uncertain and complicated, what worthwhile in her life lately had come from "uncomplicated"?

"Applebee's it is," Georgina said, and hailed a cab.

The closest Applebee's was in Times Square, near the office. Without traffic, their taxi zipped uptown, and they were seated at the bar in twenty minutes flat. Georgina was sure they were the only locals there as she looked around, spotting tourist garb everywhere— sneakers, *I Heart NY* T-shirts, visors, and too many people without warm-enough coats. But Meredith settled right in, and immediately ordered crunchy onion rings, boneless wings, and mozzarella sticks without looking at the menu.

"What do you want to drink?" Meredith asked.

"What's good?" Georgina asked, having realized Meredith probably knew the menu better than the bartender.

"I'd go with the Captain Bahama Mama, but that's just me," she said. "The margaritas are good, too."

"Captain Bahama Mama it is," Georgina said, and smiled at the boy behind the bar, who looked far too young to be serving alcohol.

The boy mixed and shook two goblets full of icy pink liquid with orange slices hugging the rims. "It's two for one," he said. "Your lucky night."

Georgina took a sip and whistled. Two of those and she'd be on the floor. When the mozzarella sticks arrived, she picked one up and dipped it in marinara sauce. "I'm all for fried cheese, but, um . . . I thought you were a vegan?"

Meredith was sucking her drink through a straw. When she peeked up, her expression was apologetic. "That's just something I tell people," she admitted. "I thought it would make me seem more interesting. Isn't that terrible?"

"It's certainly a unique approach," Georgina said. "What's wrong with the real you? She's pretty interesting."

"She's not." Meredith returned to her straw, sucking so hard her cheeks hollowed. "I'm a nobody girl from upstate. I was trying to fit in here, I guess. Here being—" She waved her arms around the room as though meaning to say, *This place.*

"Applebee's?" Georgina asked.

Meredith laughed. "No. I fit in here fine. I mean the big city."

Nobody called Manhattan "the big city" outside of a Disney musical. It was endearing. Meredith was just a girl from upstate, and as Georgina watched her dive into the onion rings, it suddenly made sense. Meredith felt like an imposter. She'd tried to hide it by becoming someone else, and Nathan had taken advantage of her quest to prove she belonged. Georgina felt a surge of hatred toward him and allyship with the girl sitting beside her. When Meredith finished her drink and ordered another, Georgina said, "Me, too, please," thinking how bizarre but strangely fun this was.

"I have five siblings," Meredith was saying, "but we're very different. They never wanted to get out of town like I did. My three sisters got married super young and had kids. I have twelve nieces and nephews, can you believe that? To be honest, I can't remember all their names."

Georgina laughed. She'd never heard this many words come out of Meredith's mouth, at this volume, with this much honesty.

"They're all super religious," Meredith went on, pulling apart a mozzarella stick to let the steam out. "One of my brothers is a pastor. The other one is in jail, but he *used* to be a pastor. It's sort of a long story."

"Do you see them often?" Georgina asked.

"No." Meredith dropped the mozzarella stick back into the basket. "Every summer, we used to go to the lake and sleep in a two-room cabin. Now I barely speak to them. Fucked-up, right?"

"I don't talk to my mom often either," Georgina said. "We're also very different. She paints pet portraits in the Outer Banks. I used to find that career too unstable or not serious enough. But actually, she's super talented. People from all over the country order her stuff online, and she was on the cover of *Modern Dog* magazine."

"Do you miss her?" Meredith asked.

"I do."

"I'm a terrible aunt," Meredith said drearily, resting her chin in her palm.

Georgina hesitated, then patted Meredith's shoulder. It wasn't as searingly painful as she'd thought it would be. "It's not too late to start being a good one."

"You know when Kathleen said today that she wanted her kid to have a sister?" she asked. "That got to me. I wanted to set myself apart from my sisters, but now I'm just . . . alone. I don't have any friends."

"That's not true," Georgina said. "Someone signed your cast *unstoppable*. She seems like a good friend."

"I wrote that," Meredith admitted.

"Oh." Georgina's chest tightened. "I hear daily affirmations can be really . . . effective."

The boy-bartender was back with their refills. On his black collared shirt, he wore a button with Nicolas Cage's face on it. Was he old enough to know who that was? "Is that it for you ladies?" he asked, and Georgina swore his voice cracked.

Meredith was hunched over the bar, licking buffalo sauce off a spoon. This was supposed to be a celebration, but she looked so forlorn. "For now," Georgina said, and held up her fresh goblet for a toast. "To killing it on your first deposition."

Meredith flushed. "I did kind of kill it, didn't I?"

"You slaughtered it." Georgina sipped and sputtered at the sweet, antiseptic taste. Then she cupped her hand around her mouth and shouted to the rest of the bar, "She killed it on her first deposition!" A kind tourist eating a burger alone gave them a double thumbs-up.

"Stop!" Meredith cried, and covered her bright pink face with a menu.

"It's a good thing you didn't quit," Georgina said. "What if I never figured out they were cousins?"

"You would have," Meredith said.

They picked at the food baskets in companionable silence for a while.

"How do you do it?" Meredith asked suddenly.

"Do what?" Georgina dipped an onion ring into ranch dressing.

"Be so perfect."

Previously, she would have rebuffed this compliment with polite—albeit fake—humility, because she had thought she was perfect and did everything perfectly. Now when she scoffed, there was nothing fake about it. Was perfection even a compliment? Or just a sad, placatory assurance?

"There is no such thing as perfect," Georgina said. "There is only trying to survive and having some fun while you're at it."

When Meredith smiled sincerely, Georgina realized how glad she was for this day. Recently, she'd been finding herself in so many unexpected places—strangers' homes, strangers' beds. Back in Whitaker's life. A patron at a sex club, and now the Times Square Applebee's with the woman who'd slept with her husband. None of it ever would have happened without the lifestyle, and she wouldn't give it back for all the perfection in the world.

"Can I give you one last piece of advice?" Georgina asked. "Then I promise I'll stop."

Meredith nodded, slurping the last icy dregs of her Captain Bahama Mama.

"You've got the instinct. You'll be a fierce lawyer. But only do it because you love it, and not because you like how it sounds."

Meredith considered that for a moment. "Do you love it?" she asked.

Georgina swirled the straw in her watery pink cocktail. "I've never really thought about the answer to that question before. But no, I don't think I do, to be honest. You know what I love?" She looked at Meredith. "This. Mentoring. Working with the juniors. It helps me channel my desire to boss people around into something productive."

"I used to find it patronizing," Meredith said, "but I couldn't have survived today without you."

"Too bad there's no job for somebody who wants to mold the next generation of young lawyers," Georgina said dryly.

Meredith laughed. "Um, I think it's called a career counselor."

As Meredith's suggestion sank in, Georgina frowned at the last lonely onion ring. Becoming a career counselor had never occurred to her, but the words felt right as she repeated them in her mind. *Career counselor. Career counselor. Career counselor.*

When the check came, Georgina reached down to grab her wallet.

"Wait!" Meredith announced. "Hold on." She dug in her purse and emerged triumphantly with a wrinkled black-and-red business card. "My punch card—I have free wings!"

After Georgina signed the receipt, the lights dimmed, and a multicolored electronic disco ball started flashing blue, pink, yellow, and green lights around a small dance floor in the corner. The boy-bartender had put on a backward baseball cap and stood in a DJ booth, talking into a microphone he apparently did not realize was off. When he turned up the volume on "Independent Women Part I" by Destiny's Child, Georgina looked at Meredith and smiled. Her identity as a swinger didn't feel so different from her identity as a person anymore, and if there was one thing she had learned in the lifestyle, it was that to let go and feel good, sometimes a person just needed to dance.

Chapter 21

Georgina's lunch with Whitaker was arranged for Friday. When her alarm went off that morning, she beelined for the shower. If she had one conversation with Nathan, she feared she'd confess everything—their secret history, the rooftop kiss, the phone call, her invitation to have not-dinner. And probably she should have confessed. What she was doing was wrong, but she couldn't not do it. It made it worse that she'd been the victim of this exact behavior. Nathan had lied to her, snuck around behind her back, and harbored secret feelings for someone—and it had nearly destroyed her. Now she was guilty of the same, knowing how much it hurt, knowing what damage it could cause to their marriage. Nevertheless, she got in the shower, got dressed, put on makeup, and left without saying a word.

Was she doing this to get back at Nathan? Had her real goal been hurting him all along, despite denying it?

If that were true, she could have used any man as her pawn.

This was Whitaker.

This, she knew in her heart, had nothing to do with Nathan.

At ten, she went to a hearing downtown. To look nice for lunch, she'd put on her favorite suit and so carefully blown out her hair that now she felt more like she was posing for law school graduation photos than attending a boring hearing. Thankfully, she'd invited a first-year associate named Stacy to take notes because she could hardly pay attention. While the judge spoke, her thoughts wandered to Whitaker as she stared at the elaborate molding on the courtroom's ceiling, decorated with a Greek key design and golden rosettes. Every time someone said a word that sounded remotely like her name—justifiable, jurisprudence, and worst of all, George, the lead attorney's name—she jumped and dropped her notepad on the floor.

"Are you hot?" she whispered to Stacy. "It's a sauna in here."

Stacy shook her head with wide eyes and her mouth slightly ajar, terrified to be alone with a partner.

"Why is this taking so long?" Georgina asked.

"It's only been fifteen minutes," Stacy said.

Georgina checked her watch to be sure. Ten forty-five. One hour and fifteen minutes until she met Whitaker. She wasn't sure she could stand one more second. Why had she come today? She was one lawyer of fifty in a joint defense group on a sprawling bankruptcy that had been going on for ten years and would never, ever end. It was painfully pointless.

When the judge finally adjourned, Georgina thanked Stacy, stuffed her blank notepad into her briefcase, and hurried from the courtroom as fast as her heels would allow, taking the stairs because she was too impatient to wait for the elevator.

Whitaker had suggested they meet at a diner on Lafayette and Spring Street. She sped toward the subway stop on Canal, dodging hot dog stands and tourists, passing stalls of fake Gucci. The skin on her little toes stung and her neck grew damp under her scarf, but this lunch felt too urgent to slow down. One minute late meant one fewer minute with him.

She rode the train a few stops, unable to keep still, bouncing from a bench to the center pole to a space by the door, where she leaned against the sign reading *Do not lean on door*. When she got off, she bolted the last few blocks, sweating in earnest and panting by the time she arrived. Outside the diner, she unzipped her coat to let the cold air calm her. After a smudge of lip balm, a deep breath, and a quick armpit sniff for good measure, she went inside.

The diner was decorated for Halloween, Thanksgiving, Christmas, and Hanukkah all at once. Multicolored bulbs wrapped the windows, which themselves were covered with stretched white cotton like spiderwebs. On every table and along the bar, small pumpkins were painted with spooky faces, and from the ceiling, plastic turkeys wearing pilgrim hats dangled. Next to the cash register sat a silver menorah and a bowl of chocolate gelt. Georgina ran her eyes across the room until they landed on Whitaker at a booth in the corner, reading a magazine.

She sat down opposite him. "Very festive in here," she said.

He looked up and smiled. The very existence of his face still surprised her. She couldn't believe he'd returned to her life, or how good-looking he'd remained all these years later. He wore a flannel shirt underneath a turmeric puffer jacket with an olive-green scarf hanging around his neck like the hottest model for outdoor goods in a Patagonia catalog.

"You look nice," she said.

"So do you," he said. "I'm not used to seeing you in all these suits."

"I'm a partner now," she said. "I have to lead by example."

"I know you are," he said. "I kept one eye on your career. I almost sent you an email to say congratulations, but I wasn't sure you'd want to hear from me."

Georgina sipped her water. She wouldn't have wanted to hear

from him. It would have been an interruption to her then-perfect life, or what she'd thought was a perfect life. Now all she could see was what she'd been missing. Him. This. The feeling of sitting across the table from someone she couldn't take her eyes off.

"I've never asked you what you're doing for work these days," she said.

Whitaker smiled, folded his hands, and leaned forward. "I noticed. Tried not to let it hurt my feelings too much."

When he didn't go on, she said, "So . . . what are you doing for work these days?"

"If I said a little bit of this, a little bit of that, would you mock me?" he asked.

"Mercilessly."

He laughed. "Fair enough. I've spent most of the last ten years working on campaigns and consulting. But now I'm starting the magazine."

"I'm sorry," she said. "I didn't realize it was that serious. Randolph is usually full of hot air."

"Couldn't agree with you more," Whitaker said, "but this time, he wasn't exaggerating."

"Congratulations. Are you past the seed stage?"

Whitaker looked amused. "This is starting to feel like an interview. Should I have dressed up?"

"Sorry. I'm nervous." She took off her coat and stashed it in a rolled-up ball on the seat cushion, still too warm from her hurried walk over. "I'm not exactly sure what this is."

"I was hoping you'd tell me," he said.

Georgina lifted her plastic menu to hide her face, which she felt burn crimson. "What's good here?"

"The matzo ball soup," he said without missing a beat. "If you don't order it, I'm never speaking to you again."

She peered at him above the rim. "You're very controlling."

One corner of his mouth lifted. "Gee, I wonder who I learned that from."

After a woman with teased hair stopped by and took their orders, they were quiet for a while, occasionally glancing up and grinning sheepishly at each other before looking away again. They were behaving like middle schoolers on their first date ever. Surely one of their moms was about to roll into the parking lot in her minivan and honk the horn.

"We don't need to be weird," Georgina said.

"I didn't think I was being weird," he said, but his expression was teasing. He was having fun messing with her. She returned the sentiment by rolling her eyes.

When their soup came, she realized that as soon as they were finished eating, lunch would be over. That was how lunch worked. Too much time had passed already, and she hadn't said what she needed to say. But what did she need to say? She was anxious to get the words right, to not waste a second, but had no idea where to begin or what she wanted. This filled her with an existential dread. They'd already lost so much time—thirteen years of time.

"This is the best soup in the city," Whitaker said. "Prepare for your life to be changed. I eat it every year on Thanksgiving. It's family tradition."

She didn't want to talk about Thanksgiving, but it was the best option she had. "Why? You don't like turkey?"

"I tried to cook a turkey for my mom and brother a few years ago, but I'd just moved into this new place and it turned out my oven only cooked on one side, so half of it came out raw. I ran around looking for something open, and came back with this soup and ice cream from CVS. Turned out to be the best Thanksgiving we ever had."

"That sounds perfect." For the last eight years, she and Nathan had been hosting a very formal and very boring Thanksgiving dinner for business connections.

Georgina picked up her spoon and scooped oily broth into her mouth. It was savory and rich, but her tight stomach left her with no appetite. She set her spoon back down. "Why are you here if you're the one who told me we can't see each other outside of parties?" she asked in a rush.

Whitaker set his spoon down, too. "I said that to protect myself."

"From what?"

"This."

It was difficult to read the expression on his face. For once, he didn't look at ease, but he didn't look away either.

"Imagine you're me," he said. "You've had one all-consuming love in your life, and she broke your heart. But you've never stopped thinking about her. Whenever you see her name online or hear about her through a friend, it sticks with you like nothing else. You forget about other people, but you've never forgotten about her. Is it just because she was your first love and you were young and you never got to see it through? Maybe. But if you try to find out, then you're right back where you started."

"Believe it or not," Georgina whispered, "I can imagine that pretty easily."

They looked at each other for a while, her head swimming with memories in the background, but focusing only on each line and curve of his face in the foreground. She wanted to memorize it so she could conjure it in her dreams. She had the sudden and alarming feeling that this might be the last time they saw each other.

"Now it's my turn to ask a question," he said. "Why are you here if you're trying to save your marriage?"

"I shouldn't be. I'd called to tell you we couldn't spend time together anymore, but those weren't the words that came out of my mouth." She pushed the matzo ball around her bowl, feeling its doughy weight. "I don't know what that means. I just know it was a lot easier to think my life was perfect before you were in it."

The woman stopped by and offered to refill Whitaker's coffee. "You don't like your soup?" she asked Georgina.

"It's delicious. I'm just not hungry."

"Suit yourself."

When the woman was gone, Georgina asked, "Have you ever wondered what life would have been like if I'd gone with you?" She couldn't look at him as she waited for his answer.

"Of course," he said. "But I think it was for the best, to be honest."

She hadn't admitted to herself that she wanted him to say, "It would have been amazing," or something along those lines, until he gave a different answer. Wasn't that reminiscent of their unpredictable, often confusing dynamic? She'd assume he wanted one thing, then he'd surprise her by doing another. She'd thought he would reject marriage because he didn't want to be tied down, but apparently, he'd gotten hitched. He'd invited her to Peru, but refused to come with her to New York, and now he lived in New York. That was what had made their relationship scary and what made a future with him scarier still. What if he didn't want to be with her like she thought he did? All he'd promised her was this lunch, nothing more. At least Nathan had sworn to be a better husband. At least Nathan wanted a future as permanent as a baby.

"If you'd come, you'd have resented me for giving up law school," he said. "This way, you got to have your dream and I got to have mine."

"And here we are now," she said. "Having not-dinner."

"I needed to find a life that didn't revolve around you."

"Did you?"

"Yeah. But that doesn't mean I wouldn't have preferred a place for you in my life at all."

"Hm, let me translate that double negative." She pretended to think hard. "So you miss me?"

He laughed. *Answer the question*, she wanted to say. *Give me some assurance*. But he didn't. Maybe, she realized, he wouldn't because he couldn't. There were no guarantees in life. Hadn't Nathan showed her that? There were only moments like these, and trying to have as many of them as possible.

Her soup had grown viscous as it cooled, and she trailed her spoon through it. Whitaker had eaten his matzo ball and carrots, and with only broth left, he tipped the bowl into his mouth and drank it.

"Were you surprised to see me at the party?" she asked.

"I feel like I can't answer that without offending you somehow."

"Try me."

When he spoke, it sounded more like dirty talk than an answer to a question. "In some ways, yes, and in other ways, no. You viewed life like a game you could outsmart. And I think that's what you're doing with the lifestyle. And I'm not sure it's going to work, because that's not the point."

"What is the point?"

"Sex would be the obvious answer to that question, but the truth is I'm not sure anymore."

"Why did you join the lifestyle, then?"

He leaned back and thought about it. "Mei wanted to. Our marriage was mostly about sex. I'm sorry if that's weird to say, but it's the truth. Once that started to fade, we both realized there was nothing there to sustain us, so we turned to what we knew."

"But you stuck with it," Georgina said, "even when it didn't save you."

"At the time, I thought, why not? It's fun, it's sexy, I'm single. But I was lying to myself. The lifestyle is to some degree about detachment from sex and everyone you're with. That was what I wanted."

"Is that what you want now?" she asked.

"No," he said. "I would prefer to attach."

She looked out the window onto Spring Street and watched bundled-up New Yorkers passing by. It was warm in the diner and cold and windy outside, and she wanted to stay in that booth with him forever, but she sensed their conversation nearing the end. There wasn't much more to say without someone getting hurt.

"If we were together," she said, "I couldn't be part of the lifestyle with you."

Setting down his coffee, his movement skipped, as if he were a reel missing a frame. "Why not?"

"I couldn't share you," she said.

The waitress brought their bill, and Georgina insisted on paying because it was her idea to have lunch, and she worried she'd made things worse somehow. It was all over so quickly, and Whitaker looked deeply sad all of a sudden.

"How about a walk?" she suggested.

He checked his watch. "I have a meeting uptown, but let me walk you to the subway."

Back outside the diner, the light filtered gray through the clouds, and the wind made the cold temperature feel colder. It was the time of year when a nice day meant not raining and not snowing. They walked silently, not touching but connected by their body heat. The closer to him she walked, the warmer she felt. At Prince Street, they turned left so she could take the R to Times Square.

She stopped at the entrance underground and looked up at him. The wind had ruffled his hair and reddened the tip of his nose. "Do you want to see me again?" she asked. "I mean, not at a party?"

Whitaker reached up and tugged on the collar of her pea coat as if that were the only part of her he was allowed to touch. After an excruciatingly long wait, he said, "No. I can't."

Georgina turned away fast and started walking so he wouldn't see her eyes fill with tears. She didn't stop until she reached her office forty-three blocks later, where she wiped her face and went upstairs.

Chapter 22

On Saturday night at nine, an Uber dropped Georgina and Nathan off on Kent Avenue in front of a pink neon sign that read *The Velvet Mouse*. Instead of meeting at someone's home for a party, Quincy had arranged for everyone to meet at the club. When Alina had passed along the message, Georgina had asked her whether it was reserved for the group. "No," Alina had said, "it will be open to the public." Though Georgina and Nathan hadn't voiced their nerves about the evening, they'd prepared with stilted conversation, and the Uber ride had been nearly silent. They'd promised each other to try harder to rekindle their romance after acknowledging in the Berkshires that the lifestyle wasn't working its magic on their sex life, and neither seemed willing to be the first to surrender.

Despite the freezing temperature that night, a bouncer waited outside the club with a clipboard and petty cash box. He took their names and charged Nathan a hundred dollars for entry and Georgina fifty.

"This had better come with a steak dinner," Nathan groaned as he handed over the cash.

"Find someone in gloves to give you a tour," the bouncer said, and waved them toward a wall of violet curtains. It was so dark it was difficult to see, but Georgina felt for a gap. Nathan placed a protective hand on her shoulder, and together they walked into the next curtained-off room.

There, she saw a wall of cubbies, half of them full of clothes and shoes. She and Nathan exchanged a nervous glance.

"Should we . . . ?" she asked.

"I'm still defrosting," he said. "Maybe later."

They hadn't seen another person, but laughter and conversation floated from somewhere beyond the curtains. She trailed her hand along the velvet, feeling for another opening but finding none. In a corner where two curtains met, she smelled the sharp scent of chlorine. Listening hard with her ear grazing the soft velvet, she detected the bubbling jets and the suck of air into a filter. *A hot tub?* she wondered. But pushing against the curtains, she felt no exit. *Screw it,* she thought. *I'm going under.*

Bending down, she lifted the hem enough to see into the next room, and found herself face-to-foot. She moved her eyes up a bare—and oddly familiar—leg.

"Georgina! What are you doing on the ground?"

The pale leg and its curly blond hair belonged to Quincy, and she'd never been so happy to see him. "Thank God," she said. "I thought you'd invited me to a haunted house."

"Just a fun house," he said. "Come in, come in!"

He swept the curtain aside and waved them into a larger room with a giant, gurgling hot tub in the center. Inside relaxed Alina, Martin, Cynthia, Laila, Jeremiah, and Marco. Their delighted faces at her arrival brought her a pleasurable relief only momentarily thwarted when she realized they were all naked beneath the bubbles.

"Get in!" Quincy said, and pulled down his briefs in one swift motion. "The water is nice and hot."

Georgina and Nathan exchanged a look that said, *I am way too sober for this.*

"Um ... Would love to, but ... is there a bar in this place?" she asked.

"Outside the play area," Quincy said, pointing through an opening in the curtains on the other side of the hot tub. "Three rooms down. We'll be here!"

"Shots?" she murmured to Nathan.

"You read my mind," he murmured back.

They walked toward where Quincy had pointed. Certain the ground was covered with slippery substances, Georgina made sure each foot was steady before taking another step, holding Nathan's hand in a death grip. Though she'd been to La Peluche with Whitaker, this club had an aura of expectation the other hadn't. There, she felt like a spectator at Cirque du Soleil, admiring the bending and twisting bodies from afar. Now she was at the circus, in the middle of the ring, with a horny lion.

It came through on its intended bonding effect, though. Every time something unexpected arose, she squeezed Nathan's hand and inclined her head. They exchanged a laugh at the dispenser of sanitizing wipes directing guests to *Please clean up after yourself!* For the first time, they were experiencing the lifestyle together instead of side by side.

As soon as they passed the next curtain, the music faded and the volume of conversation increased. It was cooler in this part of the club, too, the air thinner without the hot tub's steam. She could breathe again. "That's better," she said. "Are you okay?"

"I'll be better with tequila," he said.

The hallway opened to what looked like a regular bar with red leather booths and shelves of clear and amber bottles. Chandeliers cast a soft glow over the crowd and framed vintage pinup posters adorned the walls—Marilyn Monroe with her skirt blowing up from the vent, a woman stepping off a horse with her skirt caught in the saddle. Only the giant bowl of condoms on every table where one might expect to see a votive candle revealed this was a sex club instead of a hipster Greenpoint tavern.

First stop, alcohol. She ordered two tequila shots and two glasses of water from a nonchalant bartender wearing a backward Yankees hat and flannel shirt, either unaware or unfazed by the fact that the entire room was there to have sex with strangers in his presence. But that was true of any bar, wasn't it? The only difference between this and the bar next door was that the people hooking up didn't have to worry about feeding each other breakfast in the morning, and the condoms were free. It was probably safer for the women here. They didn't need to go back to a strange man's apartment just to get off. Here, they had security *and* safe words.

Georgina felt a light touch on her back and a voice asked, "You two wanna play with us?" It was a small woman, midthirties, with lavender hair in a sleek bob and orange lipstick. Her partner was a stocky man with a beard and a bun. They both smiled at her pleasantly, twirling their red cocktail straws in their drinks.

"No, thanks," Georgina said. "We're here with some friends."

"Okay," the woman said, "have fun!" They wandered off.

Well, that was easy. Usually, when men approached her in bars looking for sex, no amount of polite no-thank-yous, declined drinks, or moving away from them on the dance floor would get them to leave her alone. This place was getting better and better.

The bartender placed their shots on the counter with two lime wedges on a cocktail napkin and a saltshaker. She handed him her credit card and told him to close it, feeling more comfortable already and less desperate for liquid courage. She and Nathan lifted their glasses and toasted. The tequila was sour and spicy on her tongue, leaving a warm trail in her chest as she swallowed.

"Yowza," Nathan said. "Haven't done a tequila shot in a while."

Georgina's face puckered as she sucked on her lime. "I feel like a summer associate again," she agreed.

Nathan laughed. "I don't know how we ever made it to work on time."

"We didn't," she said.

The tequila was already working its way through her bloodstream, giving her a buoyant lightness. "I was nervous to come here tonight. Were you?"

"I'm not sure I'm ready to characterize my nerves as in the past."

"It doesn't seem so bad."

"That hot tub was pretty small for all those naked people." He gestured to the bartender, then pointed to his shot glass. "Do you want another?" he asked Georgina.

She shook her head. "We don't have to hot-tub. We can hang out here. It's great people-watching."

"The only person I'm here to watch is you," Nathan said. "I want to focus on us tonight."

"Me, too," she agreed, and for good measure, she stuck out her hand, and they shook on the deal.

Nathan's second shot was gone as quickly as it had arrived. "Okay. I'm ready to be adventurous now."

She laughed. The lifestyle was finally working for them. Standing beside him, she did feel a little like a teenager at prom, and he was her date, and they were going to try something together that neither had done before. It was thrilling and provocative, the daringness of it, the promise of soon being touched in a new way. She was so consumed by the environment she wasn't even thinking about Whitaker. Or at least, she wasn't thinking about him until she realized she wasn't thinking about him, and then she was thinking about him.

Looking around for someone in gloves to give them a tour, she spotted Felix standing alone in the corner by an old-fashioned juke-box. "One second," she said to Nathan, and approached him. "Hey. What are you doing over here?"

"I was waiting for Norah," he said. "Have you seen her?"

Earlier, Georgina had texted Norah to make sure she'd gotten the invitation, but she'd texted back, *We're not coming*, with a smiley face, as though that were good news. *I hope you do, though!* she'd added, that time with a winking face. "She's not going to be here," Georgina said. "I figured you knew. Sorry."

Felix said nothing. He stared in the direction of the play area, where the hot tub waited. "Did you see Alina in there?"

"She's with everyone in the Jacuzzi. Why don't you join?"

He shook his head, sipped his beer, and flipped through the metal pages of songs in the jukebox. His face was a mask of misery. *Here we go again*, she thought grimly, remembering the conversation they'd had in the corner of Quincy's living room, when Felix had insisted he wasn't just in the lifestyle because Alina wanted to be, but the nause-ated look on his face as the keys were drawn said otherwise.

"I assume Norah told you about the whole no-kids thing," he said.

"She did," Georgina said. "Are you okay?"

Again, Felix said nothing. He dug in his pocket, emerged with a quarter, and plugged it into the machine. A5, he punched. "No," he said. "I'm sick of this."

Georgina glanced over her shoulder and saw Nathan watching them. She held up a finger, asking him to wait.

"Sick of what?" she asked.

"Sick of not being myself," he said, not looking at her. "I really want kids. And I really don't want to be here."

"Then you have to go, Felix."

"I'm going to lose her if I leave."

"But what will you lose if you stay?" she asked.

It'll be worth it, she expected him to say, or, *Forget I brought it up.* He loved Alina in spite of himself, and maybe it was enough for him to love others without return. But to her surprise, he set his beer down, straightened, and said, "Everything. Tell Alina I've gone out for a sandwich." He gave her a quick hug and shouldered through the patrons until she couldn't see his black hair anymore.

She smiled, knowing that was the second time in Felix's life he'd left for a sandwich and would never come back.

The lifestyle helped everyone differently. For Felix, it had been a catalyst. For Ari, a wake-up call. For Norah, a sexual liberation. For Georgina and Nathan? Tonight, she would find out. Their promise to each other made her wedding ring heavy on her finger. This was the last chance for the lifestyle to ignite passion between them. If she and Nathan couldn't come together even in this electric place, the lifestyle would never work for them.

On their way back toward the play area, they passed a woman wearing gloves. They were disposable latex gloves, like the kind surgeons wore, not the elbow-length black silk gloves Georgina was expecting when the bouncer first mentioned it. The woman was short with curly black hair, and she wore sneakers, jeans, and a plain blue T-shirt. "Hi," Georgina said. "Are we supposed to ask you for a tour?"

"That's me," she said. "Raquel. First time?"

Georgina nodded. "What's with the gloves? They're a little . . . murdery."

"I'm on the cleaning crew," Raquel said. "We make the rounds every ten minutes to wipe down surfaces, pick up condoms, change the linens, put out clean towels, and spray with disinfectant. It's cleaner than a hospital in here, I promise you."

"You must have seen some stuff," Nathan said.

"I don't notice it anymore," Raquel said. "Follow me."

She led them through yet another curtain into a locker room. "Here's where you can keep your valuables if you like. Next time, I'd recommend you don't bring any. It can break up the mood for some people when they're about to head upstairs and they decide they need to lock up their jewelry."

Georgina looked around the small lockers, wondering how many people stashed away their wedding rings or whether that was only necessary outside these walls.

"Next we've got the BDSM rooms," Raquel said, waving them through the next curtain. "The folks who come in here know what they're doing, so if you're just curious, watch the first time and tell them you're new. Trust me on that one. Some people get in over their heads."

They entered the largest space yet, a lounge with black leather couches lining all four walls. In the center rose a tall structure, like a squat rack from the gym, but adorned with whips and chains. A woman in a leather bodysuit covering her from neck to wrist to ankle was tied to a pole. Georgina waved, and the woman smiled and waved back.

"What's upstairs?" Georgina asked.

"Private rooms and group rooms. You can reserve them ahead of time or whenever the mood strikes. They cost extra."

Next they entered a mirrored room resembling the ballet studios Georgina went to when she was little, except this one had mirrors on the ceiling, too. In the center, there were several beds full of occupants. She took Nathan's hand and raised her eyebrows. "What do you think?"

Blue-toned light rendered his features corpse-like. "I think we start with a private room."

"You can make your reservation at the bar," Raquel said. "I've got to start my round, but if you keep following this hall, you'll find all the themed rooms. We've got a 1920s room, a medical room, a school room, a safari room, a space room, a dungeon room, and a princess room. Bathrooms are to the left, clothing cubbies are at the front. We're not responsible for any lost valuables. Did you sign your waivers?"

"Is that required?" Nathan asked.

Raquel reached into her bag of cleaning supplies and pulled out two clipboards with pens attached to metal ball chains. "He should have made you sign at the front door. This says you've got clean health, you'll follow the rules, and if you get hurt in the BDSM room, you won't sue us."

They signed their waivers and handed back the clipboards. Raquel wished them a good time and left through the door they came from. Georgina and Nathan were alone in the mirrored room—alone with eight naked strangers.

"Should we stay, or . . . ?" she asked.

Nathan hesitated, looking around at the people. There were five on one bed together, three on another, and one empty. He scratched the side of his nose. Eventually, he put his hands on either side of Georgina's waist and bent down to kiss her. It was chaste at first, then his tongue pressed against her lips, trying to open her mouth. She could tell he was doing it because he thought it was what she wanted—it wasn't his usual way. It was impossible for her to kiss him without comparing it to her kiss with Whitaker, which had been a perfect synchrony of lips moving and sliding together. But lust had never been her marriage's defining characteristic, and that was the problem, so she leaned into him and tried to focus on what was nice about the kiss. His lips were soft. His body familiar. She imagined herself naked on the bed, new hands igniting her skin, and felt her body heating. It was the energy, it was undeniable, impossible to not want pleasure when pleasure surrounded her.

Then Nathan pulled away quickly and said, "Let's go see what the others are up to."

"Oh," she said. "Okay." As she followed him out, she wasn't sure what made her feel more awkward—that she'd wanted to stay or that he didn't.

Back in the humid, chlorinated room, the mood had escalated. In one corner, Laila and Marco were lost in expressions of ecstasy with mysterious origin. Something was happening below the surface of the bubbling water. In the opposite corner, a massage chain had formed between Alina, Quincy, and his wife, their lolling heads obscured behind the steam. If Georgina mentioned Felix had left, would Alina care? She suspected not.

"I'm going to get in," Georgina announced, and hastily undressed. She didn't mean to, but she looked around for Whitaker. Her pang of longing and disappointment at his absence must have shown on her face, because Nathan said, "What?"

"Nothing." She unclasped her bra and pulled down her underwear and stuffed them in her purse as a balled-up wad before hopping in the tub.

The water felt transcendent. She sank to her chin and let her hands float dreamily to the surface. Outside waited sleety misery, but in here there was only slickness and heat. Jets massaged her back and shoulders. She let her head fall back onto the edge and lifted her legs so her toes poked out of the water. Her skin was smooth and her nakedness daring. Looking around at her new friends in varying stages of bliss filled her with the bubbly warmth of belonging, and she relaxed. If only Nathan would join her, this could work. It could really work.

He slipped into the tub and ran his hand up her thigh. "You look like you're having fun."

"I am," she said. "I'm finding myself very in the mood. Are you?"

Nathan kissed her neck, and she closed her eyes. Never in a million years would she have expected her marriage to the Résumé from Kansas to have led her to a hot tub in a sex club, but she was glad it had. She craved feeling sexy now and wasn't afraid to admit it. That morning, she'd finally gone to Babeland, the brick-and-mortar store on Mercer, spent an hour browsing the inventory with a highly knowledgeable saleswoman named Amanda, and left with four vibrators. When Amanda had first suggested she consider buying more than one, Georgina had asked, "Why? Don't they all do the same thing, sort of like . . . can openers?" Amanda had laughed. "Let me give you an education," she'd said.

Georgina held Nathan's hand under the water and let him rub her lower back and kiss her shoulder with his warm lips, and like an overstretched rubber band snapping, the past released. They were different people now from who they'd been before Meredith. Tonight could be a new beginning.

Then a flash of brown hair startled her. *Whitaker*, she thought, and a wave of desire made her stomach flip. But it turned out to be Marco returning from the cubby area with a towel around his waist.

Georgina gently extracted herself from Nathan's arms. "I'm going to say hi to Quincy," she said. "I'll be right back." She swam across the tub. "Hey, Quincy," she whispered. "Where's Whitaker?"

Quincy kept his eyes closed as Alina rubbed his shoulders. "He's not coming anymore," he said. "He's decided to move on."

"To another group?" Georgina asked.

"No," Quincy said. "He's done."

Despite floating in hundred-degree water, her blood felt icy. "What? Why?"

He opened one eye and peered at her. "You tell me."

"But I don't know."

Quincy contemplated her face, and she sensed he knew more than he was letting on. "It's not giving him the satisfaction it used to. I think he wants more."

"Oh." The libido she'd had a minute ago was instantly gone. She was only embarrassed and hot and empty. "He didn't tell me."

"He didn't give me the details," Quincy said. "But I know he felt it was the right choice."

She moved away, feeling Nathan's eyes on her. She should go to him, kiss him, make love to him in the hot tub like she'd planned, but she couldn't. The water made her weightless, bobbing uselessly through her own life. As fast as her limbs would allow, she pushed through the water and climbed out of the tub. The air on her bare skin was freezing by comparison, and she shivered, so exposed. From a stack in a bin by the curtain, she grabbed a towel and wrapped it around her body. Her clothes stuck to her wet skin as she yanked them on. Ignoring Nathan calling her name from the tub, she ran out.

Chapter 23

The next morning, Georgina pretended to sleep until Nathan went to the gym around nine. When he'd found her fully dressed by the entrance to the Velvet Mouse the night before, she'd lied and told him she was ill and needed to go home.

"You can stay," she'd said. "I promise. It's fine." The truth was, she'd wanted to be alone.

"No," he'd said. "Of course I'm coming home with you. I'm only here to be with you."

Then she really had felt sick.

To keep up appearances, she forced a few coughs while she lay in bed as Nathan rummaged around in the closet for his gym clothes and brushed his teeth. On his way out the door, he kissed her forehead and whispered, "Feel better." As soon as he'd gone, she called Norah and begged to have breakfast.

"I have the kids," Norah said.

"Bring the kids," Georgina said. "Please?"

"Let me see if Ari can drive Rachel to soccer. Hold on." A whispered discussion occurred out of earshot, and Norah returned. "All right, where?"

An hour later, Norah appeared at Alice's Tea Cup on Sixty-Fourth and Lexington with her two youngest children bundled into matching blue puffers and knit hats resembling a frog and a kitten.

Georgina waved. "Don't you two look adorable!"

Norah sliced her hand across her neck. "Simon does not want to be called *adorable*," she whispered. "We are only allowed to say he looks *handsome*."

"Got it," Georgina said. "Simon, you look extremely handsome in your frog hat, and Hannah, you look as cute as a kitten."

"No," Norah whispered. "You're not supposed to tell little girls they look cute! Tell her she looks smart."

"Right, sorry," Georgina said. "Hannah, you look extremely intellectual in your kitten hat. Can we go inside now? I'm starving."

Norah gave her a level glare. "Don't say you are starving when there are actual—"

"Please don't finish that sentence. I'm having a sh—" Georgina glanced at the frog and kitten and smiled. "*Bad* day."

Norah folded her stroller and left it by the café door with several others before shooing the kids inside. "Hurry up. Auntie Georgina is hangry."

The miniature, whimsical space in the bottom floor of a brownstone smelled like orange, cinnamon, and chocolate scones. They maneuvered around the to-go line toward a rear table underneath a window facing a small, wet alley. "There," Norah said, and collapsed into a chair. Finding a place to sit in New York City was a personal achievement worth celebrating. She pulled Hannah onto her lap and handed her the small plastic menu to play with. In his chair, Simon had already turned on his video game.

"So what's this about?" Norah asked.

"Can't a girl just miss her friend?"

"Sure, but you look all jittery and weird."

A woman in cat-eye glasses stopped by, and Georgina ordered a cinnamon scone and black tea.

"Simon, do you want a croissant?" Norah asked.

He looked up. "Does it have bacon in it?"

"No, sweetie. It's a pastry."

Simon turned back to his game, which apparently meant yes, he would like a croissant, thank you very much, because Norah ordered him one. "I'll have the blackberry scone and a latte. Do you have anything gluten- and dairy-free?"

"No," the woman said, and left.

"We missed you last night," Georgina said.

Norah opened a small Tupperware of blueberries. "I doubt that."

"Are you quitting?" Georgina asked.

"I wanted Ari and me to move past our issues, and now we have, so we don't need it."

"But what about you?"

Norah glanced up from the coloring book she was opening for Hannah. "What about me?"

"I thought you were doing it to stop acting like a left foot," Georgina said, "and start acting like a bad*a-s-s*."

Simon frowned, his small brow furrowing.

"He can spell pretty well, you know," Norah said. "And that wasn't my reason. That was your reason."

They were interrupted by the woman delivering their drinks, and Norah busied herself stirring sugar into her latte, punching straws into juice boxes for the kids, and looking everywhere but at Georgina.

"I'm not one to talk, I guess," Georgina said, and blew the steam from her tea. "I'm quitting, too."

That caught Norah's attention. "No way," she said. "I thought—what changed?"

"Nathan and I need to focus on each other. I thought the lifestyle would help, but it's become . . . a distraction." Georgina took a deep breath and stared at a puddle in the alley. "Maybe I was wrong about counseling. Nathan and I need to get to know the real versions of each other."

"I didn't come prepared for this level of crisis," Norah said. "I thought you wanted to tell me about some crazy role-play that happened last night."

"I ended up fleeing," Georgina confessed. "It was humiliating. I can never show my face there again."

"Yikes. Do you want a coloring book?" Norah asked. "I heard they're therapeutic or something."

Georgina laughed. "Sure. I'll take what I can get."

Norah tore off a page with the Little Mermaid on it and handed it over with a red crayon. She was right; it was nice. Georgina colored in the mermaid's hair.

"Does this have to do with you-know-who?" Norah asked, coloring the Genie from *Aladdin* with a blue crayon until Hannah started pulling paper napkins from their holder and flinging them on the ground. "People use these, Hannah," she said with calm authority. "They are not toys." Hannah started wailing, and Norah dipped one hand in her diaper bag for a stuffed koala while the other collected napkins from the floor. When her kids were around, Norah's hands were in constant motion—patting, wiping, zipping, playing. It seemed to require no effort on her part, like Olympic gymnasts doing flips on TV. Georgina had never given her proper credit for that. She desperately wanted Norah to become a lawyer, but her current job looked much harder.

Their scones arrived, fresh from the oven. Georgina took a huge bite and relished the simple comfort of the buttery warmth.

"Did something happen?" Norah asked.

Georgina pointed at her mouth, chewing as slowly as possible.

"Don't think you're getting out of this one," Norah said. "I can tell you're hiding something."

She swallowed the buttery pastry with a mouthful of tea and peered up at Norah. "We had lunch."

Norah raised her eyebrows. "That's it?"

Georgina took another huge bite of her scone.

"I'll guess," Norah said, "and you can shake your head yes or no."

Georgina nodded.

"Did you sleep together?"

She shook her head.

"Did you kiss?"

She nodded again.

"More than once?"

She tilted her head side to side to say, *Sort of yes, sort of no.* Did making out on the roof count as more than one kiss if it lasted for some indefinite period because she'd lost all sense of time and space when his lips were on hers?

"Are you in love with him?" Norah asked.

Georgina looked down at the table.

"Are you in love with Nathan?"

"How could I not be in love with Nathan? He's my husband."

"Crazier things have happened," Norah said, and reached across the table to squeeze Georgina's hand. "You've been through a lot. There isn't one right way to feel about this."

"Are you in love with Ari?" Georgina asked.

"Yes," Norah said with no hesitation. "Is that so hard to believe?"

"No," Georgina said. "I get it now. Honestly."

Norah rocked Hannah, stroking her hair. "He makes me feel like he did when we were twenty-three. That's why it's been so hard. It can hurt to love this much."

Georgina sipped her tea and said nothing. Did that explain the sickening ache in her chest she'd been having since lunch with Whitaker?

Simon tugged on Norah's sleeve, whining and squirming. "I have to poop," he said.

"Can you handle her by yourself?" Norah asked, and passed over Hannah without waiting for an answer. She helped Simon to his feet and gently pushed his shoulders toward the bathroom.

When they were gone, Georgina glanced down at the child in her lap. The top of Hannah's head fit right below her chin, and she could feel curly baby hair touching her neck. It was so soft it felt luxurious, like cuddling a rabbit. She dared to bend her head a fraction and take a whiff. Yes, it definitely smelled like baby head. That was a real thing.

Terrified Hannah would start screaming and she wouldn't know what to do, Georgina sat monument-like, hoping Hannah would keep dozing and never notice her mother was gone. But instead she tilted her head back and looked right into Georgina's eyes with her big, brown, curious orbs. Her face broke into a gigantic smile, and Georgina smiled back. For a moment, she pretended she was Hannah's mother and Nathan Hannah's father, just to see how it would feel, and she didn't hate the idea but wondered whether "not hating the idea" was how one should approach having a child. It would require some mental readjustment, she told herself. Nathan had sprung this on her, but he was right. Georgina had been wrong about the lifestyle—it hadn't magically cured their marriage. Wasn't it Nathan's turn to make a suggestion and her turn to play along?

Norah was back. "Simon clogged the toilet," she whispered. "How about a walk?"

They quickly donned their coats and scarves and absconded like bandits, leaving behind a generous tip in repentance.

―――――

In Central Park, they meandered the winding paths until they stumbled on a tucked-away gazebo with a bench overlooking a small playground, to which Simon and Hannah sprinted. There were endless secret spots in the park, even for a lifelong New Yorker like Georgina.

"So what are you going to do?" Norah asked.

"What is there to do besides move forward?"

"Move backward. Move sideways. Move to Japan," Norah said. "Just kidding. Please don't move to Japan. I'd really miss you."

Georgina shook her head. "No. Japan is not the answer. There is no 'answer,' is there?"

Norah blew out a raspberry. "I wish there were. Although the lifestyle gave me exactly what I wanted, I have to admit. SIMON! Don't you dare jump off that!"

Fifteen feet away, Simon slid down the slide instead of launching himself from the top of the ladder.

"Why do you think it worked so well for you and Ari?" Georgina asked.

"It's like that expression," Norah said, " 'You don't know what you got till it's gone.' "

Georgina thought for a second. "Isn't that a Joni Mitchell song?"

Norah scrunched up her nose, then laughed. "Oh yeah, the parking lot song." Soon, they were belting out the words—*Don't it always seem to go that you don't know what you've got till it's gone, they paved paradise and put up a parking lot*—and Simon stared at them, horrified, from the playground.

"He's only five years old," Norah said, "and I swear he's going to demand to ride the subway alone soon. He's worse than Rachel."

"How is it like Joni Mitchell, exactly?" Georgina asked.

"Because Ari took his life for granted," Norah said. "Hearing about me and Felix made him realize he could lose me." She looked over at Georgina and shrugged. "It changed the dynamic, just like you said. I hate when you're right."

"But . . . that sounds like Ari is jealous," Georgina said.

"So? Jealous people work harder to protect what's theirs."

"Making Ari jealous was not the point," Georgina said. "I wanted you to feel strong and independent and powerful so Ari wouldn't keep seeing you—"

"As the left foot," Norah interrupted. "You've made that clear. Anyway, I do feel powerful, because I manipulated him."

"By having sex with Felix?"

"By pretending to have sex with Felix."

Georgina watched Hannah scoot down a two-foot slide as Norah's words sank in. "Wait. What? You're faking it?"

"I *was* faking it," Norah said. "We're done now, and it worked, so what does it matter?"

"Because . . . because—" It mattered *so* much that Georgina couldn't find the right words to articulate how much. "Because you have less power now than ever! You let your husband sleep with other women!"

"I did it to keep my family together," Norah said. "How is that different from what you did?"

"Because I *participated*."

Norah began to repack her diaper bag like she had somewhere urgent to be. She snatched a package of wet wipes from the ground and shoved them inside. "KIDS!" she yelled. "We're leaving!"

"So that means Felix was faking, too?"

"All I know is he wasn't having sex with me," Norah said, wrapping her scarf around her neck.

Georgina remembered the plug-in sex toy. "But if you were faking it, why was I hearing about you and Felix watching porn together?"

"You said to tell Ari about what I did at the parties and make it hurt," Norah said. "Guess what? That hurt."

Simon pumped his legs for a few more seconds on the swing set before sailing through the air and landing on all fours in the wood chips. As Georgina watched Norah maneuver her children into their coats and hats, she was crushed. She'd thought the lifestyle had emboldened Norah to demand better from Ari, go back to school, and embrace her suppressed naughty side with Felix, and that it had all been thanks to her.

"I don't understand how you could let Ari participate while you sat out," Georgina said. "That made you weaker than ever!"

"Stop!" Norah dropped her diaper bag with a thud. "I am not weak."

"But you wanted Ari to stop treating you like a left foot—"

"That was you," Norah said. "You're the one who keeps saying I'm a left foot, and to be honest, that has hurt me more than anything Ari's ever said."

Hannah and Simon had picked up on the sharp notes in Norah's voice and gazed up at her with round eyes. It was probably the first time they'd ever heard her use her scary mom voice on someone other than themselves.

"I'm not Ari's left foot," Norah said. "I'm his wife. And you don't know anything about our marriage."

"I wanted you to have more."

"More than what?" She gestured at her kids. "I have everything."

"That's not what I meant," Georgina said.

"I think it is," Norah said, and knelt down to help Hannah with her mittens. "It's obvious you think my choices are pathetic, that I'm not fighting against the man enough or something. But what you want doesn't matter as much as what I want. It's my life."

"You're right," Georgina said. "I did think that. I wanted you to leave Ari."

"Trust me," Norah said wryly, "I knew what you were up to. You're not as sly as you think you are. Let me give you some advice for once: fixing everyone else's problems isn't going to help you hide from your own."

Georgina sat on the bench, staring at her hands and feeling the cold air settle into her bones. "I spied on Ari's computer."

Norah froze in the middle of opening a ziplock bag full of presliced apples. "Please tell me you're kidding."

"I'm not. It was in the Berkshires."

Norah sat back down on the bench and pressed her fingers to her temples, bracing herself. "How bad was it?"

"Not at all. He'd googled 'how to be a great dad.' I felt like complete shit about myself. I still do."

When Norah looked up, she had tears in her eyes. "Now do you get it?"

If Georgina could have made a list of everything Norah had given her and everything she'd given Norah in return, it would have been Norah, one million and counting, Georgina, zero. "I'm so sorry I got you into this mess," she said.

"Don't flatter yourself too much. I make my own choices, whether you like them or not. You think I've been watching TV at the parties? Felix has been helping me study for the LSAT."

Georgina covered her face, half groaning, half laughing. "Perfect. So my life is the only mess."

"Hate to break it to you," Norah said. "But you've always been a mess. You've just been excellent at hiding it. But now you don't have to. It's very freeing. Watch this." She cupped her hands around her mouth and screamed, "I'M A MESS!" into the surrounding trees and boulders. "I FORGOT TO BRUSH MY TEETH THIS MORNING!"

"That's gross, Mama," Simon said, and Georgina laughed.

Norah turned, bright-eyed and grinning. "You try."

"I don't know," Georgina said. "People can hear!"

"Who cares?" she said. "Simon, you go."

Simon didn't need telling twice. He ran to the gazebo's edge and screamed, "I AM A BACON MONSTER!" at the top of his lungs.

"*Go*," Norah insisted, shoving Georgina's shoulder.

She walked to the railing and leaned out. Her hair whipped in a sudden uptick of wind. "I'M A MESS!" she screamed to the world. "I'M WEARING YESTERDAY'S UNDERWEAR INSIDE OUT!"

To her amazement, an unseen man yelled back, "I JUST PEED IN THE PARK!"

Norah jumped off the bench. "Okay, kids. Time to go!"

Norah had planned to meet Felix for LSAT prep and lunch at the South Street Seaport, a gathering of cobblestone streets bordering the East River with sidewalk cafés and a staggering view of the Brooklyn Bridge's underbelly, and Georgina decided to tag along.

"Are you sure I'm not crashing?" she asked.

Hannah belted out one long note to hear her voice vibrating as her stroller bounced around on the rough cobblestones, and Norah unwrapped a lollipop to shush her. "Crashing what?"

"Your lunch date with Felix."

"It's not a date."

"A date is a romantic arrangement!" Simon chimed in.

Georgina raised an eyebrow and asked, "How does he know that?"

"Ari's been planning dates," Norah said casually, but her smile betrayed her.

"Like what?"

"We watched the game at a Mets bar in Queens—his idea,

obviously—but now he's coming with me to the Jagged Little Pill Twenty-Fifth Anniversary Tour, and I'm buying front-row seats. He doesn't know that part yet."

"Married couples are allowed to have secrets," Georgina said. "Simon, what's your idea of a romantic date?"

His little face turned comically serious. "Jelly beans," he said, counting each demand on his fingers, "a swimming pool, an airplane that goes to space, my teacher, and fifty hundred dogs."

They were twenty minutes late to Front Street, and still they beat Felix. That was so unlike him Georgina nearly called 911, sure that he was splattered across Houston. Norah parked Hannah's stroller away from the flow of pedestrians. "I'll call him," she said. But as she dug for her phone in her massive diaper bag, Georgina saw Felix striding toward them—wearing a black suit, white shirt, and black tie—on a Sunday, and Felix didn't go to church.

"Oh no," Norah whispered. "Funeral?"

"Please don't let it be his own," Georgina said. "You don't think he's gone back to the firm, do you?"

There was no time for her to answer because Felix was two steps away, waving at Simon. Georgina and Norah exchanged a look in which they must have agreed not to press the issue because neither commented on Felix's unusual dress.

They picked a warm pub with a view of the East River. Felix colored on the paper place mat with Simon while Norah took Hannah to the bathroom and Georgina surreptitiously peered at Felix to figure out what he was up to.

When Norah was back, they ordered burgers and a basket of sweet potato fries to share. Eventually, Felix leaned back against the black vinyl booth and gestured at himself with a playful smirk. "Aren't you going to ask about the suit?"

Norah and Georgina exchanged a glance.

"We weren't sure we wanted to know the answer," Georgina said. "Does this mean you've gone back to the firm?"

"I had an interview," Felix said. "Can't stay unemployed forever, can I?"

Somehow Felix going back to the firm, where he'd been miserable and anxious and aging prematurely, felt like her fault, too. If Alina hadn't rejoined the lifestyle because of Georgina, then Felix wouldn't have felt so rejected by her. He'd never have left the club in search of his identity and, when he couldn't find it, returned to the one place he knew. Had she given her friends *anything* worthwhile?

"I may not get the job, though," Felix said. "Funemployment might continue against my will."

"Of course you'll get the job," Georgina said. "They already know you'll bill yourself sick for them. Why wouldn't they hire you back?"

Felix lifted his tie. "You think this is for the firm?"

"You're not wearing that suit to have lunch with us, are you?" Georgina asked.

He smiled with a glint in his eye. "I'm not going back to the firm. I had a job interview for a teaching position at Fordham."

Norah dropped the last quarter of her burger and clapped. "This is the best news ever!"

"It's all thanks to you," he said. "Helping you with the LSAT was the most fun I've had as a lawyer, ever. It made me realize teaching is what I really want."

Norah embraced him and said, "You're going to get so many chili peppers on RateMyProfessors.com."

"They don't do that anymore," he said. "I'll have to save my sexy shirts for the dating game."

They spent the rest of lunch reminiscing about law school and forcing Felix to grill them with the Socratic method to see what they remembered about property and con law, which, it turned out, was almost nothing. Then Georgina took the kids to the water's edge and strolled up and down while Felix and Norah practiced LSAT games. As she rode the subway home a few hours later, she realized why she hadn't been able to stop grinding her teeth since Felix's news. She was jealous. He'd had the courage to examine what he wanted and go after it, which was a lot harder than she was willing to admit.

Chapter 24

Georgina and Nathan were eating take-out sushi at their dining room table and typing on their laptops when Nathan said, "Friday is our anniversary."

"Yes," Georgina said, "I'm aware."

"I'd like to plan a date, if that's all right with you."

"You know how I feel about surprises," she said, still typing, not looking at him. She was finishing an email she was desperate to get out.

"I promise I won't take you trapezing or anything," Nathan said. "Just somewhere nice."

She hit Send as a huge yawn possessed her. "Okay. Sure. Thank you. Are we doing gifts?"

"You certainly don't need to get me one, but I think I owe you a gift or two, yes."

"Gifts it is," she said, and powered down her computer.

"I'm glad we're doing this," Nathan said. "There's something I've been meaning to talk to you about."

She paused in the restacking of her work papers. "What is it?"

"Nothing bad," he said. "It's good news, I hope."

She let the papers fall from her hands. "Come on, you can't do that."

Nathan closed his laptop. "Now is not the right time to talk about it. Don't worry, though. I shouldn't have brought it up."

"No, you shouldn't have," she said. "This is downright cruel."

They went to bed according to their usual routine.

For the next two days, Georgina obsessed about what Nathan might say. If he categorized it as "good news," she figured it couldn't be related to Meredith. Maybe it had to do with moving on from the lifestyle. Since she'd faked sick at the last party, they hadn't broached the subject of returning, and for that, she was grateful. She couldn't think about the lifestyle without thinking of Whitaker. Most likely, though, Nathan's "good news" had to do with work. "Good news" and Nathan usually related to a new client, a raise, or a business opportunity. So by Friday at five, she had it all but written in stone that Nathan was being headhunted by another law firm that was going to pay him more and give him more freedom, and he wanted her opinion on whether he should take it. Whatever the firm was, Meredith wouldn't work there, so her answer would be an emphatic yes.

On Friday evening at five, she put on her coat and dialed Nathan's extension. She hadn't gotten him the promised gift, and their mystery date was starting at seven.

"I have to run out for an errand," she said. "Where should I meet you?"

"I don't want to ruin the surprise," he said. "I'll text you the address."

She rode the S to Grand Central and the 4 to Fifty-Ninth Street to wander Bloomingdale's until she found a suitable present. Nathan was being so protective over his surprise. It must have been significant. *Hamilton* tickets? A harbor cruise? Maybe they were taking a car to the Hamptons and staying at a nice hotel with a vineyard.

Riding the escalator down to the men's floor, she thrilled at the possibilities. She needed a distraction, a fun and frivolous evening to take her mind off Whitaker. And it was her wedding anniversary, after all. Quality time with Nathan wasn't prophylactic at this point—it was a lifesaving intervention.

She found a wool overcoat that would match Nathan's gray suits and had it gift wrapped while she perused. In the lingerie section, she held red lace and black ribbons up to her body in the mirror. But anniversary or no anniversary, she couldn't picture herself wearing any of it with Nathan.

When she left the store with the gift-wrapped coat in Bloomingdale's famous brown sack, it was dark and she could see her breath in the cold. She called Nathan.

"I'm finished with my errand," she said. "Can I have the address?"

"All right," he groaned. "Fine. I'll ruin the surprise if you insist."

Man, she thought, *must be good*. She wondered whether her gift was sufficient. Should she have gotten more creative? Spent a little more money?

He gave her an address and said, "Type it into your phone, and you'll see what it is. I'm leaving now, so I'll be there in twenty."

She hung up and did as she was told, a slight flutter in her hands and extra beat in her heart. He was right, this was fun.

Then she saw it was a restaurant.

"Why am I not surprised?" she grumbled. But she had no right to be disappointed, did she? A man who planned dates at nice restaurants was exactly what she'd been looking for when she'd found Nathan. She hadn't wanted the man who was risk-taking and wild. She hadn't wanted the man who spontaneously planned twenty-five things to do in the snow that were more fun than errands. No, she hadn't wanted that man.

The place was called Niri, and it was a Japanese restaurant. She'd never been there, but several of her colleagues had told her to take a client so the firm would pay because it was so expensive, so when she arrived, she wasn't surprised that it was overly formal and full of men in suits. The environment settled on her with inevitable resignation. *This is the rest of my life*, she thought, and craved matzo ball soup.

Nathan arrived shortly after she was seated, wearing a gray suit and light blue tie, with his hair combed in the usual way. He resembled every other man in the room. "I'm psyched about this," he said. "What do you think? Good surprise?"

"Very," Georgina said. "Everyone raves about it."

"I know," he said. "I thought it was perfect."

"Here." She set her package on the table. "This is for you. Open it."

He used his butter knife to slice the tape, then unfolded the coat. "Impeccable taste," he said, "as always. Now open yours."

He handed her a package wrapped so pristinely it was obvious he'd asked Danielle to do it. Inside was a hand-knitted wool blanket in a pink rose color. It was beautiful and luxuriously soft. She touched it to her cheek. "This is amazing," she said.

"My mother made it for you."

"Wow, it's lovely," she said. "I'll call her tomorrow to say thank you."

Nathan's mother had never completely warmed to Georgina because she'd expected Nathan to move back to Kansas eventually, and Georgina was a New Yorker through and through, with no intention of ever leaving. But it wasn't fair because Nathan's ambition included becoming a partner at a Manhattan law firm. He'd told Georgina from day one that he wanted to stay in New York. But he'd never set his mother straight, so Georgina had accepted it. It was probably easier for her to take the blame. This blanket, though, meant something had changed.

What, she wasn't sure.

"We should do the prix fixe with wine pairing," Nathan said. "This is a special occasion."

"That makes it easy," she said, and closed her menu. "I'm not in the mood to make decisions tonight anyway."

Nathan frowned.

"What?"

"Nothing." He picked up his water glass and drank it in a few gulps. "Do they have waiters here or what?"

Georgina glanced around. A busy staff bustled by. "We've only been sitting here a few minutes."

"Well, I'm starving."

She thought of Norah's parenting warnings and smiled. If they were going to have a baby, she should start practicing. "You mean you're hungry," she said, but Nathan was occupied stopping a young man in a black vest carrying a water jug to ask for their server.

They sat without speaking, waiting for someone to come. Georgina examined the décor. A square stone fountain, ferns on glossy black podiums. The walls were papered with an iridescent floral pattern. It was elegant and manicured, but all she could see was the absence of personality. No string lights, pumpkins, spiderwebs, or bowl of gelt, for example.

They ordered from an older man with a bald head. She thought Nathan might tell him they were celebrating their anniversary so they'd get a candle in their dessert, but he either forgot or didn't want to. That would have been embarrassing in a place like this anyway, she supposed. The old her wouldn't have wanted it.

The first course arrived—three small squares of beef on toothpicks with a sweet-and-savory dipping sauce. It was, as promised, extraordinarily flavorful, but she was left with an unexplainable emptiness after she ate it. It satisfied nothing while creating a need for more. She drank her wine more quickly than she'd intended, and her leg bounced uncontrollably up and down. Every time she made a conscious effort to stop it, the other one started.

"What did you want to talk to me about?" she asked. "Was it counseling? Because I've been thinking we should give it a shot."

"Sure," Nathan said. "I suggested counseling a long time ago. But you weren't interested."

"I wasn't. But I changed my mind. I'm sure whoever Norah and Ari see could recommend somebody. It would be weird if we saw the same one, right?"

"Actually—"

But Nathan was interrupted by the second course, a miso soup wafting salty steam between them like gray fog. Georgina glanced around, a little embarrassed, as Nathan slurped it audibly. Immediately, he complained it made him thirsty and waved down the young man with the jug.

"So that was it?" she asked. "Counseling?"

"What?"

"The good news," she said.

"No. What? No. How is counseling good news?"

Georgina sighed and leaned her head in her hand. Finishing this meal was beginning to seem as physically exhausting as walking up a flight of stairs with a refrigerator strapped to her back. "I don't know, Nathan. You tell me."

He reached across the table for her free hand and stroked it lightly with his thumb. "I've been doing a lot of soul-searching these last six weeks, trying to figure out how we ended up here. And the answer is . . . I'm miserable."

She sat up straighter. "Excuse me?"

The bald man returned to collect their bowls and deposit new chopsticks and spoons. She and Nathan sat silently while a young woman delivered their third course, a cucumber salad. They were stuck in a bad comedy act, it seemed. Every time they were getting somewhere, they were interrupted. When the woman had gone, Nathan reached for Georgina's hand and said, "It's this job, this city, this person I've tried to become. None of it is making me happy. I feel completely . . . lost. I was searching for something with Meredith, with the lifestyle . . . but I'll never find it here. I need to get out."

"To where?"

He took a deep breath. "To Kansas."

"You're moving to Kansas," she repeated.

"*We're* moving to Kansas," Nathan said. "I hope."

"But . . . why?"

"I need to go home. If I take away all these distractions, I can focus on what's missing and what's important in life. I can get one of those lawn mowers you can drive."

"None of this makes sense." She was shaking her head; she couldn't stop. "You're quitting your job?"

He pushed a cucumber around with his chopstick. "I already did."

"How could you not talk to me about this?"

"I wanted to show you how serious I was about making a change in our life."

Georgina caressed the blanket in her lap, which now made perfect sense. Nathan had already told his mother they were coming home and probably having a baby, too. "Nathan, listen to yourself. You're saying this city doesn't make *you* happy. You're saying *you're* missing something. But I love this city. My best friends are here, my dad, my whole life. I don't want to leave."

He looked at her in disbelief. "You're the one who said you'd never give up on our marriage."

"And you're the one who said you'd do anything to fix what you'd done."

"And I meant that," Nathan said. "This is anything."

The server returned with the fourth course, and this time, she was grateful for the interruption. It was the main dish, a strip of sea bass with a jalapeño chutney. She watched Nathan scrape the chutney off the fish because he didn't like spicy food. That was one of the thousands of things she knew about him after twelve years together. All those traits she'd tabulated to decide they were the right match for each other, none of which mattered in the end. The only thing that mattered was whether she loved him so much she would do anything for him, the way that Norah would do anything for Ari and vice versa. But she would not move to Kansas for him, and the thought of him going without her didn't hurt the way it should. In retrospect, his affair hadn't hurt the way it should have either. It had felt like an insult rather than a heartbreak.

It struck her that there was another time in her life she was unwilling to sacrifice her own plans, but in contrast to the apathy she felt now at the idea of Nathan's departure, she'd spent years staring out the window of her law school dorm, wondering what the weather was in Peru. She wasn't going to make that mistake again. It turned out there was someone in her life she'd move to Kansas for.

It just wasn't her husband.

"No."

Nathan looked up from his plate. "No, what?"

"No, I will not move to Kansas with you. We should get divorced." She stood up so fast her chair fell backward. "If you'll excuse me, there's somewhere I need to be."

Chapter 25

Georgina was already in the back seat of a taxi by the time she realized she had no idea where Whitaker lived.

"Where am I going, lady?" the driver asked.

"Downtown?" Whitaker didn't seem like an uptown sort of person. "Maybe Brooklyn. Just head that way."

The man grumbled as he pulled away from the curb and drove south on Second Avenue. She scrolled through her calls until she found the 646 number Whitaker had called her from that Sunday in the Berkshires. Over the last few weeks, she'd opened her call log at every quiet moment and stared at that number, willing it to ring. But it was never going to—she was the married one, she had to make it ring. Her hand shook as she pressed Send.

Whitaker didn't answer.

"Seriously, lady. I need to know where we're going," the driver said.

"I don't know!" she snapped. For the first time in her life, she had no idea where she was going. "Please hold on."

She dialed again, trying not to panic. So soon after abandoning her life, she was lost.

Then, on her third try, Whitaker answered, and she nearly cried with relief.

"Sorry," he said. "I was in the shower. You okay?"

But she couldn't answer, her mind occupied with visions of Whitaker's bare chest slick with hot water.

"Hello?"

"I'm coming over," she blurted. "Where do you live?"

He paused, then made a sound somewhere between a groan and a sigh. "Georgina, of course I want you to come over, but—"

"No," she interrupted. "You don't understand. I left Nathan. Literally, at a restaurant, I left him there. We're not together anymore."

"153 Mott Street," he said. "7A."

"See you soon," she said, and hung up. After typing the address into Google Maps, she told the driver she was going to Mott between Grand and Broome. He grunted his acknowledgment. She sank into the vinyl cushion, deliriously high on her escape, as if she'd busted out of jail, hightailing it away from the police. As her taxi weaved through traffic downtown, she couldn't sit still. She rolled down the window, rolled up the window, sat on the right side, then scooted to the left. After what felt like a hundred years, her taxi braked in front of a seven-story gray building with an Italian restaurant on the street level, and she threw cash into the front seat like people did in the movies and leaped out.

"7A," she chanted aloud, "7A." She couldn't get there fast enough. Thirteen years had passed, but one second more might kill her. She pressed the button for his apartment again and again until the click, followed by static, and then a long, ear-grinding buzz. She threw her body into both doors and ran up the emergency stairs to the seventh floor, too pumped with adrenaline to wait for the elevator.

When she made it to the top, he stood in the hall wearing a white T-shirt and gray sweatpants, his hair damp from the shower. "I heard you pounding up the stairs. What's the rush?"

"This," she said, and flung her arms around his neck and pulled his mouth to hers, tasting toothpaste and warmth. His hands ran through her hair and tugged, tipping her head back to expose her neck, and when he grazed it with his lips, she breathed a sound of such blissful pleasure that he laughed against her skin and said, "Let's go inside. I have neighbors."

He took her hand and pulled her into a small vestibule. The door clicked behind them, their aloneness pressurized by the weight of what she wanted to happen next, but he did not kiss her again. She hung up her coat and peered at a plant, at a bronze floor lamp, the interruption having allowed her nerves to catch up. "This is nice," she said.

"You'll be pleased to learn I no longer use an upside-down bucket for a nightstand," he said.

"But you still sleep on an air mattress, right?" she teased.

They smiled at each other. He took one step forward, and so did she. There was urgency, but also time. Finally, time. She lifted one hand gently to his chest and relished the pound of his heart.

"I love you," he said. "You know that, right?"

The words were relief in her gut, lightning to her pulse, desire between her legs. "I love you, too," she said. "No one has ever compared, for the record."

His eyes were darker, hungrier than she'd seen them before. No amusement there, only fire. The air was heady with restrained longing. Then, his fingers were on her waist, under the hem of her sweater, sliding it over her head, and they were kissing again, her back against the wall, her fists knotted in his shirt, hooked in his waistband. His skin emitted heat, as if sunburned. He said it again, *I love you*, whispered against her collarbone. Again, trailing his kiss between her breasts. Again, with his open mouth against her stomach. Again, lifting her skirt, running his nose along her hip, her thigh. Her fingers twisted in his hair when he met her on his knees, and she pulled, too hard, but she couldn't help it. The contact was a full-body shock, wet to wet, heat to heat. Pleasure replaced awareness, replaced courtesies, replaced self-control.

He worked his way standing, his hands on her waist, hard against the place where she ached with a deep throb. In a swift movement, he gripped the backs of her thighs and lifted, wrapped her legs around him, and held her hips to hips. They did not stop kissing as he carried her deeper into the apartment. They stumbled into the wall, knocked over a pile of books.

She broke away. "How long is this hallway? Are you carrying me across town?"

He laughed and kicked open the door to a dark bedroom. A black-and-white photograph hung over the bed. His teeth scraped her earlobe and her eyes fluttered closed.

He set her on the mattress. When she didn't feel his touch anymore, she opened her eyes and found him kneeling between her legs. The lights were off, but the glow of the city filtered through the windows and cast them in a faint white light, almost celestial. He unzipped her boots with a painstaking slowness that made her want to shove him out of the way and kick them soaring into the wall. He set them upright on the floor like the feet of an invisible woman.

"Are you trying to torture me?" she asked. "Or have you become a neat freak in your old age?"

"I've been waiting thirteen years for this," he said. "Let me enjoy it a little."

His hands skimmed up her calves, over her knees, along her thighs. Heat followed each press of his lips against exposed skin. His fingers eased open the zipper of her skirt, guided it over her hips, onto the floor. The warmth between her legs was unbearable. She pulled him onto the bed, onto her, hands shaking as she lifted his shirt, tugged at his pants, less elegant and more desperate.

He drew back, smiling. "Patience is a virtue."

"If you've taught me anything, Mr. Mentor, it's that the rules were made to be broken."

His chest was as muscular and smooth as she'd remembered. The only difference to mark the passage of time were the few gray strands in the light pattern of hair as she ran her fingers through it, as she bent to kiss the hollow at the base of his neck. She paused before taking him in. Her eyes roved his face—his jaw, his lips, the sweat on his brow. If there was ever a moment to doubt her choices, her decision to abandon a husband with clear intentions, it was now, before she remembered what it was like to have him inside of her, their bodies intertwining and moving together.

She pulled his mouth to hers.

Her back arched at his first press, her pleasure a shuddering, blinding heat. The headboard slammed dangerously against the wall, but there was no slowing down. She drew him deeper, he pressed in harder, faster, carrying her toward the tumbling pleasure of truly letting go. His was a deep and rolling thrust. Hers, a rising temperature, a tightening around him, a rushing release. He grabbed her hand, intertwining his fingers with hers, raised their joined fists above her head, and followed with his face buried in her neck, his breath on her throat. A kiss beneath her jaw. Her body exhaled. He did not move. She could have held him like that forever.

When their bodies were spent, they lay beside each other on the bare mattress, the bedding having fallen to the floor. Her hand rested on his stomach, his draped across her leg, their chests wrung out and panting. The city was alive below; they were alive inside. Breathless, but alive.

She laughed out loud, thinking that she'd never need anything else until the day she died, not food, not water, not clothes. She would never leave his bed. She knew it, Whitaker knew it, everybody at the Italian restaurant downstairs knew it.

"You were killing me with all that teasing," she said. "I almost got out my vibrator."

"You brought your vibrator?"

"One of them. It's travel-size. For emergencies."

He laughed and lifted her hand to kiss it. "You should have told me. I could have had fun with that."

"There's always next time," she said.

"How many do you have? It's only fair if we test them all."

She rolled onto her side to face him. "I went shopping after I learned about Quincy's treasure chest, and I bought four."

Whitaker touched one finger beneath her jaw and trailed it languidly down her neck, over her breast, and along her stomach as he said, "What do they do? I need to know the competition."

She pressed her body along the length of his and traced his ribs with her fingertips. "They're pretty scientific. I'm not sure you can beat them. I swear one has a G-spot radar."

"Let's find out," he said, his mouth against her ear, and slipped his fingers where she was still slick. "Like this?"

She closed her eyes and nodded, bending her knees to let him in, refusing to admit there was no competition in case Whitaker thrived in a challenge.

At some point later, Georgina confessed that she'd never eaten dinner. He grabbed his pants and pulled them on so fast she hadn't yet lifted her head from the pillow. Her body was so pleasurably exhausted from the last several hours that she wasn't sure she could.

"I am more than a booty call," he said. "Get dressed. We're going on a date."

"It's eleven o'clock at night," she whined. "Can't you just make eggs or something?"

"Nope. I insist."

Her vision went dark as her skirt landed on her face. "Is anything good open?"

"This is New York City," he said. "I know the perfect place."

Reluctantly, she dressed her loose limbs and scooped her tangled hair into a bun. Had she and Nathan ever ventured out at eleven o'clock at night for food—and they had not—she probably would have put on makeup and fretted about her outfit, despite knowing that everyone eating at 11:00 p.m. would be too drunk to care what she looked like. She marveled at the fact that nothing compelled her to do that now. She wanted to be her most authentic, messiest self for the man who'd always given that to her in return. After she pulled on her mismatched socks, she held up her feet and twirled her toes. "Remember these?" she asked.

"The first time I saw your mismatched socks was the first time I knew I loved you," he said, and knelt down to help with her boots in the same tender way he'd taken them off.

In the hallway, she stopped to admire his photographs. They were intimate and artistic, not the cheesy portraits and fake smiles most people's hallways had. One was a woman playing the piano with a cat on her lap. "My mom," he said. "And that's my grandfather." He pointed to a dated photograph of a man in a military uniform, smoking a cigarette. She reached out and touched the sweetest one, a shot of a little boy in a basketball jersey at least four times his size. "My nephew," he explained. "He plays for ASU now. Go, Sun Devils."

She peered into his living room. Tall windows, a bricked-up fireplace, and a cowhide rug. Cluttered in a warm, lived-in way. Over a brown leather couch hung a shelf filled with more photographs, books, and a stereo system circa 2005, CD player and all.

"Does that work?" she asked.

He shook his head. "Call me a sucker for nostalgia."

A guitar leaned against the wall. "Do you play that?"

"Never," he said. "I'm too worried my neighbors will have me evicted. Don't you remember how bad I was?"

She zipped her lips, and he laughed. "I appreciate that," he said.

Whitaker locked the door behind them with one hand because he was holding hers with the other and stroking small circles on her palm with his thumb. When they walked past the Italian restaurant downstairs, she swore some patrons eyed her knowingly.

"They didn't realize they were paying for dinner *and* a show," she murmured.

Whitaker kissed the back of her hand. "And it's only intermission," he said.

They walked north to Broome Street and turned right. The night was unseasonably warm and the streets still crowded. He pushed open the door of a pho shop, and a small bell jingled. Inside, chili lights dangled from the ceiling above two square plastic tables. A man in a white paper hat waved from behind the counter. "This is Giang," Whitaker said, "and this is the best restaurant in the city."

The options on the menu were beef, chicken, squid, fish, and pork, then plain, medium, and spicy. Georgina ordered beef and medium, and Whitaker ordered squid and spicy. When they sat, Giang brought them a silver teapot and two mugs with a delicate orange pattern. He poured them steaming cups, and they cheersed, smiling at each other. Looking into his eyes was like watching a fireworks show reflected back at her. She couldn't believe they were back together, but at the same time, it made perfect sense. Reality just needed to leave her alone so she could exist in a worry-free bubble forever, having orgasms and eating soup and losing herself in his arms. The things she had wanted—stability, safety, success—seemed so stupid now. She finally got it, whatever *it* was. Life? Love? The pursuit of happiness? But at the same time, she wouldn't be with him if she hadn't learned

those lessons the hard way, when the things she'd sought didn't make
her happy, when they proved themselves superficial and unfulfilling,
when the man she'd chosen because he checked her boxes ended
up wounding her more than the passionate love story she'd so long
feared. All she wanted was the feeling of fullness now in her heart,
which swelled so big it almost hurt, so for the first time in her life, she
wasn't the one to ask, "What now?"

Whitaker did.

"I have no idea," she answered. "It feels good."

"Do you need a place to stay?" he asked. "Because I know a guy
with a bed."

"What's the rent?"

He kissed one of her knuckles. "We can work something out."

Giang brought them enormous bowls full of steaming broth and
noodles, and a tray of smaller bowls with vegetables and sauces to mix
in. Whitaker showed her how to prepare it, and she scarfed down the
salty noodles until her veins ran warm. When he gave her a spoonful
of his, her eyes watered and her lips burned. Giang had to bring three
glasses of water, which she chugged while Whitaker clapped her on
the back and lovingly called her a wimp. But even with her throat on
fire, she laughed. That would be life with him. Burning hot. Hilariously funny. Sweetly comforting.

While Giang rang them up, Georgina had an idea and grabbed
Whitaker's shoulder. "Hey," she said. "Do you want to go to Thailand with me?"

"When?"

She tapped her lip, pretending to think about it. "Um . . . I should
check my calendar, but maybe . . . tomorrow?"

He snaked his arms around her waist and kissed her ear. "You
know I will," he said, his lips grazing her skin.

Georgina pulled out her phone. "Great! Let's book."

"Wait. Hold on." Whitaker pushed the phone down gently and brushed her hair away from her face. "I can't believe I'm saying this, but maybe we need to sort a few things out first? You just ended a marriage. I know what that's like. You need time to grieve, move out, hire a lawyer. Deal with the details."

"It can wait," she said. "None of that matters."

"You're running away."

"I'm prioritizing."

Giang handed Whitaker his change, and Whitaker thanked him and promised to come again soon. Back on Broome, he tucked his wallet in his pocket and cupped Georgina's face in his hands, looking carefully into her eyes. "Are you okay?" he asked.

She wrapped her arms around his waist. "I'm fine, I promise. This was a long time coming. I should have left him as soon as he cheated. But, hey, then I'd never have run into you."

Whitaker's hands dropped from her face. He stared at her, blinking. Then his eyebrows pulled together, and he said, "Nathan had an affair?"

"With a junior associate," she said. "It's what started this whole thing."

She took a step toward his apartment. It was almost midnight, and she was tired and cold. A shower, a borrowed T-shirt, and Whitaker's bed sounded like heaven. Tomorrow they would get croissants and coffee from a bakery in Little Italy and go for a long walk to Battery Park while planning their Thailand vacation. But then she felt him gently remove her arms from his waist and knew something was wrong.

"What is it?" she asked.

"You never told me that," Whitaker said.

She tried to reach for him, but he turned away and started pacing the sidewalk. Her hands fell pathetically to her sides.

"It wasn't relevant," she said.

"It's relevant to me," he said. "Is that all this is?"

"Is *what* all this is?"

"Revenge," he said. "A rebound. You're using me."

A frantic panic possessed her. "Not at all. I chose you."

"You didn't choose me," he said. There was no fight in his voice, only resignation. "You came back to me after your husband abandoned you."

"You're wrong," she said. "Nathan wanted to have a baby, but I want—"

"Your next quick fix."

Her head felt constricted, like she was being pulled deep underwater, and a ringing built in her ears that made it difficult to think straight. Their conversation was going in the wrong direction. She'd *chosen* him, she'd given up everything for him, she'd left her husband in the middle of dinner for him. But he was hung up on a detail that didn't matter. Nathan had cheated, but that was a *good* thing. Meredith or no Meredith, she and Nathan were not in love, not like she and Whitaker. How could she make him understand? *No, no, NO!* she wanted to scream. *You don't get it! We're going to THAILAND! Where we'll have loud sex that SCARES THE NEIGHBORS!*

Whitaker's back faced her, his palms pressed against the wall beside Giang's. "I asked you one thing," he said. "Whether this was real. I told you I wouldn't be the guy you come to before heading back to your husband. But that's exactly what I am to you. That's all I've ever been."

He pushed himself upright, gave her a chaste peck on the cheek, and started walking toward his apartment. She wanted to chase after him, but her limbs were numb and useless. "I'm sorry!" she called instead.

He stopped. Without turning around, in a quiet, kind voice that pierced her, he said, "Don't be. This is my fault. You made it clear years ago I'm not the one."

He left her alone beside two rusty metal doors in the sidewalk, an overflowing trash bin, and a fire escape on which an upstairs tenant smoked. Shock kept her sobs at bay until he'd disappeared around the corner, the man she loved. Then in waves, they rolled out of her. She sank onto the stoop beside Giang's, holding her scarf across her mouth to muffle the sound. By the time she finished, her skull was pounding and her rib cage ached. She was dried up and swollen. But she was sobbing on the street at midnight because her heart was broken, and not because she'd let it get broken. She had no regrets about that.

On shaky legs, she stood up and dusted off her coat. It was time to admit defeat. Georgina wasn't the expert on love, but she knew two people who came pretty damn close.

Georgina pulled out her cell phone, and her father answered on the first ring.

Chapter 26

On Thanksgiving, Georgina woke up in her childhood bedroom. Little had been done to change it since she'd graduated from high school. Collages of shirtless models torn from *Seventeen* magazine and Abercrombie shopping bags decorated the sunflower-yellow walls. Photos of her friends from camp smiled at her, people she rarely spoke to. Some had reached out to her over the years, but she'd put no effort into reconnecting. A text here and a promise for lunch there, all meaningless. She was too busy, too important. Now she was taking a good, hard look at her life taped to a wall, seeing how much she'd missed out on.

The question mark of her future was an opportunity, she told herself. She'd been single before, in college and law school, but never as a real adult. She could reexamine her priorities. Did she want to move to Brooklyn? Maybe! Did she want to decorate her apartment in shabby chic? Definitely! Did she want to become a sober vegan cat person? No, not really. But the point was she could if she wanted to.

She threw back her comforter, a white blanket with black velvet roses she'd thought was the coolest, most art deco, Audrey Hepburn thing she'd ever seen in her life when she'd gotten it from Macy's in 2002. In sweatpants, she ambled to the kitchen. It was eight thirty. She'd become a late sleeper by her old standards. Buppha was already at the stove reading from the cooking schedule she'd prepared the day before. Though everything in Georgina's life had unraveled, she was not sorry to be spending Thanksgiving with the best cook in the world.

"How can I help?" she asked.

"You can eat this," Buppha said. She used a giant yellow spatula to scoop a cinnamon bun the size of a dinner plate. "Fresh from the oven."

"Aren't I supposed to save room for later?"

"No. You're supposed to warm up your stomach. Like a training round. Coffee?"

Georgina nodded. In four days, she had reverted from her hard-driving self to helpless child with a sore throat. Buppha made her soup, brushed her hair, and brought her coffee in bed before climbing in next to her and complaining about the neighbor downstairs who left his stinky shoes in the communal hallway.

"Here you go." Buppha poured Georgina a half-full mug. "Not too much. It will give you ulcers."

"But I love coffee," Georgina said. "I'd rather have ulcers than not enough coffee."

Buppha lifted her eyebrows. "You say that now." She returned to the stove and dropped an entire stick of butter into a cast-iron skillet. "Start chopping onions. Before the day is over, I plan to use at least five. There will be no kissing in this house!"

"Don't worry," Georgina said. "I've got nobody to kiss."

She shoved a forkful of cinnamon bun dripping with warm, sugary frosting into her mouth before pulling open the fridge. It was overflowing with Buppha's fresh groceries, which she'd driven up to

Westchester to buy from local farms—squash, onion, pumpkin, eggplant, fresh eggs, Manchego, thick white yogurt, and a fat pink turkey already soaking in green herbs and chicken broth. Georgina grabbed the bag of onions, found a cutting board, and set to chopping.

She was lost in the rhythm of her movements, down, up, swivel, down, up, swivel, when her father entered wearing a gray T-shirt with a cheerful cartoon turkey on it. He gave her double finger guns. "Why are the cranberries bright red?" he asked.

"They're super fresh," Buppha answered over her shoulder.

"Because they saw the turkey's breasts!" her father said.

"Very funny," Georgina said, and kissed his cheek. "Happy Thanksgiving."

He walked to the kitchen table on his crutch and fell heavily into a chair. Since his ankle was still healing, they hadn't gone to Thailand yet. "I don't think we've spent the holiday together in twelve years."

Georgina looked up from her cutting board and smiled. "Not since I set up you and Buppha."

At the stove, Buppha turned around, her face scrunched up. "You didn't set us up."

"Buppha catered my birthday party," her dad said. "Don't you remember? I asked her out after the first tray came out of the kitchen." He grinned, cheeks turning pink.

"Right, but I'm the one who booked her. I knew you two would get along."

Buppha waved her wooden spoon, sending a dash of tomato sauce flying. "That is not the same as setting us up. You made a lucky guess."

"I did the real work," her dad said. "You think it was easy asking out a pretty face like that?"

"You never would have met that pretty face if not for me!" She spoke animatedly with a massive chef's knife in her hand. "I did this!"

"Sweetheart. Thank you for booking Buppha as my caterer, but you're not going to take this one away from me. I even came up with a clever way to ask her out by writing a message on the whiteboard she'd been using to keep track of the courses."

"I wasn't so thrilled about that when he erased my menu," Buppha added.

Georgina started chopping again, slower. For years, she'd gotten so much self-satisfaction out of having arranged her dad's happiness, just like she thought she'd given Norah happiness and Felix, too, but it turned out she'd given them nothing.

Onion fumes stung her eyes, causing tears to cascade down her cheeks. She clamped them closed and ran to the sink to rinse away the burning pain.

"It's the onions," she said, "I swear. I'm fine."

Her dad clapped her on the back like she was choking. "No need to be ashamed, sweetheart. You've been through a lot."

"It's the onions," she said again, and it was, at first. But the more the tears came, the more their origin shifted. She started thinking about all the problems, so long ignored, that had all caught up to her in one day. Where did she go from here? How did someone who hadn't once asked herself what she really wanted finally figure it out? She wanted a palm reader to look at her hand and tell her what to do, to shed light on her destiny. But that was just another solution to ignore doing the real work. Another get-out-of-jail-free card.

"It's the onions," she said, "and everything else."

"Sit down, sit down." Her father squeezed her shoulders and led her back to the cluttered kitchen table. "Want more coffee?"

At her father's kindness, she started to cry in earnest. "Buppha says it'll give me ulcers!" she wailed.

"One day won't kill you." Her father refilled her cup, and Buppha came to join them at the table. "What is it? You miss Nathan?"

Georgina blew her nose unceremoniously into a paper napkin. "No. Not even a little bit."

"Yeah," Buppha said. "Me either."

Georgina stopped blowing. "What? You don't like Nathan?"

"We never liked Nathan, to be completely honest," her father said.

"Hated his guts," Buppha added. "I could tell he was spineless the day I met him."

"Why didn't you say something sooner?"

"How do you tell your daughter you'd rather her husband go pound sand?" her dad asked.

Georgina looked between them for a hint that they were kidding, but saw nothing. She hadn't even told them Nathan had cheated, just that they'd grown apart and it would no longer work between them. For her entire life, she'd convinced herself that she knew better than to make the same mistakes her parents had, but mistakes are necessary. Mistakes make you smarter. Mistakes make you see what you didn't see the first time.

"Well, you were right," she said. "I was wrong about him. But that's not why I'm crying." She picked up her warm mug and held it to her chest. "The person I wanted to be with was not Nathan. It was someone else. A man I used to know and . . . reconnected with."

Buppha's face exploded. "A man! Tell me everything."

"His name is Whitaker, and it's over. So it doesn't matter."

"Let me be the judge of that," Buppha said.

So Georgina told them the whole story, though she left out the part about the lifestyle and the multiple rounds of life-altering sex they'd had. When she was finished, Buppha said, "You got in a fight. So?"

"It was a pretty bad fight," Georgina said. "He told me I'd made it clear he wasn't the one."

"Did you tell him he was wrong?"

"Yes!"

"How many times?"

"Once?"

"Total cop-out," Buppha said. "Do I accept your father's apologies on the first try?" She laughed and slapped her knee. "No, I make him work for it. You barely tried!"

Georgina looked down at her coffee, which had turned into an unappetizing, lukewarm sludge. "I don't know what you expected me to do. He walked away so fast."

"Isn't it obvious what this man wants from you?" Buppha asked.

"Is it obvious to you?" Georgina asked.

"Yes," Buppha said.

"It's even obvious to me," her father said.

"You've never chosen this man," Buppha said. "You rejected him when he asked you to go to Peru with him, and now you made him feel like a backup plan. You've got to choose him!"

"I thought that's exactly what I did," Georgina said. "I told him again and again—"

"You tried to force him to listen to you. But this isn't about making him understand what you understand. This is about listening to the way he feels, and he wants to feel chosen."

"But I told him I loved him," Georgina said. "I said I was sorry."

Buppha scooted her chair closer to the table and leaned in. Her face was soft and warm, but there was no bullshit in her eyes. "This is classic you, I'm sorry to say. You think you know everything, so you don't listen."

Georgina looked between them. "So what do I do?"

"You try again," her dad said. "Harder this time."

"I'm scared," Georgina said.

"What's the worst that could happen?" Buppha asked.

"He says no."

"And then?"

"Then I'll be alone."

Buppha laughed. "Now I know you're full of shit. You've got us."

Georgina carried her empty plate to the kitchen sink to wash it. "Hey, when are you two leaving for Thailand?"

Her father patted his ankle. "Hopefully, December 7, if all goes to plan with this old bag of bones."

"I'd like to come with you," Georgina said. "If the offer stands."

"We'd be ecstatic, sweetheart," her dad said. "But I hope this isn't you running away."

Georgina dried the dish, mulling over Buppha's advice. Whitaker's thoughtfulness, not his words, had made her feel chosen over and over again. She dried her dish as the glimmer of an idea came to her, feeling hope for the first time since watching Whitaker's back disappear around the corner. "Not running away," she said. "I just think it's about time I had a vacation."

Chapter 27

Georgina waited until it snowed. Snow was essential. Every blue-skied day that passed over the next two weeks was excruciating, and every gray-skied day was a torturing exercise in hope and disappointment. But she listened to Whitaker's advice and used the time to sort out her new life. She moved her belongings into storage while she looked for an apartment, enjoying living with her dad and Buppha in the meantime. A friend from law school agreed to help with the divorce, and she cut five inches off her hair and got highlights because that was the thing to do when starting over.

Finally, one Saturday morning, she awoke to a Manhattan partially hidden under white. Swirling flakes clouded the view outside of her bedroom, and she grinned like a kid learning schools were closed.

Today was the day.

Today also happened to be the day of Norah and Ari's vow renewal ceremony, but there was time. Now that Georgina had stopped sprinting through life, she'd realized there was endless time.

She got dressed in wool tights, thick socks, and rubber boots with fleece lining. She put on a skirt and a sweater and zipped up her warmest coat. In the mirror, she brushed on mascara, combed her eyebrows, and dabbed on concealer, but she skipped the blush, finding her face already flushed pink.

On her desk patiently waited the list—a sheet of lined paper torn from a spiral notebook, on which she'd written every one of Whitaker's "twenty-five things to do when it's snowing that are more fun than errands" she could remember:

> *Bake cake from a box*
>
> *Tic-tac-snow*
>
> *Walk someone's dog*
>
> *Shower sex*
>
> *Bedroom sex*
>
> *Kitchen floor sex*
>
> *Bathroom counter sex*

And so on until she reached . . . *Get a tattoo.*

She couldn't remember all twenty-five activities, so she'd added a few of her own. Anyway, she doubted she'd be able to have sex in more than four locations by the time she needed to get ready for Norah and Ari's party. That was, if Whitaker wanted to have sex at all. If he could trust her again.

Her father and Buppha were reading at the kitchen table when she walked in, the newspaper for her dad and a crime novel for Buppha. They'd finished eating something syrupy, their empty plates brown and glistening.

"Good morning," Buppha said. "Do you want a waffle?"

"I would love a waffle," Georgina said. She'd learned that when she said no to Buppha's cooking, a plate ended up in front of her anyway. "A quick one. I haven't got much time."

"Big day?" her father asked.

"The biggest." Georgina made a cup of coffee with milk as Buppha poured batter into the waffle maker. Side by side, they watched it gently steam.

"It's snowing," Buppha whispered. "That's a good omen for love."

"Is it?" Georgina asked as the light on the waffle maker blinked from red to green.

"No," Buppha said. "I made that up. But this will work out for you. Nobody has been through as much as you have without getting their happy ending."

Georgina had ended up telling Buppha about Nathan's affair, and she was glad she had. Nobody who'd learned the truth had been anything but understanding, and she was embarrassed for worrying so much about protecting her pride. Relationships didn't always work out, but that didn't make them failures.

"I might not get my happy ending," Georgina said, "but that's okay. I just want to give it a chance."

She sat at the table with her waffle and doused it with maple syrup. "What time is your flight?" she asked her dad. His ankle had healed, and they were taking off for a rainy, warm winter in Thailand.

"Four thirty," he said. "We land on Monday morning."

"Make sure you call me."

He smiled. "I thought I was the parent here. We'll see you in two weeks, right? You all booked?"

"One-way to Bangkok," Georgina said.

"Flying by the seat of your pants," her father said.

"The new me." She scarfed her fluffy waffle in a few gigantic bites. "Now if you'll excuse me, I have some business to attend to, and if all goes the way I hope, you'll be gone before I get back. So"—she kissed her father's cheek, then Buppha's—"safe travels, and thank you. For everything."

———

She picked her way along the slippery sidewalk toward the subway station on Seventy-Second and Broadway, walking as fast as she dared without breaking her tailbone on the ice. The list, folded into a square, she clutched in her gloved hand. If she loosened her hold a fraction, the wind whipping through the buildings would steal it away.

Looking through the subway car window into the dark tunnel, spotting the occasional flash of graffiti, she was strangely at peace. So many things could go wrong today. Whitaker could refuse her. He might not be home. He could have plans with someone—a date, even. But the point wasn't to win anymore. She was only after that participation ribbon.

The weather had gotten worse by the time she exited the subway on Prince Street. Snowflakes flew sideways, and the wind stung the exposed skin on her face. She kept her head down, placing one foot in front of the other. The streets were relatively quiet for New York, the storm having forced everyone inside. Only a few bundled-up dog owners traipsed miserably along while the city's unsung heroes—the food delivery corps—wove through them with insulated backpacks. Georgina turned right on Lafayette, left on Broome, and right on Mott, where she wiped ruined mascara from her wet face.

The Italian restaurant downstairs was open but empty. The floor beneath her tilted as she remembered all those patrons who she'd sworn heard her rejoicing at the altar of Whitaker's tongue. It would hurt if he said no. She wouldn't be fine, but she would survive.

She pressed the buzzer.

"Hello?" His voice through the intercom sounded surprised.

"Hi," she answered. "It's me. It's Georgina. Can I come up?"

The pause that followed was excruciating. "Okay," he finally said, but she sensed he wasn't thrilled about it.

When the buzzer sounded, she pushed open both doors, but held the second one while she stamped the snow off her boots in the vestibule. Her heart was no longer peaceful. It thumped against her ribs as she ascended the elevator, and her palms were clammy despite their numbness from the cold. In the doors, she spotted her wet, messy reflection, and had just enough time to finger-comb her hair before they split open.

This time, he wasn't waiting for her in the hallway. But he wasn't there to serve her feelings—she was there to serve his. When she knocked on the door, he answered it quickly. Though she would have thought it scientifically impossible, her heart beat harder and faster at the sight of him. He wore his black-framed glasses and the same gray sweatpants she'd ripped off his body two weeks ago. Dampness rumpled his hair and sleep lined his cheeks. When she looked into his eyes, the same color as the cloudy sky outside, she searched for derision, anger, even hate, but only saw curiosity and a hint of his chronic amusement. That gave her enough hope to push forward.

"I know it's early," she said. "But I was wondering what you're doing today."

He waited, the corner of his mouth twitching. He wasn't going to give in so easily, and she didn't want him to.

She pulled the list out of her pocket with a trembling hand and unfolded it. "Because in case you were planning to do errands on this boring Saturday, I bet I can come up with twenty-five things that are more fun."

He suppressed his grin and folded his arms, leaning one shoulder against the doorframe. Still waiting, still not letting her in, still making her work for it. Her nerves slowly gave way to excitement. She couldn't be in his presence without feeling giddy.

A smile fought to escape, but she cleared her throat and forced solemnity. "Number one: bake a cake from a box."

Hooked onto her right arm, she had a grocery bag full of supplies. She set it on the floor and withdrew a Pillsbury box of Funfetti cake, a dozen eggs, one bottle of canola oil, and a pint of milk. Hugging them awkwardly to her chest, she looked up at him. "What do you say?"

"I'd like to hear what else is on your list before I make up my mind," he said.

"Number two," she read, "tic-tac-snow."

He nodded. *Go on.*

"Number three: walk someone's dog."

"Whose?" he asked. He was playing with her now, and she was more than happy to play along.

"We're going to the shelter to find a furry friend," she said. "Number four through ten are—"

Whitaker tugged on the pocket of her coat as he moved one inch closer. "I remember what those are. What else?"

She dug in the grocery bag for the black Sharpie and tore it from the package. She took off her coat and rolled up her sleeve as far as it would go. Whitaker watched her with entertained interest as she drew his name on her skin in giant black letters from elbow to wrist. For a little extra oomph, she drew a black heart on each end.

"What do you think?" she asked.

He ran his hand along her arm, smiling at his name temporarily tattooed there, then kissed each lopsided heart. "I think you should leave it to the professionals," he said.

"There's one more thing," she said, and the painful thumping in her chest returned. With a shaking hand, she reached into her bag a final time. She'd made him smile with her game, her cake, and her Sharpie, but had she made him feel chosen? Was it enough?

She handed him a blue-and-gold kurta she'd bought online from Norah's uncle's store. "Tonight, Norah and Ari are renewing their vows at his parents' house on Long Island. Would you be my date?"

He fingered the intricate gold pattern, saying nothing for so long she wanted to crawl into his ear to spy on his brain, but instead she took deep breaths and waited. Like Buppha said, this wasn't about her feelings.

"I'm sorry I didn't tell you about Nathan," she said. "It was selfish. You always put me first, and I never showed you the same respect, which was especially cruel considering you showed me what love is, and it took refusing Peru, getting married, and becoming a swinger to realize that."

When Whitaker put one hand on the doorknob, her stomach lurched sickeningly into her throat. He was saying no. He was closing the door. It was over. Her knees started to weaken just as he said, "I've never been the type of person to turn away from love."

He wasn't closing the door to kick her out. He was opening it to let her in.

She stepped into the halo of his body heat. "I used to be that person," she said. "But I'm not anymore."

Chapter 28

Felix, Georgina, and Whitaker caught the 5:00 p.m. LIRR to Great Neck, where Ari had grown up. Felix was single again, but unlike after most of his breakups, he was more confident in his decision than resigned to his fate. He'd even said he wanted to stay single for a while and avoid rushing into a new relationship—the Felix equivalent of swearing off PBS and national parks in its shock value.

After the Berkshires weekend, Norah had secretly brokered a deal with Ari's parents. She requested a five-year pause on Ari's repayment plan so she could finish law school. Then *she* would pay them out of her salary so Ari could quit the job he'd hated for a decade and find a career he loved. They'd apparently been so embarrassed that Norah had learned their dirty secret, and so impressed with her fierce love for their son, they'd called off the whole arrangement. When Ari asked them to use the house for a last-minute vow renewal party, they'd not only said yes but rented a heated tent for the backyard. Ari's dad wore a kurta and his mother a sari.

The train was mostly empty, so they scored a corner with two benches facing each other. Though each side sat three, Georgina pressed so close to Whitaker that two more people could have fit beside her. After their morning in bed, she was so addicted to his body against hers that separating would have been like ripping off a Band-Aid. As the train left Penn Station, she held his hand and kissed his face and draped her knees across his legs. Whitaker caught her eye, and the compartment faded away. They were alone in his shower, her body molding to his, his fingers trailing her spine—

"I've never seen you like this," Felix said, and she jolted out of her fantasy, having forgotten he was there. "To be honest, it's disgusting."

"Sorry," she said, and sat on her hands. "I'll try to control myself."

Whitaker laughed. "Please don't."

"He just looks so handsome," Georgina said. "So do you, Felix."

Whitaker wore the blue-and-gold kurta she'd given him earlier. Felix's was a deep purple. Norah had lent Georgina an emerald sari with a gold top and a tikli with ruby-colored stones that draped through her part.

"You look beautiful," Whitaker said. "Did I say that already?"

"Only about fifty times," Felix groaned. "It's going to be a long ride. Good thing I brought supplies."

From his backpack, which had made a comeback now that he'd returned to the classroom, he pulled a bag of popcorn, three beers, and a deck of cards.

"So did we," Georgina added, and withdrew a Tupperware of Funfetti cake and three forks. They played Bullshit, Go Fish, and War, then had a competition to see who could catch the most pieces of popcorn in their mouth, which quickly devolved into a drinking game. Felix couldn't catch a single piece, and his second beer was fast gone.

"I surrender," he said. "I feel like it's a bad look to show up drunk to your ex-girlfriend's wedding."

"Ex-girlfriend?" Whitaker asked. "I didn't know that."

"It was a long time ago," Felix said, and leaned his shoulder against the window as blurry white houses whipped past.

"Do you ever wish things had turned out differently?" Georgina asked.

"With Norah and me?" He lifted his feet onto the opposite seat— the most rebellious thing he'd ever done. "Yeah, sometimes. But there are a lot of ways to have someone in your life."

Georgina slipped her hand into Whitaker's and squeezed. He squeezed back. Until the train reached Great Neck, she rested her head on his shoulder and closed her eyes, so thankful he was back in her life.

The heated backyard tent glowed with string lights, votive candles, and red paper lanterns. Everyone gathered around the dance floor for the ceremony, craning their necks to see Ari, Norah, and the kids forming a circle in the middle. Rachel let Norah hold her hand, and Georgina smiled. Soon, Rachel would start high school and wouldn't hold her mother's hand for all the front-row Taylor Swift concert tickets in the world.

Ari waved to the guests, and everyone quieted. They'd decided to lead the ceremony themselves, no pandit or rabbi. Just family. Norah wore red, with crystals braided into her hair. She was incandescent as she beamed at her husband. Ari wore cream, and when he kissed Norah's hand and started to speak, his voice trembled with such emotion that Georgina had tears soon streaming down her face.

"Norah," Ari began. He stopped and cleared his throat at least three times. "When I saw you in torts on the first day of law school, I knew I had to be near you, but I was terrified. You were so smart, so beautiful, so kind to everyone and generous with your time. I asked Georgina if I could join your study group. To be honest, yeah, I needed help studying—" Everyone laughed, even Ari's parents, who looked so overjoyed it was difficult to imagine them trying to convince their son to abandon his pregnant girlfriend. "But that wasn't why I asked. I wanted an excuse to sit next to you. But I never thought you'd end up marrying a schlub like me."

Georgina was so shocked she laughed. She'd thought she lied to Norah about Ari wanting an excuse to spend time with her, but that had been true all along. Norah had never needed her help to begin with.

"I'm the luckiest guy in the world, and I'm so sorry—" Ari's voice broke, and as he collected himself, sniffles chorused around the room. "I'm so sorry I haven't made that clear to you. If I've ever made you feel small, it's because I feel small, but I want you to stand on my shoulders and have the world."

Norah smiled through tears, nodding up at him with unguarded love and acceptance in her eyes, as if to say, *Yes, I understand, I forgive you.* For as long as they were friends, Georgina had wanted to give Norah strength, to push her to stand up for herself, to inspire her to finish her degree. But it turned out Norah had her priorities straight. She gave herself wholly to love. Norah was the role model. Her marriage, the pedestal.

"Ari," Norah began. "We've both sacrificed for our family in ways we didn't expect, but I would do it all over again, and again, and again. Otherwise, we wouldn't be standing here, and here is the only place I want to be."

Ari smiled, wiped his face, and kissed his wife. When Rachel passed them their matching gold bands, the guests clapped and cheered, Georgina the loudest. It was one of the most joy-filled moments of her life. To think she could have felt so hardened and hollowed out when she'd walked into Nathan's office that night but bursting with light two months later seemed impossible. But that was life, she understood it now.

For their first dance, Ari, Norah, Rachel, Simon, and Hannah—as best she could at two—did a choreographed dance. Hannah bopped around, got distracted by the disco lights, touched a hot bulb, and started screaming. Rachel was so good at the hip-hop portion of the routine that jaws were hanging open, and both Ari and Norah stopped dancing to watch. When Simon had the floor, he performed a pirouette he'd learned in ballet, then bowed so deeply he fell over. On the whole, it was a success, and if it didn't go viral on YouTube, there was something wrong with the Internet.

When the dance floor opened to the guests, Georgina was drinking a glass of water by the bar. She'd cried so much during the ceremony, she was dehydrated. Someone put a hand on her shoulder, and it turned out to be Nathan. He was one of the only men there not wearing a kurta.

"I hope it's okay that I came," he said.

"Of course it is," she said. "They're your friends, too."

He gestured vaguely to the dance floor. "One last dance?"

She hesitated, then thought, *What the hell, why not?* There was no animosity on her end. When she looked at the man who'd been her husband for seven years, she felt only gratitude. He was what she'd needed to learn that safe wasn't so satisfying, that the reward was in the risk.

He extended his hand in a formal gesture and led her to the busy dance floor. She put her left hand on his shoulder, and he rested his on her waist, and they danced with at least a foot of space between them. It wasn't so different from how they'd danced at their wedding, a boring, traditional waltz they'd learned from an instructor. They'd been focusing so hard on keeping in time with the music that in their wedding photos, they weren't even smiling.

"So," Nathan said, "I see you brought a date."

Georgina glanced at Whitaker, who'd been getting them a plate of appetizers from the buffet. He gave her a small nod before striking up a conversation with Felix. "I have to be honest with you," she said.

"No need," Nathan said. "I could tell there were feelings there. I have no right to be mad."

"That's not it. I mean, yes, there were, but . . . we knew each other. Before. I was completely in love with him in college. It was a coincidence that he was in the group, though. A lucky one."

Nathan swayed to the music, quiet. His face was thoughtful.

"But even if we hadn't run into each other," she went on, "you and I wouldn't have made it. We weren't in love. It explains everything. We just weren't in love."

Nathan nodded, his bottom lip poking out in the same expression he usually made when there was something on his mind.

"If you're in love with Meredith," she said, "it's okay. I understand."

He looked at her, shaking his head. "No. I wasn't in love with Meredith. But . . . there is someone. And you're right. It's different."

"That's great," Georgina said. "Do I know her?"

An expression she had never seen Nathan wear overcame his face. The guardedness in his eyes, the charming but forced smile, the anxiety in his forehead—it evaporated. His was a look of pure wonder. "It's Alina."

Oh no.

"We ended up together at the second party. You were too distracted to notice, and that's okay. But we didn't even touch each other. We stayed up all night talking, and it was amazing. She's amazing."

"Does she feel the same way?"

"I don't know," Nathan said. "I hope so."

Georgina gave him a hug with a friendly pat on the back. Meredith, Kansas, a baby, and now Alina? It seemed Nathan had been searching for something, and he searched still. She felt sorry for him, but wasn't that patronizing? Who was she to prescribe what Nathan needed? Maybe he did love Alina, maybe she was the one, and they would live happily ever after in Topeka, where Alina would become the local wellness guru and Nathan could drive on his mower. "I'm happy for you, Nathan. Good luck."

Georgina sensed Whitaker's presence before she saw him. His body had become her magnet.

"May I cut in?" he asked.

"She's all yours," Nathan said, and nodded his goodbye.

As Whitaker took Georgina in his arms and swayed her to the music with his lips against her hair, humming along, she closed her eyes and remembered that wedding she'd been to with Nathan, where all the couples were dancing but them, and she'd refused to admit that all she wanted was to dance with a man she loved.

Acknowledgments

A million thanks would not scratch the surface of my gratitude to those who brought this book to life, but here goes! To Jamie Carr, for championing this book with energy, passion, warmth, and expertise. Your faith and friendship changed my life, and I thank the universe for you every day. To Caitlin Landuyt, for your brilliant edits and the hours we spent on the phone psychoanalyzing these characters and having a blast doing it. Georgina and the gang would be lost without your genius brain.

To the Anchor Books team, including James Meader, Angie Venezia, Jess Deitcher, Annie Locke, Julie Ertl, Sara Lynn, Marisa Melendez, Steven Walker, Paul Thurlby, Maddie Partner, Edward Allen, Suzanne Herz, and Edward Kastenmeier—you are my heroes.

To Catapult, for making me a writer, especially J. Courtney Sullivan, Weike Wang, Taylor Larsen, Elissa Bassist, Jennifer Close, Lynn Steger Strong, and Lindsey Lee Johnson, and all those who workshopped the swingers.

To Chelsea Bieker, for making my dreams come true. To Stefan Merrill Block and Nicola Kraus, for your cheerleading and insightful feedback, which kept me going when writing a novel felt impossible.

To Crystal Hana Kim, Liz Robau, and the Better Borough Writers, for your dear friendship and early reads.

To Alex Hahn, for teaching me what funny is. To my friends, for understanding when I said I couldn't hang out for two years because I was writing a novel. To my family, for your humor and love, and for telling everyone I wrote a book. To my grandmother, for being a lifelong, voracious reader. And to Mike, for always believing in me.

About the Author

Taylor Hahn is a writer and lawyer who lives in Los Angeles. She is a graduate of Loyola Marymount University and Fordham University School of Law. *The Lifestyle* is her first novel. Visit her online at www.taylorhahn.com.